D0463393

ORBIT

*Also by John J. Nance
in Large Print:*

Saving Cascadia
Fire Flight
Headwind
Blackout
Medusa's Child

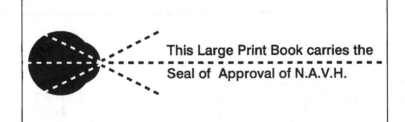

This Large Print Book carries the
Seal of Approval of N.A.V.H.

ORBIT

John J. Nance

Thorndike Press • Waterville, Maine

Published in 2006 by arrangement with
Simon & Schuster, Inc.

Thorndike Press® Large Print Core.

The tree indicium is a trademark of Thorndike Press.

The text of this Large Print edition is unabridged.
Other aspects of the book may vary from the original edition.

Set in 16 pt. Plantin by Christina S. Huff.

Printed in the United States on permanent paper.

Library of Congress Cataloging-in-Publication Data

Nance, John J.
    Orbit / by John J. Nance.
        p. cm.
    ISBN 0-7862-8634-2 (lg. print : hc : alk. paper)
    1. Space flights — Fiction.   2. Space vehicle accidents —
United States — Fiction.   3. Space rescue operations —
Fiction.   I. Title.
PS3564.A546O73 2006b
    813'.54—dc22   2006007290

To my mother,
Margrette (Peggy) Nance Lynch

As the Founder/CEO of NAVH, the only national health agency solely devoted to those who, although not totally blind, have an eye disease which could lead to serious visual impairment, I am pleased to recognize Thorndike Press* as one of the leading publishers in the large print field.

Founded in 1954 in San Francisco to prepare large print textbooks for partially seeing children, NAVH became the pioneer and standard setting agency in the preparation of large type.

Today, those publishers who meet our standards carry the prestigious "Seal of Approval" indicating high quality large print. We are delighted that Thorndike Press is one of the publishers whose titles meet these standards. We are also pleased to recognize the significant contribution Thorndike Press is making in this important and growing field.

Lorraine H. Marchi, L.H.D.
Founder/CEO
NAVH

* Thorndike Press encompasses the following imprints: Thorndike, Wheeler, Walker and Large Print Press.

Chapter 1

Five miles south of Mojave, California,
May 16, 9:23 p.m. Pacific

For Kip Dawson, the risks associated with being shot into space in a few hours are finally beginning to seem real.

Am I really going to do this? he thinks, braking the SUV hard, foot shaking, as he casts his eyes up to take in the stark blackness of his destination, amazingly visible through the windshield. This last evening on earth — the very eve of his windfall trip into space — feels too surreal to grasp emotionally. He's sure of only one thing: At long last, it's scaring as much as exciting him.

He winces at the irritated blast of a trucker's horn and pulls to the side of the highway, letting the big rig roar past before climbing out to stare into deep space. He's oblivious to the sharp chill of the desert night, but aware of the double white flash of the beacon at Edwards Air Force Base a few miles to the east.

To the west, the barest remains of ruddy

orange undulate on the horizon, a razor-thin band along the crest of it, whispering a vestigial message from the sunset. But it's the deep velvet black of the cloudless night sky that's entrancing him, and he hasn't seen the Milky Way so startlingly clear since he was little.

The highway beside him is quiet again, but the sky is full of silently twinkling strobe lights from the arriving and departing airliners frequenting LAX, a kinetic urgency energizing the lower altitudes above him. He feels like a child as he contemplates the vastness of all that void. Provided there's no explosion on the way up, he'll be there in person in a few hours, encapsulated in a tiny, fragile craft, closer — even if only incrementally — to all those stars.

There is no productivity in stargazing, the dutiful part of his mind is grousing, but he suppresses the growing urge to leave. The air is quiet and perfectly still, and he hears the song of a nightbird somewhere distant. A moment earlier a coyote had made his presence known, and he hears the animal call again, the howl almost mystical.

How small we are, he thinks, as he stands beneath the staggering scope of a billion suns strewn at least ten thousand light-years across from horizon to horizon, trying to embrace it — even the largest of his personal problems seeming trivial by contrast. There's a barely remembered quote . . . perhaps something Carl Sagan once said: "Even though earth-bound and finite, the same human mind that can declare the cosmos too vast to physically navigate can at the same moment traverse its greatest distances with but a single thought."

His cell phone rings again, the third time in an hour, but he tunes it out, thinking instead about the details of ASA's space school he's attended for the previous two weeks and the awe he still feels when he sees the famous *Apollo 8* picture of the Earth rising over the lunar landscape. Everything in perspective. It's the way he's been told every NASA astronaut feels when the sound and fury and adrenaline of reaching orbit subsides — three g's of acceleration end abruptly — and it's finally time to be weightless and breathe and look outside.

He recalls the video of sunrise from space, the colors progressing through the rainbow to the sudden explosion of light over the rim of the planet, all of it proceeding at seventeen times the speed of dawn on the ground — where the Earth's surface turning velocity is less than a thousand miles per hour. He'll see four sequences of that during the flight.

An incongruous desire for coffee suddenly crosses his mind, and he realizes he's longing as much for the tangible feel of something earthly and familiar as the drink itself. But he has a responsibility to achieve the sleep that coffee won't bring. Morning and caffeine will come soon enough. He should head back.

In some recess of his mind he's been keeping track of the number of times his phone has rung, and the newest burst is one time too many. He feels his spirits sag. Angrily he punches it on, unsurprised to hear his wife's strained voice on the other end. Like a wisp of steam, the humbling, exhilarating mood is evaporating around him, leaving only a duty to resume feeling guilty. He wonders if they're going to pick up at the same point in the argument.

"Sharon? Are you okay?"

There's a long sigh and he imagines her sitting in the dark den of her father's opulent home in North Houston where she's fled with their children.

"I may never be okay again, Kip. But that's not why I called. I just wanted to wish you well. And . . . I'm sorry about the argument earlier."

For just a moment he feels relieved. "I'm sorry, too. I really wish you could understand all this, but you do know I'll be back tomorrow afternoon, right? As soon as I get down, I'm going to fly directly to Houston, to you and the girls, and we can fly back to Tucson together . . ."

"You make it sound so routine. No, Kip. Even if you survive this madness, don't come here. Just go on back to Tucson. I'm too upset to talk for a while. We're going to stay here until I decide what to do."

He keeps his voice gentle, though he wants to yell.

"Sharon, keep in mind that this is probably the only time I've felt the need to . . . not honor your wishes on something big."

"Yeah, other than your so-called career."

He lets the sting subside and bites his tongue.

"Honey, you've been asking me to throw away the dream of a lifetime, winning a trip into space. I just wish you'd stop acting like we're in some sort of marital crisis."

She makes a rude noise that sounds like a snort, her tone turning acid. "Your wife takes the kids and leaves because her husband won't listen to her and the marriage is just fine? Wake up, Kip."

"Look . . ."

"No, dammit, you look! I only called to say I hope this thing is all you expect it to be, because the price you're paying is immense."

"Sharon . . ."

"Let me finish. I wanted to say that I hope you make it back alive, Kip. You've always belittled my premonitions. I want you to come back alive, regardless of what happens to us, but I don't expect you to. So I have to face the fact that this is probably our goodbye in this life."

"Sharon, that's nuts. I respect your premonitions, but they're not always right, and ASA does these trips twice a week. Over a hundred and fifty so far and no one's even been scratched." He says the words knowing the facts won't change her mind, but he has to keep trying. He's been trained that logic should trump emotion, whether it does or not.

"I've loved you, Kip. I really have."

"And I do love you, Sharon. Not past tense, but now."

Silence and a small sob answer his words, followed by the rattle of a receiver searching for the cradle.

He lets himself slump back against the side of the SUV in thought, working hard to overrule the guilt-fueled impulse to give in, call her back, cancel the trip and drive all night and all day straight through to Houston.

That would be the Kip thing to do, he thinks. The way he's always responded. Must repair everything. Must atone for the sin of taking her away from Houston and not following her plan for his professional life.

From the south he hears another large truck approaching, probably speeding, the whine of his wheels almost alarming as the driver hurtles the big rig northbound. But Kip's attention pulls away from the present and he's suddenly back two months before in his den in Tucson, the memory of the late-evening phone call from American Space Adventures still crystalline.

A gently burning pine log had suddenly readjusted itself on the fireplace grate that evening, startling him, even though the "thud" was as soft as a sleeping dog rolling over in the night. He'd been wasting time in his father's old wicker chair and wondering with a detached calm what, if anything, life had left to show him. After all, even though he'd always followed the path of a responsible man, the promised land was eluding him.

Watching the flickering orange rays play-

13

ing off the paneled walls of his den had been mesmerizing until Sharon walked in, naked and desirable beneath the ratty terry-cloth robe she knew he hated, and she opened the robe and flashed him as she shook her head, a signal that she was mad and that there was, once again, not a chance in hell of sex this evening. It was a weapon she'd grown too used to wielding as their lack of intimacy had progressed. There she stood, preparing to verbally batter him over something. Tonight, he figured, it was either the evils of the cigar he was smoking, or his pathetic recent campaign of systematically investing in lottery tickets.

The lottery.

She was right about that one, but he couldn't tell her how desperate he was for a windfall or any reprieve from what was becoming a conjugal prison. He was even becoming desperate for sex. But he couldn't win on any front, and he'd concluded that, at best, the universe was not listening to his needs.

At worst, it was plotting against him!

And the growing pile of dead lottery tickets was irritating the daylights out of Sharon Dawson.

The late-evening phone call had come as a welcome interruption, a lovely female voice on the other end asking a few identifying questions before getting to the point.

"And, Mr. Dawson, you did enter an Internet-based contest with American Space Adventures, to win one of four seats on one of our spacecraft into low Earth orbit, correct?"

"Yes. It's always been a dream of mine, to fly in space."

"And, you charged the entry fee on your Visa card?"

"Yes. Is there a problem?"

"No, sir. Quite the contrary. I'm calling because you've won the trip."

It was hard to remember exactly how much he'd whooped and smiled and jumped around in the moments afterward, before explaining the happy call to Sharon. Carly and Carrie, their five-year-old twins, had come running in to see what all the noise was about, followed by thirteen-year-old Julie, his daughter from his first marriage. Sharon had shooed them back to bed without explanation before turning to Kip, and he'd been stunned at the look of horror on her face, her eyes hardening as she forbade him to go.

"Excuse me?" he'd said, still smiling. "What did you say?"

"I said you're not going! I have this gut

feeling and it's really strong, Kip. I don't want to be a widow."

Within minutes it became an argument spanning the house, and then it turned somehow to encompass everything wrong with him and a marriage he'd refused to see as imperiled.

"Once again all you think about is yourself!" she wailed. "You're never here for me and the girls and now you want to go kill yourself in *space?* Then go!"

"Sharon, for God's sake, I'm never *here?* That's BS. I don't even play golf anymore. What time do I take away from you?"

"All you do is work! The girls are suffering."

"Name one school function I've missed."

"Even when you're there, you're thinking about business."

"Sharon, I sell pharmaceuticals. I'm a regional sales rep for a huge drug manufacturer. What's there to think about?"

"You could have been in the oil business, but no! You had to go be a peon for Vectra and work your rear off for no recognition, no advancement, and no time for us."

"Of course. I didn't go to work for your father. That's always it, isn't it? I don't measure up because I went out to get a job on my own."

"Stupidest decision you ever made."

Except marrying you! he'd thought, careful not to let his face show it. The thought shocked him, somehow defiling the very walls of the den he had shared with Lucy before her fatal accident. But that was long ago, before Sharon came along and caught him on the rebound. Before he caught himself growing numb.

It ended as usual with her storming off to bed alone. But for once, this time he didn't follow her like the usual whipped puppy begging to be forgiven. He'd returned to the wicker chair and sniffed the sweet woodsmoke he loved and made the decision that for perhaps only the second time in his adult life, Kip Dawson was going to stay the course and cling to his dream.

Kip's thoughts return to night in the high California desert, and he realizes he's been clutching his cell phone with a death grip as he leans against the SUV. He checks his watch, grimacing at the late hour, but pausing halfway into the front seat to watch the beacon at Edwards AFB for a few more sweeps, spotting a late-night flight lifting off, maybe a test run of some sort. He thinks of Chuck Yeager and Scott Crossfield and the other early Edwards flight test pioneers, wondering if they ever stopped like this in the early desert night to stand so deeply humbled by a celestial display?

Maybe, he decides. But they'd probably never admit it. Believing in a personal aura of invincibility was important to test pilots who routinely challenged the edge of the envelope. And besides, he thinks, men like that were constrained by the *code* from discussing feelings.

The cell phone rings yet again and he answers without looking at the screen, letting his voice convey the weariness with this game she's playing.

But the voice on the other end is different.

"Mr. Dawson, Jack Railey at ASA. We couldn't find you in your room, so I thought I'd phone you."

Kip chuckles. "Is this a bed check? Am I in trouble?"

"No, sir. But we have a problem. Could we come talk to you about it?"

"What problem, exactly?"

"I'd rather not go into it over the phone. We do have some options, but I need to speak with you about them in detail."

A kaleidoscope of possibilities, few good, flash across Kip's mind, depressing him. "I'm just a few miles south. Where can I find *you?*"

He listens to the brief description of Railey's office location before promising to be there in fifteen minutes, his voice heavy with concern before he disconnects and stows the cell phone. Sleep, he thinks, may not be necessary after all.

Chapter 2

As Kip approaches the airfield, the tails of nearly fifty mothballed airliners rise from the desert like a ghostly fleet of square riggers. The buildings of the Mojave International Aerospace Port come into view as well, the ramp awash in a sea of artificial orange light. He spots the specially outfitted Lockheed 1011 that ASA uses as a mothership to launch its spacecraft, the old jumbo jet sparking an unexpected stab of anxiety — as if finding it parked on the ground means neither he, nor it, will be flying in the morning after all.

It isn't hard to figure out, he decides. Something technical has gone wrong and the launch has been canceled, and now they want to give him his options for rescheduling. He's not sure whether disappointment will be worse, or embarrassment over not going up as planned. He can depend on one negative at least: Rescheduling will give

20

Sharon that much more time to complete her campaign to wear down his fragile resolve.

It always seemed too good to be true anyway, winning this trip.

ASA's headquarters are housed in a new glass-sided six-story building and finding Railey's office is simple. He's not surprised to find that the other face at the conference table is Richard DiFazio, owner of ASA. DiFazio gets up to shake Kip's hand as he enters.

"I didn't expect to see you again this evening, after the party," Kip says, recalling the founder's appearance at their prelaunch celebration in a local restaurant. DiFazio had planned to just drop in, a regular courtesy to his customers, but he had lingered through dessert to talk with one of Kip's flightmates, Tommy Altavilla, an extremely wealthy Seattle industrialist and raconteur who'd kept them laughing for hours.

"Kip, just after you left, Tommy had a heart attack."

"Oh no!"

"Right on the front steps."

"Is he all right?" The smiling faces of Tommy and Anna Altavilla are vivid in his mind.

"He will be. It was a relatively mild attack

and we got him to the emergency room fast enough, but he's been airlifted to Cedars-Sinai in L.A. and Anna, of course, went with him."

"God, I'm sorry to hear this."

"I know it. I mean, our first concern is Tommy's welfare, but after that, we've got to address the empty seats on the flight, and it just got more complicated an hour ago when Tariq, your other fellow passenger, got a call from Riyadh to get back there fast. He couldn't tell us why, but his Gulfstream lifted off thirty minutes ago, and I hear the House of Saud is teetering on the brink of a revolution."

Middle Eastern politics are of no interest to Kip and besides, he hadn't bonded with Tariq al Ashad.

Tommy and Anna, however, are another story.

"Three empty seats," Kip replies. "I see the problem. So, when can I reschedule?"

"Well . . . that's why we wanted to talk to you, Kip. This trip is already unique because we have a small commercial payload scheduled for tomorrow . . . essentially an industrial, scientific experiment we're being well paid for . . . and we've made the decision to launch with or without passengers. So, if you're still up for it, you'll have the craft and your pilot, Bill Campbell, all to yourself — which means you'll get much more window time."

His hesitation, if any, is measured in nanoseconds. "Hell, yes, I'm up for it! I was afraid you were going to . . . what's that word you use?"

"Scrub it," Jack Railey replies. "Comes from the World War II use of grease boards for scheduling. When you canceled a mission back then, you literally scrubbed its listing off the grease board."

"I'm ready, at any rate," Kip says. "I don't want to reschedule."

DiFazio gets to his feet with a tired smile.

"Great! That helps us, too, you know, not having to displace a paying passenger later." A worried look crosses DiFazio's face as he realizes the implications of the phrase "paying passenger" in front of a contest winner. "I apologize for that reference, Kip. You're an honored guest, and I didn't mean . . ."

"No problem. I'm glad it works out. This is, after all, a business."

"I appreciate that," Richard replies, his concerned look softening as he nods and extends his hand. "Okay, then. Someone will be banging on your door at zero three hundred. I hope you'll have a wonderful, memorable flight, Kip. We're all very glad you won

23

the contest, and I've got to tell you on behalf of all of our folks that you've been a delight to have with us during training." He starts to turn away, then turns back. "Kip, I agree completely with Diana Ross, by the way, that given your enthusiasm for private space flight, we need to talk later about involving you in some of our advertising."

"Can't wait."

He walks back to the plush ASA guest quarters and his assigned suite, his mind alternating between Tommy and Anna Altavilla and the flight. He wonders whether he should try to call Anna at the hospital in L.A., and decides against it for now. Despite their bonding during training, the economic and social divide between them is immense — though the Altavillas never paid heed to it.

DiFazio's mention of ASA's publicity director has sparked a warm flash, and in the privacy of his room, Diana Ross's face returns to his thoughts — especially the memory of the first time he saw her.

He'd been a nonswimmer in deep water at a big ASA reception in New York, and she'd been the lifeguard — though he hadn't known it at first. It was early evening with a cold rain and sharp wind whipping the umbrellas from the hands of the locals, and the cab ride from his hotel had been wet and fast, his suit pants still damp from getting in and out of the downpour. The ballroom at the Waldorf was full of elegant women that evening — polished, poised females with a serenity about their beauty that made him feel like a stammering sophomore. One such young woman in particular had caught his curiosity as she glided effortlessly between conversations, greeting friends, her smile warm, her persona inviting. Her long, black hair framed a flawless, oval face, her eyes amazingly blue and unforgettably large, and he'd been shocked when she turned and smiled at him. Even across the room he'd averted his eyes for a moment from this long-legged beauty, but when he looked back he let himself notice an abundance of cleavage framed by an expensive, gold-trimmed gown and matching heels — the trappings of a confident woman.

Suddenly, she headed across the room straight for him, which was confusing, and he'd sidled closer to an enormous floral arrangement as if to hide while a flurry of prohibited thoughts flitted through his head.

"Why, Mr. Dawson," she'd said with an endearing smile, "is that you in the potted plant?"

There was no way to know she was an officer of ASA assigned to mentor him through the preflight publicity process, and his discovering that had been a small letdown.

"I'm Diana Ross, ASA's director of publicity, and, yes, I've heard every possible joke about my name, and no, I don't sing."

"Glad to meet you, Diana."

She'd immediately turned to the business of asking him to sit for several TV interviews.

"So, the thing is, I'm in trouble here and I need your help. This soiree . . . this reception . . . is my idea. Oh, of course the primary purpose was to welcome you as the winner, but this party is really to get the media excited again so they can get the rest of the country excited. *But* . . . all we've been able to draw are two local TV camera crews and one reporter. Pathetic. I could generate that with a bake sale in Des Moines, for God's sake."

"I'm sorry to hear that."

She shrugs. "We didn't expect private space flight to become quite so *routine* quite so soon. But here's the thing. I really need to have you participate in a couple of on-camera interviews with the two crews who were kind enough to straggle in. It'll be painless, I promise. Just be yourself and tell them what it was like to win, and how you feel about going into space." She cocks her head, her eyes on his. "So, how *do* you feel?"

"I'm excited," he'd replied. But Sharon's angst was uppermost in his mind, muting his reaction.

"Excited, huh? Could have fooled me."

Kip remembered laughing in mild embarrassment before returning his gaze to her. It felt slightly disturbing, as if she could read too much, and there was an instant attraction beyond the physical, especially when he'd felt her businesslike facade falter as well. "They'll ask me that? If I'm excited?" Kip had countered.

"Sorry?" she'd replied, distracted for a moment as she studied his eyes. Her recovery took a few telling seconds.

"Oh. Yes. They'll ask you that and more. Brace for silly questions." She adopted a stylized voice deeper than her own, a smarmy tone coming through. "So, Mr. Dawson, how does it feel to be going into outer space?"

"Outer . . ."

"Too many local reporters don't know there's a difference between low Earth orbit and so-called 'outer space.'" She'd laughed. "Of course, we fly in low Earth orbit."

"I know that," he'd replied. "Even my *cat*

27

knows the difference between outer space and a low Earth orbit."

"But, you see, they often don't. Tomorrow morning, however," she'd said with pride, "you're going to be on *Good Morning America*, and those folks know all about this stuff."

His jaw had dropped. There hadn't been any mention of national TV. Just the reception.

"Isn't that great?" she'd continued, searching for an approving response. "My one big success in this campaign."

But his pained, almost panicked expression had been undisguised. Sharon Dawson never missed *GMA* and made no secret of being in love with the host, and she would see Kip talking about the very thing that had sent *her* into orbit.

He'd tried to find a way out. "Diana, I don't think you want me on national TV. I'm kind of a private person."

"Nonsense. Oh, by the way," she'd said without missing a beat, "I was sorry to hear that your wife couldn't be with us tonight. Forgive my prying, but, is she worried about your flight?"

"You might say that," Kip had responded, irritated that she'd dragged it out of him. But there it was, dammit.

"Anything I can help with, in terms of providing information, making her feel better?"

He'd looked away for a moment, trying not to send the ungracious message that he'd like to run, but suddenly wishing she'd leave him alone. There was a slight New York lilt in her voice. Were all New Yorkers this brutally direct? He'd forced his eyes back to hers before she got any closer to the truth.

"Diana, I'd prefer to stay in the background. I'd rather not do that show."

"Please don't make me beg! I might have to buy you dinner, and I'm already over budget."

The thrill he'd felt at that moment had nothing to do with national television and it surprised him, making him blush. It had been the radical thought of dining with her. But he'd covered his embarrassment — and his interest — with a laugh.

Minutes later Diana had guided him to an anteroom where she effortlessly greeted a young woman reporter while a bored cameraman with a pigtail waited to pin on a microphone and position Kip just so. At last the cameraman indicated to the reporter that she could fire the first question.

"So, Mr. Dawson," she'd asked. "How does it feel to be going into outer space?"

★ ★ ★

Kip's thoughts return to the ASA suite, his eyes on the clock. It's almost 11 p.m. but even though he's tired, sleeping is going to be difficult. For some reason his mind has locked on Diana and his conversations with her in the weeks after New York, as well as the dinner she flew him to in her own airplane — a delightful evening for just the two of them that felt dangerously close to a date. It had ended with a proper handshake back in Mojave, but not before they'd discovered how much they had in common, and he'd been thrilled to hear her say his enthusiasm for what ASA was doing was so infectious, she was thinking of making him their "poster boy." The publicity, he thought, didn't matter to him as much as the chance to work with her. If there had been a mutual attraction in New York, the dinner had endorsed it, and each subsequent verbal spat with Sharon in the weeks that followed breathed more life into the reality that there were other women out there who might actually like him just as he was.

Kip sighs as he places his cell phone by the bedstand and scans the small screen, surprised to find a message symbol blinking. He checks the call list and feels an instant loss at finding a Colorado Springs area code and his oldest child's phone number at the Air Force Academy.

Jerrod almost never calls, and to miss one of those rare moments hurts. Especially now. His son has always wanted to fly, and perhaps be an astronaut. But never in his wildest thoughts has Kip expected to beat Jerrod into space.

He retrieves the voice mail, expecting words of support. But Jerrod's message is angry and hurt, and it hits Kip like an unexpected haymaker.

Dad, I'm having to talk to your goddamned voice mail again. Julie called in tears tonight, Dad, and said you were going ahead with that spaceflight and that Sharon says you're going to die, and that you haven't paid any attention to their worries. They're all torn up down there. My sister says you aren't listening to anyone. I'm tired of you thinking about no one but you, Dad, and . . . if anything happens to you, you'll be leaving an awful mess behind. I don't want my sister crying! Call me before you take off. I'm really mad at you! Julie doesn't deserve to be treated like this. Neither do the twins.

Kip hears the catch in his son's voice, but the words are clear enough. He knows there's been hardly a moment since his first wife's death that Jerrod hasn't been mad at him. And that never changes. Nor does it make the hurt easier to bear.

He punches up his son's phone at the academy and listens to it ring through to voice mail, but he's too stunned to leave anything but a cursory message.

Kip folds his cell phone and puts it on the nightstand, taking the time to be deliberate so he won't have to react too quickly to the renewed doubts Jerrod's words have shoved back in his heart. He feels the slide toward his old habits, the need to yank out his phone again and rip-snort through however many numbers and command posts are necessary to get his son live on the other end.

Laughter reaches him from somewhere down the hall. More happy customers, he figures, scheduled to fly sometime later and anticipating their incredibly expensive flight to space. Tommy and Anna Altavilla and Tariq, a Saudi royal, each paid a half million dollars. Yet the Altavillas in particular welcomed their contest-winning freeloader as a full partner, and he'll miss sharing this with them.

He should lie down, he thinks. He's running out of night.

Fifty feet down the hallway, Diana Ross stands and debates with herself yet again. She knows Kip Dawson has been back from the meeting less than fifteen minutes, but she's also aware he has less than four hours to sleep.

Yet for some reason, the thought of his going to orbit alone with Bill Campbell is unsettling, and she can't think of a single reason why — other than the unusual nature of having only one passenger aboard. Maybe the gear collapse on ASA's other spacecraft several weeks back is making her nervous.

She poises her hand to knock and finds herself hesitating. Is this business or is this personal? She's not sure. Maybe there's some of both: Protecting her "investment" in him as a potential spokesman, and at the same time, maybe scratching an itch?

Not that he's under her skin or anything. She smiles at the idea. If she wanted companionship or marriage, she wouldn't be thinking about a married guy from Tucson.

Yet there's something about him.

She knocks gently and waits in vain for an answer before knocking again, unwilling to put much energy into it lest she wake any adjacent occupants — all of whom she's met.

Minutes elapse before he opens the door just inches, and she smiles to see him leaning at an angle so she can't see what state of dress he's in.

"Kip! Sorry to bother you so late . . ."

"Diana! Hello. This is a pleasant surprise . . . I think. Is anything wrong?"

"No, no. I just . . . wanted to wish you a good flight, and maybe give you some pointers on what to expect." *How lame!* she thinks, knowing the ground school has already covered everything she could possibly tell him and far more.

He opens the door wider and motions her in and she enters, amused that he's holding a death grip on his bathrobe. He carefully reties it before looking up at her and then closing the door awkwardly. She heads for the couch and sits.

"I was just about ready to dive into bed . . . I apologize for the bathrobe."

"No problem at all! A swimsuit would cover a lot less." She feels off balance, as if someone of greater maturity was going to burst through the door and demand an explanation as to why she's invaded this married customer's bedroom in the middle of the night before his big flight.

She sees the sudden look of doubt trending toward minor panic, the expression transmitting that he's attracted to her and he's getting worried about having her all alone in the same room when here he is naked beneath his bathrobe. The message is so clear it might as well be crawling across a marquee, and she has to suppress a laugh.

"What I want to urge you to do is think about the fantastic sights you're going to see through the eyes of a poet, which I think you may be."

"I've never written poetry, Diana," he says, looking like he's failed to prepare for a test.

"No, I don't mean as in writing poetry, but as in looking at things as if through the eyes of someone who can appreciate the ethereal, the beautiful aspects, the emotional impact, and then put it into words."

"That's a tall order for a mere salesmen of pills."

"But you can do it."

"I'll try."

"Good."

Their eyes are locked for a few intimate moments of pregnant silence and she sees the sparkle of panic mixed with interest again as he suddenly looks away, as if embarrassed.

She gets to her feet suddenly. "Well, I've got to go and let you get . . . ah . . ."

"Sleep. Yeah, I'm pretty tired."

She looks at his eyes again, a smoky aquamarine color. She realizes for the first time that she's holding his arm to steady either herself or him, she's not sure which.

He smiles.

She sees the smile at close range and cocks her head unconsciously, forcing herself to release his arm as if it had suddenly become dangerously hot.

"Well . . . I'd better go," she says.

"I appreciate your coming by."

"And thanks for letting me in." She pulls herself away from his eyes and opens the door, hesitating as she turns.

"See ya. Have a ball up there tomorrow."

And she's back in the hallway, walking with careful dignity in her heels until she's through the outer door.

There's a bench just outside and she sits on it for a moment, wondering what just happened. That moment of eye contact had transmitted something between them, something exhilarating if indefinable, and she gets back to her feet with a smile she can't completely explain, wholly unaware that she's left behind a deeply confused male, who's also smiling inexplicably.

Chapter 3

Mojave International Aerospace Port,
Mojave, California,
May 17, 6:40 a.m. Pacific

Kip knows it isn't so, but the interior of the spaceship named *Intrepid* appears to have shrunk, and it scares him.

He sat in this very seat just last week in the hangar, with Anna Altavilla on his left and Tommy Altavilla and Tariq in the back row — the seating order a result of drawing straws. It was bigger then, the interior. He'd swear to it. But on the day of his actual flight he was too excited to even think that it was going to feel like being crammed into an oil drum with windows.

Can this thing really fly?

His thought is accompanied by a nervous laugh, but he's having serious doubts. It seems as flimsy as a toy, moving in all directions at once whenever either of them moves an arm.

He tries scooting his rear around in the seat he's been carefully strapped to, but real sideways movement is all but impossible, and with Bill Campbell — his pilot/astronaut companion — already belted into the command seat in front of him, Kip can barely even lean forward.

A one-two-two configuration, they call it, with the pilot/astronaut in the forward center seat, his head in the low curvature bubble canopy, and the occupants of the second and third rows given small windows on each side perfectly aligned with their eyes by seat height adjustment.

The other three seats are gone now, removed to reduce weight, which should make it look more roomy but doesn't. He can smell plastic and cleaning chemicals and something else he finally realizes is the evaporating remnants of his own cologne.

He looks to the right, checking his window alignment, aware that his eyes are squarely in the middle of the small, thick sandwich of glass and plastic that will have to protect him from the vacuum of space and the incredible speeds which will be mere inches away at the peak of their flight.

An amusement park–style retention bar would complete this feeling, he thinks with a laugh, recalling the first time he agreed to take Jerrod on a modern roller coaster — a steel monster engineered for upside-down excursions and three-g turns. The thought that he wasn't going to survive the experience had coursed through him when the retaining bars were clicked into place, but he sat there anyway, as if chickening out in front of his boy was a worse fate than being tossed out upside down and dying.

This feels pretty much the same, he thinks, this feeling of needing to see it through, despite the gut level scream from his body and mind that no way could any human survive an attempt at spaceflight in such a tiny, flimsy, *puny* craft.

But Bill Campbell has logged thirty-nine successful missions, he reminds himself. That means no unsuccessful ones.

Yet.

"So how're you doing, Kip?" Bill is asking, grinning as he glances over his right shoulder at his only passenger.

"Just fine."

"Yeah, right. You look green around the gills. Relax."

"No, no! I'm . . . fine. Really."

"It feels like a science fair project when you first strap in, doesn't it?" Bill prompts, familiar with how a tiny spacecraft designed to be lightweight can feel, well, lightweight. He's also aware that without any other passengers to talk to and identify with, *this* passenger is feeling really isolated.

"It just seemed far bigger and more substantial the other day in the hangar."

"It was. Something happened on orbit and it came back like this." Campbell is waiting for him to laugh but for a few embarrassing seconds Kip is actually processing the statement. He catches on and winces. "Oh, jeez, okay."

"You'll be fine. This is an amazingly good piece of engineering. Best I've ever flown. But here's the thing. This is a ship you strap on, not one you get into."

"I believe it."

"Say, Kip. Did you tell me you were a licensed pilot back in class?"

Kip laughs at the aeronautical gulf between them. "No, unfortunately. I've taken glider lessons and soloed, so I know basic stick and rudder, but I never quite got time to finish my license."

"Just wondered how much to explain and that tells me. Relax for a few, or you might even want to take a brief nap. I just heard Mission Control say we're delayed fifteen minutes."

"A problem?"

"Yeah, one of the mothership pilots forgot his lunch."

"Another joke?"

"Yes, Kip," Campbell chuckles. "Boy, you need to get loose, buddy. It's all okay. They just need a bit more fueling time."

"Bill, have time for a question?"

"You bet."

"Everyone keeps saying 'on' orbit instead of 'in' orbit. Is that a space thing?"

"Yep. Mainly started at NASA, but there's good scientific reason to call it that. In brief, we have to get on speed and altitude to be there, so we're on orbit, like being on a perch."

Campbell returns to his preflight duties as Kip lets himself think back through two weeks of ground school, wondering what he's already forgotten.

It was amazing how efficient the ASA ground school had been in prepping people like Kip. Within an hour of reporting for class, he'd had his new name tag clipped to his shirt and been greeted, briefed, equipped, supplied, introduced, and seated in ASA's version of Astronaut 101, taught by the various astronauts themselves. American Space Adventures had accomplished the impossible in less than five years, they were told, and they had no intention of being shy about telling their story.

The company's chief astronaut, George

Andrews, opened the first day. A former NASA astronaut with one shuttle mission, he moved around the classroom with the ease of an experienced professor, inspiring confidence by his just standing there, his youthful appearance the result of keeping a fifty-year-old body in top condition, though his hair was clearly graying.

America's Space Prize, Andrews explained, was created after the first private suborbital flight won the Ansari X prize in 2004. Burt Rutan's Scaled Composites had teamed with Microsoft billionaire Paul Allen to pull it off, using a Rutan-built air-launched craft called *SpaceShipOne* carried aloft by a mothership from the same Mojave airport. Once the realization had sunk in that private spaceflight was a new, fledgling reality, another prize, ten times larger, was announced. The Bigelow Aerospace Corporation — a start-up organization with big dreams to orbit and operate space hotels — would need a way to get customers to and from their inflatable space stations. The fifty-million-dollar prize they posted came with a stringent list of rules. To win, a privately funded company had no more than five and a half years to figure out how to build, with no government money, a private spacecraft that could fly at least five people into a two-hundred-fifty-mile-high altitude for a minimum of two orbits, and do it a second time within thirty days.

ASA had tackled the challenge like NASA had tackled the moon in the sixties. They won the prize handily nearly a year ahead of schedule with a winged, double-tailed craft that looked like an overfed version of *SpaceShipOne*, and within six months were in full commercial operation.

"Our machine is a bit of a miracle," Andrews told them. "We couldn't just fire it up to sixty-five miles and let it glide back to Earth like Burt Rutan did with *Space-ShipOne*. We had to figure out a way to carry enough fuel to get it to at least two hundred and fifty miles up, *then* accelerate it to seventeen thousand miles per hour orbital velocity, *then* find a way to lose all that monstrous buildup of energy without constructing a battleship of heat tiles like NASA's shuttle or running the risk of incinerating ourselves like *Columbia* if something went wrong. And we had to build in enough life support and backup systems for staying in space long enough to dock with one of Bigelow's future orbiting hotels."

The key, they discovered, was to air-drop the ship from a Lockheed 1011 jumbo jet, then use a very large load of rocket propellant to blast up to speed and altitude, and the same propellant to blast back to zero velocity before descending.

"That meant we needed a far more efficient fuel system and a lot of fuel, and thanks to thinking way, way out of any known box, we did it."

"How about the dangers of all that fuel?" one of the class had asked.

Andrews had laughed. "Nowhere near as scary as sitting on top of a virtual bomb, which is what the space shuttle does on every launch. I mean, is it risky? Of course. This isn't an airline flight. That's why we've got a half day of release forms and informed consent instruments our lawyers require you to sign. But don't forget, I . . . or one of our other astronauts . . . will be up there, too, and just like you, we all have families to come back to."

Some of us do, Kip remembers thinking sadly.

"Okay, Kip. We're starting the checklists now," Bill Campbell says, pulling Kip back to the present.

There is a point, Bill has already explained to him, when a professional pilot submerges a large part of his conscious will into his procedures and checklists, and Kip watches that moment arrive. Campbell now becomes the smooth professional running through the complicated predeparture checks without a flicker of emotion.

Kip, however, is the wide-eyed amateur, and for him, no amount of ground school or simulation can make what's about to happen feel routine. In fact, every motion, every noise, every radioed response between Mission Control and Campbell is just below the threshold of startling.

One of the pilots in the mothership has triggered his radio. "*Intrepid, Deliverance.* Comm check all channels and lock."

Deliverance is the name of the highly modified Lockheed 1011 that engulfs them, the carrier aircraft from which they will hang as an appendage until the four mechanical releases are triggered open at sixty thousand feet.

"Roger, *Deliverance*, checks in progress, showing nominal and green all channels. Telemetry initiation confirmed . . . and all checks cycled and complete with green."

"Roger."

Kip has his own headset, and his microphone is set up in such a way that when he speaks, Bill can automatically hear him — as can the support technicians on the ground. But remaining quiet is something he dearly wants to do, not wishing to interfere in any way with Bill's sequence for doing things or run any risks of helping something go wrong.

The checks are suddenly over, the radio channel quiet, and he hears in place of the chatter the sound of *Deliverance*'s huge high bypass jet engines starting up, the entire exercise sounding no different than any routine airline departure.

Which is, Kip thinks, rather like what this is. What's amazing is how fast this kind of private spaceflight has become so reliable and so routine. Crank the engines, fly to altitude, drop *Intrepid*, which does its thing at three hundred ten nautical miles above the Earth, then comes home after making two million dollars. Clockwork.

He *feels* the 1011 start taxiing rather than sees it. *Intrepid* is suddenly bobbling back and forth on its four attach points, like they've scrimped on the attachment hardware and tied *Intrepid* to *Deliverance* with baling wire.

Kip looks out the side window and back behind them, seeing enormous tires rolling slowly. Craning his neck to see through Bill's bubble canopy nets little more. Basically he has a great view of the 1011's belly.

Bill flicks a switch toward the end of the runway porting the regular air traffic controller-to-pilot channels into Kip's headset.

"*Deliverance*, Mojave Tower, you are cleared for takeoff Runway Three-Zero, fifteen thousand nine hundred feet available. Winds are two nine zero at six, gusting twelve."

So now it really begins! Kip thinks, still not believing where he is.

"Roger. *Deliverance* is cleared for take-off, and we're rolling."

Physical noises and motions like he's never experienced course through his body and head, shaking and galvanizing him as the oversized engines wind up to their seventy-thousand-pound thrust level. Slowly at first, or so it seems, the aircraft-spacecraft combination rolls down the runway as if it were reluctant to go, gaining speed slowly, every bump and uneven section of the concrete surface magnified by the time it's transmitted through the attach points to *Intrepid*. Kip feels his eyeballs wobbling with each jolt, the startling vertical accelerations feeding the feeling that they're also fishtailing down the runway.

The frequency of the gyrations and bumps increases as they pass a hundred knots, steadily working their way up to the one-hundred-sixty-knot speed, which is the point at which *Deliverance*'s captain eases back on the yoke and causes the huge Lockheed wings to cant up into the wind, producing, at last, more lift than there is weight to be lifted.

And suddenly they are airborne, the washboard bouncing and yawing gone, the craft swaying gently on its attach points as the ground drops away below.

A new series of thunks and lurches course through the spacecraft. Kip dares a glance over his right shoulder in time to see the immense right main landing gear retracting toward *Intrepid*'s hindquarters. Logic dictates that the main landing gear will clear *Intrepid* as it retracts, but for a second he mentally braces for impact, surprised as the gear thuds into place somewhere behind them, and the gear doors close.

The pilots are reducing the engine power now as he's been taught they will, setting up for a forty-minute climb to altitude, and Bill Campbell turns around to check on his passenger again.

"Still with me?"

"You bet."

"Okay, not much to do for the next half hour now as we gain altitude. But once we're dropped, things are going to happen fast and heavy."

Kip nods and gives him a thumbs-up, but Bill continues.

"Let me go over the sequence again for when we get there, okay?"

"Sure," Kip responds, wanting instead to watch the desert drop away from his window.

"*Deliverance* will stabilize our flight level four-three-zero — forty-three thousand feet — and turn onto the launch heading. We'll do our final checks, get final clearance from Mission Control, and *Deliverance* will light her booster rockets and pull up to a twenty-two-degree climb angle, trading airspeed and power for altitude. She'll push over at flight level six-one-zero as the rockets burn out, and she'll hold there for just long enough to drop us. You saw those guys get aboard in pressure suits, right?"

"Yes, I did."

"That's because we can't pressurize a huge 1011 safely enough to guarantee they won't have their bodies exposed to blood-boiling pressure altitudes, so we solve it by making them very uncomfortable. As we taught you in class, we don't need to wear space suits here inside *Intrepid* since this capsule is triple-redundant and self-sealing."

"But you've got yours aboard, right?"

"Well, sure. It's all compressed flat and stored, just in case some impossible event might present the need for me to float around outside and repair something. But don't worry, it's aboard. Checking it is part of my preflight routine."

"Good."

An unexpected shuddering rattles the spacecraft — and presumably the airplane carrying it — and they're shoved sideways for a few seconds. *Routine,* Kip tells himself, but Bill hesitates, his eyes darting to his panel as he gets quiet for a few seconds.

"What was that?" Kip asks.

"Don't know. Upper air turbulence, or CAT 1, I suspect. Clear air turbulence. Whatever it was, no worries."

"Okay."

"Where was I? Oh yeah. We'll confirm our clearance as we're dropping away, light our motor, confirm forward vertical clearance from *Deliverance*, and we're off."

"Hey, Bill," Kip ventures, feeling serious.

"Yeah?"

"Is it really routine for you? This sequence?"

He can see the astronaut/pilot start to repeat the company line but stop himself, the curtain of professionalism parting for just a second as a large smile covers the man's face and his eyes flick away to the windows.

"It's Christmas morning every time, Kip. My dream comes true every launch."

Kip is nodding even after Bill turns his attention back to the forward panel.

"I'm glad to hear that. I don't think I'd want to fly with someone who wasn't as excited as I am."

The half hour evaporates and Kip hears Bill once again running through a checklist, *Intrepid*'s altimeter steady on forty-three thousand feet. The same basic countdown he listened to from Cape Canaveral on so many launches winds down in his car.

"Kip, the mothership's rocket motors never quite fire at the same moment, so there will be a sideways lurch for just a second, and then she'll steady out."

Kip nods, too overwhelmed with the sensations and the impending drop to find his voice.

"Two, one, ignition."

The outboard rocket-assist motor mounted under the left wing of the 1011 lights first and they yaw amazingly to the right as the opposite one kicks in, as advertised.

The pilot's voice from the 1011's flight deck is utterly unemotional.

"Thrust nominal, commencing pitch-up and countdown."

More numbers counting backward. More lighted numerals and readouts changing on the complicated liquid crystal displays in front of Bill Campbell. Kip struggles to keep his eyes on what he knows is the altimeter, one of the few he can read. It shows them now climbing through fifty thousand feet. He thinks the attitude indicator is showing a pitch-up of twenty-two degrees, but it feels like forty or more. *Intrepid* is shaking back and forth sideways and being pulled ahead and he wonders if there's any way the real launch will feel as startling.

"Release minus two minutes, mark."

There are a host of voices in his ears making sure everyone and everything is co-ordinated and ready, and their calm is almost unnerving. He thinks if the whole thing blew apart like space shuttle *Challenger* and the radios remained, Bill and his compatriots would probably keep the same tone of voice as they narrated down to the desert floor.

"Ah, Roger, Mojave we have unscheduled dual wing separation and unauthorized main aircraft body disintegration, with estimated time to extinction on im-

pact T minus one minute, ten seconds, on my mark."

"Roger, Intrepid, we copy the end of life as you know it."

He shakes himself free of the maudlin thought, although for some reason it does seem amusing. There are thirty seconds left and the big aircraft holding them close is pushing its nose down to level now as it slows, the altitude topping out at sixty-one thousand feet where the 1011 was never designed to be.

Kip knows about the tiny window of time to launch. If something hiccups, they have no more than twelve seconds to figure it out and fix it before scrubbing the launch and letting the 1011 pilots fly the mothership back to the low forty-thousand-foot range.

He almost misses it, the call is so routine. The drop clearance — his clearance to fly to space — is issued from Mission Control below, the count now less than ten seconds. Kip finds himself mouthing the descending numbers.

"Hang on, old buddy," Bill says. "It's about to get interesting."

"Three, two, one, release."

Kip thinks he's feeling time dilate. Nothing seems to be happening.

Wait, nothing *is* happening! Time is slowing for real now, and he waits, expecting to feel any microsecond the sensation of being dropped toward the desert below. But they're still attached!

He looks at Bill for confirmation that he hasn't missed it all, but the astronaut is busy triggering his transmitter.

"We have negative release, *Deliverance*. Select prime backup and confirm."

"Shit!" Is the singular response from above, as another voice intones "Eight seconds in the window."

"Primary backup selected, counting two, one, release."

Something shoves them around, or so Kip thinks, but they're still merely a mechanical appendage of the 1011.

"Selecting secondary," one of the pilots above says, the slightest trace of stress in his voice.

"Three seconds to abort," another intones.

"Pressurizing."

"Two, one, release, dammit!"

This time the whole world changes. Whooshing sounds of a pneumatic backup system force the jaws of the four primary hooks open in slightly staggered fashion. *Intrepid*'s nose drops first as the forward hooks release, followed by an uneven release of the rear two. In an instant Kip's stomach has declared itself in freefall. His fingers dig a deathgrip into the armrests of his seat as he watches Campbell's right hand holding the primary ignition control.

"*Intrepid* away," Campbell says.

"*Deliverance* in pitch mode," is the response, the 1011 sharply turning and slowing to get out of the way.

Aren't we going to ignite our engine? Kip's mind is screaming.

"Cleared for ignition," says someone somewhere on the ground, and suddenly ignite is exactly what the rocket does — the engine kicking the living hell out of his back as Kip hangs on and wonders how Bill Campbell can even react, let alone casually look up and back as he checks his controls.

"Ignition confirmed."

"Cleared to climb, *Intrepid*. Godspeed."

"Roger."

They're being propelled forward with incredible force and speed and suddenly they're also pitching-up, on their own, like a teenager driving away in his new car for the first time, leaving stunned parents waving from the sidewalk.

The previous pitch-up while they were attached to the mothership, Kip thinks, was sandlot ball compared to a round with the Yankees.

This is amazing!

They're almost vertical now. He can see the little black dot in the attitude indicator coming into the center of Bill's target, and while he knows it's only three-and-a-half g's he's feeling, it seems infinite.

And the shaking! Nothing in the ride up on the 1011 even remotely prepared him for the crackling and shuddering and bouncing of the little craft as it streaks straight up. He's too frightened to be scared.

"Passing Mach 2, one hundred thousand feet."

"Copy," says the same voice on the ground.

Mach 2, Kip thinks. *That's . . . that's about twelve hundred miles per hour!*

He can feel his heart racing, almost pounding out of his chest, his head locked forward by the ground-school caution that if he turns his head to look out the window, he'll never be able to turn it back.

But in his peripheral vision, he can already see the Earth's curvature.

"My . . . God!" is all he can manage as he moves his eyes as far right as possible to take in the sight.

"So far," Bill continues, "I've been flying

the controls like an airplane, but now they get strange, and things almost reverse. When we get up higher, we'll have only the reaction control jets to keep us pointed in the right direction. Okay, passing one hundred fifty thousand feet, and Mach 3."

Kip knows that's about as fast as they're going to go before pitchover, before they're so far above the denser air molecules of the atmosphere that increasing speed won't cause frictional heating problems.

"Two hundred thousand feet, Mach 3.2," Bill intones, adding a postscript. "That's thirty-two nautical miles, Kip. We're technically not in space yet."

It sure looks like space to me, Kip thinks, keeping his eyes on the horizon as the g-forces decrease.

"Are we slowing?" he asks. They've already taught him the answer, but he can't help it. The last thing he's going to pretend to be up here is a seasoned professional blasé about the details.

"Not yet," Bill is saying. "We'll start our throttle-back at sixty miles and reduce speed as we climb to two hundred miles, then do the pitchover and accelerate."

"Got it." He wants to yell, "Whee-oooh!" as loudly as possible, but it would be undignified and might startle the pilot. Not a good idea, he decides, to startle the pilot while flying an eggshell into space.

The Earth's surface curves away like a huge ball now, even though they're just passing the so-called threshold of space, around sixty-five miles. The steady force in his back begins to lessen as Bill pulls the throttle to half thrust, using the ship's immense momentum in the absence of most air resistance to partially coast, partially thrust, up to the three-hundred-mile point.

Five minutes go by slowly, but on the other end of it Kip feels Bill pushing the craft over, using the control jets now, throttling up as soon as he hits the right attitude, the g-forces reasserting themselves as the nose continues to drop slowly in relation to the horizon.

"Now the speeds get really industrial strength," Bill is saying. They pass through four thousand miles per hour, then six, then eight and ten, the actual digits familiar from training but incredibly difficult to accept. Faster than a speeding bullet. In fact, far faster.

Take us into orbit, Mr. Sulu!

The gravity he feels now isn't gravity at all, but the acceleration of the engine as it thrusts *Intrepid* through the airless void toward seventeen thousand four hundred miles per hour. His mind replays every *Star Trek* clip he can recall of the Starship *Enterprise* streaking toward the speed of light. This feels like that looked.

"Stand by for a bit of a shock," Bill calls.

"What? Is there a problem?" Kip's reply is too sharp, too instantly concerned, and it triggers a laugh from Campbell.

"No, no. It's just time to throw it into neutral." He pulls the throttle back and cuts the rocket motor, the sudden disappearance of thrust and acceleration leaving Kip feeling like he's falling again, but forward, this time. Bill Campbell hears the anticipated gasp.

"We're weightless," Bill announces. "And congratulations, man." He's reaching back now to shake Kip's hand. "You have officially arrived on orbit above our planet."

"We're here?" Kip turns to stare out his side window before Bill can answer.

"We sure are. We're almost welded up here in an orbit so stable it might not decay for forty or maybe as many as sixty years, give or take a few sunspots."

Kip falls into awed silence, his hands still death-gripping the armrests, his stomach still confused about which way is up. At long last he lets himself breathe, a runner exhaling at the end of a long jog. *Sixty years,* he thinks, missing the reference to the sunspots.

"Magnificent."

"Sorry?"

It takes a few seconds to find his voice, and Bill waits in a familiar indulgence.

"For this moment at least," Kip says, "I feel like the luckiest guy in the world."

Chapter 4

The administrator of the National Aeronautics and Space Administration stares in abject disgust at the U.S. senator from Massachusetts, wondering if the inane slip in his last question is the result of a momentary distraction, or the pickling of too many brain cells from too many years of excessive drinking.

Geoff Shear loves being the head of NASA, but he hates like hell having to deal with the worst of the hypocrites on the Hill — senators and congressmen who convince the public that they support the space program while behind closed doors trying to emasculate it.

He scoots a bit closer to the microphone, letting the full force of the senator's embarrassing mistake impress itself on the rest of the subcommittee and the media. The man

61

is apparently unaware of what he's said, and his staff seems equally confused.

"Senator," Geoff begins, forcing a puzzled look on his face, "I'm sorry, but I may have missed something. I'm singularly unaware of any U.S. policy that supports funding the goal of eventual human colonization of Venus. If I'd known, I would have recommended against it — especially since the surface temperature on Venus is hot enough to melt lead."

Good! he thinks. The senator looks befuddled as a horrified staff member rushes forward to whisper the right information in his ear. The aging liberal jerks his head around, wholly disbelieving, then grasps what he's done to himself and that the NASA administrator has gleefully added to the embarrassment.

"I, ah, think you know very well, Mr. Shear, that I meant Mars, when I said Venus by mistake. I meant Mars. Of course we're not going to go to Venus."

"Only taking you at your word, Senator," Geoff replies. "I thought I could do that safely." *Take that, you duplicitous SOB,* Geoff thinks to himself as the senator mumbles a retort and returns to his staff's list of questions. It's the tiniest of paybacks for the senator's leading a fight to all but scuttle NASA's budget, but it feels good. No, it feels *damn* good, and he doesn't need the windbag anyway. The senator is part of the disloyal minority now, his opposition to NASA programs essentially impotent.

Geoff all but sleepwalks through the remainder of the hearing, the thrust of the opposition's efforts completely blunted. His budget figures are correct, and he is not, he tells them, going to stop turning to the media to complain about Congress every time it cuts down the space program.

The subcommittee's Democrats and a few of the Republicans make it known that they are shocked and offended at the administrator's defiant tone, but it's obvious the media doesn't care, and the opposition's artificial outrage ends abruptly.

Geoff gathers his papers and stands confidently, knowing that the President approves of his pugnacious tactics. Even better is knowing that his methods are having the desired effect and putting unsupportive lawmakers in a corner.

"Eventually," Geoff tells the two staff members who've shepherded him to the hearing, "those who vote no are going to have to do so in front of the same constituents who have listened to them praise every launch and every success NASA has ever had."

Confidence is good, Geoff thinks, making sure the expression on his face mirrors serene self-assurance.

But minutes later when he's alone and in the backseat of his chauffeured government car, he catches himself once again wondering how much longer he can continue using the Joseph Goebbels method, the big lie, presenting mediocre NASA programs as grand "accomplishments." He can't be the only one who sees that the world's preeminent space agency is dying.

No question that NASA's record over the past decade is wimpy at best: No return to the moon, a manned mission to Mars about to be scuttled in the wake of the Russian space agency's impending mission to the red planet, the man-in-a-can excuse for an international space station still an expensive facade, the space shuttle replacement program in deep and probably terminal trouble, and a growing, dangerous feeling on the part of the American public that private corporations can do space better and cheaper than a huge, hidebound government bureaucracy.

And then there's Richard DiFazio's ASA

and DiFazio's personal campaign to undermine NASA at every turn. Bad enough that the fabled Burt Rutan — admittedly an aeronautical genius — always referred to NASA as "Nay Say," but DiFazio has made a career out of embarrassing Geoff Shear. What's worse, the public believes him.

The fact that DiFazio is probably right about privatizing space is immaterial. It's Shear's mission to keep NASA funded, alive, and relevant in the public eye, regardless. But there are times he wishes the job of NASA administrator brought with it a license to kill. No question who'd be first on his list. In too many ways, winning the private versus public battle has become his personal war.

Welcome to my life! he thinks, acutely aware that the agency is living on the edge and no more than one accident or scandal away from programmatic oblivion.

His driver swings smoothly into Washington's afternoon traffic, heading back toward NASA Headquarters at 300 E Street SW as Geoff pulls out a sheaf of briefing papers he has yet to study, recognizing the top one immediately as the one thing he does not want to see.

Especially today.
Dammit to hell!

He's known for weeks that if *Newsweek* decides to disregard the warnings from NASA's friends and run a particularly hated article as a cover piece, the damage will be cruel. And now here it is, as bad as he expected, its pseudo-question begging its own conclusion:

CAN NASA COMPETE WITH PRIVATE SPACEFLIGHT COMPANIES? How the pioneering space agency is losing the battle for relevance and cost-efficiency.

He scans the four pages of verbiage before yanking out his cell phone and punching the speed dial for his secretary and instructing her to pull in his department heads for a war council. DiFazio has to be behind this one, too. The rag will hit the stands in four days, and he'll need a preemptive strike to defuse what they've written.

His headquarters slides into view and the car stops, but he isn't ready, and the driver knows better than to ask. He imagines the man now waiting for the magic phrase. "Okay, Billy," he'll say, and the chauffeur will get out and rush back to open his door. For now, though, he can sit in silence and think.

And what he's thinking is disturbing. The whole nightmarish subject is out of his control, but there it is, still in his head, the same image that dawned like a revelation while he was fly-fishing in Colorado just two weeks ago.

What if, he'd thought then, *one of their shoe-box, slapped-together, backyard, two-bit excuses for a spacecraft goes down?* What if American Space Adventures — what a stupid name for a supposedly professional organization — has an accident and loses one of their only two pretend-a-shuttles? Their stock would crater and their business dry up, and the world would have graphic confirmation that the extreme dangers of spaceflight simply *must* be left to the might and wisdom of the U.S. government.

No, no. To hell with convincing the *world*. All he needs to do is convince Congress.

Standing in the middle of that peaceful stream, he'd let an attack of conscience bring him up short, a moment of uncertainty, the horror of someone actually learning his terrible thoughts. My God, of *course* he didn't really want anyone to die just to convince Congress to fund NASA! The corrective edit had coursed through his mind and it had distracted him long enough to miss hooking the trout who'd picked that exact moment to nibble on one of his best flies.

But he had no control over a private spacecraft. It wasn't, after all, a *wish,* merely an observation, and one that made him very squeamish. Moral compunction thus satisfied, he'd yanked the line hard enough on the next nibble to hook a fat rainbow *and* flip the startled fish completely out of the water with the same motion.

Geoff Shear looks around, aware that he's been lost in thought. The staff will be waiting for him upstairs.

If a private spacecraft goes down, he'll need to be ready, he'll need the right things to say, words already drafted and rehearsed with the right statistics to cite. Maybe he should even be ready to recommend that Congress put stringent restrictions on anyone but NASA attempting spaceflight?

No. That would anger the President.

The White House is too committed to the free market. No, if the worst happens, Geoff concludes, NASA will simply be there in sorrow to sympathize, and then soldier on for all mankind.

The last line to his favorite Robert Frost poem springs to mind, a phrase he's driven himself with for years: *"But I have promises to keep, and miles to go before I sleep."*

He leans forward, sorry to lose the solitude.

"Okay, Billy."

Chapter 5

Three Hundred Ten miles above
the Atlantic Ocean,
May 17, 8:32 a.m. Pacific

A sharp, almost metallic "plink" echoes through the interior of the spacecraft.

Kip doesn't want to tear himself away from the reverie of what he's seeing out his window, but the sound is too loud to ignore, and he feels a pressure fluctuation in the cabin.

He begins to turn his head back forward, realizing at the same moment that something wet has sprayed the back of his neck.

"Bill, what was that?"

Campbell is facing forward, but not answering. Kip can see the astronaut's headset askew, his hands sort of floating up in front of him.

What on Earth?

"Bill?"

No answer.

"Bill!"

Is he pulling a joke? If so, this is not funny.

"Bill, come on, answer me!"

Kip leans toward him. There is a spot, almost like a hole, in the back of the pilot's seat toward the top, and there's a reddish mist floating around in the zero-g atmosphere of the cabin. He feels his stomach twisting up as he looks behind and spots a splatter of red on the aft bulkhead, along with what has to be another hole.

He begins clawing at his harness to release it so he can lean forward. Bill Campbell is still silent. Why?

The seat harness mechanism gives way and he launches himself forward too fast, floating over Campbell's right shoulder, twisting like the zero-g amateur he is, his back coming to rest against the instrument panel with a soft thud, his eyes fixating on his companion's blank expression.

Bill's eyes are open wide and fully dilated, and in the middle of his forehead is a small, red-tinged hole.

"Oh, *God!*" Kip hears himself gasp as he claws for something to hold on to, aware he may be kicking dangerously sensitive controls. He grabs hold of something with his left hand and shakes Bill with his right, praying for a quick and cogent response.

But there is none. The astronaut looks gone, a lot of blood leaking from the exit

71

wound in the back of his head. He's beyond hope. What Kip felt on the back of his own neck is apparently Bill's blood.

Kip feels himself recoil in pure panic, as if he's preparing to run.

Oh my God! Oh God! What happened?

Somewhere inside he already knows the answer. Something — a tiny space rock, a discarded piece of space junk — *something* has smashed into and through *Intrepid* at an incredibly high speed and passed like a bullet through Bill's cranium, killing him instantly. Keeping a small hit from exploding the craft or leaking out all the air was a major engineering challenge they were told about in training. That was the very reason the spacecraft was built with self-sealing walls.

But he never took the threat seriously. No one has ever been killed by a space rock before, especially not inside a warm capsule. Have they? What are the chances?

Kip floats himself back toward his seat shaking with confusion.

This simply can't be happening!

He grabs the mouthpiece on his headset and begins calling for help in a higher-pitched voice than his own, before recalling that he has to press something to transmit outside the spacecraft. A switch, a button, something he was never supposed to need. Where the hell is it? He scrambles around the side of his armrest and finds it, stabbing at it and calling again.

"Mission Control, ah, *Intrepid.* Emergency! Mayday! *Mayday, Mayday, Mayday!* I have a big problem!"

A big problem? What a pitiful understatement, he thinks, as he waits for the response. A big problem would be an astronaut with an upset stomach.

"Mission Control . . . ASA Mojave . . . *somebody* . . . please come in. This is *Intrepid.* We have a big fucking problem up here!"

Nice touch, he thinks, adding a guilty feeling to his growing résumé of horrors. *My first communication from space and it's the "F" word.*

Between checking to make sure he's really pushing the transmit button and boosting the volume control to hear the response that isn't coming, a small lifetime passes — accompanied by the mental buzz of what has to be his sky-high blood pressure pounding through his brain.

He looks out the window, recognizing the Arabian desert moving by smartly beneath, realizing he's as isolated now as if he was sitting without a radio or water in some trackless sand dune three hundred ten miles below. No, he isn't working the radios wrong. The radios just aren't working.

So now what?

The frantic calls stop and Kip forces himself away from his seat and backward to the far right-hand corner of the tiny compartment, as if a wider angle view will illuminate the big picture at last, showing him the passage back to the place he was before.

Which was newly on orbit. Happy as hell! Privileged.

The luckiest guy in the world! he recalls thinking, mocking his own words of minutes before. From a lifelong dream to the worst nightmare in record time. The irony is almost funny.

There's a handhold near the corner of the compartment where he's hovering and he grips it tightly now, his eyes on his deceased companion, his mind still slogging through the beginnings of a deep denial that's already being challenged by something vaguely remembered from the previous two weeks in training. Something about emergencies. Something about going to the laminated checklist.

Yes! Get the checklist!

But which one? He can't recall any checklist labeled IN CASE YOUR ASTRONAUT/ PILOT IS KILLED BY A SPACE ROCK!

The checklists and detailed procedures, they'd been taught, are all contained in the master computer screen in front of the pilot. But there are physical versions — laminated duplicates — stored in a side compartment and Kip launches his body in that direction, coming in too fast again and thudding into the sidewall. He works the latch and yanks out the bound stack of pages, rifling through them far too rapidly, his thoughts near hysterical and his hands shaking too much to focus on what he's looking for.

Calm down! he tells himself, the command having little effect. Somewhere in these pages is a solution. He can feel it. But *where?*

He finds procedures for dealing with loss of oxygen pressure, failures of this or that instrument, and flight-control-system problems, and he finally seizes on one dealing with radio failure, ripping the pages back and forth as he tries to focus and deal with the information a step at a time.

No, dammit! Not the right one!

More page turning. He's aware that Saudi Arabia has slipped away and he's approaching the Indian subcontinent, flying over the Persian Gulf. Geography has always been a love, but there's no time now to do anything but take note. Whatever he has to do to get help . . .

For the first time since whatever object it was smashed through his world, Kip stops himself. His hands are still shaking, his heart racing, but his thoughts turn to a very obvious reality. There *is* no help! Even if he gets the radios working, physically no one can come up here and bring him home, because it's been made very clear that none of the governmental space agencies will lift a finger for a private space adventure.

Even NASA will ignore him.

No, he decides, he knows what he's got to look for now. If he can't reestablish contact with the ground, then it's up to him to do the same things Bill would do — throw the same switches he would throw — drop them out of orbit at the appointed time. And there has to be at least *some* time to figure it out. They haven't even completed one orbit.

We're supposed to come down after four orbits. A bit less than six hours from now.

He's breathing rapidly and he wonders if he'll deplete all the oxygen if he keeps it up.

But Bill isn't breathing at all anymore, so he's got double whatever they'd have had together. In any event there should be enough for six hours.

Also, he thinks, the electrical circuits are still on. The panel's still functioning. Lights and a heater are keeping him warm.

He looks forward, searching for the point of entry and finds it at last, just below the command window frame and forward, one of the few places something could have come through without exploding the glass and plastic forward window. Whatever it was blew out through the back wall and into the equipment bay behind them, where it either stopped or left the spacecraft. And the automatic layer of sticky sealant has obviously worked. He can hear no hissing, no obvious loss of air pressure.

He worries for just a moment about any other unseen, undetected damage back there, back where the engine and fuel tanks are located. But if there was damage to the fuel, wouldn't he be dead now? Wouldn't there at least be flashing red alerts all over the elaborate liquid crystal displays?

They show nothing, and he finds the fuel status selection and does his best to read the fact that as predicted, half the fuel remains and is safe a few feet behind him.

Once again he starts pawing through the checklists, selecting the ones on communication failure and reading carefully down each category, checking circuit breakers when he can find them and changing settings, each time expecting to hear the comforting voice of the controller back in Mojave.

But the headset remains silent.

He's ignoring the floating remnants of Bill's spilled blood he hasn't been able to mop up with a series of tissues — just as he's forcing himself not to think about having to cover the astronaut's leaking head with a thin silver, mylar blanket before pulling his body out of the command chair. What was Bill Campbell is now a macabre hooded form tied to the back wall of the small cabin while the capsule's only living occupant sits in front of the panel searching desperately for a way to talk to the planet below.

And with Sri Lanka and the east coast of India sliding by beneath him, Kip finally exhales and sits back in the assaulted command chair, letting the checklists float listlessly in front of him as he struggles through the cobwebs of his panic and pulls the last curtain of denial aside.

Dear God, I am alone up here. And I've got five hours to learn how to get myself back.

Chapter 6

ASA Mission Control,
Mojave International Aerospace Port,
Mojave, California,
May 17, 8:53 a.m. Pacific

The whine of jet engines filters into the stunned silence of the sound-insulated control room. Smoking has never been permitted here, but several occupants are wishing for an exemption. The level of tension is palpable.

Outside on the ramp, the Lockheed 1011 named *Deliverance* is returning to her parking spot, one hundred and fifty thousand pounds lighter — her missing appendage now halfway around the planet.

Video and audio feeds carry what's happening inside the computer-rich mission control room, but the TV images are going only to the Internet and a bank of digital recorders, since no news organizations have requested them. With few exceptions, the world is neither watching nor listening.

Here the response to what at first seemed

a momentary communications glitch has become disordered, adrift, the assembled professionals milling around like a troop of actors who've run off the end of their script. They stand and look back and forth, consulting their monitors and each other for answers to questions they're having trouble even phrasing. Ultimately, all eyes migrate to one man.

Arleigh Kerr stands at the flight director's console, searching the faces of the eighteen men and women arrayed before him for signs of deliverance. A veteran of the same sort of control room at NASA in Houston, his thinning hair and angular features on a six-foot frame are well known in spaceflight circles. An admirer of NASA's unflappable Deke Slayton, Kerr is working hard now to find a way to stay the calm leader, the man with the answers — but he, too, is floundering.

Intrepid achieved exactly the orbit planned for it, and they all know exactly where the ship is at the moment. What they don't know is why virtually every communications circuit in the ship could have failed simultaneously.

It's like someone yanked a plug from the wall up there, he thinks to himself, embarrassed at the simplicity of the simile.

"Arleigh, we're cued up on the rerun of the last thirty seconds of telemetry," one of his engineers is saying in his ear.

"You have something?"

"Not sure. You want to punch it up on your monitor?"

He nods before remembering to reply.

"Yeah. Channel Twelve. Got it."

"Okay, Arleigh, watch parameters forty-eight and ninety-six. I've highlighted them. Forty-eight is capsule atmospheric pressure. Ninety-six is internal structure vibration monitor."

The graphed lines crawl across the screen in routine manner until one second before the communication link ends.

"*There,* Arleigh. See that? Pressure drop at the same moment we've got a loud vibration, like a noise in a multiple of frequencies."

"I see it," he says. "But what does it mean?"

"Stand by. We're coming to you," the engineer replies, and in a few seconds, four of them are arrayed around the flight director, their faces ashen.

"What? *What?*" Arleigh demands.

"We think we may have lost a pressure seal. Explosively. Pressure drop, vibration — probably a loud noise — then nothing."

"But why no radios? Why no telemetry?" Arleigh asks, his irritation leaking into his resolve of steady leadership. "Even if we've lost Bill and his passenger, how can a blown seal have knocked out *all* communications? They don't need to be . . . alive . . . for the telemetry to keep working."

Glances are exchanged before their eyes return to him.

"The other possibility, Arleigh, is that we collided with something."

The thought had haunted him.

"Collided with *what?* We did all the usual NORAD checks before launch and we're live online with them right now for any space junk updates. There's nothing out there."

"That they know about," one of the men corrects, looking sheepish and bracing for the defensive retort he expects.

But Arleigh feels already defeated. They've voiced the ultimate heresy: no routine or noncatastrophic explanation for losing all the comm circuits at once. The lump in his throat is growing.

"We have a handheld Iridium phone up there, right?" Arleigh asks. "We've checked it? We've called it?"

The Iridium satellite phone has its own battery. For a spacecraft, it's a low-tech backup that should have worked if Bill Campbell had lost all other means of communicating.

"Yes, we called it," is the reply. "And we checked with Iridium's control center. There's zero indication Bill has pulled it out. Which . . . may indicate he can't."

Arleigh Kerr surveys their faces, seeing they all share the same horrific vision. He turns to Ian McIver, another NASA veteran.

"See if you can get one of NASA's high-powered cameras to look at him during the Australian transit. Let's see if we can confirm *Intrepid* is intact."

"I'll have to scramble," Ian says, already doing just that.

"And the rest of you rerun the tapes and see if there's any indication of anything out of the ordinary *before* that last second. Some parameter going south we didn't catch."

"We're getting NORAD involved to look at their debris tracks just before signal loss, too."

"Good."

"Arleigh, you *are* going to call general quarters, aren't you? Bring in Mr. Di-Fazio?"

Arleigh is already nodding, the act of

alerting the company's chairman a painful call he made less than ten minutes ago.

"He's out of bed and on the way."

No point in discussing *Intrepid*'s inability to automatically take itself out of orbit. From the first they've taught their passengers in ground school how to do the deorbiting job themselves in the event an astronaut dies, but it was complicated and never supposed to be necessary, since all the commands can be sent by remote and *Intrepid* can even be flown down to a safe landing remotely. The arguments they've had over the terrible things that could go wrong with a civilian at the controls still haunt them, disasters like spinning off into deep space or thrusting into an immediately incinerated reentry, or managing to slow and descend only to crash on landing from lack of pilot skills. The argument for a minimum of two astronauts on each flight had even worried the Federal Aviation Administration — until Congress swatted the FAA and decided that the word "aviation" did not include the word "space."

So the ability to remote-control everything aboard *Intrepid* was their ace in the hole, but an ability that depended on the communications links working. The idea that they could all go down at once is one nightmare they'd never fully faced.

And now?

Arleigh picks up the phone and punches in the cell number of ASA's chairman and CEO, who is racing north from Lancaster in his car.

"Any change, Arleigh?" Richard DiFazio asks.

"No, sir. The bottom line is, we have zero communication, no ability to remote control, and no knowledge of whether either of our two people up there is conscious . . . or even alive."

"Keep the lid on this. I'm ten minutes out."

"We do need to ask NASA for help. I . . . already gave the order to do so."

"Oh God! That will go straight to Geoff Shear."

"Sir . . ."

"I know, I know. It's okay. Do what you have to do."

Office of the Administrator,
NASA Headquarters, Washington, D.C.,
9:10 a.m. Pacific/12:10 p.m. Eastern

When the administrator of NASA calls an emergency meeting of his senior staff with

85

outlying members suddenly yanked from their offices and piped in by video tele-conference, the entire neural network of NASA begins to vibrate.

That pleases Geoff Shear.

He enters the conference room next to his office and sits surveying the faces around the table and those on screen from Houston and the Cape. There are several large liquid crystal screens on the far wall, each bearing the NASA logo, which now dissolve into various images.

"So ASA wants us to look at their space-craft," he begins. "Why? Are they in trouble?" Geoff is working to control his ex-pression, keep it serious and concerned, but no one carrying a NASA badge in the Beltway is unaware of the personal war of Geoffrey Shear, and Providence has just handed him a gift he dare not acknowledge.

One of the managers at Johnson in Houston answers.

"Yes, sir. They've lost all their communi-cations."

"Telemetry, too?" Geoff asks.

"We can't pick it up if anything's coming down. All their comm links went dark as soon as they arrived on orbit."

"Have we visually looked at them?"

Heads nod and there's a sudden switch to

a videotape of the spacecraft in flight, a fuzzy, indistinct image shot with an incredibly long lens from a ground station in western Australia.

"So what am I seeing?" Geoff asks, leaning forward.

"The craft appears intact, and we're reading livable heat on the other side of the windows. That could be just the window heaters we're detecting, but most likely she's still pressurized and survivable. We don't see any visible damage, but . . . there's this."

"Who's speaking?"

"Ed Rogers from Houston."

The picture changes to a composite of black and white imagery and what appears to be a digital radar display.

"What am I looking at?" Shear demands.

The same voice responds.

"This is from NORAD's array, just as ASA's ship reached orbit. This is about a minute and a half after engine cutout. I'm going to go frame by frame here, because we have just two radar hits on what appears to be a very small object approaching very, very rapidly from in front of the craft, then one single radar hit of it on the backside, in a slightly different trajectory. At the same point, on the visual image, there's a small burst of light that might indicate ejected debris aft of the capsule corresponding with the backside trajectory."

"And in English, Dr. Rogers?"

"We think they got nailed by something NORAD wasn't tracking."

"And that's where the radios went?"

"Sir, it apparently passed through the equipment bay of their ship, and God knows what damage it did, but knocking out virtually all their communications and their propulsion, control, and, eventually, even life support would not be an outlandish expectation."

"Jesus!"

"Geoff, John Kent in Houston." The voice of NASA's chief astronaut, a former Air Force colonel, is not a welcome intrusion.

"Yeah, John."

"We have *Atlantis* in the vehicle assembly building at the Cape and I can work up an emergency mission plan within an hour if you'd like."

"Why, John?"

Silence fills the room and the circuits, a silence Geoff knows Colonel Kent will be unable to keep.

"If someone's alive up there, we can't just sit on our hands, can we?"

Geoff gets to his feet, his well-honed ability to put subordinates in their place virtually second nature.

"Thanks, everyone," he says on the way out of the room, answering the question by default. He knows the effect on his staff, and he should thank Kent for the opportunity to once again demonstrate how an iron-ass leader wields his power. Those who press beyond the limits of what Geoff Shear wants to hear will be ignored and embarrassed.

Besides, he thinks darkly, Kent knows damn well what the policy is on rescuing privateers in space.

Chapter 7

So Sharon was right after all.

Kip thinks of little else. The hope that he might somehow remember how to blast himself back out of orbit and find a way to land seems beyond overwhelming. He looks at the pile of checklists in his lap, having read over several trying to get a mental image of the long litany of technical duties that he'll have to perform at the right moment in the right way to direct the rocket motor in precisely the right direction to lose all that speed they gained.

He sighs, shaking his head at the image of himself getting tangled up in what switch to hit next. Even if, somehow, he gets it all right and everything works, he'll then pop out in the lower troposphere and have an on-the-job learning experience trying to dead-stick an engineless spacecraft down to a runway somewhere without colliding with something hard and unforgiving.

No, Sharon is going to be right, he decides. But there is still the slightest glimmer in his mind that he could escape. A shred of hope, like believing your football team can somehow use the last five seconds of the game to Hail Mary their way through ninety yards of determined defenders to the winning touchdown.

Possible, yes. Probable, no.

Okay, most likely I'm going to die.

And the hell of it is, he can't even call Sharon to apologize.

He looks at his watch, then at the Earthscape passing below. He's in darkness now somewhere over the Pacific, wondering why he has to wait for three more orbits before trying to leave. Maybe he should plan to try the retrofire sequence at the end of the second orbit, instead of waiting for the third? Or would that bring him down in the wrong place? To fire it right now, for instance, would probably mean a very wet and fatal landing a thousand miles east of Hawaii.

Wait a minute, dammit! he thinks, responding to a small wave of anger that punches at him, causing him to clench his jaw in self disgust. *What am I doing? Giving up without a fight?*

This defeatist attitude, he's grappled with it before. The "Eeyore Syndrome," he's labeled it, a determination to find the worst in every situation. Hasn't he warned the girls against it? Jerrod, too, until Jerrod literally rolled his eyes at him one day.

And here I sit programming myself to fail and die. Bullshit!

He takes a deep, if ragged, breath and forces himself to sit up, to comply with this newfound determination, but not really believing it. His mouth is cotton dry and he reaches for the water bottle by his seat, drinks deeply, then recaps it and slips it back in one of Bill Campbell's seat pockets.

Okay, so what do we do first?

He pulls the checklists back to his lap, ignoring his shaking hands, and starts through the lists of steps again, determined this time to figure out and practice exactly what needs to be done.

I've got five hours before planned re-entry. That's an eternity. So what if it's hard? I have to try.

The reward is survival. Possible survival.

After all, he reasons, *they wouldn't have taught this stuff in ground school back in Mojave if they didn't think a passenger could handle it. So all the keys have to be right here!*

The first sequence will be to turn the ship around, pointing the engine nozzles in the direction he's traveling. There may be an automatic system to do just that, he figures, since it's referenced in the verbiage of the checklist. But then how to initiate the maneuver on the panel? He imagines he may also have to use the control stick, the fighter-pilot-style, video-game type hand-control mounted on the right edge of the armrest.

Once more there's a low whooshing noise in his car, and he realizes he's been hearing it periodically. Whenever it happens, he feels *Intrepid* move slightly.

The reaction jets!

That's what it has to be. And there has to be an automatic system making them fire, keeping the ship pointed straight ahead. It's floating in a three-axis, three-dimensional environment, with yaw, pitch, and roll. Without air outside to operate against flight controls, the only way to move the ship around those three axes is firing tiny jets of whatever propellant *Intrepid* uses. He remembers the briefing clearly.

But there's only so much propellant aboard, and he'll need to make sure he doesn't use too much. Without those little jets, there will be no way to position the ship for reentry or even slow down.

He stares harder at the forward panel, determined to find the appropriate switches and learn how to use them, and slowly, very slowly, some of the nomenclature begins to make sense. Just not enough.

ASA Mission Control, Mojave, California, 9:25 a.m. Pacific

Richard DiFazio has never walked into Mission Control in a real crisis, simply because there's never been a real crisis. A few scary moments, yes, but nothing like this.

Careful not to usurp the flight director's authority or give any of his gravely worried crew even more worry, DiFazio stays by Arleigh Kerr's side and merely nods an affirmation when any of the other technicians look his way.

The briefing has been chilling, and the time in transit from his home in Lancaster has provided no relief, no indication that it's all a false alarm. Bill Campbell's fate, Kip Dawson's, and the fate of the entire operation is anything but assured, and he can just imagine NASA's Geoff Shear monitoring this same information — and even doling it out to ASA.

He knows Shear all too well and loathes him. A Machiavellian, master bureaucrat.

94

"Are they helping?" he asks Arleigh regarding NASA's role.

"So far, whatever we've asked for, they've provided."

"What are our options, Arleigh?"

The question seems to stun the flight director into silence. DiFazio watches his face turn pasty, sees him swallow hard and struggle to find the appropriate answer.

"Well, sir . . ."

"Too soon to ask?"

This question is a welcome rescue and Arleigh nods energetically. "Yes. Too soon. We need to exhaust all other explanations first."

"Is *Venture* unusable? Could we get her ready to go up?" DiFazio asks, referring to the only other spacecraft ASA has, the ship now sitting with a damaged landing gear in one of the hangars.

"I don't know yet."

"If I have to send it up in less than perfect shape to get them back, I'll do it. It's guaranteed that no one else is going to help us."

More engineers are gathering in front of Arleigh now, and DiFazio pats him on the shoulder, announces that he'll be in his office, and steps away, rather than stand like a rock in the river, disrupting the flow of their urgent consultations.

The news coming into the control room is no better, the info from NASA and NORAD confirming that something was seen streaking in and apparently striking the spacecraft just as communications were lost.

"In twenty minutes," Arleigh decides, "I want us all in the conference room with any and all ideas about what we should do and how we should proceed. Any ideas. Okay?"

He turns them back to their consoles and resumes his position, the iron-jawed leader standing at the helm in hurricane force winds, undaunted by the ferocity of the storm.

But inside he's dying.

Johnson Spaceflight Center,
Houston, Texas,
9:40 a.m. Pacific/11:40 a.m. Central

Plaques, models, and framed memorials to a full if frustrating career surround John Kent. He sits at his desk and rubs his closed eyes, wondering what else he can say to the wife of his longtime buddy Bill Campbell.

"Katie, it is entirely possible that Bill's okay and working hard to get them down, and just hasn't been able to cure the communications blackout."

"I know," is the barely controlled response from the Campbell home somewhere near Lancaster, California. "I've always known the risks."

"Look . . . I've got all our people monitoring everything, and I'm . . . do not repeat this, okay? . . . but I'm working on a rescue plan if, for some reason, we need to go up there and bring them back."

The silence is long and telling. Katie Campbell knows well her husband's heartburn over NASA's official position regarding private spaceflight. And she knows John Kent doesn't run NASA.

"Thanks, John."

"I'll call you with any news. Immediately. But you hang in there and have faith."

The call ends and he sits back, his mind spinning with possibilities, his personality geared to analysis, action, and cure. The course seems clear: Prepare for the worst case, regardless of Shear's rancid attitude.

He lunges from his chair, swinging open his office door and sticking his head into the outer office where a half dozen other astronauts and engineers are waiting.

"Everybody come on in here. None of this leaves this room, but we've got to plan a rescue, just in case."

Chapter 8

There is a magnificent planet to admire just outside his window, and Kip forces himself to look up and take quick note of it. He remembers standing beneath the star field last night at the side of that desert road, wishing he was up here. Now he wishes he was back on that deserted road looking up.

But whatever happens, he made it to space, and the incredible beauty of it somehow blunts the lethality of his situation.

In other words, he thinks, *it* is *worth it, whatever happens.*

But the thought is short-lived, and he feels fear returning like a thief to steal his resolve.

He brings his eyes back to the checklist, hopeful he has his jitters sufficiently under control to begin a run-through of the procedure for automatic retrofire. The prospect of having to fly *Intrepid* manually if the automatic system flubs up terrifies him.

The autoflight panel is called something

else, but it serves the same purpose, since *Intrepid* is programmed to fly automatically. The ship was set to keep its length parallel to the planet below, the nose in the direction of flight, and rolled over on its back so that the Earth is actually the ceiling, the "up" in the up/down equation. He's verified the blinking lights and read the messages on the computer screen to make sure it's all working as advertised, and he's heard and felt the little reaction jets firing to keep *Intrepid* from turning or yawing around.

According to the checklists, just prior to firing the engine to slow down, the astronaut is supposed to feed the computer a new set of coordinates, three numbers which Kip has already found and written down. When those numbers are safely locked in the tiny silicon brain, the machine will automatically fire the reaction jets in just the right sequence to turn their tail end around almost a hundred and eighty degrees and get the ship in the correct position to fire the engine backward.

Kip looks at his watch. Thirty minutes to the turnaround maneuver, which he's decided to do about halfway through the second orbit. If *Intrepid* was programmed to turn itself automatically on the fourth orbit, he wouldn't be messing with it. But — provided he's read everything correctly — the commands have to be manually typed in or the ship will never turn around. And only if the rocket motor is firing almost precisely against the direction of flight will they be able to slow down and essentially drop out of the sky.

He feels momentarily frozen. Part of him wants to stay for the full four orbits, but another part clamors to know whether or not he's going to survive this. He feels a turf battle in his brain between those competing desires.

Maybe we should do it now, he thinks. *After all, the automatic system can hold us in that backward position for a half hour as easily as it can keep us flying forward.*

He thinks about the fact that he keeps using the pronouns "us" and "we" in every thought of what he should do and what's happening. Bill is dead. No other living being is aboard, yet he can't bring himself to shift to "I" and "me."

Not yet.

His hand hovers over the small keyboard and he pulls back, deciding to be disciplined enough to wait for the right moment. Twenty-nine more minutes. Right before the sun sets behind him, which means he'll be able to see it this time. Sunrise has been in his face, and it was incredible. But he can do twenty-nine minutes.

He takes a deep breath, the first time in perhaps the past hour. At first there were short, panting, almost hyperventilating breaths, sheer panic. Then his reluctance to breathe deeply lest floating debris from the projectile's passage get in his lungs. But while some tiny things may still hang in the weightless environment, the air is mostly clean, and he supposes the air filters are responsible.

But the air does taste a bit stale and processed. He thinks about the class ASA gave on the oxygen system and how the ingenious little devices behind him scrub the air of carbon dioxide, adding small amounts of oxygen as necessary to maintain the right balance, recirculating it all with the correct amount of water vapor and at the correct temperature. And he remembers someone saying the system can keep five people going for thirty hours before the CO_2 scrubbers fail. With one person, he guesses, that means much longer. Still, the sooner he gets the hell out of this hostile environment, the better.

He wonders if ASA will give him a second free flight to make up for this one. Sort of an overbooking penalty type of thing. Give you the damaged flight and provide a new round trip as an apology? The thought triggers his first small chuckle in many minutes. He'll have to think about how to phrase the question so they can't resist saying yes. After all, if he's to be the poster boy . . .

The image of Diana Ross at the door of his suite swims through his mind, pleasing and somewhat startling. What was it, eleven hours ago? He supposes he should be thinking of Sharon, but however suppressed it is, the realization that the marriage is over is percolating, and Diana is a great stand-in for other possibilities.

When things were going so well, the poster boy idea was great. Of course, now he'll be the very symbol and face of disaster, whatever happens, and surely of no value to her efforts. That thought adds fuel to his bonfire of anxieties.

Another deep breath and he feels himself calming somewhat, glancing again at the Earthscape passing above, and surveying his surroundings. He thinks about taking a minute or two to meditate, but he doesn't know how. Sitting quietly with a stiff scotch is as close as he's ever come, though he's always wanted to know more about achieving inner peace.

He looks down, amused at the phrase and

the idea. Astronauts in flight suits don't have time for such things though, do they? Bill Campbell had repeated the advice of a favorite Air Force flight instructor: If a pilot has time to relax, he's forgetting something. The same mental urgency feels like it's transferring to him — or maybe it's just the flight suit.

The spiffy royal blue flight suits with the large, colorful mission patches were provided to each of them on the first day of class, two apiece. He kept this one pristine for the flight while wearing the other to class, but clothes really do make the man. He *feels* like an astronaut, from walking through the classroom door in that zipper-festooned coverall with a pen in the left shoulder pocket even to sitting here now. The only thing missing, he supposes, is some sort of military flight cap.

His left ear itches and he reaches up, surprised to encounter the earpiece from his headset, still inserted in his ear. He takes the whole apparatus off and scratches his ear liberally. That's what's been missing, he thinks. Other than Bill's companionship and guidance and just human presence, all the way up he had a host of other voices in his ear, and now they're gone, and it feels, well, lonely.

All that beauty just outside the canopy bubble and side windows and who can he tell? Not that most humans on earth haven't seen hundreds of spectacular pictures from space and Earth orbit, but this is what *his* eyes are seeing, and it feels barren. A reporter without a paper. A TV correspondent without a mike.

He wishes he could show Jerrod what he's seeing, or at least describe it. Even Carly and Carrie, their little blond heads bouncing with smiles and giggles, would love his word pictures, as would Julie — even with her eye-rolling teenage sophistication.

Provided Sharon hadn't preconditioned them to reject anything he described. Funny, he thinks, running back to them excitedly with some new experience, even as a salesman, was always a joy. It's as if his delight in pretty sunsets, a fun movie, a wild thunderstorm glimpsed across a purple desert, none of it became enjoyable until he could make it come alive for *them*. He was the camera for his family, the collector of vicarious joys.

And he realizes with a start that he really doesn't know how to just drink it in for himself, and that feels sad. Especially now, when "himself" is all he has.

I should take some notes on this, Kip thinks, wondering why they never discussed a notepad. There are a few sheets of note paper in the side pocket of his flight suit by his ankle, but he'd really like a full notebook. Big, thick, empty, ready for the pen or pencil, limitless in the scope of the wonders he could record. He always loved the late August trip to the drugstore to buy those school supplies, even through college.

His eyes follow the curvature of the for ward panel to one side, where a small, three pound laptop computer nestles in a rack. He'd forgotten about that. A backup, Bill had explained, for the main computer and keyboard. That's right! He'd completely forgotten. The thing is connected to the Internet and he'd been told, along with the others, that they would be able to e-mail their families from orbit if they wanted to take the time.

There were also supposed to be two phone calls for each passenger, though on this flight — as the only passenger — he'd been told to plan for four. One call to Houston for his three little girls and an angry wife, and a call to the Air Force Academy from a number his son would not know to ignore, were his choices.

But he's already tried the built-in phone

on the side console, and it's dead. Surely the computer connection will be equally useless.

He unclips the laptop and opens it, surprised to find a garden-variety Dell which spins up just like millions of its counterparts below. He waits until the desktop screen is stable, checks to see if there's a word processing program, and then clicks on the Internet explorer icon, not unsurprised when it comes up showing no connection.

He looks around, almost frantic to be doing *something,* but well aware there's nothing more to be done until it's time to fire the main engine to leave orbit.

His eyes fall on the laptop again, and he feels the urge to communicate, even if it's only with a hard drive. His handwriting has always been just short of a scrawl, the keyboard his best means for written communication.

The little laptop is powered by *Intrepid*'s circuits, not just its own battery, and there is a word processor program loaded, all of which means he can use it as a notepad. He positions the laptop in the middle of his lap and feels it promptly float up and away from him before he can start typing.

Never thought about that aspect of weightlessness.

He looks around, letting his brain work on the problem until the long strips of velcro straps in a side compartment come to mind. He rummages around and pulls out one long enough to cinch the laptop to his lap.

Feeling almost clever, he brings up the Word program and sits for a few seconds trying to figure out a message that's suddenly appeared asking if he wants to authorize a continuous download feed.

Download what?

He shrugs, irritated at the interruption and aware it doesn't make any difference anyway, since nothing he types will leave the hard drive.

Okay, so I click on the "yes" box and make It go away.

The dialogue box disappears and he opens a blank page and starts to type, stalling out almost immediately.

Log entry — middle of Orbit 2.

Log entry? He chides himself. *What am I, Captain Kirk?*

Maybe a more personal approach.

I have less than twenty minutes before trying to turn the ship around.

Oh come on, Kip! How about a glimpse of humanity, for Chrissake?

I have less than twenty minutes before trying to turn the ship around, and I'm scared to death.

Yeah, that's more like it. But I need some description if this is going to be for the kids.

The view outside is utterly amazing, and if I wasn't so anxious to be sure I can get home, I'd want to stay as long as the oxygen lasts. It's hard to describe, Jerrod, Julie, Carly, and Carrie, how deep black the background of space is and how magnificent the Earth is as it revolves below me . . . even though "below" right now is above. All those pictures we've watched from orbit, some live from the space shuttle, can't really prepare you for what it's like in person. Worth a lifetime! Of course, I'm going to make it back to tell you all this in person, but I thought you might like to "hear" about it in words as it's happening. Your dad in space! What a concept, though in your lifetime, this may become routine.

He sits back and rereads, taking care to

save the page before checking his watch and continuing. Five more minutes. But this feels good, and someday they'll love it. Or maybe his grandkids will.

Chapter 9

ASA Mission Control,
Mojave, California,
May 17, 10:05 a.m. Pacific

Arleigh Kerr stands at the end of the small table in the conference room of Mission Control, a freshly emptied bottle of water in his hand. His gaze is fixed on his boss as he clears his throat.

"Richard, I'm sorry to tell you, but we have no rescue capability. *Venture* is down for a month or more."

"What?" DiFazio is almost out of his chair, his bushy eyebrows knitting together in a combination of pain and alarm. "A *month?* When did you find that out?"

Arleigh's sigh is heartfelt, his eyes on the papers at the edge of the table. There are only the two of them in the room, better for such bad news. He carefully places the empty plastic water bottle next to the papers, as if adjusting a family treasure, his eyes focused on the base of the bottle until he can't dally any longer.

"I just got the word from our maintenance chief. The right wing spar is cracked in addition to the gear problem. If we try to fly her, we could lose her going up or coming down. Complete wing loss." His eyes rise to meet DiFazio's.

"Can't we rush the repair?"

"You're the composites expert, Richard. Not me. They're telling me with cure times, the best they could do is ten days. Something about rebonding that spar."

"Oh my God! Without *Venture*, we can't even . . . we *couldn't* even keep to our schedule if this . . ."

"I guess the only good news is that we've only got the one passenger."

DiFazio is shaking his head in pain. "So what options, if any, do we have?"

"We can't mount a rescue mission, we can't communicate . . ."

Richard's voice cuts him short.

"No! Don't tell me what we can't do, goddammit! Tell me what we *can* do."

Arleigh's retort is just as quick. "How about pray?"

"Excuse me?"

"We don't have a lot of options, Richard. Christ, I'm not sure if we have *any* options. If we had our other spacecraft, yes, we could launch and try a rescue. But we don't. And you know NASA isn't going to help. Some other country? The Russians? The Europeans? The Japanese? I don't know. I haven't called them. But it would cost more money than our entire capitalization to buy a *Soyuz* launch from the Russians, for instance, even if they could get one together in time."

Richard is watching him, subdued now, but hair-trigger restrained as Arleigh continues. "And that raises another major, honking question."

"Which is?"

"Is anyone even alive up there?"

Richard looks staggered. Arleigh concludes he hasn't considered this. "We . . . we don't know?"

"We don't know anything, except that the ship is still on orbit and appears to be pressurized, according to NASA's analysis . . . or was it NORAD's? But zero communication, zero telemetry, no indication that *Intrepid* is doing anything more than automatically holding its pitch and roll position, and . . . and, we're just guessing."

Richard is shaking his head, eyes on the floor. He takes a deep breath before looking up. "Sorry, Arleigh. I just wasn't ready for this, I guess."

"Hell, neither am I! No one's ever taken

even a major nonfatal hit up there before. Why us? Why now?"

"You know this could kill us. I don't mean to discount those two lives, but this could put us out of business."

Arleigh sits heavily, swiveling the chair around to face the glass wall. His words are to the wall.

"Richard, you, of all people, know how risky this so-called business is. The forces involved, the explosive power, the number of life support things that can go wrong. I mean, we're vastly more reliable than the shuttle could ever be, but . . . we've been hanging it out from the first."

"I know, I know. It's just . . ."

"We've all deluded ourselves into thinking we couldn't actually lose one. We've had so many successful launches."

"But we haven't lost them yet. At least, we don't know, right?"

"True, but a word of warning, okay? I mean, I'm only your flight director, but when this blows into the public eye, we'd better not be heard kvetching about the financial losses."

"Of course not. I've got Diana inbound right now. We'll put together a quick strategy."

"It's gonna leak, Richard."

"I know it."

"It's gonna leak, and the media is going to smell blood and be all over it, and I don't have a clue what to say or do . . . other than wait and watch and lean on NORAD and NASA for more information. We're trying the radios constantly, but if we see the capsule turn around in position for retrofire, or if, at the end of the fourth orbit, it actually does retrofire, then we know for certain someone's alive up there and following the checklists and we've got a chance."

"Has someone called Campbell's wife?"

"Yeah, I have. It was brutal. She's tough, but she's scared to death."

"And . . . our passenger?"

"Dawson. Kip Dawson. We're holding off for another hour or so before we call his wife."

"For God's sake, don't wait too long. Don't let her hear it from the media."

"No. No, we won't."

"So what *are* you waiting for?"

"The end of Orbit Two. I figure . . . without any rational reason . . . I figure if Bill's alive and functional, he'll want to get the hell out of there as soon as possible, and when he passes through the window for second orbit return, that's when I'd expect something to happen."

"How much longer?"

"Twenty-three minutes from now. At least that's the end of the window. Otherwise, he overshoots California, or worse."

"But we still have two more orbits before it has to come down, right?"

"They could go longer. We figure they could keep breathing up there for, roughly three days, or a bit less."

"Before the CO_2 scrubbers saturate?"

Arleigh is nodding. "That's always the limit." He gets to his feet, leaving Richard still seated. "I'd better get back in there. I've been whipping everybody into a thinking frenzy to see if we've missed anything."

Richard nods, waving him away as he picks up the phone, then replaces it in its cradle, his eyes on the far wall as he thinks through the consequences of dialing the person he was ready to call.

Not yet. Not just yet.

Chapter 10

It's time.

Kip powers the laptop to standby mode and reinserts the machine in its holder before gathering the checklists and positioning himself in Bill's seat. A confusing feeling of excitement comes over him, a small rush before the sprint, he figures, his mind relieved finally to be at the threshold of action.

He runs back through the planned steps and reviews the three coordinates. *Intrepid* has to turn around one hundred eighty degrees to fly backward, and the pitch and roll readouts on the attitude indicator must be precisely right before firing the engine. The master keyboard is in front of him and he pulls it closer. With care he punches in the three numbers and triple checks that he's got them right. His finger hovers shakily over the "execute" button for several seconds as he wonders if there could be anything he's forgotten, then he forces his finger down, hearing a small click.

The screen changes, registering the fact that the new coordinates have been accepted, and suddenly there's a small box proclaiming that the automatic realignment maneuver has begun.

Thank God!

He holds his breath, wondering how it is that the small reaction jets on *Intrepid* can be firing so gently that he can't even feel them. It's almost as if nothing is happening, despite the announcement on the screen.

He looks at the attitude indicator, willing it to move at least in some direction, but it's static, the display as steady as if the whole spacecraft was sitting on some concrete floor back on the planet.

He takes in the screen, then the keyboard, and punches the execute button a second time, but still no movement. The annunciator screen indicates that everything should be working, the jets firing, and *Intrepid* should be turning around tail-first. Right now!

Okay, I forgot something, he decides. Complex procedures can be thwarted by one simple mistake — like getting no toast because you forgot to plug in the toaster.

What did I miss?

He runs back through the checklist, feeling a cold, creeping trickle of panic.

Focus!

One by one he reenters the coordinates, his fingers shaking visibly now as he triggers the execute button.

And once more — despite the signs on the small LED screen that all is well and working as indicated — *Intrepid* continues flying straight ahead and on her back. No pitch. No yaw. No roll.

No change.

Kip checks his watch. Eight minutes remain before the time for retrofire. If the automated system won't work, all he has left is the manual control, and he alone to manipulate it.

But he's clicked the manual control button on that joystick before, in training, electing "active mode." And in that simulator he promptly lost control so badly they had to stop the spinning simulator. All of the instructors and fellow students were holding their sides and laughing when he climbed out, and the follow-up session wasn't much better.

"Kip, I guess we forgot to tell you," the instructor had heehawed. "The object was to *stop* the spinning, not set a new record for the highest number of revolutions per minute."

He stares at the joystick, a tortuous, diabolical little tool that in the hands of a qualified astronaut is a singular thing of interfaced beauty, giving the ability to move in all three axes by just turning the wrist and hand.

But to an amateur, an invitation to spinning disaster.

I'm not touching that thing! he thinks, testing the words.

The spacecraft is still not turning. He thinks about entering the numbers a third time, but he's already done it correctly twice. It's already acknowledged his entries twice. And yet nothing automatic is happening.

I'm only on Orbit Two. I've got time to figure this out. I don't have to force it right now.

The logic of waiting is impeccable, but it's no match for his massive urge to get home *now!*

And without thinking he succumbs, adjusting his hand over the joystick and consciously punching the red button on top that reverts the spacecraft to manual attitude control.

He can hear his breathing rate increase,

but nothing much is happening. There is a little drift now to the left, just a few degrees, and maybe a bit of roll, but he's not sure.

Okay, time to try it.

He knows the controls are sensitive. The watchword will be moving in only one axis at a time, and he reviews the basics without moving his hand.

Push forward to pitch forward, pull to pitch up. Twist left to yaw left, right to yaw right. Nudge the entire stick left to roll left, nudge it right to roll right. Okay, which way first?

The Earth is still passing along above him, and it's easy to see the horizon, the Earth's curvature. So maybe he should take care of the main event first and just turn around backward before turning planet-side down.

Yaw right a full one hundred eighty degrees, putting the tail into the line of flight. Then I can fine-tune it to exactly the right numbers.

Slowly, carefully, he begins rotating the stick to the right, a millimeter at a time it seems, his muscles protesting until he suddenly feels and hears the hiss of the reaction jets yawing him in the right direction.

He releases the rotational pressure on the control stick, impressed at how smoothly *Intrepid* has begun to rotate to the right around its center of gravity. The rate is steady, and he doesn't seem to need any of the other two axis controls, at least not yet. He's turning, through ninety degrees at last, finally completing a full reversal, and he leads his arrival at the right coordinates by twisting the control back to the left until he fires another small burst to stop the turn.

But it's a bit too much, and the turn now reverses, very slowly at first.

He tries a tiny burst back to the right, but it, too, is overdone. Once more he's turning right, passing through the one-hundred-eighty-degree point and continuing on around, this time beginning to pitch up, the nose heading toward Earth.

He pushes the stick forward for a small corrective burst and tries to arrest the yaw at the same time, and suddenly he's turning back left slightly, pitching down away from Earth's surface, and beginning a left roll, all at the same time. He can feel the sweat beading on his forehead as he tries to steady his hand and oppose the motions one axis at a time, but each burst is too much, and the memory of what happened in the simulator returns like a nightmare, as *Intrepid* begins to tumble, slowly at first, then faster, the Earth beginning to gyrate and roll in front of his eyes.

Somehow he manages a glance at his watch. Four minutes left before he has to be rock-steady for retrofire.

Mojave International Aerospace Port, California, 10:53 a.m. Pacific

The chirp of her car alarm system arming behind her is all but unheard as Diana races through the front door of ASA's building and accelerates toward Mission Control in search of Richard.

Sleep had been difficult after returning home from her trip to see Kip. Nevertheless she'd had every intention of being on the tarmac as they taxied out and grossly over-slept instead.

Her cell phone is ringing and she curses quietly as she yanks it to her face, hearing a familiar name from the small list of aero-space reporters. She comes to a halt in the corridor and pulls the cell phone back for a moment, staring at it as if she's discovered a pipe bomb in her hand.

So now it begins, she thinks. She had dreamed of being an astronaut and always thought she had ice water in her veins. Now she's going to be tested.

"This is Diana Ross, ASA's PR director,"

she announces sweetly, as if it was a routine day in the office. Suddenly she's working hard to dredge up any information from her memory on this particular reporter.

DiFazio has emerged from Mission Control down the corridor and is walking toward her with a grave expression, and she waves him to be quiet. He joins her silently, listening to her end of the conversation as she tries to convince the reporter in the calmest of tones that nothing in ASA's world is amiss other than a nasty communications glitch.

"Really?" is the skeptical reply from the Beltway. "Then why am I looking at a live picture of your Mission Control and seeing absolutely no data streaming down from the spacecraft on any screen?"

"That's what a communications glitch sometimes entails. We're working on it."

"I have a source who tells me it's far more serious than that."

"Really? Could your source call us? We'd sure like to know what he knows, because we're not aware that the problem is any more serious than any other problem in spaceflight."

The reporter is sighing, well aware she's sparring with a pro. "Okay, look. I understand you're in damage control mode and probably you don't know yourselves what's happening, but let me at least get some vitals on who's up there."

"I'm just getting to work and I need some coffee," Diana says. "Give me your number and twenty minutes and I'll get back to you." The agreement is reluctant, but she ends the call and looks at Richard, taking in for the first time the depth of worry on his face, the hopelessness in his eyes.

"Richard?"

"Yeah," he sighs, nodding slowly, his eyes on the floor as he chews his lip.

"Lord, how bad is it?"

"We don't know anything new yet, but we're praying that Bill is okay and getting ready to retrofire in a few minutes. We're coming up on the end of the second orbit."

"But we can't talk to him?"

Richard launches into a quick and tense briefing that ends as they reach the entrance to Mission Control. He moves back inside with her in trail and Diana can feel the tension thick as summer humidity in Houston. The risks of making a business out of spaceflight she's long understood. At least intellectually. She can talk about it for hours, marshaling details and numbers and even orbital mechanics. She knows *Intrepid* and its grounded sister ship are tiny bubbles barely sustaining human life after being shot to impossible speeds and altitudes and brought back against incredible forces. But they've been doing it almost a year now, week after week, without fail. The thought may be silly, but it's echoing through her head: Since we know how to do this perfectly, it simply *can't* end badly.

A sudden burst of activity flutters into view at the flight director's console and she sees a receiver pulled to Arleigh Kerr's ear. He speaks quickly and turns toward the rear, spotting Richard and Diana and motioning to the boss with a staccato movement. There is no smile on Kerr's face, no deliverance in his expression, and Diana follows, feeling ill.

"What, Arleigh?"

He lowers the receiver as he searches for the right phrase.

"*What,* Arleigh?" Richard snaps.

"Okay, Richard. NASA is pulling in a live long lens picture, and it shows *Intrepid* is tumbling." He sees the question in Diana's eyes. "Rotating around its center of gravity in all three axes."

"I understand what tumbling means," she says.

"Which indicates to you, what?" Richard prompts.

"He may be out of control."

"Jesus."

They all know the rest of the equation. A tumbling spacecraft can't fire its rocket motor and drop out of orbit.

"How long to the retrofire window?"

"One minute. They're watching." Arleigh raises the receiver back to his ear and turns away, as if expecting his monitor to burst to life with good data streams from *Intrepid*. Every technician in the room somehow seems to know what he knows, and there is a collective quiet as the seconds tick away and more and more eyes turn to the flight director. He holds the receiver with one hand and rubs his eyes with the other, willing the nightmare to go away.

Chapter 11

The centrifugal forces have begun to pull Kip in opposite directions, but they aren't half as bad as the increasing frequency of alternating light and dark pulsing through the main windscreen.

He wills his hand off the joystick and realizes he's been clutching it with a death grip. He reaches over with his left hand and pries his right fingers open, working them back and forth until they feel almost flexible again. There was something one of the astronauts told him in the simulator a week ago. Something that had to do with control sticks. What the hell was it?

For the first time in minutes the rate of tumbling isn't increasing, and he realizes that it's because he isn't jamming the joystick back and forth in panic. The tumbling is remaining constant, and he's feeling increasingly dizzy and ill, his upper torso and head being pulled toward the ceiling while below the waist he's being pulled downward.

Fingertips! That was it. He said that instructors could calm down pilots having trouble with formation flight by teaching them to fly with their fingertips to avoid overcontrol.

Kip moves his hand back toward the joystick, this time placing only the ends of his fingers on the top of it and moving them in concert backward to fire the control jets in just one axis against the tumbling. He hears the jets hiss and feels the reaction, and for the first time the gyrations begin to slow. He does it again, tentatively, letting as much as a minute elapse between each burst, and finally daring to hope he might actually succeed.

He glances at the clock, hoping for a few more minutes before retrofire, but realizes it's already too late. Firing the rocket now — even if he was in position and ready, which he isn't — would bring him down somewhere far to the east of Mojave, and maybe way across the continent. No, he decides, he's stuck for at least another orbit, another ninety minutes.

And with that realization, some of his panic leaks away.

Tentatively, he tries a small burst to the left to stop the right-hand roll, and the frequency of the Earth's appearance in the side windows begins to slow. But he can't twist the control and affect the yaw with fingertips, and he tries gripping the joystick with only thumb and forefinger and finds it works. A few short bursts in that direction and the sideways turning slows, too.

One axis at a time he works at it, trying hard to keep the bursts very, very brief, letting minutes elapse between each attempt, and watching the Earth's movement relative to the spacecraft slow burst by burst, until after many very long minutes he realizes he's finally in the right attitude, flying right side up, tail first, and steady.

Kip punches at the computer screen to try to reengage the automatic attitude controller, not believing it at first when the small box on the screen suddenly glows green. But the reaction jets are hissing quietly and he feels the craft steady itself, the coordinate readings all within a few degrees of what he's supposed to have for retrofire.

Damn, I did it!

He's covered with perspiration, still breathing hard, and his right hand is aching, but he's in the right position and only that matters. A surge of confidence returns and he smiles the smile of a football player spiking the ball in the end zone.

He checks the time like a veteran. A little

more than an hour to the next window, and this time he'll be ready. He's *already* ready, though drained and still shaking. He takes the barf bag he's been issued out of his breast pocket and restows it in the zippered one by his right ankle, proud that he hasn't needed it.

Once again he finds himself looking at the transmit button connected to his headset, wishing he could tell someone below of his success. He was spinning into oblivion, but he kept his cool, remembered the training, brief as it was, and he did it!

ASA Mission Control, Mojave, California, 11:01 a.m. Pacific

Arleigh suddenly raises the phone handset over his head like a trophy, his voice booming through the control room.

"Yes!"

All eyes not already on him snap to as he shakes his head and exhales before explaining.

"He's stabilized! The craft is no longer gyrating and is apparently in position for retrofire. He's missed this window, but he's under control and alive!"

There are shouts and applause as a wide

variety of body English transmits the relief in the room. The monitors and the radios, however, are still vacant of contact and information, and the mood returns to watchful waiting, though with an improvement in hope.

"No cigars yet, people," Arleigh is saying into his headset. "But Bill's obviously on duty up there, so let's prepare for a deorbit in eighty minutes."

It takes a few minutes for Diana to remind the flight director and the CEO that the story is already leaking and she needs direction. Arleigh reluctantly leaves his console and follows the two of them into the glassed-in conference room.

"This will sound very cold, but it's my job," she says. "We have an incredible opportunity here."

"For what?" Arleigh asks, indignant. "What the hell does that mean?"

Richard has his hand out for silence, his trust of Diana's judgment all but total.

"What it means, Arleigh . . . Richard . . . is that our future as a company depends on how we handle whatever occurs next. Good or bad. If we show strength, authority, perfect honesty, and a vision beyond the moment regardless of the depth of this disaster, we will build an invaluable trust in the

131

public mind. If we show fright, hide any fact however small, sidestep questions, or appear confused . . ."

"Any appearance of weakness, in other words," DiFazio adds, nodding slowly, knowing she's right but disliking the need of it.

"Exactly," she continues. "Vulnerability breeds lasting distrust and even contempt."

"I'm not a damned actor, Diana," Arleigh snaps.

"No, you're not," she interjects before he can continue. "You're a steel-willed professional who knows private spaceflight will remain and succeed and lead. All I'm saying is, be careful to show that true face to whoever's watching. And they'll be watching every moment from here on."

Johnson Spaceflight Center,
Houston, Texas,
11:20 a.m. Pacific/1:20 CDT

"Talk to me."

In John Kent's perfect world, there is no need for verbal niceties when there's an urgent mission to accomplish. "Hello's" and "How's the weather's" are time wasters in a crisis. Nailing the point as he walks through the door of the teleconferencing suite is greeting enough for his old friend and senior manager at Kennedy Space Center, Griggs Hopewell.

"Good to see you, too, John. Okay, let's get to it. We can make it happen, but we'll need twenty-six hours a day for four days and a blowtorch to everyone's behind."

"*Endeavor* is ready, then? Enough to roll out to the pad from vehicle assembly?"

"Not as ready as I'd like, but yes. So who's going to fly, if this impossible mission comes about?"

"Paradies, White, and Malone. Tell me what you need to pull this off, Griggs."

"How about authorization for starters. You're talking tens of millions in prep expense. Shear is dead set against it and we're essentially in a mutiny here even talking about it on company time."

"Look, I don't have a green light yet, but I'll get it."

"From *Shear?* What, are the Houston refinery fumes affecting you? John, I love ya, man, and I owe you for a lot of things, but you don't run this organization."

"Neither does he."

"Jeez, John. We're talking the administrator. We're also talking about a guy who has an industrial-strength hatred for Di-

Fazio. John, he *wants* DiFazio and anyone dumb enough to fly with him to bite it."

"All true, but he doesn't make policy. The White House does."

"And they're suddenly going to go across town and politically bitch-slap their boy? I don't frigging think so."

"Griggs, ten minutes ago ASA's craft stabilized and aligned for retrofire. He may get down on his own. This is just a feasibility exercise."

There is silence from the Cape. "And if he can't?"

"He just proved someone's breathing up there and capable of controlling the spacecraft."

"John, Bill's a friend of mine, too. I also want him back safe."

"Not the point. He comes down on his own or we go up to get him. Shear will be shamed into doing it by public pressure if nothing else. But this is just a contingency exercise until we know whether we need to go up."

"Okay, a word of warning. I know what you're thinking, and who you're thinking of calling. But keep in mind that, despite nice handshakes and smiles when you've visited, there are people around the President who don't necessarily like you, John, and they were never Boy Scouts like us. Approach them with reason and logic and compassion and they'll jam it all back up your tailpipe and leave you seriously retired."

"Duly noted. Keep your fingers crossed and get a playbook together for me, Griggs. Please."

"Whoa, did I hear John Kent say *please?*"

"Kind of."

"My God, that's a first. Okay, I'll slam a plan together, but if Shear gets wind of this, neither of us will be holding NASA IDs past tomorrow morning."

"Who's gonna tell him?"

"John, I've got a Cape full of irritated, overworked employees with more dedication to spying and informing than Stalin's KGB."

Chapter 12

Aboard *Intrepid*, End of Orbit 3,
May 17, 12:30 p.m. Pacific

The countdown ends in silence.

The only roaring is in Kip's head, along with the soft hissing of the air cycle fans that are no match for the pounding blood in his temples. Kip's eyes dart around the checklist and back to the screen as he sits in disbelief, the enormity of the silence settling over him like a heavy shroud. He's been prepared for retrofire for over an hour and never considered that the engine might have other ideas.

He's heard the engine fire before. He knows what it sounds like, feels like. When *Intrepid* was dropped by the mothership so many hours ago, the rocket engine roared and shook. But whatever he's hearing and feeling now, it's not the engine.

Kip punches the manual firing button again, just to make sure he hasn't been too timid. It clicks.

Nothing changes.

Only seconds have elapsed since the exact programmed firing point. There's still time to fire, he thinks.

There must be a safety. Something else I need to throw! Obviously he's done something wrong, something that can be fixed.

The checklist items begin to blur, but he forces his eyes to take them in item by item, his finger still stabbing at the ignition button. He checks the screen, the fault annunciator display, the switch panel to each side, expecting an "Aha" moment of recognition, the easy answer. So he's a bit late. So he comes down in Las Vegas instead of Mojave. What the hell. Just get the damn thing to fire!

But still the engine remains silent, and even though it's only the end of Orbit 3, Kip feels himself losing control. He balls his fist and crashes it into the central liquid crystal screen, changing nothing. He begins flipping switches at random, snarling at the display and flailing, each wild action propelling him left or right in the zero gravity, restrained only by the seat belt.

No! Goddammit, no!

With one final burst of frustration he hurls the checklist behind him, sickeningly aware of what it's hit as it thuds into the dead astronaut's body, bouncing back to slap the windscreen, and ends up hitting him in the face.

"Shit!" he yells, the sound of his agonized voice encouraging another yell, eyes closed, fists pounding the armrests of the command chair.

But he's hurtling away from the retrofire point at the speed of twenty-five thousand five hundred feet per second, and the engine is still quiet as a tomb.

His anger subsides and in its place flows a cold and heavy fear, worse than anything he's experienced. Terror would barely describe it. No brakes, no parachute, no skyhook, no lifeline. No rescue of any sort if the engine won't fire.

Until a few minutes ago, his major concern was to find a way to pilot an unpowered gliding spacecraft with stubby wings to a safe landing somewhere flat and hard. Now even a crash landing sounds okay, as long as it involves getting out of orbit.

Kip looks over his left shoulder, as if a living relief pilot might be sitting quietly back there. He feels the bile rising in his stomach, his head spinning. The view of the Earth turning below suddenly seems an exquisite form of torture — home being dangled in front of him, but out of reach.

No! Oh my God, he thinks, swallowing

hard. *What the hell am I going to do now? I can't just sit here and wait to die.*

He yanks the barf bag from his ankle pocket just in time, and when the release is complete, he cleans his face and disposes of the thing in a side-mounted trash receptacle, glad for something rote to do, his mind still reeling with the thought that he's missed something. He opens the relief port then — a small funnel-shaped urinal dumping to the vacuum of space — and drains his bladder, before retightening the straps connecting him to the command chair.

This can't be it. I can't be stranded. There has to be a solution I haven't thought of. Calm down! This is just a machine. Machines can be made to work!

He remembers the spacecraft simulator back in Mojave. The door in and out is on the rear cabin wall of the simulator and he remembers how comforting it was to know that at any time they could just turn the doorknob and walk out of the box into the hangar to safety. Just like that. Just open a door and leave the nightmare.

The urge to turn around and look at the rear cabin wall obsesses him. He struggles against the seat belt to turn around far enough, gripping the back of the command chair, his focus snapping to the unbroken surface of the back wall.

There is, of course, no door.

That fact triggers a buzzing disbelief and panic which crashes over him like an emotional tsunami. He feels tears on his face as the images before him begin to compress into a tunnel, and then to a single point of light, just before everything goes dark.

ASA Mission Control, Mojave, California, 12:45 p.m. Pacific

Richard DiFazio takes the news from Arleigh quietly. Most of the controllers have left their stations since the realization dawned that there would be no more information on the video monitors. They stand in small groups now, scattered around the room, grim and tense as they wait for something to be relayed from cameras and sensors they don't have, the frustration compounded by their having no sources of their own.

The CEO of American Space Adventures quietly returns to the conference room and lifts a receiver, punching in the number he'd considered calling earlier, an international number he guards carefully in his PDA. The male voice answers in Russian and switches adroitly to English with a cheery greeting which changes to a serious tone at the news of *Intrepid*'s dilemma.

"And, of course, it will be a balmy day in the Bering Strait before our good friend Geoffrey is willing to help, no?"

"You've got that right. But you've got a re-supply mission coming up in two weeks, correct?"

"What you're thinking is not possible without money, Richard, and maybe not even then."

"But you'll try?"

There is a long pause and a weary sigh.

"Can your people last for eight days?"

"No."

"Then you're asking the impossible, regardless of money. Launching inside of eight days from now would be suicide."

"They're damaged up there, Vasily. Our astronaut . . . you've met him, by the way . . . Bill Campbell."

"Yes, I have, but it doesn't change the reality of what we can do."

"They were hit by something, they've lost all comm, and apparently he can't get the engine to light to kick him out of orbit. He's flown through three chances we know he'd take."

There's a long stretch of silence and the two wait each other out, Vasily giving in first. "I already knew of this, Richard. John Kent called me and our people have been monitoring, too. But even if we could get there, you have no docking collars, no compatible hatches, and only one space suit. We can't tow him back home."

"We have an airlock. We can stuff a spare suit inside the lock. Bill gets the passenger ready and out, then takes the spare suit and comes out himself."

"Perhaps. But it takes eight days, Richard. I'm sorry. Maybe NASA can move faster."

"I'm begging, Vasily."

"Don't beg, my friend. It isn't becoming. Unlike Shear, we would help if we could. But you knew the risks when you started your business, and we all warned you about rescues."

Aboard *Intrepid*, 12:45 p.m. Pacific

Consciousness returns slowly. Dreamlike, fuzzy images of an upside-down cabin slowly coalesce until Kip realizes he's floating in zero gravity around the ceiling, upside down in relation to the cabin floor. How long he's been out he isn't sure. He's

142

never blacked out before, except for one time as a kid when a larger classmate bounced an impressively large rock off his head in the school yard.

It's the same scene, the same nightmare he'd left. Bill's body, the absence of an escape door, the hiss of the air conditioning, the plastic and antiseptic smell of the interior. Everything.

He reaches out tentatively and grasps the back of the command chair, working his body into it again, facing forward. He feels foolish and exhausted. They had explained that the cabin pressure in orbit would be the equivalent of a ten-thousand-foot altitude and that too much physical exertion would net light-headedness. That must have been it.

I moved too fast and blacked out from lack of oxygen.

That's better than the alternative explanation. No way could he have just fainted.

Kip clicks the seat belt on again and looks at the clock. He's only been out a short time and nearly eighty minutes remain to the next retrofire point — the end of Orbit 4. He tries to pump himself up with the idea that he can try to fire the engine yet again, but he knows he's deluding himself. For some reason the Eagles' "Hotel California" suddenly begins playing in his head, the haunting lyrics and one phrase in particular sending a shiver up his spine.

You can check out any time you like,
But you can never leave!

He lets himself sink into the bizarre images it paints in his mind as he shivers, unwilling to believe he's hit the wall with no more options, and equally unwilling to delude himself that there are some. His anger returns, but this time there's no energy left for hitting or throwing or yelling. He sits, doing a slow burn, searching for someone to blame and coming up empty.

About as productive as blaming God! he thinks, his mind still ricocheting off a dozen possible solutions, each one of which evaporates into little more than wishful thinking.

And suddenly there is nothing left but reality, and it feels like a black hole in his soul, sucking everything that remains of him into another dimension. He sees movement in one of the side windows and looks, realizing the image is his, startled by the mirrorlike reflection of the fear in his eyes.

And the guilt! The overwhelming, crushing guilt that he's done exactly what Sharon tried to prevent. He's killed his children's father, her husband. He's walked stupidly into the abyss.

He feels tears again cascading on his face and he buries his head in his hands, eyes closed, body shaking, wishing, praying, begging for deliverance as the silent, anguished cry of "No!" fills his mind. He rocks back and forth in agony until he's stunned enough and tired enough to escape into the blessed release of a numbed sleep.

Chapter 13

On any normal day the sight of Richard DiFazio walking into ASA's maintenance office would be routine, but his sudden bursting through Mark Burgess's office door just now catches everyone by surprise. The director of maintenance turns with a shocked expression as the CEO motions him to a corner office and pulls the door closed behind them.

"We have no choice, Mark. You've got to get *Venture* ready to fly by tomorrow, day after tomorrow at the latest."

The veteran maintenance chief is shaking his head. "Didn't I make it clear enough on the phone? Richard, the landing gear is damaged and the wing spar is cracked. We could easily lose her and anyone aboard if we tried to fly. Going up and especially coming down."

"What are the chances of that?"

146

"Well, hell, I don't know! All I can be sure of is that she's dangerously weakened."

"Percentages, dammit!"

"I don't know, okay? Maybe a fifty percent chance. Maybe better."

"Fifty or better of surviving?"

"Yes. Or a fifty percent chance of the wing falling off. No one's going to be stupid enough to fly her like that."

"I already have two volunteers."

"Richard, she can't fly."

"This isn't FAA rules. She's experimental. This is a cutting-edge space program."

"The hell it is! This is supposed to be a space *line* with high reliability, and it *has* been up to now. Dammit, Richard, we've talked about this very contingency."

"Yeah, but it was just theoretical then. This is real."

"She can't fly, Richard."

"Bullshit. If I have to, I'll fire your ass and find someone to get her ready."

He regrets the words as soon as he's said them. He knows he's gone too far, but the frustration is driving him to play the "Damn the torpedoes, full-speed ahead" card.

Mark Burgess, however, is too experienced and principled to be bullied like some green lieutenant. His arms are crossed, his jaw set, his head shaking slowly. "Go ahead. Violate everything you promised."

"What did I promise?"

"To never, ever attempt to overrule my department's judgment on flight readiness. *We've* learned the lessons of *Challenger* and *Columbia* even if you haven't."

Richard sighs. He's cornered, and the defeated slump of his shoulders uncrosses Burgess's arms.

"Look, Richard, I want this as much as you, but I can't let you compound a disaster. We lose *Venture* and *Intrepid*, we lose the company, at least for a long time. No spacecraft, no spaceflights."

"How bad is she, really? *Venture*, I mean."

"You mean is there any hope of a fast repair?"

Richard nods.

"These are composite materials, laminated sheets with glue. But we're already reexamining our conclusions. I've a team crawling all over her right now."

"Good."

"Keep in mind this is not a metal bird. I can't just rivet a doubler in place like we could with aluminum."

"Try, Mark. For God's sake, try something."

"I'm not planning to just sit here drinking lattes. But you have to accept that the chances she could be ready to fly this week are near zero."

"Then Bill's chances are the same."

"You don't know that. So he missed a deorbit burn. He may make it on the next one."

"And if he doesn't, he has enough air for the two of them for maybe . . ."

"Three days, tops. Yeah, I know. We build the scrubbers, remember?"

The two of them stare at each other in pain before Richard DiFazio flails the air with his right hand and turns to the door.

"I'm sorry, Mark. Do your best."

"We will. We are," Mark says to the back of the departing chairman.

The *Washington Post*, Washington, D.C., 2:30 p.m. Pacific/5:30 p.m. Eastern

Her instincts are on high alert as the aerospace reporter for the *Washington Post* punches off the latest call from ASA, her headset relieving the need to juggle a receiver as she sits at her desk. The questions ASA are sidestepping are key, and she's traveled the arc from passing interest in a rumor of trouble to being convinced that the occupants of ASA's private spacecraft are in danger. She's already wasted a volley of calls on bad numbers and uncooperative "sources," and now, she decides, it's time for a minute of deep-think. The story — whatever the story really is — will break any second on cable networks or online services, or even on the AP wires. *Someone* is about to scoop her if she doesn't get this figured out right now.

So what do I have? Two people aboard that craft, a stable orbit, no telemetry, and no communication. Could she be lying to me about the stable orbit? Could it already have burned up or something?

No, she decides. Ross is a pro, in the game for the long haul. She wouldn't cite NASA as a source unless it was a valid claim. NASA saw them with a very long lens still in orbit.

But what's really wrong? Is communications loss the extent of it, like she wants me to think?

There's something scratching at the back of her mind and the veteran reporter twirls a pencil and looks around the newsroom to let her thoughts coalesce. Her eyes sweep past a large clock, doing visual busywork and taking in the quiet intensity of the other reporters working away on a planet full of stories.

And all she's got is suspicion and a ticking clock.

Her patience at an end, she snaps back, wondering if she's dredged up any answers.

Clock. Timeline. When did they launch?

She dives back into the Internet and checks the launch time listed on ASA's Web site, looking for the planned length of the flight and finding nothing. She Googles and selects a hit from one of the first such flights nearly a year ago, paging down through endless verbiage until the right phrase catches her eyes.

"Each flight is planned for four orbits of approximately ninety minutes each," DiFazio said. "That's enough time to not only get a lifelong feel for zero gravity, but to drink in the most spectacular view anyone will ever see in his or her life. We deorbit at the end of the fourth circuit after six hours."

Six hours.

She checks her note on the time they dropped the spacecraft from the mothership.

Eight a.m. Pacific Daylight. And it's 2:30 p.m. out there now. That's over six hours.

The reporter sits back hard, eyes wide, recalculating lest she screw up the math, then leaps to her feet to chase down her editor. Her head is swimming.

My God, they're stuck up there!

NASA Headquarters,
Washington, D.C.,
2:30 p.m. Pacific/5:30 p.m. Eastern

Geoff Shear stands behind his desk looking out the window at the Capitol and waiting for his secretary to connect a call to Houston. He's quite capable of lifting his own receiver and punching the single button that connects him to the operator at Johnson, but he has little respect for leaders who drop the trappings of power to be just one of the boys. Like Jimmy Cornpone Carter and his silly "jes' folks" act of carrying his own hang-up bag to and from the White House when Shear was a White House aide. He'd been disgusted to find out the suit bag was usually empty.

"John Kent is on line one, sir," a female voice announces over the archaic wood-boxed intercom he insists on maintaining on his desk.

"Thank you."

"Kent?"

"Mr. Administrator?"

"Well, that's right. I thought maybe you'd forgotten my title."

"I have my moments of wishful thinking, Geoff."

"And I have my moments of distasteful leadership duty."

"Meaning?"

"Let me see how I can put this delicately, Colonel Kent. How's this? Your mutinous ass is fired. Clear enough for you? You've had no authority to start planning a mission, and this is the last straw with your insubordinate running of that office. I've warned you before."

There is a disgusted sigh from Houston loud enough to echo through the speaker. "You can't fire me without a lot of congressional fallout, Geoff. Or is this just a little autoerotic exercise?"

"Clean out your desk, throw your crap in a box, and be out of the front door in precisely twenty minutes or I'll have you arrested. Your security clearance has just been canceled and you have no authority to be in a secure area."

"Cute, Geoffrey. Juvenile, but cute. You know I'll simply walk out the front door, make two calls, and walk back in."

"Well, go ahead and try. But you've been running around behind my back all day against my direct orders, trying to waste a few hundred million of the taxpayers' hard-earned dollars on a foolish mission I have not and will not authorize."

"So you hate DiFazio."

"I spend no time thinking about that huckster."

"That's still one of our guys up there. A NASA guy."

"You mean Bill Campbell? I'm not just concerned about Campbell, I'm worried about the safety of both of those men, but I warned DiFazio very clearly we do not have the resources to mount a rescue if they get in trouble."

"Yes, we do."

"Your problem, Kent, is pure insubordination. Either in government or business that's pretty much enough to justify firing anyone up to and including Jesus."

"Well, Geoff, you didn't even have the courtesy to answer my question when we had our little conference this morning. I had no idea you were prohibiting a quick feasibility check. So there was no direct order."

"I e-mailed you an hour later that you were not to attempt to construct or research a rescue mission unless I gave you direct approval."

"Sorry. Never got it. You should have called."

The sound of voices in the background from Houston are already interrupting Kent, and Shear can hear him being apologized to by security.

"Some of our very embarrassed friends from security are here, Geoff, to do your dirty work. Sorry we can't talk further. Oh, by the way," Kent adds, his voice steady and a chuckle in his tone. "If, somehow, you make this stick, be sure to watch the *Washington Post* and ABC's *20/20* in a few weeks. You'll find it all very interesting. I would strongly suggest early retirement."

"Time to write your book, Kent." Shear punches the line off and sits, pulling the receiver to him as he flips through a small notebook for the first of a half dozen congressional leaders he'll have to call before Kent can get to them. The ranks of the John Kent fan club on the Hill are extensive, and he'll be forced to rehire the smart-ass astronaut in a day or two. But those two days will make all the difference in derailing any half-assed attempts to light an emotional bonfire and accelerate the launch schedule at the expense of safety, which has to be the prime concern. With only two shuttles left and the entire program hanging in the balance, he cannot be sentimental.

Chapter 14

Headquarters, North American
Aerospace Defense Command,
Colorado Springs, Colorado,
May 17, 2:35 p.m. Pacific/
3:35 p.m. Mountain

Christopher Risen looks at himself in the mirror of his private bathroom, wondering why his father is staring back. He doesn't feel more than two thirds of his fifty-two years, but the perfectly shined four stars on his Air Force uniform would never adorn the shoulders of someone in his thirties.

He sighs as he buttons the coat, wondering for the millionth time if he should have tried to get into test pilot school right out of F-15s instead of taking the fast-burner track to the Pentagon, and now CINCNORAD, his official title, Commander in Chief of the North American Aerospace Defense Command. Back then the path to being an astronaut seemed to wind through Houston. Lately, the dawn of private spaceflight had shifted the possibilities, and now this.

The small team of senior officers and one very nerdy captain are waiting with the patience and respect appropriate to being in the presence of four stars, and Risen retakes his seat at the end of the coffee table, mindful that once again his first challenge is to get them sufficiently at ease to talk openly.

He fixes the young captain with a smile and gestures to the papers he's clutching.

"Sammy, go ahead and tell me what you found."

"Yes, sir. As you know, we reran the tapes of everything and downloaded NASA's images to take a close look at the gyrations around the end of Orbit Two. We assumed he had a control problem, but what we're seeing is all the reaction jets firing in staccato sequence. As the sequence continues and the craft stabilizes, the patterns calm down, as if the pilot is learning."

"She's not on automatic, in other words? The astronaut is on the controls manually?"

"Someone is. I mean, we're not trying to be NRO analysts or anything, sir, but if you want a guess, mine would be that those reaction controls were being manually fired by a person who did not have the training of an astronaut."

There is silence as Chris Risen glances at the two other officers present, a colonel and a brigadier.

"Bill Campbell is the pilot up there, right?"

"Yes, sir," the one-star answers.

"And you're saying that . . . like listening to a telegraph operator's patterns in the old days, you can tell that isn't Bill?"

"Not quite, sir. More like just saying that whoever's on the controls is an amateur with a very steep learning curve."

"And . . . that would be the passenger?"

"Yes, sir."

"Oh, shit. Which means that Campbell is hurt or worse."

"You know him, sir?" the colonel asks.

"It's a small fraternity, our service. Yeah, I know Bill. But what's important here is not who's alive up there but that someone is. And here's our challenge. There's a renegade rescue going on at NASA now that's already gotten the chief astronaut fired, but one of the other space programs will probably try to launch and save whoever remains. We're going to provide full support up to and just short of revealing any classified capabilities. I don't care whether it's the

Russians, NASA, ASA's other little ship, or even the Chinese, whoever wants our help in this gets it full bore."

The chorus of "Yes, sirs" fills the room as they get up to disperse. When the office is empty, Risen pulls out his own cell phone and dials a number in Houston, dispensing with the formalities as the circuit is completed.

"John, I've got some bad news about Bill Campbell's situation."

The White House,
2:45 p.m. Pacific/5:45 p.m. Eastern

Even after three terms in the U.S. Senate and countless visits to the White House, Mitch Lipensky still feels the rush of history and power when he walks into the Oval Office. He supposes it should always be so — never should he become complacent about the responsibility bearing down on anyone in this place.

The greetings and smiles befitting a white-haired committee chairman and member of the President's own party lubricate his passage through the hallways to the east entrance and the waiting President.

He's had thoughts of running for this office, dreams of being the leader of the free world and making the tough decisions. But in truth, the fire has never been hot enough in his belly, and the brutality of the campaign and the compromises which stand like huge peaks before any contender are simply beyond him.

He greets the President like the old friend that he is, refusing to call him anything but Mr. President, and they settle onto opposite sides of the coffee table before the fireplace, the Chief of Staff taking a side chair. There are only so many chits even a senior senator can call on for an immediate audience, and this one has been costly but necessary. NASA is his committee's responsibility, and the disturbing call from a man in Houston he considers an American hero has triggered a telephoned explanation and now this.

He knows Geoff Shear all too well, and sometimes even respects Shear's iconoclastic invulnerability to even the strongest congressional pressure.

But an order from the President would be a different matter.

"NORAD is telling me the pilot may be hurt or dead, Mitch. Is that what you have?" The voice is distinctive, tinged with the Virginia accent of his youth, and it's met by the equally familiar warm growl of the senior senator from Texas.

"Yes, sir. I have the same report. But the important thing, to my mind, is that someone is alive up there with a few days of air left, and he apparently can't fire his engine and get out of orbit."

"Understood. So no self-rescue. But is this something we have the ability to do?"

"We don't know, Mr. President, because our esteemed NASA administrator has rejected even the most rudimentary attempt to find out."

"You made it clear you want me to order John Kent reinstated."

"Yes, sir, I do. He's the best man to spearhead any attempt we might make. But there's a good reason beyond that. Way beyond that. All through the cold war, all through the space race, all through our history of manned — sorry, I mean *human* — spaceflight, our nation has maintained a steadfast consistency on the value of even one human life. For God's sake, even Stalin said the loss of one life is a tragedy."

"Yes, and the rest of that quote is that a million deaths is a statistic. Terrible thing to quote in part."

"I'm a doddering old senator with a selective memory. Sue me."

"Go on. I'm sorry to interrupt."

"Mr. President, we're the nation that refused to let the *Apollo Thirteen* crew die. The Russians killed dozens in their space program and refused to be moved. I submit we not change that now just because the stranded human is in a private spacecraft and is not a certified NASA astronaut. He's an American, and . . ."

"I get it, Mitch. That's an eloquent speech, but you can stop now. I get it."

Mitch's hand is out. "Let me finish. We need to have these words ringing in our minds. The business of America is business. Calvin Coolidge said that and we should be teaching it in every elementary school. Are we going to let a bureaucratic bureaucrat like Geoff Shear reject a rescue only because it involves someone shot into space by a mere American corporation and not our mighty government? Not to mention his personal animus against Richard DiFazio. If this was a current NASA astronaut up there, would there be any question? Aren't we dedicated to encouraging our companies, including private spaceflight ventures?"

"You know my stance on that."

"Then, dammit, Mr. President, you have to rein in Shear. He's out of control."

"Mitch, he's defending our ability to

carry anyone into space. How long have we been operating with only two shuttles? Six years?"

The senator chuckles with a knowing smile. "He's already called you, hasn't he?"

The President is smiling back, almost embarrassed. "Well . . . you know Geoff. He's a Beltway pro. He got to me before Kent got to you."

"That's unimportant. The order of contact, I mean."

"He's not an evil force, Mitch. He's got a point."

"He's on a personal vendetta, sir. You remember the fallout from that rather infamous hearing."

"Yes, but he still has a point."

"You going to let him cloud the bigger picture?"

The President laughs. It's more of a snort than a laugh, but he ends it by looking at his shoes before shaking his head. "Of course not."

"You still hate bureaucrats?"

"With a passion. But they have their uses."

"True. Landfill, for one."

There's a resigned sigh. "Mitch, if we lose a shuttle in this, can you steer the Senate to adopt the replacement bill at long last?"

"No guarantees, but we can probably do it. And you know we've got more than enough satellite lift capability without ever flying another shuttle."

"Sad, but true." The President slaps his thigh and stands, holding his hand out for Mitch to shake. "I'll issue the order."

"Rehire Kent and get a rescue mission ready if possible?"

"Yes. Shear may resign, Mitch."

"And, Mr. President, your point would be what?"

They both laugh as the senator takes his leave.

The President picks up the phone. Within a minute the requested voice comes on the line.

"Geoff? This is your leader. What the hell are you doing upsetting senior citizens like Mitch Lipensky?"

ASA Mission Control, Mojave, California, 3:05 p.m. Pacific

The very sound of Vasily's voice on the other end of the surprise phone call is comforting, buoying Richard DiFazio's spirits.

"There is a chance, Richard. I did not realize we were as far along in our preparations as we are."

"How soon could you launch?"

"This is the space station resupply mission, you understand. We would have room for two, and only to transport them to the station. From there, one of the escape capsules would have to be used to return."

"For one?"

"Or both. We don't have enough seats to do our mission and return two of your people."

"One may be badly hurt, or worse. We may have only one alive."

"If only one, we can bring him back after the resupply rendezvous."

"How soon?"

"Five days."

"Oh jeez, Vasily, they'll be dead by then."

"Not if they're careful. There are conservation steps, even with CO_2 scrubbers."

"Yes, but we can't tell them. We can't talk to them."

"And we cannot move any faster. But if there's only one alive, you have twice the time, no?"

Silence while Richard grapples with that possibility.

"And . . . there is one thing, Richard. I'm

sorry, but in the new Russia we still count every ruble, and this is a substantial change."

"How much, Vasily?"

"Twenty-five million."

Richard feels his blood pressure rising, simply out of the question. Unless . . .

"Can't we get that lower? This is a humanitarian rescue, an emergency. Suppose you need us someday?"

"Then you will name your price, too."

"Vasily, we don't have that kind of money."

"One of your backers, Butch Davidson, certainly does. He makes more than that every week in interest, I think. Is good idea, true?"

Why he's hearing the word "okay" coming from his mouth is a mystery. He knows Davidson's true penny-pinching nature that contrasts so gratingly with his publicly magnanimous reputation. The thought of approaching him for such a sum scares him.

"I have two million I can wire you as a down payment," Richard tells him.

"Okay. The rest you can get from Davidson."

"Please tell me you won't demand payment in full before launch."

The pause scares him again, but the

chuckle from Baikonaur Cosmodrome is reassuring. "No, we will extend you credit, my friend. But the money comes due whatever happens up there. Success or failure, you agree?"

"Yes. Five days, right?"

"Yes."

"You'll need coordinates and everything from us then?"

"No, we already know precisely, Richard. I shall e-mail you the bank account information within the hour. And then we begin."

Richard replaces the receiver in shock. Two million dollars without so much as one line on paper. Not to mention the remaining twenty-three million.

He shudders thinking of the reaction when he tells his board, which includes Davidson.

He stands suddenly, as if considering bolting. The deal he just verbally inked is based on a colossal set of assumptions, chief among them that NASA's chief is as good as his word and there will be no American rescue attempt.

What if NASA decides to do the rescue? How much do I owe the Russians then?

Clearly, the two million will be lost the moment it's wired, but it's a risk he has to take. He reaches for the nearest computer keyboard and punches up his e-mail. The bank information message from Vasily is already in place.

Chapter 15

It was inevitable, Diana thinks, and in some ways she's surprised it took this long. It's minutes past five p.m. western time and the sun is hanging low, *Intrepid* has been gone for almost ten hours.

The six flat-panel TV screens arrayed along the wall at the end of her desk are one-by-one posting their versions of a breaking news alert, adding file photos of ASA's spacecraft, first on Fox News and now on MSNBC. She's trying to keep up, toggling on the sound one by one to hear the same basic message: "A private spacecraft launched this morning has lost communication and may be in trouble."

Two secretaries are handling the rising tide of media inquiries, and she's staying out of contact to think and write a statement for Richard. She sees no easy or quick solution to this nightmare, and despite her concern for both Bill Campbell and Kip Dawson,

170

her job is to play this situation with infinite grace.

The tie-line from Mission Control rings.

"Diana? Richard. You called?"

She briefs him on the approaching media storm, before adding the essence of the storm warning, "There are satellite trucks being scrambled right now in L.A., and I'm working on a statement, but I need about fifteen minutes. You *are* going to be our face, right?"

"No. I want you to be the face."

"Not a good idea, Richard. You have the major skin in this game. They look at me as a flack."

The sigh she hears from the other end worries her. He's a good man and a good leader, but in the last six hours he's been all but falling apart. This may be a major mistake.

"Whatever you think, Diana," he says. "When do you want me over there?"

"Within the hour, if you can. Any changes?"

"No." His reply is a bit too curt. She knows something new has happened. "Who got it first?" he adds.

"The story?"

"Yes. Who broke it?"

Strange he'd ask that.

"The *Washington Post*. They slammed it

171

on their Web site twenty minutes ago and gave it to their partners, MSNBC and NBC, and it's been mushrooming since then."

"ABC and CBS?"

"They've called, too. I'm not returning calls for another hour, but the girls are handling it. Oh, Richard . . . someone did talk to Kip Dawson's wife, right?"

"Arleigh was going to."

"If he didn't, she'll find out the wrong way within minutes."

"Hold on." Within half a minute he's back. "Yes, thank God, he did it."

"Anything else I . . . need to know?"

More silence. Telling, pregnant silence, unbroken by an offered explanation, and she elects to sidestep it.

"Okay, you tell me whatever you think I need to know when I need to know it. Just don't let me twist in the wind."

"I'll be there in thirty minutes."

"Are we going to get them back, Richard?"

She fears the answer to the question she's blurted, but beneath the facade she's struggling to maintain, she feels like a frightened little girl watching the twisting trails of a shattered *Challenger* against the blue of her mind's eye.

"I don't know, Diana. I do know we're going to try everything."

Johnson Spaceflight Center, Houston, Texas, 5:12 p.m. Pacific/7:12 p.m. Central

The chief of security leans into John Kent's newly reoccupied office with a grin on his face and something in his hand, aware the chief astronaut is concentrating totally on the deluge of papers before him.

"Hey, John?"

Kent looks up, more curious than startled, and smiles. "Daniel. Missed the fireworks, did you?"

Daniel walks in, fanning the air with a small plastic security badge. "I was crushed I didn't get to escort you out at gunpoint myself."

"Yeah, right," Kent laughs, recalling the hours the two of them have spent talking about security matters on one of the post-9/11 committees.

"But I'm happy to bring you back a new badge, freshly minted with zero limitations and even a nice, fresh clip."

"Didn't know you made house calls."

"Oh, indeed. When one gets a call from the office of the President directing immediate reinstatement of even an Air Force guy, I hop to." He lays the badge on the overburdened desk, his expression turning serious. "I heard what you're working on. Can we do it? Launch that fast, I mean?"

Kent meets his eyes. "I don't know, but the President says it's a national priority to try, so . . . I'm working on it."

"I'll leave you alone, then." He hesitates halfway to the door. "I knew Bill Campbell, too, you know."

John is nodding, aware of the past tense. "Could be he's still with us, Dan, and just hurt."

"Could be."

"But we're going up regardless."

"Yeah. You might call the alternative Shear madness."

John shakes his head, a sworn enemy of puns. "Get out of here."

"Yes, sir."

The door closes and John works back through a list just e-mailed in from the Cape. His clandestine effort has now become the twenty-four/seven focus of the entire Kennedy Space Center, and the orbiter is already on its way aboard the crawler-transporter from the vehicle assembly building to Pad 39B, the nearly fourteen million pounds of launcher and spacecraft moving at less than a mile per hour.

John stops for a second, placing the pencil

he's been using on the desk and sitting back to clear his head.

He doesn't envy Bill Campbell's current dilemma, whatever it is, but he's watched the project in the Mojave with a certain longing for the last five years, knowing he's in Houston nursing a dinosaur that doesn't see the asteroid-sized meteor coming. To be able to just *fly* into space rather than blast and claw a sixteen-story building into orbit each time should have been the national focus for years. But here they are with only two ships left, both of them essentially flying museum pieces. It's no wonder, he thinks, that all versions of *Star Trek* were so popular in the space community. For NASA, watching the possibilities of twenty-third century technology each week was the equivalent of a centurion of ancient Rome getting a look at M-16 rifles, F-15 fighters, and cruise missiles.

John leans back into the calculations. It will be mid-morning before the final assessment can be made on whether an early rescue launch is possible, and the decision will not be his.

And despite his hostility to Geoff Shear and his megalomaniacal tendencies, he shares the same nightmarish worry: Another shuttle loss from pressing safety limits is unthinkable.

Chapter 16

Aboard *Intrepid*, May 17, 5:44 p.m. Pacific

It's sunset when Kip awakens.

There are sixteen sunsets per day in low Earth orbit, and at first he has no idea which one he's looking at as *Intrepid* flies backward, eastbound around the planet.

He glances at his watch, startled at how late it is back in California. He's been asleep for hours, and it's dark in Mojave, where he and the spacecraft should now be parked. He was supposed to be drinking champagne right now at a postflight party.

In sleep there were dreams he almost recalls, confused, kaleidoscopic, but dreams of his kids and meadows and for some reason a fast convertible that kept trying to get through a snow-covered pass in the Rockies with his father aboard.

But he's pretty sure what he's perceiving now is reality, and it sucks. All the excitement of being where he is, seeing what he's seeing, floating in zero gravity, is ruined by the reality that he's stranded and in grave danger.

He laughs, a short, loud expression of disgust. *Danger? Is that what I'm in? Try doomed! Try dead!*

Another small wave of buzzing dizziness passes over him and he realizes it has nothing to do with the zero gravity and his inner ear and vestibular balance system. It's his mind working overtime to reject this reality, like a kid with his fingers in his ears mouthing "na-na-na-na-na!" as loud as possible to drown out unwanted information.

So, what, exactly, is going to kill me? Am I going to run out of food, water, oxygen? Maybe die of boredom?

Kip can't believe he's chuckling, but the chuckle is building to a laugh, and he's laughing hard enough to draw tears.

That's it. I'm going to die of boredom long before running out of air!

Ground school details are coming back, and he remembers the discussion about the air cycle machines and the fact that the life limit isn't oxygen. It's getting rid of carbon dioxide — the same problem that threatened the *Apollo 13* crew.

So how long do I have? he wonders, attempting to keep the question clinical, ignoring his shaking hands.

It has to be written down somewhere, he thinks. Maybe in one of the checklists. He starts pawing through the nearest one, locating a table in the back in small print, a grid with the number of people aboard plotted against the capability of the CO_2 scrubbers.

Five days. One person, five days. So that's it. In five days I'll sit here and keel over from CO_2 poisoning. Probably not an unpleasant death.

At least, he figures, without communication he won't have to listen to Sharon say, "I told you so." That in itself is a blessing, but the forced joke falls flat and he finds himself reviewing the arrangements he's made.

The life insurance will pay, and they'll all be financially okay without him. Besides, even if there was no insurance, her well-heeled father wouldn't let her go wanting. The house in Tucson will be paid off and there will be a million left to put into investments, so they can live off the interest. He's left careful instructions.

The pragmatism evaporates, leaving his heart exposed, and he thinks about how eager he was to take this flight, and how right Sharon was to worry, and how much he misses his kids. The twins, Carly and Carrie, are barely five. Kip knows they'll remember their father mostly from family videos and snapshots. He will easily be replaced, as long as Sharon can find an appropriately obedient male to dominate, someone who by definition will be good to the girls.

Julie, however, is thirteen, and losing her dad will be devastating. She's bonded with Sharon, but never lost the effects of the trauma of her mother's sudden death.

Thank God, Jerrod is on his own now. He'll miss him the most, mainly because of the unfinished business between them, and the anger he's never been able to defuse.

Some of Bill Campbell's words return, something he said just before dying about their being in an orbit so stable they could stay up here for fifty or sixty years.

My God, Kip thinks, *Jerrod will be almost eighty before this spacecraft falls into the atmosphere and my long-dead body burns up on reentry. How awful for Jerrod and the girls to know their dead father is flying by overhead every ninety minutes your entire life.*

Or maybe it won't happen that way. Surely some spacecraft will eventually be assigned to come open the hatch and see what happened, retrieve any data files from the computers and deal with the dead. Maybe then all they'll do is give it a push toward Earth.

Or maybe he should just save everyone the trouble and when the air is all but un-breathable, just shoot himself out of the air-lock with Bill's body. The two of them would hardly be a flash in the sky on re-entry . . . or would they just be floating alongside *Intrepid* for decades?

Strange, he thinks, *that even death should be so meticulously planned.*

Every couple of minutes he looks around as if rediscovering where he really is, and with each such moment the wave of depres-sion breaks over him again, a rising tide drowning all hopes. He pushes the images of Sharon and his children out of his mind for now. The need to decide his own fate is far too strong, and he finds himself facing it with an unexpected equanimity.

Do I have any chance at all?

No rescue flight. They made that clear, but doesn't ASA have another spacecraft? He remembers their talking about it — and the fact that it was damaged. Which is prob-ably why the last-minute warning that there was no rescue potential if anything went wrong.

So the cavalry won't be on the way.

Is there anything I can do?

He already knows the answer. He's punched every button, read and reread the checklists ad nauseam, and it's inescapable that the meteorite that killed Bill also took out the engine, or at least the ability to fire it.

No, face it, kiddo. We're dead in five days. Period.

So, he wonders, how does one spend five remaining days on — or in his case, high above — the Earth? Not that the choices aren't severely limited, but his mind is sharp, even if saddened and stressed and panicked.

He remembers the notes he was starting to write in the laptop. *But no one's going to read it . . . for at least a bunch of years. Maybe even sixty.*

But surely someone will eventually find and download and study everything he puts on that hard drive. So maybe he should write a narrative and copyright it to his kids and grandkids, just in case the story could bring some money.

Who knows? he thinks. *They pay ridiculous sums to read the stories of criminals and the seriously disgraced. Why not a dead dad from half a century before?*

He remembers a fantasy he's nurtured his entire life in which he owns a beautiful wooden-hulled sailing ship at least a hundred feet long with an incredible master cabin, several guest rooms, and a small, ornate, walnut-trimmed captain's office. He sees himself every evening repairing to his little office to open a big, bound, blank notebook to write in a clear and ornate hand beautifully phrased passages about the day, his feelings, the state of the ship, and his life.

Every night, without fail! How wonderful that would be. Like being his own Greek chorus and his own reflective, calm, and intelligent critic.

But the image is too ludicrous a contrast to the reality of an overscheduled dad who has been known to fall asleep from exhaustion before even having a chance to brush his teeth.

Kip looks around, aware there's not a scrap of wood aboard *Intrepid*, but finding sudden similarities between where he is and that mythical ship's office — and his nightly journal. His imagination could panel the walls, especially now. And maybe he could even imagine the creak of heavy ropes and the slap of waves on the hull.

There's no bound, blank book, but there *is* a laptop aboard.

And there will be an audience someday.

And there are five days left, which is a lot more than would be available to some poor soul T-boned to death at an intersection on the planet below.

The word "epitaph" comes to mind.

Chapter 17

United States Air Force Academy,
Colorado Springs, Colorado,
May 17, 6:33 p.m. Pacific/
7:33 p.m. Mountain

Cadet Jerrod Dawson has never been summoned to the commandant's office before, let alone in the middle of the evening and immediately on return from a field trip. He's already reported, saluted, and waited for an explanation from a major and a lieutenant colonel in the room when one of the academy chaplains comes through the door, raising his level of alarm.

"Sir, may I ask what this is about?" Jerrod can feel his stomach contracting in fear. He's purposely avoided watching or reading any news reports during the day, not wanting to even seem to be endorsing his father's self-indulgent flight. But now . . .

"Is something wrong?"

"Sit down, please, Mr. Dawson," the colonel directs, and Jerrod sinks into the nearest chair, his eyes darting among each of them.

"Is this about my dad?"

The glances among the three confirm that much, and the colonel finally finishes fidgeting long enough to speak.

"Cadet, you are aware your father was participating in a civilian spaceflight today, correct?"

"Yes, sir. Please tell me. Has something happened?"

"We don't know if he's all right or not, but we got a call from your mother . . ."

"My mother's dead, sir. That would be my stepmother."

"Right. Well, let me tell you in as much detail as we have it what we know."

National Air and Space Museum, Washington, D.C., 8:05 p.m. Pacific/11:05 p.m. Eastern

It's late evening in the Beltway, past 11 p.m., and the black tie reception and dinner, attended at the last minute by the head of NASA, is winding down. The guests are taking their leave, winding beneath the amazing displays of space and aeronautics, past the suspended *Spirit of St. Louis*, Burt

185

Rutan's *SpaceShipOne*, the *Wright Flyer*, and the *Mercury Project* capsule. The men look sharp in their tuxedoes, their wives and girlfriends mostly stunning in their expensive evening gowns — some featuring necklines which plunge giddily.

Geoff Shear is uninterested in both the pomp and purpose, though he's made nice and uttered the appropriate comments — especially to those who've fawned over his presence. His purpose for being there is waiting just ahead in a semi-private alcove.

She turns, elegant but appropriately conservative, her last-minute invite a puzzling request to the museum since her apparent mid-level position with the Agency would hardly put her in the same league as the mainstream crowd.

"Dorothy?"

"Mr. Administrator."

"Thanks for responding at the last minute. Anybody, ah, keeping track of you?"

She's smiling, considering her answer as she glances back toward the thinning crowd. "There is one young Senate staffer who keeps trying to strike up a conversation and get lucky, but otherwise, no."

Geoff smiles and follows her glance, seeing no one in particular.

"Sorry to spoil the possibilities of the evening."

"It was yours to begin with, considering the source of the invitation. What can I do for you, sir?"

He motions her into a side room where the displays of the evolving history of rocketry are arranged in the form of an open maze. He turns, his wineglass still tightly gripped and only half drained.

"Dorothy, I have a mission for you. I've been ordered by the President to do everything NASA can to mount a rescue launch for ASA's apparently stranded spacecraft. You know this?"

"More or less."

"Okay. A presidential order is an order, but NASA cannot afford suddenly to throw caution to the wind. I need you to go to Reagan at seven in the morning and get down to the Cape. Should you ever be asked by some damned congressional committee, then these are my formal orders: You're there to coordinate and ensure safety for the Agency. You were asked to go down there by your supervisor."

"Understood."

"But . . ."

She's reaching out to him, her index finger actually touching his lips, the level of familiarity and the knowing smile a bit disturbing.

"I think I understand. I know how you think, and how you feel about these private efforts. This launch attempt must not take place if there is too much risk, and I might just discover that there's far too much risk . . . the type the boys down South just didn't see at first."

He's nodding, admiringly. "I'm glad you see it that way. As you well know, I can't trust anyone at the Cape."

"There's one thing I want."

"Go ahead."

"I've enjoyed being your fix-it agent, so to speak, especially after eight years in covert ops for the Company. At least no one's been shooting at me here. But I'm ready now to come in out of the cold, as the old reference goes. That desk you promised me?"

"You really want to fly a desk?"

"Can we make this my last assignment?"

"Why not. Although I'll need your help recruiting someone new. The one thing I learned early on in this town, Dorothy — if you don't have your own eyes and ears, an administrator can never know what's really happening in the trenches. You've done that well."

"Deal, then? Last assignment?"

"Deal."

"You want reports back from me?"

"No. We need plausible deniability at all turns. We may have said hello here at this party, but that's it. In fact, amazingly, there will be no record of your having ever been here tonight."

"I figured. In that case, I should evaporate," she says, placing her empty wineglass on a nearby ledge and leaving without another word.

Chapter 18

Cheyenne Mountain,
North American Aerospace
Defense Command,
Colorado Springs, Colorado,
May 18, 4:08 a.m. Pacific/
5:08 a.m. Mountain

"Here's our problem, General."

On one of the huge screens an amazing furball of moving blue dots is gyrating, the dots orbiting the planet they're almost obscuring. General Risen has seen this many times, the 3-D depiction representing the orbiting garbage dump of space junk whirling around the Earth. But now a single object begins to blink red, and the senior master sergeant controlling the display adds a circle around it and then drops out all but it.

"How long until impact," Risen asks, ". . . and are we absolutely sure?"

"Six hours, twenty-four minutes, sir, and the answer is yes, it'll be a high probability of a conjunction — a direct hit. There's a kind of football-shaped zone of probable flight path around it, but . . . it looks potentially fatal to me."

"How large is the object? Any estimate?"

"General, we're sure this is one of the shroud halves off a 1986 Soviet Proton rocket. That means more than a hundred pounds."

He leans forward, scanning the waiting, worried faces of the six men in front of him as they sit in the middle of the main Cheyenne Mountain war room. As commander, he's rolled his staff car through the vaultlike blast door and climbed into the six-story, spring-mounted building too many times to count, but each time there's been a crisis or an alert, a special quiet tension fills the place like nowhere else. That biologic electricity now crackles unseen among them as they wait for their commander to assess what their computers discovered less than an hour ago.

The call to his predawn bedroom brought him running.

"Did ASA use Space Command's clearance procedures for this orbital insertion? In other words, that piece of junk has been up there one helluva long time and we've been tracking it. How come they used this precise orbit and we're only now seeing the conflict?"

"Their orbital flight plan terminated yesterday, sir. They weren't supposed to be where they are."

Chris Risen drops his head and grimaces, the know-all senior commander caught in a simple but embarrassing mistake.

"And that dumb question, guys, was just my daily reminder that I'm a carbon-based unit and thus imperfect, stars or not."

"Easy mistake, sir."

"We've talked to ASA?"

"Yes, General, we've already alerted ASA's Mission Control, but . . . they have no contact and can't do anything to alter the spacecraft's course."

He nods, aware of the consternation NORAD's call will have caused in Mojave.

"Sir," the duty controller, a colonel, adds, "I'm stating the obvious, but the collision won't be survivable."

"Understood."

"And, sir . . . worse is the fact that we calculate literally thousands of individual debris orbits will result, quite a few of them becoming elliptical and threatening other altitudes. A broken-up shroud would present far less hazard than the rain of fragments from a shattered spacecraft."

Chris meets the colonel's eyes for just a moment, getting the message. There are a few top-secret defensive abilities that are known to only a tiny handful of NORAD senior officers, officially denied capabilities that are never to be spoken of in the presence of uncleared individuals. Not even the highly trained control room personnel.

Risen gets to his feet, ever mindful of the delicate balance between approachable leader and the strong, impeccable commander. "All right. Carry on. I've got some calls to make."

He makes his way to one of the glassed-in booths at the rear of the control room and picks up a tie-line maintained twenty-four hours a day by a crack team of specialists, a line that can reach the President almost anywhere at any moment. It is a capability approached with great care and some fear. Lifting the handset bypasses the chain of command, and if the reason isn't as rock solid as the mountain around them, careers can be ended.

Even that of a four-star general.

A voice most of the nation instantly recognizes comes on the other end. It's just past 7 a.m. in Washington, and Chris assumes the President is already away from the family quarters, but the sound of rustling bedcovers, a momentary comment from the

First Lady, and a deep, sleepy voice betray the assumption.

"Yes?"

"Mr. President, General Risen at NORAD. My apologies, sir, but we have a situation in accordance with your directive yesterday on the private spacecraft."

"Good morning, Chris. I'm just being lazy getting up. What's up?"

His explanation is crisp and clear, and there's a long pause from the other end before the commander in chief sighs.

"What do you recommend? And we are on a secure line, right?"

"Yes, sir. Mr. President, with the considerable damage this will do to orbital safety and the tremendous increase in debris . . . not to mention the loss of life . . . I recommend we use Longbow."

"Really? Won't our buddies across both ponds see what we're doing?"

"Sir, we have to assume they will. The Russians, Chinese, French, and perhaps the European Space Agency will probably be watching. The National Reconnaissance Office is the better one to answer that."

"But you think it's about time they knew our capabilities anyway, right? I mean, it's been thirty years and five presidents since we made a show of it."

"Sir, you're asking me a policy question I'm not qualified to answer."

"Yeah, Chris, you're right. That's unfair of me. Look, I'm glad you brought this straight to me. I know it's tough to jump the chain even in your position, but I need that direct contact. I realize this was a judgment call and not out of the Defcon procedures."

"Thank you, sir. I thought it was justified, because of your statements yesterday on television."

"You say we have six hours left?"

"Yes, sir."

"That's barely any time. Okay. I've got some tough questions to ask an array of people."

"We'll be here, sir."

"By the way, I'm told the astronaut up there is a friend of yours."

How on earth does he know that? Chris wonders, a flash of caution rocketing through his head about the source of the information and whether it was passed to the President honestly or with malicious intent. Was someone in the Pentagon waiting in the weeds for him?

"Yes, sir," he answers. "Bill Campbell was a NASA astronaut and a fellow Air Force pilot and a friend. But I . . ."

"That's what makes us a great nation,

Chris. Not that we know everyone, but that we're sufficiently family to care. That isn't an object up there, it's two of us."

"Yes, sir."

"Okay. Gotta go. Hang in there, General. You are appreciated."

Chris replaces the receiver with a smile. "You are appreciated," is a signature tag line unique to this chief executive and grossly overreported by the media, but Chris knows the man means it. And despite the fact that his Air Force peers consider it an eye-roller and call it a "warm fuzzy," the President's appreciation is, well, appreciated.

And as he stands to go, Chris Risen gives himself just a few seconds to embrace that very human pat on the head from the most powerful office holder in the world.

ASA Mission Control,
Mojave, California, 7:45 a.m. Pacific

Diana feels like rubbing her eyes, but with no time to find a mirror and assess or repair the effect a vigorous eye rub would have on her makeup, she stifles the urge, fussing with the microphone clipped to the collar of her blouse instead.

This is the eighth interview so far, she

counts, and there will be dozens more since Richard's refusal to do anymore himself. She gets into the zone mentally, summoning the vocal tone and the mental sharpness she's going to need, like an actor with the flu taking the stage and forcing away the pain and the weakness for a few hours. The right tone, the right phrases, the right balance will be critical with each interview . . . not that she isn't personally torn up and as scared as everyone else over what's happening. But "torn up and scared" would be the wrong message. What the public must see is strength, control, concern, cautious optimism, and absolute realism. In the public mind, she *is* the company, and one misstep on camera could theoretically destroy it.

She only half listens to the correspondent as he begins his report next to her, and shifts her eyes to him only on the cue of the question.

"Ms. Ross, there's been no radio contact of any sort, correct? How could that happen?"

"It's not easy for that to happen. A whole host of radios had to have been knocked out, including several backups, but however it happened, we have lost all radio contact, both voice and telemetry. Yet we're sure, through NASA's help with their long-range cameras, that the spacecraft is still powered and pressurized, and that someone is at the controls."

"Some*one,* versus both of them?"

"I'm not going to speculate beyond that. The spacecraft was obviously damaged. NASA, however, has seen solid evidence of sentient human control of the vehicle. But since we can't talk to them, we don't know what their status is. I'd like to add that I think it's pretty remarkable that, regardless of the radio problem, they were apparently struck by a high speed object and yet the craft remains livable. That's an accolade to the engineering."

"But why haven't they reentered and landed?"

"There could be a variety of reasons, not all of them bad. But again, we just do not know. What we are sure of is that all our carefully planned emergency procedures are in progress, and the entire space community is joining hands to help get them back safely."

"You can't fly another of your ships up there and rescue them?"

"We only have one other ship at this time, and that very operation is being considered as we speak, yes."

"And how long do they have? How much air?"

"Four days at least. They are in no danger right now, but we wouldn't want to see them stay up there more than a few more days."

Something catches her eye off camera and Diana glances to her right, spotting Richard, who is peeking around the corner and gesturing to her to finish and follow.

"I hope you'll excuse me, but I have to go attend to something. We'll keep you briefed."

The reporter turns to the camera as Diana unclips the microphone and hands it off, pushing past six other camera crews to hurry from the room.

Her CEO is waiting at the end of the hallway, his expression even more sallow than before, and she wonders how that's possible.

"What?"

"In here."

She follows him into an empty office and closes the door.

"Diana, they've stayed up there too long."

"Excuse me, isn't that a 'Well, duh!' statement?"

"No, no . . . I mean, our orbital debris clearance was only good for half a day. They were never supposed to be in that orbit this long."

"Richard, you're trying to tell me something. Stop dancing."

He sinks into the nearest chair, defeated. "NORAD called. There's a piece of an old Russian booster in a polar orbit that's going to take them out inside three hours."

"What?"

"They said it's a dead-on collision — they called it a conjunction — from the side at seventeen thousand miles per hour. It won't be survivable."

It's her turn to be staggered, and she leans on the edge of the desk to absorb the news.

"There's nothing we can do?" she asks.

"Maybe if we could talk to them! Otherwise, they'll never see it coming."

"God!"

"I know it."

"Well . . . do we have to tell the world? I'd recommend we sit on it for a while at least."

"Okay."

"And, Richard, there's one other thing, though it's going to make me sound even colder than before."

"What's that?"

"Which is better? A catastrophic collision we can't control instantly ending it, or a spacecraft with two dead people in it circling for a half century?"

"Good God, Diana!"

"Sorry, but think about it. Not that we can do anything."

He's on his feet and she can tell it was the wrong thing to throw at him. His frustration and panic have been looking for a target and she just handed him one.

"Don't you have any feelings at all?"

"Of course! But it's my . . ."

"What the hell's the matter with you? Damage control is one thing, but . . . but . . ."

"Richard! There are two guys up there I care about. I was trying to make you feel a little less panicked."

"Two you care about? I mean, I know you know Bill . . ."

She's blushing and can't figure out why. There's no love interest regarding Kip Dawson, but she remembers his big eyes lighting up and his little-boy enthusiasm and suddenly thinking about him being smashed to atoms after the terror he's already been through is too much. She feels the tears before she realizes they're falling, and she lets Richard gather her into his arms.

"I'm sorry!" she says, heartfelt.

"Me, too," he answers. "I apologize."

They part awkwardly and she searches for a Kleenex. "I've got cameras waiting. I'm not telling them this. And I still think you should be the one doing these interviews."

"I can't. And you're doing wonderfully."

She turns to the door and stops to look back.

"Richard, is it truly unavoidable?"

He nods sadly. "Unless we can talk to them or they light off the rocket or unless NORAD is wrong. There's just nothing we can do."

"I guess we can pray. I haven't done a lot of that for a very long time."

Chapter 19

For just a moment several hours back Kip saw a glimmer of something on the horizon, a momentary flash just enough to convince him that he isn't yet resigned to his fate. During the next entire orbit he'd strained to see it again, whatever "it" had been, his hopes telegraphed through a pounding heartbeat that maybe, just maybe it was a rescue craft. But by the fourth hour after the flash, his hopes evaporated.

This time his sadness and the letdown are muted, as if he should be embarrassed for even raising the possibility of deliverance again, and especially for crabbing backward along the emotional arc he's tried to travel to reach a state of acceptance.

Before that flash — that glimmer of hope now dashed — he'd slept some more, shaken by the realization that more than a day has elapsed since launch.

The laptop has been opened and closed several times, but the words he wants to type seem stuck in his heart. Yet, once again he pulls the weightless machine to him, secures it to his lap, and stares at the keyboard for the longest time before his fingers move to the keys.

A strange message pops up asking his approval for some sort of connection and he answers yes without thinking, then can't get it back.

What the heck was that? he wonders, taking a quick detour into the Windows Control Panel to see if something's unusual. But nothing jumps out and the connection utility shows the computer connected to nothing, no networks, no modems, no other humans.

He calls up a word processing window and begins anew.

Anyone out there?

Of course not. At least not in my lifetime, which will be short.

But let's pretend you are there, whatever year it is when you finally read these words.

For the record, I suppose I should yell Mayday, Mayday, Mayday! (At least I think that's the right phrase.) I'm a passenger on the private spaceship *Intrepid*, which launched from Mojave,

California, and we were hit by some sort of small object which came right through the cabin and right through my pilot's head, killing him instantly. No one can hear me on the radios, and apparently I only have four days of air left.

And this isn't fun anymore.

I probably had more days of air than five at first, but I used it the first day panicking, crying, raging, and generally acting like an idiot. But it's okay now. Death happens. I know intellectually that there's no chance of rescue or survival, and I realize that there will be no reprieve, no heroic stretching of the available air supply, and no magic solutions derived by teams of sweating scientists below in the eleventh hour. This won't be *Apollo 13.*

When I won this private spaceflight, they warned me very carefully that if anything happened, neither NASA nor any other country's space program was going to attempt to save me. I accepted the risk, and I'm sure what happened was beyond anyone's ability to foresee, as far as I can tell. But now . . . here I sit, knowing I have four days left to say something to a mute disc drive, and the worst part is I can't even say good-bye to my family and friends or anyone else, even though I'm passing over their heads every hour and a half.

What's wrong, by the way, is that because of the thing that hit us, the retro rocket won't fire. So I'm stuck in a stable orbit and sick with guilt over the fact that my wife, Sharon, begged me not to take this risk. Turns out she was dead right, pun intended. It was an unforgivably selfish act. I expect my son, Jerrod, will never forgive me either, since he already continues to blame me for his mother's death, and my little girls will never have the chance to hear directly from me why this all happened, and why I decided to come up here and ended up depriving them of a father.

Then he considers addressing his words to Diana, and the thought surprises him. She's the first name that pops into his head, and he decides it has something to do with hers being the last smiling female face he saw before launch.

For the tiniest moment, the idea of her feels like a focal point, an inspiration, a reason to struggle hard to come back.

And just as quickly that sparkle of thought evaporates.

At my ripe old age of forty-four, I'm that worst of all white Anglo males, the middle-aged dad with a mid-life crisis, and I've been feeling for a long time like I've wasted the last twenty years, or at least that I went down the wrong road somehow.

No, no, no, he thinks. *I'm not going to sit up here and whine in print.*

He pauses, aware of a vague pain in his stomach, at first not recognizing the symptoms of simple hunger. There's a selection of protein bars and other packaged food in a side compartment that he's already raided, and he pulls one of the stowed bars out of the ankle pocket of his flight suit and wolfs it down with a water chaser from his squeeze bottle. Food is one of his lowest priorities.

He's distracted by the sun disappearing over the horizon again, the beauty of the rapid change from ruddy red to deep purple and inky, star-studded black absolutely amazing. He wonders whether, when it's all over and he's . . . wherever . . . beauty like this can still be perceived. Maybe it's even prettier there. Wherever "there" is.

Heaven. He has his own definition, probably born of too little intimacy in the last few years. He's enjoyed poking fun at straight-laced male friends who still think sex is a four-letter word. "Heaven's right here," he's fond of saying as he enjoys the shock value, "in the arms of whatever pretty female you can find."

But in his early years he'd occasionally fallen in love so deep he couldn't eat or think for weeks.

There was, for instance, Linda Hammel, and he smiles at the warm memory, wondering where she is. He has never discussed her with anyone. His folks would have been scandalized, and her father would have killed him. But now . . .

He looks at the keyboard, suddenly excited at the prospect of reliving those moments, even if only through a dreamy window of words.

All right, let's begin unconventionally. I've got to start somewhere, and both I and whoever I mention will have been long dead by the time you, my reader, find these words, so I think I'll tell you about my happiest times, my teen years, and my first real love.

Chapter 20

Situation Room, The White House,
May 18, 8:00 a.m. Pacific/
11:00 a.m. Eastern

The President pauses before unlocking the bathroom door and walking back into the world. He shakes his head to think that the only privacy the most powerful leader on the planet can have is in his private water closet, but too often it's true.

He rummages through his pants pocket for a breath strip, aware of his growing case of coffee breath, and does a quick reassessment of his image in the mirror before drying his hands and opening the door. As usual, several people are hovering right outside and waiting for him, this time the number includes the White House Air Force liaison officer.

"Ready, Mr. President?" she asks.

"Yes, Kim. Lead the way."

They quickly move into the inner chamber of the Situation Room, a small conference room festooned with communications equipment and liquid crystal screens.

Colonel Kim Wallenda lights up one of the screens, a real-time image of an Air Force hangar complex in Nevada undulating in the morning heat. One of the hangar doors is open, with nothing but black visible inside.

"Good show and tell, Kim, but why?"

She looks taken aback, but she knows this President and knows it's not a challenge.

"Just an establishing shot, sir. To be honest, I just put it up there to show off our real-time video capabilities."

"Let's get to the details."

Charts and tables alternately fill the screen with the top secret deployment details of a standby force ordered quietly into existence by President Reagan in the early eighties.

"As you know, sir, Longbow has been on pad alert since its inception as an antisatellite killer, and our planes have been scrambled only twice, but never used for an actual kill. We have a total of fifteen of these specially modified F-106s ready in six different locations, all shown on the screen. The original tests used F-15s, but the 106 has a bigger weapons' bay. The one for this mission has to come from Holloman in New

210

Mexico, because of the target's orbital path. The only real challenge is computing and flying the precise path to lob the missile into the right window. We can reach as high as a six-hundred-fifty-mile orbit."

"And the thing we're trying to hit is at three hundred ten miles, right?"

"Yes, sir. Now, what you've essentially asked us to do is change the course of this rogue object by a kinetic kill. There will be an explosive charge on the missile's second stage, but we're relying on the energy transfer of the kinetic impact to blow the shroud off course just enough to miss ASA's spacecraft. But just fragmenting it isn't enough, so we're using an oblique trajectory, almost forty-five degrees to its course. Hopefully, not even fragments will remain on the same collision course."

"Are we absolutely sure . . . is NORAD sure . . . that the collision course is valid and that we really need to do this?"

Another woman at the far end of the table in civilian clothes nods.

"Yes, sir. I just spoke with General Risen at NORAD. Their continuous orbital path reassessment still shows a high probability of a dead-on collision if there's no change."

"Very well. Jim? Objections on this decision from the Pentagon's perspective?"

"Nothing new, Mr. President. As far as our overseas friends and adversaries, we're going to show 'em our . . . ah . . ." The President can see the Deputy Secretary of Defense suddenly realizing there are women present, tough and professional as they may be, and it's momentarily amusing to watch him founder as he looks for an expression less earthy than what was on his lips.

"Showing them our what?"

"Muscle, sir."

"Uh-huh." Even the two women are chuckling under their breath as he tries to continue with some dignity. "It's . . . a worry, revealing what we've got, but we've long since made it clear we were not going to comply with archaic treaty restrictions that are questionable, anyway. And this is not hostile use."

"As soon as we're done, I'll phone Moscow and explain what's happening. Him first, then NATO. So, how about State? Kevin?"

"No objections, sir. The only countries able to perceive what we're doing by direct observation probably need to be warned we have this capability."

"It's thirty-year-old technology, Kevin. I doubt even popular science would be too impressed."

"Yes, sir, but we pretended to abandon it. So, whether we're using Star Wars–pulsed beam plasma systems or throwing large rocks with a guidance package, it all comes down to the same thing. If it's up there, we can bring it down."

The President closes his notebook and looks at each of them. "All of us understand that this will solve only one of the problems. What I've ordered NASA to try to do is far more problematic and risky, but if there's anyone breathing up there . . . and we all think there is . . . we've got to do our best to bring him back. Kim, let me know the moment you launch."

Her "Yes, sir" is spoken to his back as the President swings out the door, trying to imagine for a second how it would feel to be trapped in a spacecraft with no communications. The news that most likely the civilian passenger is the only survivor continues to chill him.

Holloman Air Force Base,
New Mexico,
8:50 a.m. Pacific/9:50 a.m. Mountain

Owen Larrabe feels the excitement building as he sits in his pressure suit on a box beside the F-106 and studies the top-secret flight plan he figured he'd never get the chance to fly. Two crewmen are hovering at the ready, one holding his helmet.

"I'd better get in," he says, getting awkwardly to his feet. The two crewmen are instantly at his side, walking him to the ladder for what will be a brief but arduous job of sliding into the seat and attaching himself with straps that he won't have enough mobility to reach. F-106 cockpits were not designed for pressure suits.

Owen pauses to survey the interior of the secret hangar, built to look like a dusty warehouse on the far side of the well-worn Air Force base. When they're ready and the security police have chased off everyone who might otherwise be looking, the entire false front of the allegedly old brick building will open, allowing him to taxi quickly to the adjacent end of the runway for a quick takeoff to the west. By the time he plugs in the afterburner, the building should have returned to normal, protected by the anonymity of its uninteresting appearance and a host of sophisticated sensors and monitoring devices.

Like an astronaut who never thought he'd fly a mission to space, Captain Owen Larrabe has always thought of his weird, secret assignment as a pain. Three years stationed at Holloman supposedly flying a revived continental defense mission in one of the few remaining F-106 squadrons, while secretly maintaining proficiency for this mission and spending too many weekends and evenings practicing getting into and out of the pressure suit. Two other pilots here have the same mission and the same problem, with wives and families who just don't understand where they go all those extra evenings when the rest of their squadron is at home or having barbecues.

The last strap is being snapped in place and the young crew chief runs over his checklist, showing the removed ejection seat pins and getting the requisite nod from his pilot.

At least, Owen thinks, the air conditioned temperature maintained in the hangar is a blessing. He'll taxi into the desert heat in comfort.

The side of the hangar is in motion now, large hydraulic arms moving the counterbalanced facade up and over as he runs the checklist and starts the engine, timing the start of his quick exit for the moment the marshaler signals the door is clear. His takeoff and flight clearance have already been granted on a special UHF frequency

and the airfield is silent, awaiting his departure. He finishes the last checklist item and
smoothly swings the Delta Dart onto the
runway, bringing the power to maximum
and then plugging in the afterburner as he
accelerates, the unusually long missile held
snugly inside the weapons bay. He passes
eighty knots with a glance to his left. The
building is a building again, the door closed,
the crew invisible, and he pulls the bird into
the air, cleaning up gear and flaps and
burner as he turns for the intercept point
somewhere to the southeast.

The missile has been designed to launch
itself, just like the original test back in 1985,
but at nearly ninety thousand feet. And the
trajectory is not what they've practiced. Instead of a head-on shot, it will go for an intercept from a forty-five-degree angle from
the back.

He's already had the classified briefing on
what they're trying to do, and there'll be
only one chance. If they miss, on the very
next orbit ninety minutes later the old Russian missile shroud will impact the spacecraft, obliterating both.

But his equipment is improved from the
old days. The first and only successful test
had none of the sophisticated onboard guidance computers he has now, and the missile

was more or less a dumb infrared tracker. The pilot of that test plane, Doug Pearson, had become the first and only "space ace," the first to shoot down a spacecraft.

And now, Owen thinks, *I've got the chance to be the second. Sweet.*

Yet, the seriousness of the mission is not lost on him. The stakes couldn't be higher. He's trained to take out an enemy's orbiting eyes or an orbiting nuke if anyone is ever stupid enough to put one up. But this is a different type of shooting.

Owen engages the trajectory computer and locks his global positioning satellite system into the data stream, pleased to see the green light flash on his screen. The flight director pops into view and he places the dot representing the F-106 in the middle, following the computer commands to the start point. The mission is to be flown in radio silence, except for his transponder and an open satcom channel to the mission commander back in the Pentagon. He's closing on the hold point where he'll fly a racetrack pattern for thirty minutes waiting for the precise moment to start the run, and he looks over to check the fuel remaining, momentarily disbelieving the figures.

What the hell?

He should be reading a full tank but it's

coming up short. Disastrously short, and he wonders if the fuel totalizer could be wrong.

A quick mental calculation deflates that possibility, and he toggles the UHF radio back to the ground crew's frequency at Holloman, triggering a series of messages that end with the realization that someone screwed up big-time.

I don't frigging believe this! he thinks, his heart pounding. *Twenty years to practice and the one time we get a mission we blow it for insufficient fuel?*

There's no time to scare up a tanker. He runs the numbers again, the planned fuel burn during the antisatellite launch run and the fuel between now and then, plus the fuel back to the base.

They don't match. If he uses the most fuel-efficient speed to hold, he'll still flame-out on the way back down from launch altitude.

Okay, but can I dead-stick her back to the base?

The thought is chilling, shoving an engineless F-106 back through the stratosphere and stretching the energy enough to make the home runway.

But that, too, won't work. He'd end up crashing in the desert fifty miles short or worse.

The call to the command post in the Pentagon is tough but crucial, and there's a momentary flurry of confusion until a general comes on the line.

"Bluebird Two-Three, Stargazer. You do realize we have no other options on this mission?"

"Roger, Stargazer. I can't believe we're short. I don't suppose there are any tankers airborne nearby?"

"Negative. We just looked at that, and there's no time to go back. Can you make the launch work?"

"Yes, sir. That I can do, but I'll flame out on the way down."

"We're considering a punch-out scenario here."

Owen's finger freezes on the transmit button for a few seconds. Punch out of a perfectly good F-106? Worse, a specially modified F-106? A hundred million dollars or more reduced to junk because one of his team failed to read the tanks?

Not acceptable, he tells himself.

"Stargazer, there's an alternate airport below my flight path. Civilian and short, but I can probably make it in dead stick."

"Which one?"

"Carlsbad Muni, sir."

Silence for a few seconds before a cautious reply reaches his ears.

"Your choice, Bluebird Two-Three. You are authorized to leave the ship or take it in without power to Carlsbad. We'll scramble a team there right now just in case."

"Roger."

"Hey, Bluebird . . . a personal note from an old fighter pilot, okay? Don't wait too long if you have to leave her. Eject inside the envelope. Got it?"

"Roger, sir."

Chapter 21

Kalgoorlie-Boulder, Western Australia,
May 18, 8:55 a.m. Pacific/11:55 p.m. WST

Satisfied that his parentals have quieted down at long last, Alastair Wood slides out of bed and quietly pads across the cold floor of his room. He pulls on a thick robe before sitting at his desk and firing up his most prized possession — a computer with a flat screen monitor and the high-speed Internet connection that was his main gift for his just-celebrated twelfth birthday.

The sleepy look and deep circles under his eyes he carries to school these days are worth it for the midnight hours he usually spends at the keyboard, but tonight has been a disappointment. It was shaping up at first to be a bonus with his father and mother doing their lock-the-door intimate thing at ten, but two hours have gone by. Now all he'll have is three uninterrupted hours before having to hit the sack as usual at three to be up by seven.

While so many of his school chums have

their heads buried in video games, he's touring the world real time every night. And it *is* the whole world that pours into his personal portal, filled with information on just about anything he would ever want to know.

His father will never understand of course, and he's tired of being called a geek whenever he's discovered hunched over the keyboard at some ungodly hour. He loves his dad, even though he knows he's a hopeless dinosaur when it comes to computers and communication, thinking his GSM cell phone is cutting edge. Alastair can't bring himself to tell him that they've had the same phones in Africa for over a decade.

The operating system goes through its start-up routine and he waits it out, reviewing his surfing plan for the next few hours. A new bulletin board from England, a number of Web sites in the U.S. — including one featuring bikini shots of famous actresses — and an attempt to hack into a poorly protected Internet e-mail provider are all on the agenda.

The house is quiet as a tomb, and he double checks to make sure the volume is zeroed before running the risk of a burst of noise — a big mistake he made a few weeks ago that brought his father flying up the stairs.

There's a parcel of e-mails from friends, including one with a link he's never seen before, some sort of Internet router service.

Oh what the heck, he decides, clicking on the address and waiting for the screen to stabilize.

A long list of active e-mail accounts parades by, and he selects a few at random, watching a stream of 1's and zeros without being able to discern their meaning.

Right! A challenge!

He selects a translation program and tries it with no effect, then pulls in another, and on the third try someone's real-time transmission is crawling across his screen, some teenage girl complaining about a feckless boyfriend.

Boring.

He pulls back a level and scrolls down to the very bottom, finding a message in progress without a coherent address.

Hm-m-m. Let's look at this private, personal communiqué.

He triggers the translation program again, and the words assemble themselves in English, the transmission apparently still in progress and scrolling across his screen.

. . . record, I suppose I should yell Mayday, Mayday, Mayday! (At least I think that's the right phrase.) I'm a passenger on the private spaceship *Intrepid*, which launched from Mojave, California, and we were hit by some sort of small object which came right through the cabin and right through my pilot's head, killing him instantly. No one can hear me on the radios, and apparently I only have only five days of air left.

And this isn't fun anymore.

Alastair sits back, scratching his head. The syntax and tone don't match any of the hackers he knows who might try to pull such a stunt, but then he can hardly know all the tricksters on the planet. Someone, however, is trying a sophisticated scam, and he triggers a save program to record whatever comes and sits back to watch what the trickster will try next.

Private spaceship. Yeah, sure.

Just to be certain, he triggers the Google search engine and throws the words private spaceship and *Intrepid* into the search box, expecting a cascade of gobbledygook.

Instead sixteen thousand hits come back with the starting point the official Web site of American Space Adventures. Alastair sits forward slowly as he pages past the home page and reads about — the launch one day before — the name of the craft: *Intrepid*.

What the hell?

A smile spreads across his face. *Buggers almost got me!* Whoever the hacker is pulling the stunt, he's cleverly used the right names and references.

Can't fool me! he thinks, watching the evolving message once again. After ten minutes, he decides, he'll run the whole thing through a matching program and see where in reality it came from.

Help, I'm trapped in a Chinese fortune cookie factory! Yeah right. A new twist on the oldest scam in the book!

Cheyenne Mountain,
North American Aerospace
Defense Command,
Colorado Springs, Colorado,
9:25 a.m. Pacific/10:25 a.m. Mountain

The chief master sergeant toggles another command and turns to the NORAD commander. "Sixty-seven minutes left before impact, General, and thirteen minutes to target intercept."

The special liquid crystal display he's

been controlling in a closed conference room changes views.

Chris Risen nods at the duty controller as he scans the orbital threat to ASA's *Intrepid*, now displayed on the screen. The effort he set in motion is now approaching the critical moment, and with the Situation Room maintaining an open line for the President, it's eating at him that there's nothing NORAD can do but watch and hope.

"What will they see in the main control room?" Chris asks.

"They would see a launch, sir, but we've nulled it out of the computer, so it will not show."

"And if it impacts the target?"

"They'll see the debris with no explanation."

"What's the status of the ASAT launch?" He's very aware of the serious fuel mistake.

"Bluebird Two-Three has elected to continue, sir, despite the . . . ah . . . problem. He's positioning now for the run."

"We have radar on him?"

"Yes, sir. I'll bring it up."

The track of the F-106 appears to be moving in slow motion relative to the track of the oncoming piece of Soviet space junk streaking south on its polar orbit. The Delta Dart is flying at just under six hundred miles per hour now while the target approaches at seventeen thousand. A digital readout next to the F-106's target depiction shows his heading changing and his speed increasing as Chris settles into one of the command chairs to watch. It will be up to him to call ASA if the attempt fails, and it's a call he does not want to make.

"He's starting his run, sir."

Bluebird 23,
9:31 a.m. Pacific/10:31 a.m. Mountain

Owen Larrabe tries to ignore the persistent itching on the side of his face in a place he has no hope of reaching. Sealed inside his pressure suit, it will just have to itch, he decides. But the damned itch is leaching away his attention at a critical moment, and he summons up the willpower to combat the distraction as he nudges the throttle into afterburner. He's level at thirty-five thousand and keeping the flight director target dead center as he lets the Delta Dart accelerate smoothly through the speed of sound, the airspeed indicator winding up toward the needed airspeed of 1.22 Mach. He sees the Mach-meter already at 1.2 and accelerating and pulls back the throttle, holding constant at 1.22 as he mentally counts down to the pull-up point, now just five miles and less than twenty-five seconds ahead. He checks his lateral flight path, reconfirms that the missile arming sequence is complete and precisely on target, pulls the F-106 into a sharp 3.8-g climb until reaching sixty-five degrees nose up, holding the attitude as the airspeed remains constant with full burner, the fighter climbing at more than forty-six thousand feet per minute, the altimeter more or less a blur as he shoots up through fifty thousand, then sixty and seventy, slowing slightly as the engine gulps for air and fuel and flames-out.

Oh, shit! Too soon! I hope the missile can compensate.

He's coasting now up through eighty-five thousand feet, gravity slowing him rapidly. He feels the F-106 jump slightly and hears the whoosh of the missile's rocket motor as it releases itself and starts its climb, its silicon brain aware that the launch speed is slower than it should be, the altitude more than five thousand feet shy of the mark.

He's got worries now beyond the missile's fate, and he tunnels in on the task of getting down safely. Bailout is always an option, but one he doesn't want to use.

Owen pushes the stick forward and lets

the F-106's nose fall through the horizon and steeply downward as the speed builds again. He flicks open the speed brakes as he tries to restart the engine, but one glance at the fuel indicators confirms that there won't be a restart. The engine has sucked down the last drop of fuel in the full afterburner climb, and he's now flying a delta-wing glider with one solitary chance at a safe landing.

Only a few thin cumulus clouds dot the landscape below as the Delta Dart plunges earthward, the speed stabilizing at just under Mach 1, a small Ram Air Turbine providing the only hydraulic pressure to the flight controls. He punches up Carlsbad Muni as his destination and does a quick calculation.

Okay, the runway is twenty-eight miles east, so plan to enter a high key down the runway at eight thousand feet.

He swings the fighter's nose to the appropriate heading, watching carefully as the altitude unwinds through forty thousand.

A bit high and fast, he decides, banking the jet into one back and forth S turn, and then resuming the course. He dials in the VHF frequency for Cavern City Unicom, the common radio channel for the airport in the absence of a control tower, and rechecks his energy profile as he triggers his transmitter.

"Pan, pan, pan, Cavern City Unicom, Carlsbad Airport traffic, this is Bluebird Two-Three, I'm a flamed-out Air Force F-106 making an emergency approach to Runway Zero-Three, Carlsbad. All traffic please stay clear. Pan, pan, pan."

A puzzled voice with a heavy West Texas accent comes back almost instantly.

"Air Force F-106, this is Cavern City Unicom. Sir, your winds are two two zero at eighteen knots, gusting twenty-two, so I suggest you use Runway Two-One."

"Roger, Cavern City. Thanks. Bluebird Two-Three changing to a high-key left traffic downwind for Runway Two-One, Carlsbad."

A flurry of quick mental recalculations leads to the sudden realization that he's no longer too high and too fast.

Okay, enter a high downwind and meter the turn to final at two miles, ah, northeast at four thousand. Gotta turn at four.

He's dropping under ten thousand now, worrying about pulling the nose up and stretching his flight path as the Delta Dart slows below four hundred knots on the way to three hundred, which he'll use as his maneuvering speed. But that speed is coming off too fast, and he can't figure it out. The airport is just ahead by four miles and he turns to parallel Runway Zero-Three on his left, letting the jet slow to two ninety before continuing the descent, dropping through eight thousand as the field passes his left shoulder. At this rate, he thinks, he'll have to turn inside one mile and delay the landing gear.

What the hell? Why am I slowing this fast?

The answer comes in a flash of embarrassment.

Oh, jeez, the boards!

He flicks the speed brake closed and feels the jet's aerodynamics improve instantly from those of a boulder to something more resembling a flying machine.

The field is a mile back to his left now, the altitude at five thousand, and he calculates the wind and decides to make an early turn, sliding the F-106 around to the left with his eyes on the end of the runway and lining up, checking his speed before committing the landing gear, which will slow him even more.

The speed is just above target, the end of the runway moving beneath his nose less than a mile out as he aligns with the concrete ribbon and drops the gear. The runway numbers stop moving forward in his windscreen, and he meters the jet over the threshold fifty feet high at a hundred and seventy, using the speed brake to help him settle onto the concrete, which is disappearing fast.

He's on the wheel brakes, metering the pressure, wondering if he should have used aerobraking, the craft slowing through a hundred with less than two thousand feet of runway left. He presses harder on the pedals, worried about blowing the tires but slowing as the far end of the runway hurtles toward him.

And just as quickly he's at the end, rolling the jet off on a taxiway at twenty knots and bringing her safely to a complete stop clear of the runway.

Owen powers open the canopy, runs the shutdown checklist, and starts removing his helmet — aware of a flurry of vehicles approaching from the southeast part of the field. He pulls the helmet free just as several Air Force cars pull into view and turns quick attention to scratching the place on the right side of his face that's been bugging him since takeoff.

A crew chief is placing a ladder now to his left.

"Did we make it?"

"Sir?"

"The shot. Was it successful?"

Cheyenne Mountain,
North American Aerospace
Defense Command,
Colorado Springs, Colorado,
9:36 a.m. Pacific/10:36 a.m. Mountain

Chris Risen doesn't feel like a four-star general at the moment. More like a green lieutenant watching something momentous but completely out of his control as lines and vectors merge on the small screen. Outwardly his image is as secure and professional as ever. Inside he's on edge, his heart in his throat.

"Status, Chief?" he asks quietly of the chief master sergeant.

"Missile at one hundred seventy-five miles and climbing, sir. It's . . . a little off profile, but closing."

"Show me the intercept solution, please."

New lines appear on the display, one red, one blue.

"General, the blue line is the missile, the red, as you know, the proton shroud."

"Am I seeing that right? Are they going to miss?" He hates to believe it, but the computer is projecting the missile to pass *behind* the oncoming shroud.

"That dot is the current projection . . . I

mean, without the missile speeding up. That's where the missile will be along the shroud's orbital path as it crosses. But the missile should speed up."

"God, I hope so."

"The corrections are real time."

As they speak the display shifts, the intersect point moving closer to the shroud, overtaking it slowly from behind, the digital readout of the missile's speed indicating a steady acceleration.

"The second stage has a thirty percent reserve boost capacity, sir."

Another jump in the missile's speed registers as the altitude continues upward.

Come on, come on! Chris thinks. Less than five hundred miles separate the two objects, the missile racing to close at a forty-eight-degree angle.

Once more the computer updates, moving the intercept dot within a mile of the shroud, still to the rear. The speed of the missile is over seventeen thousand nine hundred miles per hour, and as he watches, the display upgrades it to eighteen thousand.

"Almost, sir."

"Time to impact?"

"Thirty seconds."

"Jesus, I'm too old for this."

"Yes, sir. I am, too."

"Like waiting to find out if your girl-friend's pregnant."

The chief turns with a smile and a puzzled look, unsure how to take this. Just as quickly he returns his gaze to the closing race.

"Twenty seconds."

The red intersecting projection dot is less than a quarter mile behind the shroud as the two objects close within seventy miles of each other.

"Fifteen."

The predictor dot moves to a tenth of a mile behind the target, the missile's speed still increasing.

"Ten seconds."

Goddammit, FLY, you bastard! Come ON!

The gap between dot and shroud closes a bit more, but still not colocated. The speed readout on the missile is now eighteen thousand five hundred.

There's no margin for failure here! God, please help us make this happen, Chris thinks, his teeth clenched as the two icons converge in real time on the screen.

"Five, four, three . . . " the chief intones.

The predictor red dot is almost on top of the shroud's icon now.

"Two, one . . ."

The dots merge and the computer-generated picture freezes.

"Now."

"Now *what?* What happened?" Chris demands.

"Stand by, sir. Switching to real-time radar."

The screen flashes black and then to a two-dimensional display of NORAD's radar, which is tracking an exploding spray of objects that seem to be at an angle to the original track of the proton shroud.

"We *got it,* sir! Direct hit! Damn, that's a beauty!"

"Direct hit?"

"All the debris is flying off at a twenty-degree angle."

"Everything?"

"I'm looking, General. Yes, *sir!* We freakin' did it! Everything!"

"Holy Moly."

"Yes, sir! Woo-hoo!"

"I'll second that, Chief. That was too close without a defibrillator standing by. And if you're sure, tell the Sit Room while I call ASA."

"They'll make it, sir. No impact. Not even a bolt."

Chapter 22

Kalgoorlie-Boulder, Western Australia,
9:40 a.m. Pacific, May 18
12:40 a.m. WST, May 19

The sudden resumption of noises he doesn't want to know about from his parents' bedroom startles him for a second. But Alastair's attention quickly returns to the screen and the alert he's about to send to thirty-three of his e-mail friends, what were once called pen pals around Australia and the world. Especially Becky Nigel, the only girl he really likes, who keeps in touch despite her British father's moving his family all the way back to the U.K.

Hey, mates! I've stumbled on a really cool, hardworking scam artist trying to wind me up. He sez he's stranded in a private spaceship. LOL! The bloke's creative, I'll give him that. And other than the mushy stuff about his first love and all, thought you might want to have a look. It's coming across as a continuous scroll so you have to record it yourself. I'm sending the first stuff I captured.

He includes the Web address and triggers the screen back over to the evolving message from Kip.

Sorry to break the narrative, but something really strange just happened up here. Of course, here I am apologizing to a hard drive. But hey, a human will read this someday, won't you?

Yesterday I got all excited when something glimmered on the horizon and I started thinking about rescue craft. I won't make that mistake again, but I swear I saw an explosion in the same direction a few minutes back . . . some sort of a burst of sparkles, of what looked like sparkles, as if metal was reflecting in the sun, which is behind me at the moment. Then it seemed to move to the left and disappear. Poor Bill would probably have known what it was . . . some space phenomenon all astronauts consider routine but gets an amateur like me all excited.

Anyway, where was I?

Oh yes. Growing up in my ideal family. At least I thought they were ideal, and I loved my folks, both of whom are gone now. Dad was an executive with a big mining company and an upright, reliable, serious, and dedicated father, who defined life as a series of challenges a man met with responsibility for those who depended on him. But I guess when he was programmed as a child, someone forgot to include the concept of fun and self.

The symbol for new e-mail pops up in the right-hand corner of his screen and Alastair opens a window to read it while still watching the evolving narrative.

To: Alastair
From: Becky
Message: Hey, blockhead! Guess what? There *is* a private spacecraft in trouble right now on orbit, and there are two men aboard, an astronaut named Bill and a passenger named Kip Dawson. Don't you ever watch the telly? You're too cynical, you know that? Ever consider this might be *real?*

Alastair triggers the reply button.

You're kidding, right? This could be real?

He sends it back through cyberspace to Becky wondering what she's doing on her computer at two in the afternoon in London, but before she can reply a host of other e-mails start snapping in from his friends, all apparently tuning in and reacting to the strange narrative.

If this is real, he thinks, *the guy says no one can hear him on the radios. Do the space officials know about this?*

He sits back, suddenly uncertain, as if he's just witnessed a momentous adult event like a serious crime or terrible accident and he should be the one to alert the authorities.

He wonders how upset his dad would be if he tapped on their bedroom door now and asked for help.

No, not a good idea.

Maybe he can handle it himself, but he's getting a really creepy feeling.

ASA Headquarters,
Mojave, California, 10:20 a.m. Pacific

Dammit!

Diana is already coming through the door

when Richard spots the bottle of tawny port he's left on his desk. He's not a teetotaler, but he abhors the idea of anyone thinking he needs to drink to get through even a day like this.

But she's already spotted it and gone straight to the bottle, lifting it to examine the label.

"Good brand. Can I mooch some?"

"Be my guest. I was just, ah . . ."

Her hand is out, accompanying her shaking head.

"No explanation needed, Richard. Frankly, I'd worry about you if you weren't drinking." She pours an inch into a tumbler as she hands him his glass, then raises hers in a quick toast. "To NORAD and NASA and God knows who took care of that object."

"I know."

"So . . . who did?"

He's shaking his head. "They won't tell me, other than to say that the threat has been terminated and we would be best advised to never mention it."

"Hookay. I'll drink to that."

"Still doesn't get them back down."

"No, but it sure solves the immediate problem."

Richard looks at her, calculating whether to remind her that a few hours ago she'd found a positive side to a quick ending. No point, he concludes. It would sound like a slap, and she was only doing her best. Putting the best face on anything up to and including disaster is what she does.

His cell rings and Richard keys it on, a strange look crossing his face as he asks the caller to hold and raises his eyes to Diana.

"I hate to ask you . . ."

"But you need some privacy. No problem. I'll be down the hall."

She picks up the bottle of port and shoots him a questioning look.

"May I?"

"Please."

"Good stuff," she says on the way out.

Richard pulls the phone back to his ear. "Go ahead, Vasily."

"Well, my friend, it has been a busy last few hours, no?"

A cascade of caution stops his response. *Do the Russians know what the Air Force just did?*

"Which, ah, nightmare of mine are you referring to?"

There is a chuckle on the other end. "That NASA has decided to get the shuttle ready to go up and do what you've retained us to do, Richard. I had a long talk with John Kent. I believe this would be STS193."

"They'll never make it in time. At least, I don't think they will."

"We don't think so either, but you know what happens when NASA has a blowtorch to their ass. They usually move. In fact, in my humble experience, that's the *only* way to get NASA to move fast."

"But . . . you're still going to try, right?"

"Of course. But things have changed. Now it has become a political matter and a matter of Russian honor."

"Excuse me?"

"Our president, Andrei Kosachyov, has become involved, and when he discovered that NASA was going to try and probably fail, and that we were getting ready to do this for you for a price, he directed us to cancel the charge and be the ones to pluck your people back as a humanitarian gesture."

"Really?" Richard replies, thinking of his two million dollars now in a Moscow bank. "Without charge?"

There is a pause and then brief unrestrained laughter. "Yes, Richard, without charge, and your deposit is already being wired back to you. Good for you, no? Bad for me. No commission."

"Hey, I can take care of that."

"No charge means no charge, but we are

on schedule now. I thought you needed to know."

"Thank you, Vasily!"

"Oh, one other thing. The Japanese Space Agency's Hiragawa just called me. He said the Chinese are about to make a similar decision to help."

"You're kidding?"

"No. It may get crowded up there."

"Well, aren't you guys going to coordinate?"

"If coordinate means defer to them, the answer is no. We have our orders. We will get your people. This is no time for the Chinese to be messing around."

Aboard *Marine One* en route
from the White House to Andrews
Air Force Base, May 18,
10:30 a.m. Pacific/1:30 p.m. Eastern

People first, Ronald Porter thinks to himself, smiling. It's the reason he came aboard as Chief of Staff, jumping political parties for a man who keeps earning his respect.

The President doesn't notice Ron's smile. He's talking to one of his Secret Service agents whose wife has just been diagnosed with Parkinson's, comforting him as best he can.

They're passing over Bolling Air Force Base on the east bank of the Potomac as the President turns his attention back to why Ron has decided to hop aboard a routine *Air Force One* flight to New York.

"So how is the Commerce Committee going to vote?" the President asks.

"That's . . . they're with us. But there's something else we need to discuss." He hands the President a one-page summary of an intelligence report less than an hour old.

"What's this, Ron? The Russians?"

"Our buddies in Moscow have decided to ride to the rescue and go after the ASA spacecraft."

"A special launch?"

"Actually, they're moving up a scheduled ISS resupply mission."

"Don't they know we're going to send the shuttle?"

"They don't believe we can."

"Well, hell, Ron, get someone on the phone to set them straight. Have Shear make the call."

"It all started with Kosachyov a few hours ago. He's determined to be the white knight. So, should we stand down?"

"Cancel our effort?"

"Yes. I talked to Shear. He heartily advises it."

"I'm sure he does. I had to order him to get cracking."

"He may have a solid point."

"About safety?"

"Safety and cost. As he says, we only have two shuttles left, and when you push something on an emergency basis, you cut corners and take additional risks."

The President sits back in thought, his eyes watching the forested beauty below as the *Marine One* pilots begin the descent to the presidential ramp at Andrews, where one of the two specially built Boeing 747s used as *Air Force One* is waiting.

Suddenly he's forward again, in Ron's face.

"There's a principle here, Ron, and in my view it's worth the risk. One, we protect our own, civilian or government. Two, we may have only two shuttles left, but we don't have to plead for help because we're afraid to use them. Three, this goes to the heart of American trust of and pride in our capabilities, and in NASA, and four, I know what Kosachyov is up to. There is a commercial purpose behind it I can't ignore. This is like letting Airbus snag a U.S. Air Force contract, something that will never happen on my watch."

"So, we fly?"

He's nodding. "Damn right we fly. Unless there's a solid, no-foolin' safety concern beyond the routine."

"I'll tell Shear."

"Oh, we need to do more than that." The President's already pulling the receiver out of its cradle in his armrest.

"You're calling Moscow?"

A naughty grin that would fit a much younger man breaks across the President's face.

Kalgoorlie-Boulder, Western Australia, 10:50 a.m. Pacific, May 18/ 1:50 a.m. WST, May 19

The connection to the Web address carrying the alleged transmission from space has apparently frozen, and Alastair thinks he knows why.

The e-mails pouring into his own mailbox from addresses he doesn't recognize have overloaded it.

And now the frozen transmission.

He pulls up another screen and calls up a bulletin board he's found, a site for people

nuts about space travel. Sure enough, the message from the man calling himself Kip is there, too, *and still actively scrolling!*
Right! They're retransmitting it.
Another excited message from Becky has made it to an alternate mailbox and he opens it quickly.

So why are all my messages to you on the normal channel getting bounced? I don't want to see another of those @%!^#$ "Mailer-Daemon" things! If you get this, let me know. Your stranded spaceman's transmission is exploding. Someone's retransmitting it everywhere and I've already seen it on eight sites. And Ali-boy, I think the poor guy IS really up there and is really, REALLY screwed! And the story he's telling is so amazingly rad.

Me

Alastair checks the time, amazed to find it's nearly two-thirty in the morning. He feels like he just sat down. The only light on in the room is the gooseneck over his keyboard, but suddenly he feels the need for more. It's chilly and he's already pulled on a sweater, but it's not enough. He snaps on the ceiling light, aware of how closely his dad monitors the electrical bill, but there's still too little heat and he pulls a small ceramic heater from the closet, the one he's been told never to use, before sitting back down at the keyboard.

Whatever all this is, he decides, it is way more than he can handle now. But there is one thing he hasn't done yet that just has to be accomplished. He checks his notepad for the e-mail address he wrote down of the company in California that launched the spacecraft, and writes as simple a message as he can.

Dear American Space Adventures,

I don't know if it's real or not, but there's a guy saying he's a passenger in your spaceship *Intrepid* and he's sending a continuous letter into the Internet, and I'm forwarding the Web site address. It's frozen up on me, but you can see it being retransmitted at two other places. I'm sending a file with my record of the first part of what came in.

If there really is a problem, I hope everything turns out okay.

Your friend, Alastair Wood.

Kalgoorlie-Boulder, Western Australia

Jeez, what would it feel like to be up there

all alone? he wonders, knowing that some of the words he first read — words he thought were part of a scam — might hold the answer to that.

Maybe he should reread them.

But first, he decides, he'll take a look at his jammed-up mailbox. He opens the long list and pages to the latest one, not believing the address: ABC, the Australian Broadcasting Corporation, his national network.

Dear Sir or Madam: We have been forwarded a copy of an e-mail you sent to several friends last night with a Web address that apparently is the only live transmission from a stranded space tourist on an American craft in orbit. If this is true, and you are the one who somehow found it, we would very much appreciate the opportunity to interview you this morning as soon as possible. We would like very much to know how you managed to come across such a transmission, and how you reacted. Won't you please call us at our toll-free number in Sydney? Wherever you are in Australia, we can send a camera crew to you.

James Haggas
Executive Producer

The number is at the bottom and Alastair sits there staring at it, wondering what to do and remembering that the way this thing started was by his hacking into a private transmission. Not terribly legal.

I should get on the telly and tell the whole bloody world? I don't think so!

Suddenly the urge to shut down the computer and hide overwhelms him.

Can they find me through an unregistered e-mail address? he wonders, his stomach contracting with worry. *Dad will kill me.*

He snaps off the ceiling and desk lights and dives under the covers. The bedcovers always feel like the best defense against a world gone mad.

Chapter 23

ASA Mission Control,
Mojave, California,
May 18, 1:18 p.m. Pacific

For the previous agonizing day and a half, Arleigh Kerr has had to deal with the reality that without communication a flight director has virtually nothing to direct. Two of the staff have kept Mission Control operating in the hopes that somehow a data stream or other useful information will once again start pouring through their monitors, but nonetheless it's felt like a deathwatch.

And now, from the most unlikely quarter, contact?

Arleigh stands at his console, waiting for the room to fill, as his people rush back in, each wearing cautious expressions. When the room is back up to strength, Arleigh leans down and looses a flurry of keystrokes into his computer keyboard, then glances up at the largest of the screens before them, waiting for the text to appear.

"What's this, Arleigh?" the flight dynamics controller asks.

"It's coming in through an obscure site on the Internet, one of the servers we've used for e-mail. We would have never seen it except for someone way out in the boonies of Australia. The guy e-mailed us a half hour ago where to find this."

"But what *is* it?"

"We think," Arleigh says, "that it's our passenger, Kip Dawson, trying to communicate. But apparently he doesn't know anyone's listening . . . or reading. I've got a lot more, and if this is truly him, it tells what happened yesterday."

Arleigh highlights the first portion about the impact and Bill Campbell's demise and lets it sink in.

"I want everyone to read everything he's written, then punch up line eighteen to pick up with his real-time transmissions. I don't know what we can learn that can help him, since we can't talk back, but I want you to scour every line for facts that might help us get him down."

"How is this being transmitted, exactly?" the woman in charge of capsule communication asks.

Arleigh shrugs as he looks around the room. "Who has the details on this computer interface to the Internet. Janet? How is this possible?"

A tall woman with her hair severely pulled back meets his gaze with a deer-in-the-headlights expression.

"Well . . . theoretically . . . I mean, we included a downlink in the S band transmitter package, which is a dedicated line out to the server, and there are no restrictions on your reaching the Internet with it, but we've lost all the S band transmitters."

"Could that be a separate transmitter?" Another of the team wants to know. She's starting to shake her head when an adjacent engineer stands.

"Yes. Yes, it is separate. We put a very small transmitter package on there to handle the volume of downlinked photo files so the passengers could reach their loved ones by Internet if they wanted. It weighs just a few ounces, and uses the same antenna array. But it's powered separately."

"Then it's two-way?" Arleigh asks, excitement building. "We can *send* as well as receive?"

"No. Unfortunately, we only set it up for downloads. The two-way function is done with a regular transmitting array that's off line. But, Arleigh, I don't understand how he could possibly know to use this. He wouldn't be getting any response. No replies, no e-mail, no indication of a successful transmission."

"I'm told," Arleigh replies, "that he seems to have no idea *anyone* is watching or reading."

"Oh, okay. Then it's just a single downlink transmitter that somehow remained online."

"But . . . how did he trigger it?"

The engineer shrugs. "I don't know, unless one of the autoconnect features on that laptop kicked it in. Wait a minute."

"What?"

"Arleigh, are you familiar with what they used to call 'spyware'?"

"No."

"Programs that record each keystroke in an endless string and store it in some nondescript little file. I think our programmers put one of those in the computers on *Intrepid* as a kind of digital recorder. If somehow the output of that keystroke recorder got routed to that individual transmitter, it would explain why we're only getting what he types when he types it."

"Somebody get the programmers who worked on this thing and find out, okay?" Arleigh asks.

"Are we relaying this to NASA?" the engineer adds.

A commanding feminine voice fills the room from behind, and Arleigh turns to find a startled-looking Diana Ross standing in the entrance.

"Arleigh? Everyone? It's not just NASA getting this. Thanks to a sharp reporter at the *Washington Post*, what we're apparently doing . . . our server, I mean . . . is relaying this to the world. Most of the media have picked up on it, and they're breaking in everywhere with it."

"Breaking in?" Arleigh asks.

"All the cable news networks. I haven't read everything that's come down yet, but . . . the poor guy thinks he's dying and I guess he's writing about his life. Very private stuff."

There's a slight glistening in the corners of Diana's eyes and Arleigh realizes she's tearing up as she turns to go. She's hoping no one reads back far enough to see a brief reference to her. Not that his kind words about her are a problem, but they're personal, and instinctively she knows that he'll be going into the most intimate details of his memories.

Oh my God, if we could only warn him or shut off that feed!

Behind her in Mission Control a stunned silence prevails as one by one the controllers read what's been written so far, then tune into the live feed. The letters are marching in stop-and-start staccato fashion, exactly as they're being written, making it seem almost like the writer is sitting right next to them composing with an imperfect hunt-and-peck technique. They can almost *feel* his fingers touching the keys, hesitating, punching some more, forming the words as he thinks of them.

As if his voice were in the room.

You know, I never knew it could be so much fun to describe moments like that one in the backseat, on that mountainside. We were lucky, Linda and me. We were too young and I too inexperienced and uninformed to worry about accidentally making babies. I just wanted her. I felt I'd go mad if I didn't have sex with her while my head — full as it was of warnings about duty and responsibility — knew that the responsible thing was to never have sex without love. So I loved her as well as *made* love to her.

And there was something else funny about those years, as testosterone-soaked as they were (something girls will never understand is the insanity of that period for a guy). I was born and bred to measure my life by accomplishments, and I really and truly considered Linda an accomplishment. I don't mean a notch-on-the-bedpost type, I mean the fact that I made her feel good, and I cared for her that summer, and she became a part of my life, however briefly, and I a part of hers. If time is really eternal, then we're still out there doin' it in the backseat of that old Chevy. Was that an accomplishment? I guess I'll find out from a Higher Source in about four days, but I always thought it was. And as long as I could point to something and say, "See, I was productive, I accomplished that!" it was okay, even if ultimately it was the wrong decision.

Kalgoorlie-Boulder, Western Australia,
3:58 p.m. Pacific, May 18/
6:58 a.m. WST, May 19

Daylight is streaming into the room as Alastair wakes up seconds before his alarm clock corks off. He reaches for the clock to silence it in time, liking that he can pull off being the last to bed and the first up, when he's startled by the sound of footsteps on the stairs. Heavy footsteps.

Dad!

The events of the preceding night are slow to return, but in a sudden rush he remembers all of it and the e-mail from ABC in Sydney, and fear looms with his father's footfalls. He can hear a television on somewhere in the house.

The door opens and Dad walks in, pulling the curtains open.

"Alastair, wake up!"

"I'm awake, Dad. What's happening?"

His father's hands are on his hips but he looks more puzzled than mad.

"I've been watching the news, son, and there's something on now you're going to want to hear. I know I'm on you all the time for being on the computer so much, but, well, get on a robe and come downstairs."

Alastair is already in motion, sliding from beneath the covers and grabbing for his robe. "What is it?"

"There's the most amazing message coming down through the Internet from a guy stranded in orbit on a private American spacecraft, and they wouldn't have found it if some hacker right out here in Western

Australia hadn't broken into someone's computer."

"R-really?"

"Yes. He's a bit of a hero and they're looking for him. They think he may be a student. He may also get a twist in his knickers for the hacking, but overall he's got a thank-you coming. Come on down and see this. Could be someone you know."

Chapter 24

A stunning young woman with shoulder-length, blond hair has been watching him for the past ten minutes. Jerrod Dawson assumes it's his uniform, because he certainly isn't exuding anything but gloom.

She can't be more than twenty-five, he figures, with a modest, tight-fitting suede skirt and an achingly feminine, well-filled frilly white blouse set off by calf-length high heel boots. Normally, he would be falling in lust. After all, the women at the academy are untouchable. His opportunities for any intimate female companionship these days are severely limited.

But the copy of *USA Today* in his lap with the headline about his father's perilous situation has numbed and deflated all that's normal, leaving him awash with guilt as he waits for his Houston-bound flight to board and tries to keep unbidden tears from showing.

Why he's even going to Houston isn't clear, and even as they were granting the emergency leave orders and helping arrange a military fare, he felt reluctant about going there at all, except to see his sister and two half-sisters. The thought of Sharon in the role of his mother is infuriating. He can barely be civil to her. While he likes Sharon's father, Big Mike, he can't believe he is actually, voluntarily, going to put himself in Sharon's presence again — and in Houston, to boot! He couldn't believe it when he found out Sharon had left his father and run back to her daddy in Houston.

And, of course, there's the small matter of Sharon never liking him. He loathes her for what she's done to his father, roping him into having two more children. As if they hadn't already been a family.

Not that he doesn't blame his dad, too.

The cute blonde is smiling at him now, making eye contact, the sort of thing that would thrill him no to end if he wasn't so completely torn up. She's on her feet and moving toward him like a beautiful wave, a whiff of expensive perfume preceding her as she leans toward him. He knows an encyclopedia of pickup lines, but nothing comes to mind, and he actually wishes she'd go away.

"Hi! Are you from the Air Force Academy?"

"Yes, ma'am." His response is flat.

"My brother is a senior this year. Maybe you know him? Bob Reinertsen?"

He does, but he's not going to admit it. Reinertsen is a pompous ass who ragged on him terribly in his doolie year — the label for the freshman hell-in-residence period at Doolittle Hall.

"No, ma'am. I don't believe I recognize the name."

"Really?" She slides into the seat next to him. "Bobby's a cadet colonel. Oh, well. Where are you headed?"

Oh, I don't know, babe . . . how about Houston, since that's where our flight is going?

He's shocked that he has no desire whatsoever to take this golden opportunity. Sex suddenly seems cheap compared to the responsibilities he'll now have to shoulder. Especially if his dad doesn't make it.

"I'm going to my . . . folks' house. I've got a family emergency."

"Oh, I'm sorry to hear that."

"And . . . I'm sorry to be rude. I really am. But . . . I'd just like some time alone, if you don't mind."

She gets to her feet, patting his arm.

"Well, if you need to talk to a sympathetic ear, I'll be around."

The one I need to talk to is three hundred ten miles above the planet and stuck there.

He fights back tears again and resumes the struggle to hide them.

Johnson Spaceflight Center,
Houston, Texas,
5:00 p.m. Pacific/7:00 p.m. Central

"Ever hear of someone named Dorothy Sheehan?"

Griggs Hopewell's voice is too recognizable for John Kent to need even a cursory introduction, and the calls between the two of them have been accelerating during the day.

"Should I, Griggs? Who is she?"

"Well, she's from headquarters, as far as I can tell. But I'm wondering just exactly what she's been sent down here to do."

"I don't recognize the name, but is she causing problems?"

"Twice today I've had safety stops declared out of the blue by people who would normally never pull the emergency brake, and she's the only new kid in town."

"I'm not following. Are you connecting

dots between her and headquarters safety concerns, or are you just being your usual paranoid self?"

"John, you, better than anyone, know they really are out to get me. I'm a principled, purposeful paranoid."

"You also ramble a lot, Griggs. So answer my question, please."

"I'm just suspicious of who she is and what she's doing here."

"What's her security clearance?"

"Total. She can go sit in the cockpit and honk the horn if she wants."

"Shouldn't be hard to find out who she works for."

"I already checked. She's a low-level safety compliance officer under Dick White-head in D.C. A long way down the food chain from our esteemed admini-shredder."

"So, aside from that, any other show stoppers yet?"

"I love the confidence inherent in your use of the word 'yet,' John. No. So far as we know at this moment we will be able to get our bird off the pad in three days. We'll set the launch window formally in a few hours. You should already have all the parameters."

"Yes, I do. And our guys should already be there."

"Your three T-38s arrived in the dark of

night some two hours ago. No, my only big worry, John, is that someone's waiting in the weeds to pull a safety stop at the very last second, and we'll lose it. The window is very tight, and the long range on the weather is not encouraging."

"By the way, Griggs, you are aware of what's happening with that live transmission from the ASA craft?"

"Haven't seen it but I'm aware of it. The passenger's the only one left, correct?"

"Yes. Bill's gone."

"Instantly, I hope."

"I'm sure."

"What's the guy up there talking about?"

"Personal stuff. He doesn't know anyone is, ah, watching, or reading, or whatever. But it's a real weeper and it's leaching away manpower here. Every woman in the place is glued to CNN."

There's a chuckle. "The foxes aren't watching Fox?"

"All the news outlets are broadcasting it live by now, and I've got a few of our number watching in case he says anything that could help us. Also, I'm ignoring your politically incorrect comment."

"John, find out some more about Miss Fem-de-Dorothy for me, will you? She worries me."

Aboard *Air Force One*,
en route to Washington, D.C.,
5:35 p.m. Pacific/8:35 p.m. Eastern

"You wanted to see me, sir?"

The chief master sergeant in charge of communications aboard the presidential jet is holding on to the doorjamb as the President looks up from disassembling a ballpoint pen.

"Yes! José, come in a sec."

He does so, standing ramrod straight in an impeccably pressed uniform and smiling as the commander in chief loses control of the parts he's fiddling with, loosing a small spring which soars past the chief into the passageway.

"Shit!"

"I'll get it, sir."

"Spring has sprung, you might say," the President adds, delighted at the pained reaction.

"I would never say that, sir," the chief replies, handing over the recaptured spring. "I could get you a few hundred workable pens, Mr. President."

"Naw. I just wanted to change the innards and keep the shell. I've had this one for a very long time."

"Yes, sir."

The President scoops the pieces together and slides them into an envelope.

"Okay, I need an update on the coverage of that stranded space passenger's message."

"Kip Dawson?"

"You've been monitoring, right?"

"I'm piping it live through the plane on Channel Three."

"And everyone but me knows his name?"

"The coverage is exploding, Mr. President. The cable news outlets were carrying it live, but now all three major networks are on and have it as a crawl across the bottom of the screen. They've all got air time to fill. ABC, for instance, put on a panel of people to kind of read between the lines. They're reporting on Dawson's background, his life, his marriages, family, and anything else they can bring into it. It's pretty much the same all over the planet."

"What's Mr. Dawson saying?"

There's an unexpected smile from the chief. "Well, let's say that any of us who are male went through the same female-chasing phases he's been recalling in . . . ah . . . rather vivid detail."

"Really? Names, too?"

"*Oh* yeah! Names and dates and where they were parked and whether they used a condom. I mean, he writes well for a guy trapped in space who believes he's dead, but I mean I'm only thirty-six and I can relate to what he's saying."

"I'm not following that."

"Mr. President, this guy sounds like all of us working stiffs. He's Mr. Everyman, with . . . with a sometimes unappreciative wife and the programming to be a good husband and father and provider and forget about anything else. I mean, I haven't read everything he's said but he's already won me over."

"Won you over?"

"Yes, sir. On an 'I can sure relate to you, bro!' basis. You know, the 'been there, felt that,' thing where you think you're the only guy in the world who's ever had those thoughts and, wow, here's someone else who's fought the same mountain lion."

"I gotta read this!"

"Channel Three, sir. Let me . . ."

The President's hand is up in a stop gesture as he swivels around and turns on the flat screen TV monitor.

"I might not be able to fix a ballpoint but I can turn on a TV."

"Yes, sir. Anything else, sir?"

"No, José. Thank you very much for the insight."

"Would you like a printout of everything he's sent up to now, sir? Because this is live."

"Live?" The President looks around, catching José's eyes. "This . . . I didn't understand that, I guess. He's typing and we're watching?"

"Yes, sir."

"Yes. I would very much like that printout."

From your description, the President thinks, *I'll probably relate to this guy myself.*

George Bush Houston
Intercontinental Airport, Texas,
May 18, 5:53 p.m. Pacific/7:53 p.m. Central

Jerrod leaves the jetway and scans the overhead signs for the way to baggage claim before recalling that he isn't carrying more than his roll-on. He starts down the concourse trying to shake off the troubled sleep that carried him here, the takeoff and landing a vague blur and the drinks and peanuts a completely missed experience.

He hasn't enough cash for a fifty-dollar cab ride, so he's had to call Big Mike's house for a pickup, but fortunately Mike himself answered and volunteered to send someone.

He sees large TV monitors broadcasting live coverage from CNN but he pays no attention, knowing that the story of his dad's plight will be in his face if he does. But there's a signboard with a newscrawl mounted over the concourse ahead he can't ignore, and he wonders why it's stopping so many passengers in their tracks, a logjam of standing people almost blocking the way.

A familiar arrangement of letters catches his attention and he, too, stops, wondering why the name Jerrod Dawson is moving across in front of him.

He turns to a tired-looking man in a business suit next to him who looks less shocked than the others.

"What's going on? What is that?"

The man barely glances away long enough to discern where the question originated and resumes watching the evolving words.

"That's a message coming down from that poor guy trapped in space. He's got an angry young son in the Air Force Academy and he's talking about how much his son's rejection and anger have hurt him."

Jerrod stands stunned and immobile as the man slowly looks back at him.

"Say, you're from the academy, too, right?"

He can barely nod.

"You know this cadet, Jerrod Dawson?"

The sound of his roll-on slipping from his hand and clattering to the floor behind him doesn't register, his eyes transfixed on the moving words.

What I wouldn't give to be able to hug my boy again without the barrier of that anger. What I wouldn't give to have my little boy back, my firstborn. I've prayed myself dry that one day he'd realize that his mother's accident was not my doing, and that I couldn't save her, and that I wasn't rejecting her memory by remarrying. Now, of course, any hope of that grace dies with me in, what, five days.

The businessman next to him is trying again.

"I was asking if you knew his son, Jerrod Dawson? Hey, are you all right?"

Jerrod is sinking to the floor, on his knees, sobbing, and he can't do anything to stop himself — or hide the name tag that the man is now reading as he turns and leans down to take the distraught young cadet by the shoulders and try to help.

"Oh my God in heaven! You *are* Jerrod Dawson!"

Chapter 25

"I have neither the time nor the patience to deal with this right now," Diana is saying with fury into her cell phone. "I'm not overdue, my bill is paid, this is the worst possible moment, and I swear if you bother me again, I'll find a lawyer and sue your ass. Good-bye!"

She snaps the phone closed and rolls her eyes before motioning to the startled young woman standing in the office doorway and holding a pair of shopping bags.

"Is this a bad time?" Deirdre asks.

"Come on in. You get dunning calls from New Delhi much?"

"India?"

"No, Iowa. Of course, India. Where all our call centers and jobs seem to be going. Half the time I can't understand what they're saying, and they never have anyone in charge to complain to."

Deirdre walks into the room tentatively

273

with one eye on the door, as if she'll need to run back out.

"What am I, dangerous? Bring that here, please. Did you get everything?"

"I think so. All your hair stuff and dryer, curling iron, the clothes you wanted, and a change of lingerie . . . and those Atkins breakfast bars, which, in my humble opinion, you're about the last person to need."

"I like them. They like me."

"I worry about you."

"What else?"

"Everything on your list. And Mr. DiFazio's bathroom and shower are yours when you're ready."

"Thanks. I feel like I've been camping for a week in the same clothes."

"Diana, has something new happened? It's been a shock per hour around here."

Diana sighs. "Richard and the team in Mission Control are fielding requests now from the Russians, NASA, the Chinese, and the Japanese about how to enter *Intrepid* and get our poor passenger out without killing him. We don't have a compatible docking system, so it's a big problem."

"Wait, *four* of them? Which one is actually going up?"

"Would you believe all four say they are?"

"That's nuts!"

"The Russians won't back down, nor will the White House."

"Well, that's good, right?"

"Maybe. As long as we get *someone* up there to get him, yes. But at this rate they're going to need to send a space-suited traffic cop as well."

"I'll get back out on the phones. You won't believe it, but they're even feeding Kip Dawson's transmission over that moving sign at the bank."

"No!"

"It's everywhere, Diana. Every radio station has someone reading it. I've never experienced anything like this."

"None of us has. And the media are shifting now to Kip's background, intimate details we can't answer. I'd tell you I've lost control of this story, but I never for a moment had it."

The intercom feature is ringing again with a relayed call, and she answers, shaking her head.

"Tell Oprah's producer thank you, but I cannot fly to Chicago at this . . . Oprah *herself?* Well . . . sure. Put her on."

Aboard *Intrepid*, 5:50 p.m. Pacific

The cereal bars are beginning to get tiresome, and Kip wonders if there isn't at least one freeze-dried version of a real meal for his last.

Even condemned serial killers get something better than cereal bars!

It's one of the few thoughts he hasn't entered in the computer. So little time, so much to say.

I had no idea I was so . . . so verbose.

The pause to munch another bar and drain more water has brought him back to the present. He has to live here for a few more days, but the hours he's just spent wandering through his past have been therapeutic. He's been back there reliving his teen years and jumping around from good memory to better, whole hours spent ignoring the inevitability of CO_2 scrubber saturation. But for the time it's taken him to eat something and use the relief tube again, reality has claimed him, and he feels the almost desperate need to start typing again.

Kip looks up, taking note of another brilliant sunset, the price for which is realizing how few are left. Better to tackle his adult life. Not just the good parts . . . he's been doing that. But he needs to track how he got to age forty-four with such feelings of worthlessness.

No, not worthlessness, he corrects himself. *Hopelessness. Disinterest. Terminal apathy.*

He takes one more squirt of water, stows the bottle, and resumes the keyboard.

I didn't have to get married at twenty-two, but I was told it was the right thing to do. Lucy was an orphan who'd raised herself, and I came from a straight-laced family. And it just seemed that she was the logical one to marry. We agreed on that. We discussed it, like my father would have done. We agreed we were probably sexually compatible. We enjoyed each other's company in a passive sort of way, plus we both wanted two-point-three children and two cars in the garage and the great Middle-American lifestyle. In other words we agreed to marry our middle-aged selves at age twenty-two and twenty-three. How pathetic it seems now, not that I didn't love her and grow to love her more, because I did. But that we did the practical thing and decided that waiting to fall in love with someone was a silly waste of time, because, undoubtedly, you'd eventually fall out of love, and then what do you have? So, we just bypassed the passion and fast forwarded to rocking on the front porch.

And life? It took one look, rolled its eyes, and moved on, leaving us there.

Jerrod and Julie would hate to "hear" me say this about their mother, but the truth does sometimes hurt. She was a wonderful mom (despite battling the depression she tried valiantly to hide). But neither of my kids grew up witnessing parents with the kind of passion for life I see all around me now at forty-four . . . guys and gals who, despite being married or just together, love being spontaneous and can still hold decent jobs and professions. Lucy and I were incapable of just *doing* something on the spur of the moment. And yet, isn't that where life gets fun? When it's not so meticulously planned? Why didn't someone tell me? Where did I get the wrong instruction manual?

And of course the answer is: I was reading my dad's book. That doesn't mean it's his fault. I just followed the wrong plan, and I'm responsible. Boy, am I responsible!

Chapter 26

ASA Mission Control, Mojave, California,
May 19, 7:02 a.m. Pacific

"Diana, exactly when did I lose control of this control room to you?"

Arleigh Kerr has his hands on his hips, but there's no anger in his voice. Merely deep fatigue.

It's just past 7 a.m. and only three of the control room staff are present, all watching the multiple television signals their public relations director has been assembling on the screen that covers the entire front of the room. Where normally an orbital map would compete with lists and graphs and a live shot or two at different times in a launch and return mission, TV morning shows are in progress, every one devoting their coverage to the phenomenon of a public transfixed by the journaling of a man about to die.

Kip has been "silent" for more than an hour, the live transmission still flashing the last words of the last sentence he wrote before, presumably, going to sleep.

Diana straightens up from one of the consoles and smiles an equally tired and tolerant smile at their flight director. "Am I interrupting any other work here, Arleigh?"

He pauses and shakes his head. "Naw. I guess I'm just pulling your chain. It's just . . . with a bird still up there . . ."

"I know. It feels all wrong. Just like my complete inability to control even the smallest part of this story feels all wrong."

"What are they yammering about?" Arleigh asks, gesturing irritably to the silent TV images, each of which has the now-stalled crawl of Kip's writings across the bottom of each screen.

She punches up the audio from NBC and adjusts the volume, then punches it off again.

"I'm not a sociologist, Arleigh, but this is fascinating. I grew up in broadcasting, and I think you're looking at the beginnings of a kind of phase two. Phase one was a passenger trapped in space and facing death, and they're largely still on that phase. In phase two, the story becomes this unprecedented situation of his writing so freely without knowing the world is reading along with him."

"And phase three?"

"If I'm right . . . and I'm just guessing . . .

phase three will be when the story becomes *what* he's saying. The substance of his thoughts and how they relate to all of us, not just the fact that he's writing them."

Arleigh is looking at her quizzically.

"What?"

"Diana, doesn't this feel a little . . . sordid? You know . . . I mean I'm just a technical guy, but doesn't the word voyeuristic come to mind?"

"A prying observer seeking the sordid or scandalous?"

"Yes. Exactly."

"Doesn't that more or less describe us as a people? Certainly the networks and cable companies think so, paying gazillions of dollars to *be* voyeurs. I mean, Arleigh, look at it. It's everywhere! From that thoroughly idiotic 'O.J. Low-Speed Chase' that none of us could turn off, through that murderer's trial before the world's stupidest jury, through the plague of reality shows and the unbelievable things now broadcast on cable."

"Not a good commentary on humanity, I agree."

"And it's not just us. We've taught the world to be voyeurs and they've gleefully joined us."

Arleigh gestures to the multiple images. "But this just feels dirty, Diana."

"I know this guy, Arleigh."

"Personally?"

"We've talked. But I knew from the first moment I met Kip that his level of enthusiasm for what we do was very special. You should have seen his eyes light up when he was on *Good Morning America*, talking about how this was the dream of a lifetime. I'd already suggested that he'd be a great public relations icon for us when he got back."

"I was getting the feeling you had a special concern."

"I do feel protective of him, not that I can do anything."

Arleigh smiles and cocks his head. "You're not dating the customers are you, Diana?"

She feels her face redden. "Arleigh! That's beneath you."

"Sorry." He has both hands up in apology and she nods, embarrassed that he's identified exactly what she'd been thinking the night before, that Kip Dawson was a man she could get interested in.

Diana clears her throat, more like a short growl of terminated disgust.

"The point I was getting ready to make, Arleigh, is that one reason the public is already resonating with him is that he's an average Joe, a good guy from Middle America, who knows for an absolute fact in his mind that he's dead in a few more days."

"That is incredible."

"How would either of us feel? And how would we react? His thoughts are uncontaminated by hopes of rescue, contact with the ground, anything. So what we're reading has a quality about it . . . and there's a word I'm searching for . . ."

"Eloquence?"

She nods, tearing up slightly. "Yeah. Eloquence. That's exactly it. Even if his writing isn't brilliant, what he's saying, how he's *dying,* is eloquent. If that makes us voyeurs, dying along with him, then so be it."

"You . . . don't think he's going to make it, then?" Arleigh asks, looking deathly pale, as if she's got the key.

"Do you?" she asks, equally off balance. They stare at each other for a few seconds like microwave antennae transmitting volumes of unseen information for which no vocal narration is needed. There is hope of rescue, but their passenger doesn't know it, and neither of them has enough faith that it can be done.

"Can you turn the sound back on?" Arleigh says, yanking them both away from the subject.

"Sure."

She punches up NBC's *Today* again, catching the host in mid-sentence.

". . . excerpts we just showed you coming down from the private spacecraft *Intrepid*, many very personal stories have already been told, some with the names of friends and lovers he hasn't seen since his teen years. In one passage, Dawson writes about his first love, a girl named Linda Hammel, wondering where she is now. This story is so deep and personal that we felt someone should search out people such as Linda, and amazingly we found her living right here in New York City. She was gracious enough to join us this morning to give us some insight into this remarkable man. Linda, good morning."

Diana shakes her head and punches up *Good Morning America* just as the host comes on.

"In the broadcast business when there is what we call a breaking story, we refer to what we do as 'continuing coverage,' but this is an extraordinary story that plows new ground. So, while asking you to bear with us as we try to figure out the best way to report what is clearly an *evolving* story . . . and while it's continuously writing itself across the bottom of your screen . . . we're going to spend the next hour giving you as much background as we can on who Kip Dawson is, as a man, a husband, a father, a salesman, a friend. All this would normally seem invasive. But considering that most of us have eagerly been reading his words as they come down on a radio link to the Internet from orbit raises the question of whether we should have been doing so in the first place.

This morning we'll talk again with Kip's wife, Sharon, from her family home in the Houston area, but first we go to a gentleman who's worked with Kip Dawson for many years in the pharmaceutical sales business, Dell Rogers, who joins us from our ABC affiliate in Phoenix."

Diana kills the volume and brings up a succession of other network shows, each struggling to craft their own portrait of Kip, before switching the sound off again and gaining the attention of the three staffers sitting one tier in front of her.

"I've got the various audio tracks on the

comm switcher, so you can listen to whatever you want."

"Diana," Arleigh interjects, his eyes on the screen.

"Yes?"

"He's awake."

"Sorry?"

"Kip's typing again."

Aboard *Intrepid*, 7:22 a.m. Pacific

There's apparently no choice now about growing a beard. One doesn't pack a shaver on a three-hour tour.

Kip rubs his hand over the stubble threatening to morph into something he's sworn he would never wear. It itches, and he itches, pretty much all over, and even though he's already stripped once and sponged himself off, he thinks a hot shower would be a good substitute for a last meal.

The dream he's awakened from has ended again with a falling sequence. But the fact that he's remembering his dreams is extraordinary, and he hurries to write this one down, knowing how ridiculous it will look to his future reader if he doesn't explain it.

He shakes his head to clear the fog and takes some more water, deciding to save the next delectable cereal bar for a few hours from now. There will still be cereal bars and water when there's no air left.

The shroud of sadness that is his companion greets his awakening. He's getting used to it, like learning to relax and play a few rounds of poker with the grim reaper during a five-day hiatus in his morbid duties, even though he knows he's the next client on his list. The waking sequence is like a fast-forwarded version of his first day up here: a bolt of terror and startled uncertainty, denial, struggle, and anger, and then acceptance that his fate is a done deal, his demise a matter of a few days.

And then he remembers the keyboard, and for some reason he can't fathom, he's developing a feeling of responsibility toward that future reader, the man or woman ten or fifty or a hundred years hence who first reads the words he's writing.

Responsibility! If I could have a tombstone, maybe that should be the inscription: Here lies a really, really *responsible man!*

The phrase "three-hour tour" keeps rolling around in his head, a direct product of the dream, and he wonders how many even remember the old campy TV show that spawned that oft-repeated warning: "Never,

ever, go on a three-hour tour." The entire dream was about the S.S. *Minnow* and Bob Denver's *Gilligan's Island*, with some emphasis on Ginger — of the long evening gown and killer body — standing with him on the beach with a shovel having a debate about digging for hidden passages back to Honolulu.

Must be the cereal bars, he concludes, though he's eager to escape back into the process and, at least for a while, leave *Intrepid* to orbit by itself.

I grew up feeling guilty. I think maybe most of us did, and that seems a sad commentary on the process of growing up American. My Mom was Lutheran, and thus had a long-standing knowledge of guilt and precisely what to do about it. My Dad was Southern Baptist, and guilt in his view seemed to trigger outrage — at himself and anyone else not towing the line. I loved my folks — I think I said that before — and I kind of feared my Dad's anger and definitely was terrified of disappointing him. That kind of fear is probably needed to keep the boundaries in place and keep a kid out of trouble. But what I didn't need — and got in spades — was an Atlas-sized load of institutional guilt for almost everything else.

A sudden beeping courses through the spacecraft, bringing Kip's attention to the front panel. Lacking the experience to scan the complicated array of instruments and see an anomalous indication instantly, his eyes dart back and forth looking for a blinking light or an indication in motion or something.

The beeping continues unabated. Kip, trying to zero in on the source of the sound, slowly works past the echoes around him and finds himself laughing almost uncontrollably for a few seconds.

He reaches out and cancels the alarm he set himself on a sophisticated little clock on the forward panel and looks up in time to catch the next sunrise before turning back to the keyboard.

Where was I? Oh yes. Guilt. I was supposed to feel guilty, especially about any sexual feelings, let alone my doing anything about them. I was a teenage boy awash in testosterone driving me to find a girl to couple with, and I'm told that my feelings are dirty and bad. Sex, they taught me, was just barely tolerable in private in the dark and in shame, even within marriage. What a crime, the concept of using "sin" to describe the most beautiful act in life. In my family, original sin was a concept humans earned all the time, and every instance of failure of mine — whether grades or conduct or thought-crime — would engender reminders not that I was merely human and thus fatally flawed, but that I should pity myself because of those flaws. I was supposed to grow up on my knees — not worshipping my Maker, but apologizing to Him for His own act of making me imperfect. Talk about confused! No wonder we spend so much money and time as a people on psychological analysis.

What is that?

Something has changed, Kip realizes. The sound of the air conditioning, pressurization system more or less wobbled for a second. Once again he scans the panel, his heart in his throat. If that system goes down, or the fuel cells fail, the end will come a lot quicker.

But once more everything appears stable and his ears aren't clicking, and when he finds it, the cabin pressure indication looks normal. Slowly — as if looking away would allow the indications to start going sour and only continuous scrutiny could prevent such — he disconnects once again and forces himself back to what he was writing.

Despite all the dour messages I got as a kid, I grew up kinda liking me. That was actually a big victory in itself, because if I had applied all the religious terror that both sides of my parental equation taught me, it was clear I was on a fast-track to hell, mainly for being an average teenage boy. In truth, I was a pretty good and honest kid, but since I was made to feel guilty about pretty much everything, that set the stage for my thinking as an adult.

When the very act of being a normal human is labeled bad and sinful, your guilt becomes an ever-present companion. Like Eeyore and his tail. I feel guilty for so much in my life, and sometimes I feel guilty even for feeling guilty. Thoreau said in *Walden*: "The mass of men lead lives of quiet desperation." Good Lord, yes, that's been me. And when it comes to courage to break out, yes, I've been a failure. Don't abused women do that, too? Just take it and hope things will get better?

Feeling guilty was engineered into my mental operating system, but you know something? How can we really be all that bad if God put us here? Aren't we defaming Him to suggest such a thing? Where does society get off deciding that *human beings* are inherently so bad and flawed and evil that we have to spend our lives feeling guilty about being us?

Here I sit, three hundred and ten miles and an impenetrable distance above my planet, and it's literally like pulling the lens back and getting a broader view. My God, it makes me want to yell at everyone down there: Don't waste time feeling bad about being an imperfect human. Acknowledge your mistakes, correct them, and go on, but take the risk of enjoying what you've got, and be brave enough to change what doesn't work. Don't be depressed by those who want us all to feel guilty, about being busy, about being American, or about not conforming to someone else's stereotype.

And if I truly did have a bullhorn loud enough to be heard down there, I'd say one more thing, loud and clear: Tell your kids how much you love them and how proud you are of them, and spend as much time with them as you possibly can (it's so sad how few of us really do that well). You see, I'll never have another chance to tell my son and my daughters how much their dad loves them. But all those moms and dads down there still do. What a gift.

Chapter 27

Kalgoorlie-Boulder, Western Australia,
May 19, 7:45 a.m. Pacific/10:45 p.m. WST

The chances of remaining anonymous being slim to none, Alastair forces himself to head downstairs in search of his father. Scenes from *The Green Mile* come to mind as he contemplates the potential ferocity of his dad's reaction.

Dead boy walking! he thinks, feeling ill.

It was hard enough to feign innocence this morning before school, especially with the arrival of two more e-mails from ABC, quickly deleted. But the live narrative from space he illegally uncovered is now a worldwide story, and even his father is captivated by it.

Dad has spent the whole evening in front of the telly, darting to the kitchen to grab his food and return, one eye kept on the words crawling across the bottom of the screen.

His mother, too, is hooked — worse than any soap opera. She, too, wanted to stay in front of the screen, so dinner became a can of heated chili.

According to his father, the local search for the hacker who started it will be successful.

"Why, Dad?" Alastair asks, trying hard to keep his voice from shaking.

"Because, ultimately, the police will force the Internet provider involved to divulge the owner's name. They may want to thank him, but they'll probably prosecute him, too. If he was my kid, I'd probably strangle him with the cord to his mouse."

It was all Alastair could do to keep a plastic smile on his face and nod as his stomach twisted. He flew to his room, but another round of pleading e-mails from the Australian network pushed him past the tipping point, convincing him to confess now, rather than fessing up after a public discovery as they haul him to the nearest jail.

"Dad?"

His folks' bedroom is dark and the door is open, and as he lets his eyes adjust, he can just make out his mother's form under the covers, her long, sandy hair spilling over the side of the bed. His father's side is empty, so he continues down the hallway to the living room, practicing his opening line.

Dad, there's something I have to tell you.

*No. Dad, I need to tell you something im-
portant. Dammit, no. Dad, sit down. I have
a confession to make.*

The TV is still on, of course. He could
hear it from his room. And his father is still
in the same spot he was an hour ago, on the
couch, leaning forward, his hands clasped,
concentrating lest he miss reading a word.
He's wearing a pullover, and as Alastair
draws closer he can see his father holding
what looks like a handkerchief.

The message on the screen is only one line
long and moving, but he lets his eyes follow
it for a second, recognizing enough to know
that the man stuck in orbit — Kip — is
talking about his son in the Air Force
Academy again. Alastair doesn't understand why the son is so angry, but the father's remorse touches even Alastair's tough
father.

"Dad?" he says, tentatively, barely above a
whisper, as if failing to be heard could be an
escape pass and he can flee back to his
room.

There's no response, so he narrows the
distance to five feet and tries again, forcing
himself to speak louder.

"Dad?" he begins again, and this time he
sees his father's broad-shouldered form
jump slightly.

"Yes, son?" He's still riveted on the screen, and all Alastair can see is the back of his head.

"I . . . have something to tell you, Dad."

"Something to sell me?"

"No. No, *tell* you. Something to tell you."

"Right. Go ahead."

Weird, Alastair thinks. *Why isn't he turning around to look me in the eye like he always does?*

"Dad, that kid they're looking for? The one who found that space tourist's transmission?"

"Yes?"

"I . . . should have told you before . . ."

His father is turning around now and Alastair can see his father's eyes are red-rimmed, his face damp, as if he'd been crying. He's never seen his dad cry, so maybe it's allergies. The thought takes him away from his terror.

"Should have told me what, son? You know who the fellow is?"

"Yes."

"Well, tell me."

He swallows and dives off the high board, sure he'll hit cement.

"It was me, Dad. I did it. I'm so sorry! I know I promised I'd never hack into anything again, but I . . ."

His sentence is interrupted by the frightening speed of his father's six-foot frame rising from the chair in a heartbeat and covering the distance between them. Alastair flinches and tries to step back, totally unprepared to be scooped up in a bear hug.

"Dad? Are you okay?" Alastair asks after a few seconds of pure shock, straining to breathe.

His father nods at first instead of speaking, which is strange. When he finds his voice it's a strained, reedy version of it.

"I'm so sorry, Alastair."

Utter confusion crackles through Alastair's brain, the words making no sense. His father should be angry, stern, gesturing red-faced, and working his way to some sort of punishment. Some yelling wouldn't scare him half as much as this.

Yet he's standing here almost holding me off the ground and crying.

"Dad, I don't understand."

"It's hard to explain, son."

"Could . . . could you try?"

"I just want to hug you for a second, okay?"

"Sure, Dad."

"There was a time I could put you on my knee, you know?"

"Uh-huh."

"You're too big now, but I miss that."

And at last Bob Wood holds his son back at arm's length and smooths his hair with one hand while keeping a steely grip on his shoulder with the other.

"I'm the one who's kind of taken things for granted, son. I've been hard on you, even when you've done such a good job in school. I tell you when I'm upset with you, but I haven't told you enough when I've been pleased."

"You're *pleased?*"

His father is nodding, smiling, his big wet face looking like some benevolent alien rather than his strict dad. He thinks about asking, "Who are you and what have you done with my father?" but he's too shocked to be funny.

"I've let myself get too busy to be there for all your games and plays and things. And we haven't gone walkabout for a year."

"You've been to almost everything, Dad, and I know you're busy."

"So was the poor fellow you discovered, Alastair. He was very busy, and he missed some of his son's stuff, too, and there he sits in orbit, dying, can't tell his kid how proud he is of him, and how much . . ." The sentence trails off, incomplete.

"Dad . . ."

"And about the hacking. Did you tell the authorities what you found when you found it?"

"Yes, sir. I e-mailed the space company in California and they thanked me."

"Then I couldn't be prouder of you."

The bear hug starts again, along with words he can't recall ever hearing.

"I love you, son!"

Alastair can feel him shaking slightly, and he pats his father's shoulder.

"That's okay, Dad. Really. I love you, too."

Pad 39B, Kennedy Space Center, Florida, 8:25 a.m. Pacific/11:25 a.m. Eastern

The Deputy Space Shuttle Program Manager stands on an upper gantry bridge and adjusts his death grip on the railing. So far, even after three decades at the Cape, no one knows he's a hopeless acrophobic, and he intends to keep it that way.

It would be useful to look over the side to the base of the launch pad some one hundred and fifty feet below to see whether Jerry Curtis had stepped into the elevator yet, but Griggs Hopewell is not about to try it. What happens to his head with such a view is a nightmare he's smart enough not to revisit.

Ever!

Predictably, Curtis — the Director of Safety and Mission Assurance — was anything but pleased about being called out to the top of the launch complex. They haven't gotten along for years, and though Griggs tries to keep the volatile manager's feathers unruffled and tries to listen to his department's constant dithering, there are times he has to pull rank, and this is definitely one of them.

Griggs smiles at his memory of their brief conversation.

"Well, why don't you just come to my office?" Curtis whined.

"Nope. High-level meetings are best held in high places. Gantry, top tier, Pad 39B in twenty minutes. That's an order, Bub!"

Griggs takes a deep breath. "Where the hell is that insubordinate bastard!" he growls to himself. The delay is wearing thin, even though he'll never tire of standing beside the monstrous form of the shuttle, especially when it's mated to the solid rocket boosters and external tank and poised, ready for launch, as it is now.

There's still a chance they can make the launch window, but with each new delay, that hope becomes more iffy. After a cut cable, a safety stop, two personnel complaints about overtime that spilled all the way up to D.C., and the latest dust-up over the fueling schedule, he's beginning to detect sabotage in the air, although, given the fact that the rescue involves Richard Di-Fazio's company, some forms of sabotage even from the administrator himself would be unsurprising.

Griggs shakes his head, thinking of the Ahab-like determination Geoff Shear has shown to find the fatal flaws in private spaceflight in general. But in the case of DiFazio — perhaps the only man to publicly unmask Shear's deceptions in front of the Senate and the public — his little company has become the white whale, the Moby Dick Captain Ahab is determined to find and kill.

His thoughts snap back to the gantry and the present, and the presumed interference aided by Curtis, who seems to be rubber-stamping even the most flimsy concerns as genuine safety problems.

The elevator is rising now, and Griggs readjusts his grip and waits, watching the gulls soaring lazily in the mid-day sun.

The elevator cage door opens and disgorges Curtis who appears spoiling for a fight, yet smart enough not to start one.

"Okay, Griggs, I'm here. What?"

"Jerry, see this big old thing we're standing beside?"

"No, Griggs, I see nothing," he snaps, the sarcastic tone barely contained. "Must be your vivid imagination. Come on, man, you didn't call me up here to admire the damn launch vehicle."

"Well, I called you up here to answer a very simple question."

"Yeah?"

"You want to launch this thing on time?"

"What? Of course!"

"You understand the go order comes from the President of these here United States, right? And he's the ultimate boss?"

"What are you saying? That I'm doing something to frustrate this launch? Have you forgotten the basics of system safety?"

"We had a cut cable this morning. How'd it get cut?"

"I don't know. I've got an investigation going. It doesn't look like anything but a mistake."

"I'm getting a work-to-rule headache out here, too, with those two clowns filing their complaint last night."

"It's handled."

"Yeah, but why now, Jerry? I checked those two. They've never, ever, been upset by the very thing they jumped on this morning. Someone ask them to complain, perhaps?"

"I don't like your implication, Griggs."

"Well, I don't like delays unless they are truly safety-related, and the reason I called you up here is so I could say this to you clearly and without excessive ears around. If you or any of your people — including that little gal from D.C. who's been lurking around . . ."

"Dorothy?"

"The same."

"She's just doing routine safety audits."

"Right. And I've got beachfront property in Phoenix for sale. If anyone starts using artificial safety reasons to delay this launch, Shear won't be able to save the culprit from professional oblivion, you included."

"Are we done here?"

"I hope so. I just want to make sure you understand. A presidential order means a national priority. If it's really a safety issue, I'm with you. If it's artificial, I'll strap your ass on one of these SRBs and launch it myself."

Chapter 28

North Houston, Texas,
May 19, 1:55 p.m. Pacific/3:55 p.m. Central

Jerrod enters the smoky den tentatively, like his invitation might have expired and he doesn't want to get caught gawking at the animal heads and plaques and other artifacts on what Mike Summers calls his "I Love Me Wall."

He's spent most of the day with Julie watching his father's story and words. Even Sharon was decent to him, and he feels beaten down enough to appreciate that, putting his discomfort around her on hold so as to support his dad with his attention and his remorse.

"Sir?" he asks, pretty sure he sees Mike Summers's form in a large swivel recliner across the den. Sure enough, the recliner turns and Big Mike spots him, getting to his feet and motioning him over.

"Jerrod. Come over here."

"You want to talk to me?"

"I sure do. Come sit down. Would you like

something to drink?"

"I'll take a Coke if you have one."

"Also have stronger stuff, son, if you'd like. As far as I'm concerned, you're entitled."

"Maybe a beer, then. Thanks."

Mike gets a couple of longnecks from a small refrigerator and hands one to Jerrod before motioning him down and returning to his chair. Jerrod twists off the top and settles onto a small couch opposite, and they stare at each other in silence.

"You been watching all day?" Mike asks.

"TV? Yeah."

"TV, and your dad's writings?"

Jerrod nods, his eyes now down. He's noticed the large stack of printed pages by Mike's chair.

"I ditched going to my office today and pulled up a record of everything he's said so far . . . there must be a thousand Web sites keeping track . . . and I printed it, and read it, and son, I gotta ask you something directly, man to man. All right with you?"

"Yes, sir."

"It may be harsh."

"Okay."

"I'm pretty direct, Jerrod, so I'm just going to say this . . . as soon as you look at me, that is."

Jerrod looks up and meets his gaze.

"Okay. Now, just what the hell are you so angry about?"

"I . . . with all due respect, sir . . ."

"Can the bullshit, Mister! Just talk to me. Why are you so damned furious at him? For marrying my daughter?"

"No, I mean . . . no."

"Another pile of manure! Of course you are."

"I don't dislike her."

"Son, listen. You don't like her at all. Hell, she's my daughter and half the time *I* don't like her, either! And I know it's not because of who she is, but because he brought her in to replace your mom, right?"

He's nodding. A good sign, Mike figures.

"Okay, and some of that's natural. And I know my little girl, and I know she's probably made a mess out of trying to get to know you, and with you not liking anyone female he brought in . . . I get it. That doesn't bother me much. But what I want to know from you is, why are you so mad at your old man that you've . . . you've stomped his heart flat? Huh? What'd he do to deserve that?"

Tears are welling up now and Jerrod is trying to hide them, as well as hide his anger at being cornered.

"I was wrong, I guess. I should have for-given him."

"For what?"

"For . . . you wouldn't understand."

"No, I would, and I want to hear you say it. Why? Not because he found a girl and married her. Not because he asked you to respect her as his wife. Then why? Does it have anything to do with your mom's fatal accident?"

"I'd rather not . . ."

"You think he set that up somehow?"

"Of course not."

"She decided to go driving that day all by herself, didn't she?"

"I suppose."

"In fact, it was all her fault, wasn't it?"

"No!"

"No? Why not? You tell me why. We both know she was sick that day and had no busi-ness driving. She told you she had the flu, right?"

"He made her drive! Okay? My sister was waiting at her school for hours for Dad to pick her up, but he couldn't break away, so he leaves Mom to do it, knowing full well she was too sick." The words are a snarl, and exactly what Mike wanted to elicit, and with the native abilities of an oil field negotiator, he eggs Jerrod on.

"That's all bullshit, son!"

Jerrod is on his feet, his eyes aflame. "No, it isn't! You don't know anything about it. You weren't there, and I was!"

"I don't have to have been there. I know what you're saying is bull. Your mama had no business driving that day. She killed herself."

"No!" Jerrod's eyes are closed, his arms in the air, fists clenched, his body shaking, as he tries to control the response, tries to avoid punching his in-law grandfather or throwing something at the big-mouthed bastard. He can hear his teeth grinding in pain and anger but doesn't hear big Mike Summers rise quickly from his chair to suddenly grab him by the shoulders and swing him around.

"It's okay, Jerrod. Those are the things I wanted to hear you say."

Jerrod looks stunned and Mike continues, nose to nose.

"I wasn't there, but there's a lot more to the story you never knew, and your dad never told you, and it's time you heard the truth."

"What?" Jerrod's voice is subdued, suspicious, like he's just been maneuvered into a scam, yet Mike Summers is close to a force of nature and he can't bring himself to completely disbelieve.

"Come here and sit." Mike guides him back down and scoots his own chair as close as he can.

"I know you heard the crash, Jerrod. I know you ran to the end of the block, saw her car in flames, and ran the rest of the way to the wreck. I know you burned yourself trying to get her out, and that you watched her burn to death. I can't erase . . . no one can erase those terrible images. But, son, your mama was having a hard time psychologically. She was, in essence, emotionally disturbed and taking several drugs from several different doctors, none of whom knew about the other. Two of them . . . a very powerful antidepressant and a drug called Ritalin . . . should never have been taken together, because one of the dangerous side effects is making really bad decisions, and hallucinating."

"Hallucinating? Like . . . like on LSD?"

"Or worse. Or maybe just seeing things that weren't there, or not seeing things that were. Like a stoplight. Like the one she ran through."

"I didn't know this."

"I know you didn't. And your dad wrongly believed that if he told you, you'd be even angrier with him for slandering your mom."

There is a long silence as Jerrod searches Mike's face for any sign that he's being lied to.

"But here's the rest of the story, Jerrod. That day, Julie had already been picked up safely at your dad's direction by a family friend, but he couldn't get your mom to accept that. She was paranoid and thought he was lying, and despite the fact that she had been warned not to drive, she did it anyway."

"I remember Dad called, but she said it was to tell her he wasn't coming for Julie."

"Yes, that's right. He wasn't coming because she was already picked up, okay?"

"He said that . . . he told me some of those things, but I never believed him. I asked my mother once weeks before if she was taking something because she seemed so out of it, but she said no and I believed her. And . . . and that day, I only heard her side of the conversation, and she was furious and told me Dad wasn't going to pick Julie up because he couldn't be bothered."

"In fact, when he was on that phone call — the part you didn't hear — he was begging her to understand what he was saying. When she sounded so strange, he left work and screamed toward home, and it's fortunate you didn't lose both of them that day.

Didn't you ever wonder why he showed up at the accident site so quickly?"

Jerrod shakes his head, stunned. "I never knew it was quick. I was so . . . horrified . . ."

"I understand."

"How do you know all this, sir?"

"Your dad sat right here one night a few years back and told me the whole story. He felt . . . just like he's been writing up there in space about guilt . . . he felt so guilty that he didn't see it coming, didn't know about her doubled prescriptions. See, guys like him and you and me, we get this idea that if anything happens on our watch, it's all our fault, regardless. Especially where women are involved, 'cause, see, we're supposed to protect them."

Jerrod is nodding slowly, numbly, as Mike continues.

"Your dad later sent me copies of the prescription drug labels, Jerrod, and I had a friend validate the effects. This isn't exaggerated."

Jerrod buries his head in his hands. "Oh God, I never gave him a chance, and now . . ."

"Okay. Look, I think they'll get him down from there. I have a lot of hope for that, and you should, too. But there's something else. What's really been going on with you,

Jerrod, is that you keep blaming yourself even more than him. You think deep down inside that if you'd been faster, stronger, smarter, or what-the-hell-ever, you could have pulled her out of that car before the fire killed her. You know why I know that? 'Cause you're a male, and that's the god-dammed way we think. Especially about our moms. Son, I *saw* the pictures, okay? The post-fire pictures shot by the coroner."

"How?"

"Before your dad married my daughter I had him thoroughly investigated, and I wanted every detail of that tragedy to make sure he had no culpability. Jerrod, she was trapped in a tangle of metal. There was nothing you could have done!"

"I could have pulled her out of the window."

He sighs deeply, his eyes on Jerrod, considering whether to push on.

"Okay, dammit . . . I'm going to show you a picture, Jerrod, if you truly want to see it. It's gruesome as hell and it will probably do you more harm, so I beg you not to ask, but you're an adult now. If you want to see it, I'll show it to you, but it was taken after her body was burned beyond recognition. It shows clearly that she had been completely impaled on the steering column after the wheel broke off. Run through, Jerrod, all the way through to her backbone. Even if you'd had superhuman strength, all you would have been able to pull out was her upper torso."

"I . . . saw her look at me . . . her mouth moved . . . she was screaming . . ."

The only grandfather he's ever known moves to sit alongside him, putting a big arm around the boy and pulling him into a hug, hanging on as the tears finally flow.

Aboard *Intrepid*

The so-called terminator — the line of demarcation between night and day — is crawling across the middle of the United States again, but Kip has to check his watch and think to realize that it's been two days since he should have returned to Earth. He's checked the oxygen and CO_2 scrubber saturation tables twice now, and he figures he has two more days before breathing begins to get difficult. Maybe he should just depressurize the ship and finish the job, freeze drying himself and his dead pilot with the vacuum of deep space and eternal cold.

Bill is about to become a problem. Kip

knows it instinctively. A body in room temperature for two days has already gone through rigor mortis, and despite being sealed in plastic as well as Kip could manage, he fears that soon he'll be inhaling the telltale odor of decomposition. Earlier, he stopped writing for a half hour to search out Bill's pressure suit, wondering if perhaps putting him in it and sealing everything wouldn't be the best course of action. But he's convinced he's waited too long; were he to open the sealed plastic now . . .

Besides, he might decide to go for a spacewalk and just end it out there as his own satellite.

But for now the air remains okay and he's way too far into the story of his life to waste the remaining forty-eight hours pulling and hauling on a space suit that — given Bill's slightly smaller frame — probably wouldn't fit him anyway.

The pull to get back to the keyboard is great, and this time not because of the escape it provides, but because he's worried about the import of everything he's chronicled, frightened that it doesn't amount to as much as he thought. An autobiography of mundane occurrences and banal sameness, and an embarrassing lack of significant achievements. He isn't happy with the way his life looks so far, and he's hoping it will get better, rounding the corner of the last ten years. There have been happy times, he's sure of that. But somehow, in print, as a chronicle, it seems so ordinary, and he's caught himself wanting to lapse into fiction a few times, spice up a few things here and there. After all, who on Earth would know, so to speak?

But the fact that it is, or was, his life forces him to stay honest about the details, even some that he would never have spoken about on Earth.

There's an incident in particular a few years back that still bothers me to the point of losing sleep, something I did nothing about in order to save my job. I didn't find out until too late, and when I discovered the corporate leaders knew about it, I was convinced they would can me if I said anything. I just stowed the evidence away quietly and sat on it like a coward. I'll never know how many people, if any, have been injured or maybe even killed. But a corporation that knowingly ships a bad, completely inactivated lot of a major antibiotic just to avoid the costs of a recall has to be committing a criminal act.

Kip stops, wondering whether to risk putting the details down in print for the first time, knowing it could put several executives of the American branch of the company in prison. But who will care twenty or fifty or whatever years from now? And if by some miracle he does get rescued, he can quietly delete it.

Ah, what the hell. No one's reading this but me anyway.

I think I want to tell you in detail exactly what happened, and how I found out.

The White House,
4:18 p.m. Pacific/7:18 p.m. Eastern

Ron Porter makes it a point never to charge out of his office like the West Wing is on fire. He knows about the adrenaline that races into bloodstreams when a Chief of Staff looks panicked, and now is no exception — even late in the evening with most of the staff gone.

He strolls to the desk just outside the Oval Office still occupied by the President's secretary and catches her eye. Technically, she works for Porter, but he wouldn't dare fire or chastise her without the President's permission. She's been working for the man for twenty years.

Not that she needs chastising or firing, but sometimes Elizabeth Delacourt can be a bit too harsh as a gatekeeper.

"Is he ready, Liz?" he asks, glad for the relaxed smile in return as she waves him in.

He expects to find the President behind his desk, but instead sees him in front of the TV, quietly reading the latest words from Kip Dawson.

Ron, too, has been caught in that distraction all day, canceling any productive work as he watched the words on his computer screen.

"Pretty amazing, huh, Ron? Just one guy, but I can't quite stop reading him. And . . . frankly, he's making a lot of sense on some things."

"Mr. President, two items. First, the Chinese have just let it be known that they're going to launch on Saturday to go get him regardless of our plans to launch *Endeavor* Saturday around noon, and the Russians plan to launch Saturday at the same time. On top of that, the Japanese Space Agency says they're preparing an emergency launch for Friday."

"You're kidding!"

"I wish I were."

"This is ridiculous. What are they going to do if they all make it up there? Draw straws? Has Shear tried to discourage them?"

"No. He's *en*couraging them. The Russians in particular. He says it's because *Endeavor* may not be ready, even though they're already on the extended countdown."

"Call Shear at home, will you, and tell him now's the time to pare this down to one reasonable backup launch. I know he can't control those folks but he can beg and wheedle."

"I'll tell him."

"And the second item?"

"Nothing we can do about it, but we just celebrated a completely unexpected, undeclared national holiday. Actually, more like international."

"What are you talking about, Ron?"

"A large segment of our business community is reporting massive absenteeism and the retail sector is reporting plummeting sales. Everyone's staying home to read what Dawson is writing."

"Really?"

"There are estimates out there right now

that over two thirds of our people are actively watching this, word by word, and probably close to a billion worldwide."

"How is that possible?"

"Mr. President, there are live feeds coming through beepers, moving sign boards, radio, television, cable, AM, FM, Web casts . . . you name it. In China, too, it's virtually everywhere, with simultaneous translation. You remember we've remarked how fast the world can become a global village?"

"Yes."

"Well, now add all these other forms, including PDAs and the galaxy of so-called Wi Fi 'hot spots' around the nation. Cell phone screens, too. I've even heard that one of those advertising blimps is hovering off Malibu right now and scrolling Dawson's words."

"A *blimp?*"

"Yes, sir. If this continues, we might as well shut down any form of transportation not connected live to this thing. We have wire reports about hundreds of travelers changing their flights at the last minute to airlines that have live TV aboard. If it goes through Saturday, it may paralyze most of the civilized world."

"Good heavens."

"The AP is carrying a tale about an international flight on which one of the flight attendants remained on one of the audio channels for the entire thirteen hours reading the transcript aloud as the pilots downloaded it from the cockpit."

The President is silent as he's drawn back to his own TV screen, Dawson's words snagging his attention.

"Wait, I want to read this."

I have to admit I feel guilty about this, too. So much so that if I were able to survive and return, one of my first acts would be to go to the nearest U.S. Attorney and give him a copy of everything I just wrote. And the sad part is that now that I go back through it, I realize I do know where the evidence is . . . where the bodies are buried, so to speak. Right there in my filing cabinet in my den under the 2004 tab. The folder with the red exclamation point on it and a rubber band around it. By the time anyone reads this, I'm sure everything in that cabinet will have been long since burned or buried in some landfill. But I know in my heart that there had to be at least a few patients out there who died or had a terrible time because the good old reliable Vectra penicillin they'd bought from us wasn't working. No one . . . not the doctors, nurses, or pharmacists who trusted us implicitly . . . would have ever suspected the reason was simple greed. Someone needs to be prosecuted for this.

"Did you see that, Ron?"

"Yes, sir. So did most of the country."

"Vectra knowingly sold bad penicillin?"

"We should act on this, don't you think?"

The President is nodding and pointing to the phone. "Let's get Justice moving on this in the morning. No, wait. Those records he mentions. Let's get those protected."

"FBI then?"

"Yes. Quickly." He turns back to the TV, quietly addressing the unseen writer as Porter hurries from the Oval.

"So, what other bombshells do you have for us, Kip?"

Chapter 29

Kennedy Space Center, Florida,
May 19, 5:57 p.m. Pacific/
8:57 p.m. Eastern

John Kent has lost count of how many nighttime approaches he's made to the KSC runway in one of NASA's T-38s, but this one is unannounced. He rolls the sleek twin jet onto a stable final approach, working the throttles forward and back to keep the supersonic trainer on speed across the threshold. Touchdown and aerobraking are followed by a rapid taxi to the ramp where an unmarked NASA car is waiting, the driver bringing the ladder over as John cuts the engines, opens the canopy, and finishes the shutdown checklist. The man is on the top of the ladder now and John reaches over to shake his hand before unstrapping.

"Griggs! Great to see you."

"Glad you're here, old sport. I'm beginning to feel like the French underground versus Vichy."

"World War II–speak again, Griggs?"

"Can't keep an amateur historian down. Need help outta that tin can?"

"Nope. Stand back please, and don't try this at home." He pins the ejection seat, unstraps, and stands before swinging a leg carefully over the side and climbing down.

He joins Hopewell in the front seat of the car.

"Why am I here, Griggs?"

"I need your help, John. We've got a presidential directive to launch and a soft sabotage operation being run by our dear administrator to prevent us from launching," he says, gesturing toward the Pad 39 launch complex visible in the distance bathed in lights. "I don't know why Shear is silly enough to believe he can send an operative into my space center and not be found out."

"The woman you told me about?"

"Miss Dorothy Sheehan. I've had one of my guys watching her, and where Sheehan shows, nothing goes. She's not red tagging anything herself, but throwing her HQ weight around so that anything she points to someone gets excited about. All day today it's been one crisis after another, not a one of them legitimate. I've warned Curtis, because I think he's in cahoots, but I don't have enough evidence to go over Geoff's head to the White House."

"And the bottom line is?"

"We're not going to make this window, John, if this crap continues."

"Of course he's been against this from the start. Anything involving DiFazio . . ."

"Is he wrong, John?"

"Yes, dammit!"

"But we don't want another *Challenger*, John. And, Bubba, since you is my bona fide partner in crime, I want to review everything they've fingered so far and have you take a long look at the overall plan."

"Look over your shoulder?"

"Exactly. I'm afraid of pushing too hard, even against this rotten interference."

"Where are we going?"

"Back to my office. And before you ask, yes, I've got Kip Dawson's monologue punched up on my computer. You were busy boring T-38-sized holes in the sky, but just before I came out to pick you up, he was talking about a huge scandal involving his drug company employer, and if someone doesn't end up in the hoosegow over it, I'll be shocked."

"Good Lord. He writes it there and things happen here, and he doesn't even know it. Talk about the power of the pen."

Tucson, Arizona, 7:15 p.m. Pacific/ 8:15 p.m. Mountain

It doesn't take an FBI agent to know that a moving light in an empty house is seldom a good thing. But Tucson police officer Jimmy Gonzalez can see nothing amiss as he slides up to the curb. He reads the call details again on his dash-mounted computer screen. "Next-door neighbor reports seeing flashlight beam moving around inside. Knows resident is out of town. Window involved on east side by shrubs."

There's a phone number listed for the house and he punches up the number on his cell phone, waiting until it flips over to a voice-mail message.

He closes the phone and types in that he's leaving his car and investigating. Walking carefully, he moves along the eastern side of the rambler and positions himself to peer into the window where the flashlight beam was reported to have been.

Nothing.

He shines his powerful SureFire through the pane, lighting up a den that seems intact and untouched, then continues around the back and other side of the house, checking the doors before returning to his car.

"House secure, nothing appears amiss," he types, closing the call and deciding there's no point to interviewing the complainant.

Special Agent Kat Bronsky of the FBI has never loved the desert, but Tucson has been an exception, especially the pristine resorts on the northern flank of the town. This time, however, a two-week Homeland Security assignment meant a forgettable Tucson motel from where she's spent most of the afternoon watching Kip Dawson's amazing story unfold — including the fact that his home is less than a mile away from where she's sitting. But reading that somewhere in the Dawson home is a file with evidence of criminal activity electrified her. For the past year she's been part of a special strike force investigating Vectra Pharmaceuticals.

A quick after-hours phone call to her superior in D.C. is unavoidable, if unanswered. She waits a fitful twenty minutes for a callback from the urgent beeper message she leaves, relieved when her cell phone finally rings with his number on the screen.

"If *I* just read about it, Glen, and *you* read about it, at least someone at risk from Vectra saw it. We should get a warrant and get out there now."

"Already in motion, Kat. A big alert triggered by the White House came down moments before you called. We're trying to roust the Tucson office right now."

"They're not answering beepers or phones?"

"The whole team is away in Phoenix, I think. We're working on it."

"Okay, there's no time. Let me take it."

"You don't know the local judges."

"I don't need to. There's no one covering that house while we're talking, so let me go out and at least watch the place. When you get the local team, have them get the warrant and hook up with me there."

"Kat, use the local police for that."

"Glen, that'll go out on the radio channels, and anyone interested enough to be racing in to snatch that file will be on the police scanner."

"Okay, dammit, you're making sense, as usual. But, Kat, this one is the highest priority for doing things right. We can't screw up an evidentiary grab started by a presidential order without all our heads rolling down Pennsylvania Avenue. Got it? No heroics. Do *not* go in or touch that file without a warrant."

"No problem. Message understood and acknowledged."

Finding the address and driving to 4550 East Fernhill takes less than ten minutes, and Kat parks down the street before walking back slowly, looking over the darkened residence as she approaches. *Why is a local police cruiser in front of the house?* She hesitates, pretending to search for an address, as the officer pulls away and passes her, accelerating around the corner as she makes a quick note of his plate number.

She sees mature trees in the front yard casting deep shadows against an overhead streetlight and takes advantage of the black hole to disappear alongside the Dawson house, moving carefully past shrubbery until she's at the northeast rear corner. She waits a minute to watch and listen. The house is dark and quiet, and she decides to move to the nearest window and peer in before checking the doors and finding the best vantage point from which to be sure no one enters.

The ground beneath the window is a flower bed of soft topsoil anything but native to Tucson, and she steps in it carefully and lifts her eyes above the sill, letting her vision adjust to the darkness inside.

At the same moment a startlingly bright beam of light stabs through the interior, illuminating a desk in the corner of what appears to be a den.

Kat jerks herself back to one side, but whoever is wielding the flashlight doesn't appear to be interested in looking her way. She can see him, a male of average height, holding the flashlight and moving the beam to a four-drawer filing cabinet.

There's no doubt in her mind what's happening. He moves quickly toward the cabinet like he's been there before, and she can see he's carrying something metallic. He focuses the light on the cabinet lock on the upper left-hand corner and tries to balance the flashlight between chin and shoulder while he uses what looks like a small kitchen knife and perhaps an ice pick to spring the lock.

The man appears to be alone and she watches his ham-handed fumbling with the lock.

This is not a professional thief, she concludes, unsurprised. *Whoever he is, he's got a stake in getting rid of the evidence Dawson talked about.*

The man reaches a breaking point and throws the makeshift tools to the floor in disgust, looking back and forth around the room as if the key might be hanging within reach if he could just take the time to spot it.

The desk catches his eye and he moves to it, flashlight beam on the top drawer as he rummages through it, pulling it out steadily until it suddenly falls to the floor. He's on his hands and knees now, frantically sorting through the contents, then coming up with a key. He leaps to his feet, racing back to the file cabinet but can't insert it.

Wrong key, boy, she thinks, calculating which way he's likely to leave if he achieves his objective. In the reflected beam of the flashlight when it hits his face every few moments she can see he's a Caucasian male, perhaps in his fifties, and moderately overweight.

He's back on his knees rifling through the contents of the fallen desk drawer, and Kat can see the flashlight beam shaking in his trembling left hand.

Scared to death. Probably never had more than a traffic ticket, and probably not armed.

Another key! He's back up and over to the file cabinet and this time the lock springs open. She can hear his small victory yelp even through the window as he yanks open the drawers successively until finding the one he's looking for.

FBI procedures and common sense dictate calling for police backup and intercepting the suspect as he leaves, and she reaches for her cell to dial 911 the same moment a bright light snaps on from behind and an excited male voice orders her to freeze.

"POLICE! GET THOSE HANDS UP!"

Kat can see the man inside the den turn, startled, a folder in his hand as he yanks it from the drawer and snaps off his light. She can see him bolting to the rear door in the den, fumbling with the knob and the lock, and she turns quickly, raising her hands as she sidesteps toward the corner of the house.

"Turn that light out! I'm an FBI agent!"

"KEEP YOUR HANDS UP!"

She glances back through the window, aware the intruder is still struggling with security locks and frantic to get out. She has only seconds, she figures, to calm the cop down.

She looks back at the bright light in her face.

"There's a suspect in that house and we don't have time for this. I'm going to pull out my ID wallet! Keep your trigger finger under control!"

"KEEP THOSE HANDS WHERE I CAN SEE THEM! DID YOU HEAR ME?"

She pulls the ID wallet from her jacket pocket with two fingers, bringing it out laterally and flipping it open as she hears the back door being flung wide.

"Hold it right there!" the cop is saying to Kat, his voice more uncertain now as he gingerly approaches, surprised and unprepared for her to turn around and yell toward the back of the house while still thrusting the ID wallet at him.

"FEDERAL AGENTS! FREEZE! HANDS IN THE AIR! NOW!"

"What . . . what are you doing?" Jimmy Gonzalez asks, his gun still leveled at his suspect as he tries to read the ID at the same time he's trying to see who she's yelling at.

"GET THOSE HANDS IN THE AIR, MISTER! NOW! ON YOUR KNEES OR I'LL SHOOT! DROP THAT FOLDER!"

Kat looks back to Gonzalez in a lightning move.

"Satisfied?"

"I . . . guess."

"Here's my ID. Toss me your light."

"What?"

"NOW!"

He tosses the SureFire to her, watching as she catches it and tosses him the ID wallet, covering the distance between the corner of the house and the obviously frightened man kneeling by the backdoor in a few heart-beats. She covers the suspect with a 9mm Glock Jimmy never saw her unholster.

"Officer? Bring your cuffs, please."

Jimmy responds as quickly as he can, cuffing the man as he notes the business suit and the balding head.

"Don't shoot! I'm a friend of Kip's! I have a key!"

"But not to his filing cabinet, it appears," Kat says. "What's in the folder?"

"Ah, private company information."

"Right. Half the world read exactly what you read about a particular folder with a rubber band and a red exclamation point in the file cabinet you just broke into."

"Kip asked me to protect this if anything ever happened to him."

"Sure he did. What's your name?"

No answer.

"NAME! NOW!"

"Ah . . . Robert Wilson."

"How did you get in the house?"

"I have a key. I'm authorized."

"All right, Mr. Wilson, you're also under arrest on suspicion of obstruction of justice in a federal case, for starters. Officer?"

"Yes, ma'am?"

"Please Mirandize this gentleman after

you finish cuffing him, and then get us some backup while the rest of my team gets here."

"Okay."

She turns to Jimmy Gonzalez now, asking his name, and he responds as he hands her back the ID wallet.

"Good job, Officer Gonzalez. All the way around."

Chapter 30

Coleman TV Studios, Washington, D.C.,
May 19, 8:00 p.m. Pacific/
11:00 p.m. Eastern

Matt Coleman is aware tonight's broadcast could be the definitive performance of his career. He checks his appearance, wondering why anyone would think he looks like the late Johnny Carson, although he considers it one hell of a compliment. At age forty-seven, with a full head of prematurely silver hair, a neutral Midwest accent, and a natural smile, there are a few similarities. But he understands that the comparison is the wishful thinking of a vast audience hungry for the more serious approach and occasionally sharp-witted humor he's made a trademark since he took over from Larry King, building his now-syndicated evening news, comment, and interview show far beyond the confines of CNN to span American broadcast and worldwide broadcast networks, as well as cable and Internet outlets.

And tonight — broadcasting in high definition to an estimated combined world audience of at least a hundred million people with simultaneous translation in sixteen languages, he can either own the story of Kip Dawson by walking a razor-sharp line between commentary and reportage, or end up as just another conduit for what's happening.

And Matt Coleman intends to own the story.

Tonight the computerized reassembly of his image will have him appearing for all the world as if he's actually standing in three different world capitals, complete with a shadow where the sun is shining. He takes his place for the opening against a live shot of *Intrepid* being downlinked from a high-powered NASA camera in orbit.

Good evening, and right to the point. Seldom has the story of one person dominated our worldwide attention for more than a few moments in this frenetic modern life. When that rare event does happen, however, usually it's after an event is over. Not so in the case of Kip Dawson. Tonight, I'll guide you through the significance of what's been occurring, not only some three hundred and ten miles above us on orbit, but on

337

Earth, too, as an ordinary man — an ordinary husband and father named Kip Dawson — unknowingly communicates to an amazing number of his fellow humans in real time in ways simultaneously complex, simple, and profound.

Not even when the President of the United States or the Pope speaks do so many pay such rapt, all-consuming attention. Yes, this has developed into a shared human experience, reading the words of a man who knows he's going to die in two more days. But what makes this so profound is that Kip Dawson is saying things that ring true in the hearts and minds and unspoken memories of so many . . . his angst, his remorse over things left undone, his grief and joy over relationships that form the basic sinew of life, and even one amazing instance this afternoon in which his recounting of misconduct by the company that employs him has already sparked law enforcement action that may end in indictments and prison sentences. In many things he's written, Kip Dawson is giving voice to feelings we've dared not reveal, and touching us uncomfortably in the process. Worldwide, he's sparking debates and focusing attention on ideas, some fairly far out — such as the religious debate Kip's words ignited when he recommended that marriage be limited to eighteen years past the birth of the last child. If you've been glued to your TV or computer reading every word . . . if you've called in sick or been inattentive to your duties because you're wrapped up in this, that's okay, because you're witnessing and living as it happens something we've never seen or heard before — a single voice, speaking to mankind, guileless, with no agenda, and with a blinding honesty we all need to understand. Space tends to do that to us. Our fathers and mothers stood transfixed in 1969, knowing what adults know, and watching Neil Armstrong step on the moon. Later the drama of *Apollo Thirteen* galvanized the planet, to the extent that communications were able to bring the globe together. And today? A planetary audience is reading or listening in dozens of languages to every word Kip Dawson writes. An audience of perhaps two billion — that's with a "B" — two billion members of the human family. Perhaps it takes something like this to truly remind us how connected we really are.

Okay. First, let's get to the basics of what's happened.

Hyatt-Regency, Los Angeles, California, 8:30 p.m. Pacific

With a pedestrian mini-bar scotch in her hand, in a plush Los Angeles hotel room, Diana Ross settles into an easy chair, thinking over the day's events. The TV is on, the story doing just what she'd predicted now and turning to phase three, the story about what he's saying and how he's saying it.

She shakes her head at the coincidence of Kip going silent just before Coleman's show hit the air. Intellectually she knows his producer had nothing to do with it. But it gave Matt Coleman an invaluable window of opportunity to feed the void in Kip's transmission with his own spin, and given the deep public hunger for more, the size of tonight's audience has to be a record.

Kip's last-typed words still hang along the bottom of the screen, the end of a surprisingly introspective tale of his second marriage and how the progressive withdrawal of sexual interest by Sharon Summers Dawson affected him slowly, insidiously, exacer-

340

bated by her refusal to admit there was anything wrong between them. He wrote about his frustration and his attempts to ignore it. He talked about trying to tell himself it was okay, that he could survive semi-celibacy as Sharon became sexually colder.

But she's been wholly unprepared to read that Kip fantasized about her while in training in Mojave — a revelation written with her name clearly attached that's led to an instant phone explosion and morning show bookings for tomorrow. She's gone through a series of rapid responses from shock to embarrassment to anger to a growing, deep sense of connection.

So I affected him that much!

For several hours she's been worried that he'll say more, take his fantasy into the literary bedroom or something equally tawdry. After all, he could say anything at all with the secure "knowledge" that no one in his time would read it. And when he began describing the feelings their one dinner together had sparked in his love-starved head — thoughts that maybe he should consider ending his marriage and looking for someone like her to love — it was not a welcome accolade. Half the planet has now been invited to think of her as a virtual pinup girl, if not a potential homewrecker.

How on earth am I going to deal with this tomorrow or even live this down? she wonders. Even *Playboy* is now trying to reach her. At the same time she feels guilty that she's irritated over his words when the man has less than forty-eight hours of air left and has absolutely no intention of embarrassing her. And in the end, she decides to deal with the morning show questions by laughing it off. After all, she's done nothing to encourage him, and these are only the private musings of a dying man.

Nevertheless, the same questions keep echoing in her head. *Why now? Why me?*

She knows the answer, but she's been avoiding the conclusion: She's in his head.

And now, somehow, he's in hers.

Aboard *Intrepid*, 8:40 p.m. Pacific

Waking from each nap is becoming more and more confusing.

Somehow Kip has developed the ability to fall almost immediately into REM sleep, something he could never do on Earth. But coming out of REM is a slightly wrenching experience, the dreams left behind so real and visceral that each time he has to think carefully about what is and isn't real.

But then the full reality of his situation returns.

This time the dream was all about sex and lovemaking and he hates to leave it. He wonders if there's sex in whatever dimension he'll find himself occupying in two days. If not, he thinks, maybe he'd rather not go — as if he had a choice. It was sex and the lack of making love (or even the lack of opportunity to have raw sex with Sharon), that has all but destroyed his marriage.

And of everything in this life, he thinks he'll miss sex the most.

If that's how I measure my existence, in terms of how much I've been getting, he thinks, *I was already near death.*

The thought makes him chuckle and he considers writing something really steamy in the computer, just to show his future reader who he really is, the lusty Kip Dawson, a lover devoted to the female of the species who didn't get much practice.

He poises his fingers over the keyboard, visualizing Diana Ross, wondering how tastefully yet graphically he could describe how he'd like a night with her to unfold, a menu of delights with her pleasure at the center while Conway Twitty sings "Slow Hand" in the background. "Bolero," he thinks, was never his style.

Of course he could substitute any pretty female in such a narrative, but then it would be no more than mental masturbation. No, if he's going to fantasize in writing, it should be Diana, whom he can see so clearly.

Why shouldn't I try my hand at erotic narrative? No one in her time will see it, and I've already said I was thinking about her that way.

But then he feels a twinge of Puritanical alarm, as if even his demons will be straight-laced enough to be embarrassed at his prurient thoughts. But he needs a more practical reason to stay his hand, and he finds it in chivalrous concern for Diana. Even if his words weren't found until she was a much older woman, such self-indulgent X-rated musings could embarrass her, and he would never want that.

He laughs again at how different the mental wiring is between male and female, and how abysmally unaware most women are of the simplicity of the male mind on the subject of sex.

Think driving force of life! Think the most beautiful element of life. Think I'd rather die without it.

He's had no hope of getting that through to Sharon, or getting her to understand how destructive her disinterest in making love has been, and how it's essentially doomed them.

So many things he should have changed. So many times he played it safe.

Oh, great! he chuckles. *I find the true meaning of life with less than two days of it left. Impeccable timing!*

He can see a lot of things more clearly now, having chronicled his entire life and come to the conclusion that at best he would give it a C minus.

No. Not even that good, Kip thinks. *As an adult, I give myself an F.*

Then again, what sense does it make to spend the remaining hours whining and crying and carrying on? Nothing will change as a result, except that he'll lose the chance to add to his narrative. Besides, death will be a new beginning. He believes that, doesn't he?

Kip feels a shudder ripple through him, a primal fear of what's on the other side of that one-way door he's facing. He remembers the adage that there are no atheists in a foxhole, and there are certainly none in *Intrepid*, but somehow all his philosophical thoughts about this existence and what happens next and why are being spread out on a table for some future universe to look at, and perhaps judge.

Or not.

In any event, he'll know in two days how right or wrong he was, but suddenly all those musings seem infantile and untrustworthy.

Kip closes his eyes and forces his mind back to his narrative. It's safer there, like a warm and familiar room with four walls and window shades he can pull against reality. *Intrepid* itself has begun to feel a little like that, and for two days he's been able to stay uniquely focused, living his life over again.

Amazing, that focus, he thinks. Like Samuel Johnson said, "The prospect of being hanged in a fortnight most wonderously concentrates the mind."

He shakes his head. Johnson was talking about two weeks. He has two days.

But he also has the keyboard in front of him and a hard drive that doesn't know the difference between the real life he's been writing about and the life he wishes he'd had and all the things he should have done.

Virtual reality, virtual life. What is it they say in Hollywood? Do a rewrite? Good. I'll rewrite my life the way it should have been.

The idea begins to take hold, bringing a faint smile. It would be like taking control, having the power to determine his own destiny, rather than just being along for the ride. He can get just as crazy about it as he wants. He can replace his parents with a keystroke, have the brother he always wanted — maybe even an identical twin — and when it comes to girls, the possibilities are unlimited. The cutest gals in school will be his. The homecoming queen, the sexiest siren in town. Forget Lucy, he'll marry a drop-dead gorgeous Ph.D. with a stand-up comedienne's sense of humor and a Julia Child's skill at cooking. Superwoman! Chef in the kitchen, lady in the parlor, and wild woman in the bedroom.

Maybe I'll earn a Ph.D. Maybe two. Perhaps a Nobel Prize for some discovery in one of the hard sciences, after a short but stellar career as an Air Force ace. No, not the Air Force. The Navy. I'll become a Navy carrier pilot. Top Gun.

He lets the thoughts swirl, thinking about all he's ever heard about someone creating his own reality by doing little more than what he's contemplating. Just . . . *creating* it.

If it's all in my mind, then what's the difference?

Suddenly he's paging back through what has become a massive document, looking for the place where he first began to regret the way things were going.

That would be age fourteen.

No, he decides. Earlier. Age nine, before he noticed girls.

No, he corrects himself, *I was noticing girls by age eight, I just didn't have a clue what to do with them.*

He finds the spot he was looking for around page forty and begins highlighting everything afterward, page after page of his life the way it was.

He opens the main hard drive and locates the file and deletes it, leaving the hundred twenty page document on the screen as the only remaining record.

It is as I make it. And maybe it all was a dream, both good and bad.

His finger is over the delete button now as he thinks about all he's written, two days of electronic scribbling for forty plus years of an unfinished, imperfect life. How many fellow humans have wished for a rewrite, he wonders. How many have wished for a chance to go back and do it all over again?

His index finger touches the delete key lightly, hovering there, waiting, knowing that if he presses it, all he's highlighted will disappear. As if it never was. As if he'd never lived it, never married Lucy, let alone lost her, never been devastated by his son's rejection because there will have been no son. One keystroke to do away with the lost years of obeying someone else's flight plan of what life should be like, and suddenly the bile of resentment is rising in his throat, the recollection flooding back of the lifelong, aching feeling that something was missing from an equation that, by his dad's book, was complete.

Two days to rewrite it all. Why not?

He pushes firmly, hearing the click, as over a hundred pages disappear into cyberspace.

Time to start over.

Chapter 31

Los Angeles, California, May 20,
3:10 a.m. Pacific/6:10 a.m. Eastern

The limo headed for ABC's local studios and the West Coast *Good Morning America* set will be ready in ten minutes, but Diana Ross is having trouble tearing herself away from her laptop. She knows she should have been sleeping, but it wasn't possible. Deciding to shower and get put together by midnight, she's worked the laptop ever since.

There is, she thinks, *no other subject being discussed! It's turned into an All Kip, All the Time Internet.*

In New York, through Web connections, John Gambling and Don Imus and every other major radio host are shifting from backgrounders and interviews with Kip's friends aired the day before, to open debates about sex and wifely duties and professional obligations versus time with your kids. Religious debates are raging on some of the national talk shows excoriating Dawson for accusing both Lutherans and Baptists of fostering guilt, some callers crying on the air, and a growing list of experts showing up to debate the deeper philosophical implications of a man turning away from organized religion, yet clearly embracing his Maker. Newspapers across the nation from Diana Ross's own *Washington Post* and *The New York Times* through a galaxy of small-town papers fed by syndicates and wire services have special columns on Matt Coleman's comments from last evening, the President's order for NASA to launch a rescue mission, and details about an FBI raid in Tucson that netted a Vectra regional executive trying to steal the very evidence Kip Dawson revealed from space. Every electronic newspaper carrying the front pages above the fold deal with Dawson's words and his ideas and impressions, and *The New York Times* has an entire transcript as a special section, as does *The Wall Street Journal* and *USA Today*. Instant books have been announced by a host of publishers in hopes of advance orders, and religious leaders from across the spectrum of faith are queuing up to enter their spin or engage in perceived damage control, the cleverest among them seeming to co-opt Kip's views as their own, the message they've preached all their careers. Pastors and priests and rabbis across North America are working on special sermons and homilies and scheduling special services for Saturday, some of the more progressive dangling big-screen coverage of the NASA launch as an incentive.

Diana looks down at her coffee cup suddenly as if it's betrayed her. She's drained the contents without realizing it.

Look at this! The bloggers have gone mad as well!

A quick search of the advanced Google service turns up no fewer than forty-six thousand blog sites engaged in some discussion of, or use of, Kip Dawson's name. And the number is growing by the minute.

Incredible!

She finds an unofficial estimate posted from some obscure department at the UN claiming that of the world's six point five billion humans, fully one billion of whom have access to TV and many more to radio, that at least two billion people are following the story.

And in the United States, ABC is reporting, nearly eighty percent of the population are fully engaged, meaning an incredible number of children as well as adults.

It's an advertiser's wet dream! she thinks,

wondering how fast the ad agencies are scrambling to figure out a way to leverage the coverage, and what the networks are charging.

On a whim, Diana types her name and that of Sharon Dawson in the search engine, startled that several hundred hits pop up instantly — as does an Instant Message from Richard DiFazio.

"You up?"

"Yes. You wanted me to do the morning shows, and they're at seven a.m. Eastern."

"Sorry. I was just looking at the international coverage on TV. From the BBC through Al-Jazeera to NHK in Tokyo it's all the same thing. All Kip."

"I've been seeing that."

"Did you see the latest, Diana? About his divorce?"

"His what?"

"I just caught it on TV. He's writing up his divorce filing. It just started."

Aboard *Intrepid*, 3:12 a.m. Pacific

Kip pauses, wondering why lawyers have to use such convoluted words to say the simplest of things. Drafting his own divorce filing has been relatively easy so far, though he's sure that it would disgust any lawyer. But there are no lawyers around *Intrepid*, and the process of creating a brand-new life simply has to begin with the gift of a conjugal pardon.

Once more he rereads the words, wondering if Sharon will even be alive by the time anyone actually sees what he's composed.

To the Pima County Superior Court, Arizona:

Comes now Kip Dawson in the matter of the request for dissolution of the marriage of Kip Dawson and Sharon Summers Dawson. Due to irreconcilable differences, Kip Dawson hereby requests the court to dissolve the marriage between the petitioner and the respondent. All Petitioner's personal property and all of Petitioner's share of the marital community property are hereby transferred to Respondent with Petitioner's blessing, inclusive of bank accounts, savings accounts, and all real or personal property of whatever kind wherever situated. Petitioner shall retain only his automobile, his father's wicker chair, his filing cabinet and the contents thereof, and one half of his retirement account. Petitioner requests the immediate grant of this petition. Signed electronically and certified correct in the physical absence of any living notary at this location, I hereto affix my signature, Kip Dawson.

He adds the date and sits back, wondering if he should finalize the divorce before going out with anyone on a fantasy date in his new, re-created life.

Yeah. It would be unseemly otherwise without a final decree.

Pima County Superior Court, Arizona. In the matter of Dawson versus Dawson, Petitioner's petition is granted in full as petitioned. By order of the court.

There! Now I'm truly free to start over.

Okay, now for the *real* story of my life.
I was born to a branch of the Rockefeller family and filthy rich from the get-go.

He stops, appalled by the flippant nature

355

of the words against the truly serious intent. He backspaces to erase the sentence. This may be fun, but it's deadly serious fun, if there is such a thing.

So, how do I want to have it start? How do I want to begin my ideal life?

Strange, he thinks. It should be so easy to figure out.

Chapter 32

Peterson Air Force Base,
Colorado Springs, Colorado,
May 20, 4:40 p.m. Pacific/
5:40 p.m. Mountain

Air Force wives learn early that family dinners are uncertain events. Especially when the husband is a four-star general. Such men are married to the Air Force first, leaving the wives to feel at times like little more than mistresses with commissary privileges.

Bitsy Risen checks her watch, aware she's been glued to the television all day — though her slight rebellion against complete submersion has been the piano sonatas playing gently in the background as closed captions march across the top of the silenced flat screen TV. Kip Dawson's amazing saga continues to scroll haltingly across the bottom.

"It's like the ultimate reality show and soap opera rolled into one," she's telling friends — including the equally solitary wife

357

of the NORAD vice commander who also expects to see nothing of her own husband until very, very late. They both know that a series of space launches are about to start ". . . popping off the planet like fleas off a dying dog," as Chris Risen said at five in the morning when he rolled out to find the shower. Bitsy knows the routine. When things start happening in space, NORAD wives open wine, turn on stereos, call their girlfriends, and mostly chill.

But the experience of reading the *Book of Kip*, as one of her friends refers to it, has been disturbing, and she thinks any wife would feel about the same. She sees Kip's words about wifely support and intimacy and sex, and she's surprised that it's prompting her to suddenly reassess her own, well, *performance*. It's the only word she can use within the context of Kip Dawson's laments — not that such worries really apply to her. She and Chris are still in love with each other, and when it comes to libido, they've always chased each other into the bedroom at the drop of a suggestive comment. Still do. So no problem there, right? At least none that she can sense.

Bitsy hopes there's nothing she's missing — no blind, unwarranted, dangerous assumptions she might be making.

Chris is satisfied, isn't he? As satisfied as I am?

She's kept herself trim and feminine and completely supportive of him in what they, as a team, both chose. But the whole subject is unsettling, as if she might suddenly discover that this marital bliss isn't real life, but a play in which she's become too immersed — an illusion that can evaporate as rapidly as a play reaches its finale.

Men like Chris *can* be seduced by illusions, too, she thinks. Like any pilot who bruises himself hauling on the controls trying to "save" a flight simulator that's actually bolted to a concrete floor.

But, she hopes what *they* have is anything but an illusion.

This has got to be deeply rattling a lot of women out there, she thinks, *especially those who've become lazy and forgotten to be lovers.* At the same time, she knows that the male mid-life explosion often has nothing to do with intimacy or frequency.

Sometimes it just happens.

Thank God, Chris and I escaped, she muses, already aware how rare it is to grow together instead of apart over the years. So many of their friends have long since split, leaving kids shuttling endlessly between cities and houses and sets of parents and stepparents. Not to mention the anger and divided retirement funds and the names of former spouses who can no longer be mentioned without pain.

The words begin scrolling across the bottom of the screen again after a pause. He's been working on the rewrite of his life and the thoughts and ideas and dreams are fascinating. In some ways it's been like getting a private, completely unauthorized look at the top-secret workings of the male mind.

And some of the things he's related — some of the things he's been through and felt — have brought her to tears.

The phone rings with Suzie, the vice commander's wife, on the other end. They've been talking on and off all afternoon. Bitsy takes the portable back to the couch.

"Did you see that montage Fox News did?" Suzie is asking, still amazed at the depth of the reactions through dozens of interviews.

"No. Tell me."

"I didn't know they had that many correspondents. They're flipping all around the country. For instance, there was this little beauty shop somewhere in Iowa, crammed with women who're holding kind of a vigil with the TV and hanging on to every word he writes. I swear some of those gals were sounding like rock groupies. It was strange."

"I'm not surprised," Bitsy replies. "Some of what he's said . . . you just want to hold the poor guy and tell him it's okay, you know?"

"Mother him, in other words?"

"Right. Don't you?"

"Okay, I'll admit it. But some of the women they've been talking to are thinking less of giving comfort than of getting him under one. But I don't know, I think it's *what* he's saying that's sexy. The guy is intelligent, and remember, there's nothing as sexy as a well-hung mind."

"Who said that?"

"I did. Seriously, I'll have to Google it."

"Well, sexy or not, the reactions of everyone out there are just amazing," Bitsy adds, still reading the evolving words. "What he's saying now is really thought provoking. I'm sitting here wondering about a lot of the subjects he's raised, not just how I would feel up there in his place."

"The most touching thing to me are all those people who're crowding airports and bus stations right now to race across the country and see parents or kids they haven't talked to in years, and every one they've interviewed says the same thing: I wouldn't be here if it wasn't for reading what that poor guy wrote, and realizing how little time there is in this life."

"Do they say which part, exactly, touched them the most?"

"Just the whole thing, and the anguish when he wrote about his son, I think."

"He's broken some sort of mass psychological dam, that's for sure," Bitsy says.

"You know, he wrote earlier about a dangerous intersection near his home in Tucson. For six years, he said, he couldn't get anyone in city government to pay attention to the need for a traffic light there, and three people died. Now, suddenly, because he wrote it up there and half the world read it, the Tucson City Council is debating the issue as we speak."

"I hadn't heard that. But yesterday he wrote about how much he loved Banff and Lake Louise in Canada, and almost instantly they sold out for the summer."

"You reading him right now?"

"About how he's become a well-known artist, with four kids and a beautiful, Brazilian wife?"

"Yes. His rewritten life. He wants four kids and he already *has* four kids."

"And the house in Tucson? He's put himself right back there, only this time it's a vacation residence. And the father he was going to fire and re-create? Still works for mining interests in Arizona, only now he always tells Kip he loves him."

"You know what impressed me? The guy thinks he's not brave. You probably read that part where he said he was far too timid to do anything bold. But he *is* brave. Look how much courage it took to delete everything he'd written for two days. He was really deleting his old life and moving on. How many of us could do that, even in writing?"

The sound of the front door opening catches her attention and Bitsy turns to find her husband pulling the door closed and waving. She waves back and ends the call, coming to him quickly, ignoring the prickle of the metallic buttons on his uniform as she enfolds him and holds on tight, aware he's slightly puzzled, though hugging her back enthusiastically. The hug progresses to a deep kiss and a loosened tie and shirt, and his hands begin an appreciative tour of her body as she tilts her head toward the bedroom.

"How 'bout it, sailor? Wanna get lucky?"

"Does the sun rise in the east?" he answers, grinning as he stops her momentarily. "But . . . not that I'm complaining, because

I'm sure not . . . but to what do I owe the pleasure?"

"Let's just say there's a poor guy flashing past overhead every ninety minutes who's reminding me how very, very lucky we are."

ASA Mission Control, Mojave, California, 4:55 p.m. Pacific

Arleigh Kerr replaces the receiver as Richard DiFazio comes back into the nearly deserted control room.

"Any news?" Arleigh asks, aware that the final urgent meeting between their director of maintenance and the chairman was scheduled for an hour before.

"It's final. We can't fly. I saw all the reasons up close and personal and he's right. We'd probably lose our second ship. How about you?"

"The Japanese have scrubbed their launch, pulled the plug."

"And Beijing?"

"Still scheduled for a liftoff tomorrow morning, three hours before the Russians, and four before the shuttle."

"Two down, three to go."

"He's got a fighting chance. Three launches are good odds."

"You're sure the scrubbers will hold?"

Arleigh looks at him long and hard before answering.

"No. I'm not sure. But death by CO_2 isn't instant. Not like suddenly cutting off his air. If someone can get him out of that airlock before he's too far gone, he could make it. We've briefed all of them."

"And if you were to bet?" Richard asks.

"I wouldn't. Not on this."

Kennedy Space Center, Florida, 5:05 p.m. Pacific/8:05 p.m. Eastern

There are times, Griggs Hopewell thinks, when he can almost recapture that old feeling of NASA invulnerability, those heady days when there was nothing they couldn't do.

It is night again at the Cape, the night before the launch, the frenetic preparations beginning to pay off, despite the delays. John Kent has gone to sleep for a few hours, but even he's feeling better about the prospects, and the crew is anxious to go, as most of them always are.

Griggs stands in the heavy night air, swatting at an occasional mosquito as he looks at the shuttle lit up so spectacularly a mile away. The morning he knows will be a challenge. He's aware that Miss Dorothy from D.C. has not given up, and thwarting her will take a masterful effort, the main thrust of which is just about to begin.

On schedule his cell phone rings and he answers with a quick flipping motion of his right hand.

"Yes?"

"Okay, we've got what we came for."

"Anything overt?"

"Not yet. If she's got a specific plan, it's buried in what we found, but there are some very interesting names in the database on her laptop."

"I'll meet you in ten minutes as planned."

He closes the phone, disgusted that he has to play cat and mouse the evening before a launch, just to be able to launch. But if Dorothy Sheehan makes the mistake he expects, she'll be facing criminal charges — the one element of leverage that may get Shear into another line of work.

Chapter 33

Aboard *Intrepid*, May 20, 6:00 p.m. Pacific

Kip sniffs the air again, fearful of confirming what his senses perceive.

And yes, it is there. Faint, but there, and where there is some smelly evidence of the process of decomposition, there will be more.

He's stopped typing, aware that his fanciful life story rewrite has wobbled too far afield. It's not even a good fantasy, and it feels so narcissistic. No, he decides, he should be writing about something else, maybe how he wishes the world was, rather than how rich or famous he'd like to be.

Well, not famous. That's never turned him on, though now he supposes he'll be a tiny footnote in space history: "First contest-winning space tourist dies in orbit."

With the odor, he can't get Bill out of his mind. Of course he's going to run out of breathable air anyway, but why hurry the moment?

Now, for some incomprehensible reason,

he's compelled to turn around and actually look at the bagged corpse as it floats Velcroed to the back wall.

What, he might have gone out for a stroll? Kip chides himself. How dumb that he has to actually look. But he had to.

Okay, there's the space suit idea. Put him in it and seal it, but now it's far too late for that.

He's read about the hatch and the airlock now, and knows what he didn't understand before: This isn't like a Hollywood movie where the hero can pull a handle and blow anything in the airlock into space. Someone live has to be inside the airlock to work the outer door. So that leaves him getting into Campbell's space suit, completely depressurizing the ship, opening both doors and floating Bill out, since there isn't room for two of them in the lock. He's tried to calculate how many hours of air would be lost, but he can't find the formula. At least he'd have the air pack on the suit, but when that ran out, he might have nothing.

So, I sit here and die with a stench, or just die faster in clean air. Wonderful choice.

So far it isn't that bad, though, he thinks. He has just a little over twenty-four hours anyway, according to his best calculation. So perhaps it won't matter.

To be on the safe side, he carefully hauls the sealed space-suit pack out of the side locker along with the helmet and opens it up, spreading it out and trying to remember the steps they'd been taught on what to don first.

Just in case, he thinks, putting the suit aside and returning to the keyboard. *Just in case.*

For minutes he sits quietly, listening to the hiss of the air recirculation system that is now less than a day from betraying him, and thinking about the idealized "life" he's constructed in words. He's tried to make it work in his mind as well. Bianca, his Brazilian wife who never was, not only loved him and couldn't wait for him to come home, she was the woman who was at his side in every thing, personal and professional, willing to advise him and even counter him when he headed down the wrong track, but as loving and as caring for him as he was for her.

I think so many men forget, or maybe never know, the basics of how a woman's mind works, which begins and often ends with the simple desire to be loved and cherished and not taken for granted. Expressions of love, tenderness, caring, attention, and appreciation are things we men want, so why do we forget that our ladies do, too? Yes, it's true that as a rule women give sex to get love, while men give love to get sex, but once the contract is struck, it should be kept, even if it's that basic.

He stops, thinking about Sharon, recognizing that the failures were not all hers, that he could have done so much better, even when he realized how self-absorbed and high maintenance she was.

Too bad, he thinks, *I'll never have the chance to put what I've learned into action.*

He leans into the keyboard again.

Anyway, with Bianca, I had never even imagined that kind of relationship, where you just long to *be* with each other.

Okay, look . . . I have a confession to make, future reader. I did have a previous life, but I deleted it. There was no Bianca. It's all my confused dream, my ideal, of what I would have liked my life to be like. I erased the real one because I wanted something better and more exciting, something filled with accomplishment, and I don't want to go back now and re-member — except for my kids, whom I love. My real kids. Jerrod, my firstborn,

Julie, and my twins, Carly and Carrie. More than anything else about my life, I miss them the most. All of them.

True, I did make myself a well-known artist. But why did I stop there? I could have decided to make myself a king or a dictator or a Bill Gates billionaire — someone else rich and spectacular. But suddenly I've come to the conclusion that whoever I decide to be, I'm still me, regardless of the trappings, the money, the position, and all the education in the world. I think who we are remains the same, and I think inside each one of us is a little child who won't tell the adult in us what's wrong. I'm sure there's a little girl in every woman and a little boy in every man. And very often that little child is still very upset over something that happened so far back he can't recall the details, only the hurt. So I think in this "new" life of mine, what I tried to palm off on you had everything to do with that little boy in me and what he's upset about, not Sharon, or even Lucy's loss.

No, I think in the time I have remaining, which isn't much now, if I could, I'd call my only sibling, my younger sister, and just tell her I love her. She's down there, and I can almost see her with every pass, doing that ear tugging thing she's done since childhood. But I can't reach her now. It's too late, and life's been happening for two years without contact, and even the last time I talked with her, we were still so very much at arm's length and . . . Dadlike. No "I love you's." My father never used the phrase. Phrases like that embarrassed him.

When I was born, Dad was forty-one. So many years later, here he was an infirm eighty-something, couldn't take care of himself, and Mom was gone, so I had to act. I found a good retirement facility; I knew he hated it but he went quietly and I sold the house. I was very efficient and took a month off to get everything done. I thought he'd appreciate that — the efficiency. And once I'd made sure everything was okay, I said good-bye. With a handshake, the way he always dealt with me. I was just south in Tucson and I intended to come by at least every month — he was just a couple of hours up the road in Phoenix. But something always came up, and when I'd try to call too late at night, I'd get a small lecture from the night nurse. I didn't like that, so I used it as a license to stop calling. So life slipped by and one night when I was lamenting the lack of open expressions of love in my family, I decided to go see him and tell him I loved him, words that had never been spoken between us. The decision made me feel good. I was going to take the time because I could never seem to find the right moment to call, and because he was getting very old and frail. I started looking for the right opportunity — which really means that I started making excuses why I didn't have the time. I was still playing that game when word came that he'd died. Alone. Just up the road.

Every time this spacecraft soars over Phoenix I think about him. All those years, and I could never just call and say, "Hey, Dad, you know what? You don't have to say anything, but I love you."

Terra-Net Corporation,
North American Network Control Center,
Pittsburgh, Pennsylvania,
7:45 p.m. Pacific/10:45 p.m. Eastern

The unique three-dimensional display in the middle of the circular command center is beginning to change, but only one technician sees it. The colored lines representing ground, tower, satellite, and fiber-optic connections across a quarter of the globe are shifting from green, the color of routine voice traffic, to yellow, orange, red, the colors of increased bandwidth utilization, the telltale indication that perhaps as many as a million people more than normal suddenly picked up their phones for a long distance call.

The technician keeps his eyes on the plasma display as he flails his right hand for the attention of the shift supervisor, whose eyes also go to the display. Both men stand in puzzled silence as a third checks with another major telephonic network, discovering the same sudden jump in activity there.

"Globecomm reports the same increase, including overseas traffic, and three of the cellular networks report the same. In fact, there are indications this is happening worldwide."

More of the personnel in the control center join the head-scratching as they monitor the automatic rerouting of call overloads. Landlines that are normally standby-only have snapped into use, some routing through the old, almost decommissioned, AT&T land-based microwave system that first telephonically united the country in the nineteen fifties.

A young woman with pulled back hair and thick glasses leaves her position several tiers back and comes up quietly behind the supervisor, a laptop computer in her hands.

"I know what's causing this. I just called my mother, too."

" 'Scuse me?" the supervisor says. "Everyone's calling your mother?"

"No. Everyone's calling someone they should have called long ago. It's Kip Dawson, and what he just said." She turns the laptop around so the team can read the words on the screen — as ten more trunk lines go red and a routing overload alarm sounds off somewhere in the command center.

Chapter 34

Kennedy Space Center, Florida,
May 21, 5:00 a.m. Pacific/8:00 a.m. Eastern

Once the "Enter" key is pressed, she knows there will be no going back.

Dorothy Sheehan thinks over the steps again, restraining herself from sending the benign bit of computer code into the system until she's as certain as she can be that all bases are covered. The entire assignment has been an exhilarating contest of wills, a shadow fight between Griggs Hopewell and herself, but she's thinking ahead to the good life to follow in the Beltway, with only an office job and real weekends to herself. Of course maybe she won't be happy unless she's walking a tightrope somewhere. Her years with the CIA were terrifying and wonderful at the same time, mainly wonderful because she never ended up caught or compromised.

Okay. Here goes.

Amazing, she thinks, how the tiny click of a key can be the beginning of a causal chain that blocks a billion-dollar launch. She waits for the tiny string of computer code to add itself to the appropriate program and gets the return message before signing off and shutting down. If it works as planned, the minute alteration will disrupt things just long enough to scrub the launch, the code alteration then disappearing.

At least, in theory that's the way it should go. And if it does, Geoff Shear will have to follow through on his promises.

Dorothy carefully wipes off the keyboard and anything she's touched before moving back to the door of the empty office, one she selected some days before on learning the normal occupant was out of town.

She thinks back to the close call last night and the wisdom of always figuring out from the outside of a hotel which is her window and checking for lights when she comes back. Otherwise she would have walked right in on whomever Hopewell had sent to search her laptop. There was nothing to find, of course, and she hadn't planned to use it for a mainframe insertion, anyway. Much too risky, and for the past forty-eight hours she's hoped that one or more of the legitimate problems she's found can be accelerated into an aborted launch.

But she's found that Griggs Hopewell

comes by his can-do reputation honestly, and item by item, problem by problem, he's kept working his magic and driving his team, four hours before liftoff, with everything still a go.

She waits with the office door cracked slightly until she's sure the hallway is clear, then slips out. Her temporary office in an adjacent building is sufficient for monitoring what's happening, but its computer terminal absolutely can't be used outside the boundaries.

Dorothy chuckles at the thought of the people waiting right now to catch her computer's numeric signature entering the mainframe. They'll be waiting in vain, of course, but their trap was cleverly laid, and when she got bored enough to go look for it on the mainframe, she almost didn't find it.

She checks her watch — 8:12 a.m. Eastern. The slightly delayed Chinese launch should be happening right now. She knows Shear will be calling the President for permission to scrub the second someone else achieves orbit, and if so, the little adjustment she made may never even make an appearance before it evaporates.

The possibility that Hopewell and company might somehow defeat her, or worse, catch her in the act, is unfortunately part of the game. And she fears that if she gets in trouble, Shear will turn on her completely and play mister innocent while she twists in the wind.

But that's not going to happen, Dorothy thinks. *All my bases are covered. And besides, I'm not forcing anyone to make a no-go launch decision. I'm just helping them with their rationale, and saving the nation one hell of a lot of money in the process.*

Aboard *Intrepid*, 6:03 a.m. Pacific

For perhaps the first time since his voyage began, Kip wakes up without falling.

He *is* falling, of course — continuously around the planet — his Newtonian tendency to travel in a straight line continuously warped into an orbital curve by the centripetal force of gravity pulling him down at the same rate inertia tries to take him straight on into space.

Kip rubs his eyes, aware he's getting comfortable with his weightlessness, this feeling of floating. He lets some of the explanations from high school physics replay until he's jarred back to reality.

Oh my God, this is day five, isn't it?

According to the scrubber charts — and

he's checked them dozens of times — there can't be a day six.

The panic buzzing in his head is almost overwhelming and he closes his eyes, trying to fight back hysteria. The fifth day is no longer an inestimable series of sunrises and sunsets in the future. It's today. Sometime in the next twenty-four hours it ends.

And so does he.

I'm going to die today, Kip tells himself, but the words in his head aren't believable enough, so he speaks them out loud, having to clear his throat to finish.

"I'm going to . . . I'm going to die today. So, what do I think about that?"

Reality sucks, is what I think! But there's no humor in a line that usually makes him chuckle.

I thought I was resigned to this. I thought I was ready.

But if so, why are his hands shaking? He's known for four days he wasn't going to make it, but facing it now overwhelms him.

He forces a deep breath, suddenly remembering he should carefully sample the air first. But either the odor from Bill's decomposing remains has abated or he's become used to it. In any event he thinks he can last the day now without a spacewalk.

After all, he thinks, a spacewalk would be a very dangerous thing to try.

Wait a minute! Dangerous? Jesus!

He's actually embarrassed that he's sitting here with hours left to live and worrying that a spacewalk might be an unsafe thing to do.

So what if it's dangerous? I could play with matches today, run with scissors, insult a serial killer, or rat on the mafia with complete impunity!

At least he's coaxed a chuckle out of himself.

He's read that death row inmates, no matter how brazen and sociopathic, lose their bravado just before execution, and he sees why. It's not hypothetical anymore. Leaving this life and this body is about to be his new reality. Every human's fear of what lies on the other side drowns all the neat Biblical assurances in a tsunami of doubt.

Kip works to control his breathing, which has become fast and shallow. He feels his heart rate declining.

This is my last chance to say whatever I want to say, he thinks. He's typed so much — hundreds of pages if he includes what he erased — he needs to go back and read it. But there's no time.

What happens, he wonders, when scrubbers saturate? Will he just suddenly feel light-headed? Will he keel over? Or will it be long and agonizing?

He catches sight of the unfolded emergency space suit floating near Bill's bagged remains and wonders why the idea of putting it on and going outside is tugging at him. Should he do it to die out there? Would it be any easier?

No, something else, some reason that he almost recalls from a dream and can't put his finger on.

The tool kit, that's it!

The suit has a small tool kit like nothing he's seen before. They showed the components in ground school but he barely paid attention. Now he turns and pulls the suit to him, searching for the correct pocket and pulling out the silver-plated kit.

That is what I remember! he thinks, finding a pair of wire clippers and three colors of electrical tape along with several garden-variety wire nuts. The thought about a spacewalk wasn't for hurrying his demise, it was all about trying to repair whatever had been screwed up by the object that hit them.

He can visualize himself wiggling into the suit, figuring out how to pressurize it, stuffing himself in the tight little airlock, and floating outside. Maybe another meteor will get him, fast and painlessly. Or cosmic rays sterilize him (not that there's any chance of that being a problem now). And he'd be doing all that struggling to play in-flight mechanic? Get real.

Yet he thinks, it's like guzzling chicken soup for a cold. It may not help, but it can't hurt.

Whether the fatigue he feels suddenly is emotional he can't tell, but the thought of flailing around trying to put on that complicated pressure suit is exhausting, and he decides not to decide for a few hours. After all, there's another delectable cereal bar and much more to write before he's ready to think about trying. And maybe it would be a lot more comfortable just to stay inside and slip away slowly.

But there it is again, that misguided feeling of hope, a glimmer that there could be some way out he hadn't considered as he turns back to the keyboard.

NASA Headquarters, Washington, D.C., 6:10 a.m. Pacific/9:10 a.m. Eastern

The fact that it's ten minutes past nine and his phone hasn't rung can't be good.

Geoff Shear opens the tiny instrument

and finds the symbol that confirms the ringer is set to on. It is.

The Chinese Long March missile boosting their crew capsule into low Earth orbit should have cycled through first- and second-stage cutout by now and their astronaut — all by himself in a three-person craft — should be approaching orbital velocity.

The cell phone suddenly corks off, startling Geoff who didn't realize he was that jumpy. The practiced act of sweeping the phone toward his face while flipping it open is completely unconscious.

"Yes?"

"The Chinese scrubbed, Geoff. This is Jake at NRO."

"Shit! How're the Russians doing?"

"Still on countdown for a noon-our-time liftoff."

"I knew the Chinese would fink out."

"I think they tried hard, but there was a major fuel leak early this morning, and they couldn't resolve it. One of my people speaks Mandarin and we had him patched into their comm channels."

"So they're completely out?"

"Yes. I'll call you back, as things progress at Baikonaur."

Chapter 35

Cheyenne Mountain, North American
Aerospace Defense Command,
Colorado Springs, Colorado,
May 21, 8:41 a.m. Pacific/
9:41 a.m. Mountain

"What now?" Chris Risen asks, glancing at the chief master sergeant and noting his sudden shift of attention to the commercial television feed being displayed on his console.

"The Secretary of State, sir. They were just interviewing him coming out of the White House. Kip set off another controversy by recommending a type of death penalty for countries that don't cooperate with the civilized world."

"And the Secretary has to respond."

"Yes, sir."

"Where are we on the countdowns, Chief?"

"At the Cape they're at T minus eighteen minutes. At Baikonur, T minus nine."

In the old days of the Soviet Union the idea of a live video feed from the Russian spaceport would have been James Bondish, a fantasy. But now, Chris thinks, we're sitting here watching that very video feed live and in color, as are the Russian people.

He can see the liquid oxygen venting from the Russian proton booster assembly, the gantry now moved out of the way, the scene looking very similar to the video feed coming in from the Cape.

"Chief, do we have a pool going on whether NASA will cancel if the Russians lift off?"

The chief is grinning. "A pool, sir? You mean, as in gambling? As in a chief master sergeant informing the commander of NORAD that his people are violating regulations?"

"Sorry. Of course I didn't mean that."

"Yes, sir."

"Put me down for twenty that we scrub."

"Yes, sir. But for the record, I know nothing."

Launch Control, Kennedy Space Center, Florida, 8:44 a.m. Pacific/ 11:44 a.m. Eastern

"Out of limits means out of limits, Griggs!" The launch director is standing now, hands on hips, one of his people standing beside him, the computer screen showing the excessive temperature readings displayed on his master console.

"Stand by, Cully. Do *not* declare a hold yet."

"Look at the count, Griggs! How long do you need?"

Griggs has a receiver to his ear and a prepositioned computer team on the other end, physically stationed at a hastily constructed war room one building away.

"Two minutes."

"You've got forty seconds."

Cully Jones shakes his head and turns back to the screen, rolling his eyes at the engineer waiting for direction on what to do with the temperature indication climbing in a tank that could theoretically explode if it, in fact, was to heat up another twenty-five degrees.

"Watch it like a hawk. If it tops redline plus thirty, we open the vent and hold the countdown."

"Got it."

Cully turns back to Griggs, aware of what he's doing but equally aware that a high reading can't be easily written off as just another artificial computer-generated anomaly. Like a pilot's guiding philosophy of instrument flight, safety demands belief in your gauges, until you have solid, almost irrefutable evidence they're lying.

Cully can feel his blood pressure inching up, something he can usually control, but the series of bad readings and interrupted communications that have marked the last ten minutes are either evidence of a serious, systemic computer glitch — as Griggs insists without much evidence — or a launch sliding toward disaster. This does not feel right.

Griggs turns back to him.

"Okay! Cully, check it now. We're reading raw pickup data and bypassing the distribution processor that's been causing so many bad readings."

The display blinks and the high temperature suddenly drops thirty critical degrees into the green.

"Jesus Christ!" Cully snarls, his eyes on the reading lest it rise again. He turns to Griggs. "That's real? I can trust it?"

"You bet. This is just more of the nonsense we've been fighting all morning. The basic distribution processing program is apparently corrupted and we have no time to reboot the system."

Another engineer is in his ear on the intercom, and Cully closes his eyes to concentrate on what he's saying.

"Talk to me."

"I have a complete data dropout on the SRBs. Total."

"Stand by!" Once more Cully Jones turns to Hopewell, who is still hanging on to the receiver with his emergency computer team on the other end.

"Griggs?"

"I heard, goddammit! Hang on."

"I'm declaring a hold."

The countdown is descending through T minus sixteen minutes, the tension in the control room increasing exponentially.

Chapter 36

Aboard *Intrepid*, May 21, 8:44 a.m. Pacific

Kip leans into the keyboard once more.

Having now solved all of mankind's problems (the doomed passenger says, facetiously) it's time to turn my attention to some of my own. The challenge is how and when I should pull the plug, or should I just plan to slip off to "sleep." That problem has been rattling around my head all morning (as measured by my watch, of course, rather than the continuous ninety-minute cycle of sunrises and sunsets that have me humming the song from *Fiddler on the Roof*, and shedding tears.)

The other thing that has me fibrillating is an embarrassment: If I had a boat that sprang a leak, wouldn't I at least *try* to plug the leak? Of course. But I've sat here for days waiting for Godot, assuming that nothing more can be done, even though deep down I've known all along it's not true. There is one more overt, physical thing I can do, or at least try.

I'm going to wiggle into Bill's space suit and see if there's anything I can repair outside. What are the chances? Below absolute zero. Yes, I'm somewhat mechanically inclined and I can wire up a mean set of speaker wires. Actually my BS degree in electrical engineering is really a smoke screen, since I never used it, and especially not with high-tech messes caused by high-speed objects hitting spacecraft.

And what's the worse case? I die outside instead of inside, but better with my boots on . . . space boots though they may be.

You know, I'm feeling a little punchy. I wonder if the CO_2 buildup has already begun? I feel more loose. Or maybe just feeling relieved we're getting close to the end. Relieved and scared out of my mind. That, I think, is the real reason I'm going to go outside and play with the vacuum. I need something to do besides sit here and wait for the inevitable.

I hope you understand — whoever you are and whenever in the distant future you read this — just knowing another human is absorbing all this verbiage has given me a form of companionship. I thank you for that! I thank you for sitting through my grumbling and pontificating and crying and the poor expressions of how I would do things down there if I had the proverbial magic wand.

If any of my kids are still alive when this is found and read, please see that they get the separate letters I've written to all four individually. And as for Sharon, in case she is still alive, just this: I'm sorry. I wish things could have been better for us as a couple.

And there is one last overall message I guess I want to leave.

I want for all of you a future in which every human has firmly in his or her mind the scene the three *Apollo 8* astronauts saw back in 1968 when this tiny, beautiful blue marble we live on rose over the edge of the moon as they raced along the far side — an almost iridescent oasis of beauty in an endless, star-speckled sea of black nothingness — and they realized they were looking at spaceship Earth, their home. Suddenly wars and borders and conflicts based on economics and theories seemed utterly stupid, and while in reality we're a long way from being a species that universally shares that startling view, we must — you must — keep moving in that direction.

That goal of harmony and love that a man from Galilee tried to teach us in amazing simplicity so long ago is still the goal we should strive for, regardless of what labels we put on the message. "Us" seems a strange concept, since I'm leaving. But I was a part of spaceship Earth and the human family, a pioneering species that is still relatively blind to a very profound truth that's so hard to see when you're working hard and paying bills and raising kids: We are all so very connected! Even me, here, waiting to die in space. I'm connected to everyone down there, and . . . you know, it's amazing. . . . as soon as I type these words I feel the warmth of uncounted prayers and a sea of good will and good wishes, as if the entire population of the planet was somehow telepathically saying, "Everything's okay. Regardless of what happens, it's okay." I know that virtually no one down there can discern a single thought of mine, and may never read a word of this. But since I've been up here I haven't felt as enfolded as I do at this moment. But now it's time for some pro forma struggling. Some self-help that I have to try, so that I will know I didn't just sit here and ignore options, no matter how bizarre and impossible they may be. So, if I don't get to write another word, thank you. I left this life as calmly as I could. Not bravely, just calmly. And you know, after everything is said and done, I have been very, very fortunate.

Kip sits back and rereads the last few lines, hoping to feel a rush of satisfaction. But the only closure is that now he can't wait any longer.

The space suit is floating behind the command chair as he unstraps and moves into position to use the breadth of the small cabin for the struggle. Bill was at least ten or fifteen pounds lighter and a little shorter.

He unzips and prepares it as best he can before shucking his flight suit, finding it surprisingly easy in zero gravity to pull the legs and arms in place, hauling a bit to get his head in and up through the metal helmet collar. He can feel the fabric of the shoulders pressing down firmly because of the difference in their height.

Item by item, gloves, boots, zippers, interlocks, and air packs, he assembles the space suit until the only remaining items are the helmet and pressurizing.

He checks the "Emergency Donning" checklist again, puzzling through some of the nomenclature and finally finds the appropriate lock once the helmet is in place, the white inside hood pulled over his head. The small control panel on his left arm is already glowing with a small LED annunciator, and he pushes the button to power it up and pressurize, hearing the tiny fans come alive as the oxygen mix floods the suit and the arms and legs go semirigid.

He checks the clock on the forward panel. Twenty-five minutes have elapsed.

Not bad for a rank amateur, Kip thinks, checking that the small tool kit is secured inside the Velcroed pocket before floating to the airlock.

Even for a small, naked man slicked up with grease, the airlock would be a challenge. For a moderately sized man in a pressurized space suit, it's like folding himself into a post office box, and at first Kip all but gives up.

This damn thing must be here for show only! Kip thinks after trying first an arm, then a leg, then his head through the inner door, and finding that either the service pack with the air supply and batteries or some other appendage catches on the door sill each time. He feels an urgency propelling his struggle and cautions himself to slow down. A ripped suit or damaged service pack will doom the entire effort.

Okay, then, let's go back to headfirst.

He rotates himself around until he's floating on his back and slowly guides his head and shoulders and torso inside, curling forward as he carefully pulls in his legs, folding them just enough to let the boots clear.

Like crawling into a front-loading washing machine, he thinks.

He pulls the inner plug-type door closed and works the locking mechanism until a small green light illuminates on a panel he barely can see.

There are several switches to be thrown before the pressure dump valve will motor open, and he goes through the sequence carefully until he's down to the last button push.

Kip takes a deep breath, remembering almost too late to unfold the nylon tether strap and hook it into the metal loop within the lock. He assumes the outer door is supposed to remain open while he's outside. Nothing else would make sense.

The button pushes easily and he takes a deep breath, as if the air in his suit was going to be sucked out as well. The pressure gauge begins dropping in pounds per square inch, moving toward zero, but nothing changes in the suit except the sudden increase in the rigidity of the arms and legs.

An orange zero-pressure light illuminates on the panel, and then a green light on the latch mechanism, and Kip begins rotating the vaultlike wheel to remove the latches, surprised at how easily the door just swings open into the void.

Chapter 37

ASA Headquarters, Mojave, California,
May 21, 8:51 a.m. Pacific

Like a gathering of pallbearers, Diana thinks as she glances at the stricken faces of those standing outside Richard DiFazio's office. Richard hangs up the phone and motions them in, most electing to stand, hands thrust deep in pockets, eyes downcast at the latest message from Kip.

Diana finds the couch and sits, sensing their immense frustration.

"We've thought through everything we know, boss," Arleigh begins. "Using a laser to blink Morse code at him was about the last, most desperate suggestion. But there's no way to tell him no fewer than two spacecraft are trying to get off their pads to reach him."

"He's going to die trying to spacewalk, right?" Richard asks.

The deeply weary breath Arleigh Kerr draws and exhales seems to answer the question.

"Not necessarily. We taught him — we

teach all of them — the basics about a spacewalk. If he can't get the suit on and get it inflated and tested to a green light status, he probably won't try it."

"But if he does?"

"There's no way this guy can fix a spacecraft, and he doesn't have a hand thruster, so if he forgets to connect his tether, he'll . . . just float away. Or he'll tear his suit and die trying."

"Or he'll just spend his final hour outside on purpose," Richard adds, speaking their collective thoughts. "I know I probably would. With Bill's body inside getting ripe and all."

"Well, the view's going to be better out there," Arleigh agrees.

"So, bottom line, there's no chance for him outside, and even if he succeeds in not floating off, there's no way he can fix the ship. Right?"

Several of the men shrug and Arleigh voices the response. "We don't have any idea what it would take to repair the ship, but the chances are slim to none. Anyway, if we figure an hour for him to get ready past the time he stopped typing, he should be heading for the airlock now. That means about one and a half hours and he'll either be dead or back inside and typing again."

★ ★ ★

Kip floats out of the airlock the same way
he got in: head and shoulders first, checking
to make sure the tether is tight before
turning around and facing the surface of the
Earth passing below without the constraint
of *Intrepid*'s tiny windows.

Oh my God!

Words are failing him, even in his mind.
With almost a hundred-and-eighty-degree
view from his helmet, he's simply flying
along, his own satellite, as part of Texas
slides along soundlessly beneath him. Only
the fans and the small hiss of the air supply
break the silence, and he turns starward,
shocked by the moon hovering clear and
bright above. For the longest time he just
stares, floating, flying, incredulous, and
wishing he'd done this days before.

No point in going back inside, he figures.
*What a way to leave! Thank you, God, for
this chance!*

He can see the Gulf Coast below, along
with New Orleans, and thinks fondly of the
times he's enjoyed the chicory coffee and
beignets with their snowstorm of powdered
sugar at Café du Monde, in spite of being ignored by the waiters.

Pensacola is visible to the east, as is Panama City, which triggers a few more memories. A line of thunderstorms is marching toward Atlanta to the north and he can see lightning flashing, noiselessly visible from space. Not as impressive as the thunderstorms he's seen over Africa in the darkness, lightning pulsing away over a thousand miles as if the storms were communicating in bursts. But the storms near Atlanta are impressive enough.

Nothing can prepare you for the magnificence of this! he thinks, wishing he still had the laptop in front of him and the ability to share this, too, with the distant future.

He knows there's a depressurization safety sequence to be followed in order to blow the suit when it's time. Or he can just cut off the oxygen. But he thinks a sudden depressurization might be better and quicker. The suit has approximately an hour and a half of air, and then the options expire. So he'll have one and a half hours to take all this in and . . .

Whoa, I came out here to check the tires, he recalls, pulling on the tether to rotate back toward *Intrepid* and move in from where he's been floating five feet away.

He sees no indication of meteor damage near the door, so he begins pulling himself upward and over the top of the spacecraft. But there are no handholds and suddenly he's floating up and away slowly with no choice but to pull on the tether, which starts him back toward the door.

Kip floats motionless by the open hatch, while he figures out how to get to the other side. As far as he can tell, there is no handheld thruster to propel him, and no handholds on the fuselage to hang on to. But he has a tether at least as long as the spacecraft, and the nose is only fifteen or so feet in front of the hatch.

Kip uses the open door as a launching pad for propelling himself along the fuselage toward the nose. He waits until he's just abeam of the tip of the nose before looping the tether over the top of the fuselage and around like a rodeo cowboy throwing a rope. With the line now going over the top from the door and coming back to him under the chin of the nose, he tightens his grip and pulls, letting his shoulder bounce off the left side of the nose. Suddenly he's floating back toward the door, and he uses the structure to stop himself and turn upside down before starting to pull himself around beneath the fuselage using the tether that's now snaking over the top and around the bottom. Carefully, making sure to keep his speed and momentum as slow and controllable as possible, he comes around to the right side and finds what he's been looking for.

A hole approximately three inches wide of flared metal and fiberglass sits just next to where an inspection panel has been blown away, providing access inside. The cavity is just behind the point where the pressure bulkhead divides the livable capsule inside from the service areas behind. He carefully touches one of the edges, closing his fingers around it to stop his drift. There are wires visible just inside. He can see a major wiring bundle slit in half by whatever hit them as it exited the side at a shallow angle.

No wonder the engine wouldn't fire!

He stares at the damage, wondering whether to just go back, or try for a closer look.

The small tool kit in the leg pocket of his suit contains a knife and electrical tape, both on tethers of their own. Overcoming the momentary urge to just give up and return inside, he begins assembling what he thinks he'll need as he floats to one side of the hole. He places the knife beside him and lets go, marveling at how it just sits there in mid-space gyrating slightly with each tug of the tether, its own tiny little satellite. He supposes if he disconnected it and batted it down toward Earth, it would eventually de-orbit and burn up. But right now it's obediently staying more or less where he wants it.

The severed wiring is chaotic, but as he looks more closely, he can count perhaps twenty actual wires completely cut and others merely grazed.

Okay, suppose I treat this like speaker wire? Is there color coding? Yes! Look at that! Red, orange, and green stripes go to whatever else has red, orange, and green stripes. I'll probably run out of air before I can get them all, but what the hell.

He secures himself with his left hand, which is holding both the edge of the hole and the wire, working inside the hole and letting the knife blade bite into the insulation around the first cut wire, scraping it away neatly before finding the other end and doing the same. Twisting them together and taping off the result is incredibly awkward in the inflated gloves and the worry about slicing open his suit on the jagged edge of the hole is great, but he keeps each movement under tight control and slowly works through each of the wires, going faster as he gets more familiar with the bulky gloves.

There is intense heat from the sun's unfiltered rays on his left side and he remembers to change position to keep from over-whelming the suit, which is getting warm inside.

The suit's control panel is showing twenty minutes of air left by the time he finishes splicing every wire for which he can locate a mate. He folds and replaces the knife and the tape, before pulling himself back over the top to the open airlock door, where he stops to make a critical decision.

It would be so much more meaningful to die out here, he thinks. *Just a button push. But, if I do, I'll never know if the repairs have changed anything. Is there any chance the radios could be working now and I could reach someone?*

And what if, somehow, he's reconnected the rocket?

No! he cautions himself. *Don't rekindle all your hopes! No way the engine is going to light off. That requires a professional. The best I can hope for is that somehow I've bumped something the right way and re-stored space-ground communications. But as long as I'm floating here trolling for meteors, I'll never know.*

Five more minutes, Kip decides, drinking in the view as the terminator slips by below, just past the Red Sea, and he watches the glow from what he decides must be the

Saudi Arabian desert city of Riyadh sitting like a twinkling, grounded star against the darkness of the desert to the east.

He knows by now that the retrofire point — should he need it — is just under an hour away, which means that even if he decides to test the rocket motor, he'll have to wait for that window. Not that anything is going to happen.

But he does feel the tiniest glimmer of hope.

Okay, he decides. *Let's get back in, and once I'm sure nothing's going to change, I'll come back out and end it here.*

Chapter 38

Office of the Administrator, NASA
Headquarters, Washington, D.C.,
May 21, 9:06 a.m. Pacific/
12:06 p.m. Eastern

The Russian rescue mission and the administrator of NASA go into motion at the same moment. In Russia the *Soyuz* spacecraft clears the Baikonaur launch pad while in the Beltway Geoff Shear is already speaking to the White House aide he's had holding for ten minutes.

"Okay. Put him on. Quickly."

Less than a minute goes by before the President picks up to hear that the Russians are underway.

"I urge you to let me scrub our launch, Mr. President. It's unnecessary now."

"How much time on our countdown, Geoff?"

"Coming up on eleven minutes, sir. We just came off the hold."

"Geoff, I want our guys to do the job. You know that."

"Yes, sir, but . . ."

"And I'll take the heat for the additional funds, but this is the sort of mission the shuttle was supposed to be able to do. Even if we have to compete with a parking lot full of spacecraft up there I want Kip on our shuttle. And that way the poor guy doesn't have to ride to the space station first and spend, what, ten days before coming back? I mean, he could be injured."

"He's not injured, sir. He's mentioned nothing about being injured."

"Well, psychologically he needs to come home."

"Yes, but, Mr. President, we've pushed everybody down there very hard to accomplish this emergency mission so we can comply with your directives, and frankly there have been all sorts of technical problems, and even though we've gotten past most of them . . ."

"When?"

"Today. During the countdown. And in the previous few days. We're hanging it out."

"Are you telling me the launch is unsafe?"

A contemplative silence lasts a moment too long.

"Geoff, are you saying on the record this is too dangerous? You have good reason to believe that?"

"I . . . don't know for a fact that there's any inordinate danger, more than usual, but whenever you push hard like this, things can go wrong."

"What's gone wrong?"

"Just a lot of computer problems and glitches and low readings. The countdown has been threatened over and over again. But it tells me . . ."

"But you can't say definitively that you're violating any safety parameters?"

"No."

"Very well, then. We launch, Geoff. And that's that. Get our guys up there and get Kip Dawson down safely. Clear enough?"

"Very well, Mr. President. Keep your fingers crossed."

Geoff hangs up and sits for less than a minute, weighing the dangers of triggering what he considers his own "nuclear" option — his last chance to keep the shuttle grounded. It's a no-brainer, he figures, and suddenly he's pulling his cell phone from his pocket and punching up the screen to send a coded, numeric text message:

80086672876

He checks the TV monitor on his desk. Less than ten minutes. The display loses one minute before his phone beeps and the return message appears with a simple "OK."

Kennedy Space Center, Florida, 9:08 a.m. Pacific/12:08 p.m. Eastern

Dorothy Sheehan stares at the cell phone display in disbelief, wondering if the number she's been given as a code matches what she's seeing.

She quickly checks a secure page in her PDA and feels a shiver when the number matches.

It's the same!

If Shear had asked her to have a cyanide capsule embedded in a tooth against capture she wouldn't be more surprised. The launch will be safely scrubbed, but she'll be almost instantly traceable as the saboteur.

There's no way she can use the computer in the office she's been assigned, and there's no time left to return to the vacant office and computer she was using. She snatches up her small briefcase and races to the door, confirming the hall is clear before entering and walking quickly to the far end of the corridor.

Why didn't I prepare for this? she thinks, knowing the answer. What she's already embedded can have no direct safety impact on the shuttle or the crew, but what Geoff Shear has just ordered could lead to a major computer shutdown just before liftoff. For the first time in days she feels her confidence ebbing away. Real fright is taking its place. This is her space program, too. It's one thing to influence the scrubbing of a launch, and another entirely to do so at the very last second when the readings could confuse the launch crew.

The thought of just walking away and reporting there wasn't time crosses her mind, but her deal with Shear depends on success. She knows him well. And Shear is the one charged with making the tough strategic decisions. She's merely the operative, like carrying out the Company's orders years ago. If she fails him on purpose, she's second-guessing policy, as well as screwing up her own future. Besides, what he's decided to do is keep everyone safely on the ground, and that can't be bad.

Dorothy ducks into a stairwell, her heartbeat accelerating as she tries to think of a computer terminal she could reach in time that would leave no traces of her presence. Putting the commands into the master com-

411

puter through the Internet is impossible. The NASA firewall is impenetrable. She has to use a computer connected to the main network and from inside. Shear thinks she's preloaded everything and she should have. Dammit! She really should have!

God, that was arrogant to think I wouldn't need it!

She glances at her watch. Just over seven minutes remain, and if she can't insert it before T minus three, it'll be too dangerous, both for the shuttle and for her.

Okay, think! If I use any office computer, they'll have it traced in an hour, since I was in the same building and Griggs already knows my mission. I can't get in from outside, and there's no time to . . . wait a minute!

She tries the next three office doors, finding the third unlocked, and races to the most isolated computer terminal she can find. She brings out the laptop in her bag and starts it spinning up while she pulls on surgical gloves before making the entries in the office computer.

And within a minute she's in, a connection established from inside to out through her laptop's air modem.

So, I opened my own gate to the castle from inside.

The program she needs to load is a complicated string of computer language and she checks the connection, moving through the office computer's now-breached firewall to the main NASA network, looping it around through a server to confuse where it came from.

Four minutes to go. That should be enough.

The code has to replicate over the course of at least a minute before inserting itself in the master program as a basic program patch. She takes a deep breath and hits the load button, then immediately shuts down the connection and races from the room, relieved to find the hallway empty. She returns to her assigned office and almost dives for her own office computer keyboard to type in a mundane search request, a routine act that will bear a date and time stamp and help prove that she was nowhere else when some "hacker" loaded the illicit code.

Launch Control, Kennedy Space Center, Florida, 9:13 a.m. Pacific/12:13 a.m. Eastern

"Yes!"

The report from Griggs Hopewell is accompanied by a broad grin as he lowers the receiver and turns to the launch director, the report from his computer team still ringing victoriously in his ears. "Caught her red-handed monkeying with the program, and my guys stopped the program patch she tried to install."

Cully Jones is nodding appreciatively but his eyes are on the countdown clock now ticking under two minutes while he presses his headset closer to his ear and motions Griggs to silence. "What? Which one?"

Cully leans into his screen as he triggers a series of entries before answering the reporting engineer somewhere in the room.

"Shit! I see it. Has it been steady up to now?"

Griggs punches into the same net and struggles his headset back on in time to hear the remainder of the response.

". . . no problem I can see before, but it's suddenly climbing into overpressure. The book says we've got a thirty-degree tolerance and we're approaching it."

"Go raw data and recheck it."

"I can't. This one doesn't go through the same processor."

"The readout is hardwired or telemetry?"

"That's telemetry, Cully. Fifty psi to go and still climbing. I have a corresponding temperature rise and a pressure warning on the relief valve."

Griggs flips through one of the manuals as fast as he can, conscious of the count reaching T minus one minute. A complicated wiring and transmission diagram opens before him and he goes directly to the circuit controlling the dangerous readings they're discussing before turning to Jones.

"Cully, the readings go through a computer processor. Not the same one, but equally vulnerable."

The auxiliary power units are already on-line and consuming the shuttle's hydrazine fuel supplies, and there are mere moments left before the launch is committed. Although Jones's voice is steady and controlled, the pressure he's feeling is excruciating.

"I thought your guys stopped the interference?"

"They did," Griggs says. "But something from before must have slipped through. Or this is a phantom."

"We don't know that. We can't assume that. I'm going to have to call a hold."

"Yes, we do know that!" Griggs's voice is rising in intensity. They're out of time for this argument, but the launch window is too small for a hold. "Cully, it's through the same basic switching equipment and equally vulnerable and this happens just suddenly? I don't think so."

T minus fifty-eight seconds is flashing on the screen. Everyone in the room is aware that once the countdown reaches thirty seconds the debate is over. The launch can't be stopped. Cully Jones has all but frozen in position, his eyes on the distant screen at the front of the room, his mind racing before triggering his interphone.

"Systems, what's your recommendation?" he asks.

"It's out of limits. No fly."

Griggs leans farther toward Cully, knowing he's mere seconds from a decision, outraged that somehow Geoff Shear is about to succeed.

"I vote for go. This is a phantom problem, Cully."

"Hold the count," Cully orders.

"No, goddammit!"

Jones is turning now, his eyes flashing anger. "Two words, Griggs. *Challenger*, and *Columbia*. We stay conservative. You object?"

Griggs stares into the resolve in Jones's face and shakes his head.

"No. No objection."

Cully triggers the interphone channel.

"The count is holding at T minus forty-two seconds. We have thirty seconds to decide to scrub or resume the countdown. Systems, where are we?"

Griggs can see the man stand and turn from his console two rows away, his face reflecting genuine fear.

"Pressure is out of limits, temperature approaching out of limits, and I have a report from the gantry shelter of heavy venting. We need to get the crew out, now! This is real!"

"Then we're scrubbed!" Cully barks.

Launch control explodes into action as the practiced team at the pad begins moving toward an emergency extraction of the two crew members while Cully Jones begins running through the checklist to purge the dangerously overpressurized tank before the contents can explode.

Griggs Hopewell sits quietly, watching and listening and slightly stunned.

My God, this one was real, and I led myself into the assumption that Sheehan did it.

If they had launched with a true overpressure, the remains of the shuttle and the two astronauts would probably be raining back on the launch pad right now.

Chapter 39

Office of the Administrator,
NASA Headquarters, Washington, D.C.,
May 21, 9:16 a.m. Pacific/
12:16 p.m. Eastern

Somehow, Geoff Shear is thinking, he's going to need to do something really special for Dorothy Sheehan. Not that he's given to overt displays of appreciation beyond NASA award dinners and other official stroking, but in this she's succeeded against overwhelming odds.

Word that the launch went to a hold and was then scrubbed brings a smile to his face. He assumes the scrub was for being out of the launch window, but there's the slightly puzzling news of fuel overpressure in one of the shuttle's tanks — and the call for an emergency evacuation of the crew. But even those developments can't dilute Geoff's smug feeling of restored control.

His cell phone is vibrating in his pocket and he whips it out, expecting the female voice he hears to be his wife's. But this voice is different. Frightened and tense. It takes him a few seconds to realize that he's talking to Dorothy herself.

"Why are you calling?" he asks, puzzled. *She knows better.*

"I'm in trouble, sir. I think I've been discovered."

"What did you say? I heard we just scrubbed down there. So, thanks for everything you were doing down there to keep us safe . . ."

"The fuel overpressure is real. It's . . . unexpected."

"Well, of course."

Geoff feels his mind racing. How to deal with this? Any call could be monitored and if anyone should know that, it's Sheehan, which means she's seriously frightened, and dangerous.

"Where are you calling from?" he asks.

"I'm outside now, in my car, and getting out of here."

"Why are you calling?"

"I . . . I guess I just need some coordination since my purpose here is done. All the safety checks and such."

"Well, Dorothy, your assignment was clear. Double check to make certain we weren't pushing safety limits. Just come home."

Now he hears a telling hesitation.

"Well, sir," she says, her tone hardening. "I got this call and I responded as requested."

Five seconds of silence pass before she speaks again, her voice this time low and serious and no longer pleading. "You're going to let me twist in the wind, aren't you?"

"What does that mean? Dorothy, if you've . . . done something improper, then you need to tell security about it. I have to go. And this call never happened."

He punches the phone off and erases the number from the display, a small chill climbing his back as he realizes his cellular bill will have also captured the number.

The phone is vibrating again and he sees her number and punches the button to reject the call, erasing the second record of the number before depowering the phone altogether, feeling off-balance. Sheehan was supposed to be rock solid reliable, his own ex-CIA operative with steely nerves and endless resources. How could she crack? And after all, the only thing that's happened is a launch scrub for an apparently legitimate reason. This is all containable, he tells himself, remembering the moment he decided to trigger the so-called nuclear option. The launch would have had to be scrubbed anyway! But knowing that doesn't soothe him, and with the sixth-sense survival instincts of a high-level bureaucrat, he can already hear footsteps behind him.

Aboard *Soyuz*, 10:05 a.m. Pacific

Sergei Mikhailovich Petrov is not surprised to find himself precisely where he expected to be: on orbit, four hundred ninety-eight kilometers above the planet and precisely one hundred fifteen kilometers behind the private American spacecraft.

He glances at his companion, Cosmonaut Mikhail Rychkov who is hunched over his computer display.

"Our closing rate is what?"

Mikhail punches another button and replies without looking over.

"Forty meters per second."

There will be a turnaround and a braking burst from their main engine necessary in forty-eight minutes, followed by the delicate task of carefully approaching the winged craft from beneath and slightly ahead. In the rushed briefings and preparations of the previous two days, the plan coalesced only as far as parking the *Soyuz* just above the private space plane and sending Mikhail out on a dangerous spacewalk with the spare pressure suit they plan to stuff into *Intrepid*'s airlock.

The right leg pocket of Mikhail's suit is brimming with black markers able to take the exposure to the vacuum of space. Using a white posterboard and a tethered cloth, he'll write instructions in English for Kip Dawson to read through the forward windscreen.

At least, that's the plan. The backup is equally risky, given the size of their space suits and the tiny airlock on *Intrepid*; Mikhail has substantial doubts whether he can fit inside if he has to go in to prepare Kip for the transfer.

Sergei has the high-powered binoculars out and is searching the void ahead, a smile forming on his face that Mikhail notices.

"You see him?"

"*Da!* And he's still flying backward, facing us, which will make it easier, I think."

ASA Mission Control,
Mojave International Aerospace Port,
Mojave, California, 10:05 a.m. Pacific

Had a wayward buffalo wandered into and through the control room, the effect would have been much the same. The disbelieving looks on the faces of the control room technicians accompany a stunned paralysis as their collective minds try to grasp the fact that every monitor, including the big-screen display, has suddenly burst back to life with numbers, graphs, and *information coming from* Intrepid*!*

The first technician to get to his feet glances at the door, then back at the screen, wanting to call Arleigh Kerr in from his office but not wanting to look foolish if this is some sort of hallucination.

Or maybe, Chuck Hines, the assistant flight director thinks, *we've somehow triggered one of the training simulation tapes.*

"What the hell is this?" someone else is asking.

Yeah, Chuck thinks. *That's it. A computer display training tape.* He looks away from the main display screen to answer the question, his heart still racing as if he'd jumped out of the path of an oncoming truck. "Okay, we've accidentally triggered an old simulation run, everyone. Let's stop it and figure out how it got triggered."

"Ah . . . Chuck?" One of the occupants of the front tier of monitors is standing, and she turns toward Hines, her blonde hair swinging across her cheeks from the move.

"Yes?"

"Look at the time signature."

"Sorry?"

"The time signature. Look at it."

"What's your point?" Chuck asks, fatigue masquerading as irritation noticeable in his tone.

Arleigh Kerr has entered the room and is standing now, taking in the slightly surreal scene, and Chuck can see him in his peripheral vision.

"My point is that the time and date stamp are current. Today. As in now. Chuck, this isn't a simulation. This is *Intrepid*'s live telemetry back online! Chuck, *he did it!*"

Kennedy Space Center, Florida,
10:05 a.m. Pacific/1:05 p.m. Eastern

Griggs sits heavily in his office chair, waiting for the confrontation with Dorothy Sheehan, feeling certifiably old. Despite the continued presence of the shuttle on the pad rather than on orbit, the system worked, but the net effect has been depressing.

He hears a door opening at the end of the corridor leading to his office, the assigned locus of the meeting he's ordered. It will take less than a minute for the footsteps to reach his door.

Griggs pushes a crystal paperweight around in a small circle on the desk. It's an expensive thank-you from a past launch crew, an intricate replica of the shuttle in flight on a tiny pedestal, his name engraved on a gold plaque at the base, but for some reason it feels like the stereotypical gold watch, marking the end of a career.

Admitting he's tired is hard, but he's coming to it more often these days, and the past week has pushed his limits. He'll have to think about that. John Kent has years of fight left, but — as he's loved to put it over the years — his get up and go has, this time, really "got up and went."

"Griggs? We've got Miss Sheehan here."

He snaps to mentally, being careful not to change his relaxed, almost slouched position in his swivel chair. There are times to sit on the throne behind the desk, and there are times to come around to the chair facing his small couch and be more approachable. This is one of the throne times.

"Everyone come on in."

A somber delegation files into the room and he sees Dorothy Sheehan's been cuffed. The head of security for the space center follows with one of his officers, trailed by Cully and the head of the legal staff.

Sheehan's glare is meant to melt steel, but the fear in her eyes is ruining her act.

"For God's sake, Nelson, take those cuffs off this lady. What's she going to do? Run out and steal the shuttle?"

"We did catch her trying to run out of the front gate, so to speak," the security chief says while pulling out his cuff key and unlocking her.

"Twenty miles per hour is hardly running out the front gate," Dorothy says, her voice subdued and tense.

"Have a seat, Miss Sheehan," Griggs says, motioning to the couch.

She complies, her eyes boring into his face as he looks at the others with a smile and then locks on hers.

"You're familiar," Griggs begins, "with the old term 'red-handed'?"

"Look, I don't know what you think you're doing . . ."

Griggs raises his hand, stopping her. "Honey . . ." he sees the lawyer and the human resources chief stiffen at the term and throws a smile at them. "Hey, guys, lighten up. I run this place." He looks back at Sheehan. "So, Miss *Sheehan,* would you care to tell us precisely why you were attempting to sabotage the launch of our little rocket out there?"

"I was doing no such thing!"

The moment has arrived, Griggs thinks, and he comes forward slowly in his chair, letting his stocky build shift toward her like an old grizzly leaning forward to sniff its frozen, terrified prey.

"Honey, let's get one thing really straight, okay? We have you. We have the evidence to put you in a federal prison, probably for life, and the only thing that you have to cling to right now is the hope that if you tell me who, what, where, when, how, and why — including every conversation in exquisite detail you had with Mister Geoffrey in Washington leading up to your actions — I might decide it's the bigger fish who need frying. Now you're a big girl. Nod your pretty little head if you understand, and let's cut the bullshit and get to, as they say out in West Texas, the nut-cuttin'."

"You want to deal?" she asks, triggering a broad grin from Griggs.

"You have no idea how much," he says. "So you cut the cards, Ma'am."

She nods, her eyes on her manicured fingernails drumming the table in front of her. The drumming stops and her jaw clenches. Her eyes become mere slits as she fastens them on his and speaks through tightened lips. "If I'm allowed to walk, I'll give him to you in a sealed box."

"You do that, Sheehan, you walk. You'll never set foot on a NASA installation again in this life, but you won't have to limit the rest of your days to having an intimate relationship with a cell mate."

"Please cut the sexist crap and answer one question," she snaps. "Do we have a deal?"

"Well, if you can deliver, l'il sister, then yes. We have a deal."

She nods. "All right. So happens, I have tapes of just about everything Shear and I discussed. And because of where they were made, they're admissible."

Chapter 40

ASA Mission Control,
Mojave International Aerospace Port,
Mojave, California,
May 21, 10:10 a.m. Pacific

Diana Ross stands in silent shock at the back of the reactivated Mission Control room, recalling the story of Lazarus. If Kip can be brought back to Earth, there would be room for the word "miraculous."

Yet, if he doesn't reenter *Intrepid* before an hour and a half are up, all the cosmonauts will be able to do is recover bodies.

News that the telemetry downlinks from *Intrepid* are working again took a few minutes to reach her office, and she figures it is some sort of overwrought misinformation. But there it is, she thinks, live and in color, the data streams moving across the screens as if nothing had ever been amiss — with the exception of voice communication, which has not been restored.

She thinks back to the shock hours ago upon reading of his intent to leave the ship and the frustration she felt at not being able to scream at him to hang on, that help was coming.

In the background she hears ASA Mission Control's repeated attempts to hail *Intrepid* rolling over and over again like some sort of exotic Tibetan prayer. But no answer from Kip, and no further typing, and the world is, quite literally, waiting on the collective edges of a billion seats for the next act.

Diana moves into the back of the room with a newfound ability to stand away just a bit and observe. She's had too much opportunity in the last four days to think. Endless hours in her office waiting to be useful, and she's been reading and rereading every word that her would-be poster boy composed.

The shock of *Intrepid*'s sudden telemetry reactivation is still ping-ponging back and forth among the fine technical minds in the room and despite the obvious, there is still no widespread willingness to accept the idea that Kip Dawson, a rank amateur, has actually repaired *Intrepid*'s radios.

"Is there a master circuit breaker for all the radios he could have pushed back in?" one of the structural experts asks, wondering why the rest of the group merely shake their heads as if the question is technically embarrassing — which it is. She hears the ongoing discussions of the oxygen and nitrogen mix and the CO_2 levels, the adequacy of the remaining fuel, and the fact that all systems except voice communication appear to be working as if nothing had ever impacted the ship and killed its pilot.

"The external airlock door is showing open," Chuck Hines reports.

"You didn't see that before?" Arleigh asks over the interphone.

Chuck turns and addresses him directly. "It just now came up on the telemetry readout. The inside door is still closed, inside atmosphere still breathable."

"Dammit, he's got less than fifteen minutes of air left to get back in there," Arleigh is saying, as much to himself as to the control room.

Over and over again Diana hears them returning to the almost hushed discussion of the apparent "far out" reality of how *Intrepid*'s downlinks have sprung back to life — the "impossible theory" first fueled by the startling decision Kip Dawson had written about several hours ago:

I'm going to wiggle into Bill's space suit and see if there's anything I can do outside to patch up the damage.

431

"How could he know? Do we cover how to do an emergency spacewalk in ground school, Arleigh?" Chuck Hines is asking.

"Yes, to the same extent airline passengers are schooled on emergency evacuation."

"If I wasn't looking at all this stuff streaming down," Chuck says, "I'd tell you the chances he successfully put on Bill's suit and went outside and repaired the ship are zero. But you tell me, which is more likely? *He* did it, or the problem was cured by mystical equipment self-repair uncontaminated by human contact?"

"I'd vote for Kip."

"Yeah," he sighs. "Me, too."

Diana tunes out the discussion, focusing on the numbers cascading down on one side of the screen while her mind reaches for him so many miles away. Daring to hope, just a little, where no hope had been was logical. But the startling reality is how much it impacts her. She knows fatigue is in charge now. If there's some uncontrolled, starry-eyed tendency to slide toward falling in love with him, it would be, she thinks, like falling in love with Elvis before he passed. She's mature enough to know that myth and reality are seldom connected, except in the mind.

She knows all of it, and yet Kip to her has become as compelling as gravity.

Diana shakes her head and tells her common sense to immediately search out and destroy such little-girl fantasies. After all, the man *is* married.

The thought is interrupted by a shout from one of the console positions.

"Hey, everyone! *Intrepid*'s outer door just closed, and I'm getting a pressure drop inside!"

Aboard *Intrepid*, 10:12 a.m. Pacific

Strange, Kip thinks, how climbing back inside feels like spoiling a good stage exit. He looks around the tiny, tublike interior of the airlock, working to suppress his feelings of claustrophobia.

The whoosh of air from the interior fills the tiny space quickly and he can feel the rigidity of the space suit diminish. The green light indicating equal pressure comes on and he works the inner door locks and swings it open, taking his time again in extricating himself.

For just a moment he considers leaving the suit in place and pressurized before remembering the limited oxygen in the airpack. He cuts it off and secures the little arm-mounted control panel before removing his helmet, securing it before working to adjust himself back into the command chair. The bulky space suit is a bit easier to handle when deflated, but he wishes he could have just kept it sealed. Bill's physical decomposition is now stomach-turning. All the more reason, he thinks, to take his leave outside in the most spectacular arena imaginable.

But he's agreed with himself to try the rocket one last time, on the chance it might make a difference. And now, sitting in front of the command panel, the thought hits him that if it fires, he'll then have an incredibly complicated flying machine to guide through the atmosphere but without benefit of flight training. Not to mention figuring out how, and where, to land it. Succeeding in a spacewalk repair, a deorbit burn, and a reentry, only to crash and die in a botched landing would be awful. Worth a complaint to DiFazio himself.

And the thought makes him chuckle. *Yeah. If they kill me with inadequate ground training, I'll never speak to them again.*

The humor masks the fear that's contracting his stomach, and he's already flipping through the checklists looking for the very page that turns up now, a reference to another checklist he hasn't seen — one for emergency reentry.

The discarded headset is floating to his left, disturbed by his movements, and he wonders if he should put it on and try the radios one last time.

No point in wasting time with that. Whatever I was messing with out there didn't have anything to do with the antennas.

The storage compartment for the ship's manuals is just out of reach, and he has to unbuckle again to lean far enough over to open it, worry now rising that he won't be ready in time.

There!

The checklist is in his hands and he opens it, reading too quickly, having to force himself to slow down and reread it.

God, if I'd seen this before, I could have turned the ship automatically!

Someone down there, Kip thinks, decided that with one astronaut aboard each flight, it made good sense to write the checklist so that a rank amateur could follow it.

And even with a dozen glider flights and basic stick and rudder skills, and a couple of fixed-wing flights in a single-engine Cessna in his head, Kip has never felt so much like an amateur.

He checks the time. Twelve minutes to go. Just time enough to learn how to place the small bullet-shaped icon on the attitude indicator in the arms of the moving "V" that is the flight director, the key to keeping the ship in the proper attitude on the way down.

He keeps looking for the information on how to punch an autopilot button and let the ship fly itself, but it either doesn't exist, or he can't find it. He'll have to manually follow the small, projected dot on the attitude indicator all the way and hope for the best — flipping the tail assembly into the split reentry configuration at the right moment, reconfiguring on time, and keeping the engine pointed in the right downward direction until coming through ninety miles up.

Like drinking from a fire hose, he thinks, realizing that he's actually thinking of reentry as a real possibility and getting way ahead of himself. After all, if the engine doesn't fire, the rest of it is academic.

Cheyenne Mountain, North American
Aerospace Defense Command,
Colorado Springs, Colorado,
10:38 a.m. Pacific/11:38 a.m. Mountain

"We have a live picture, General," the duty controller announces, bringing Chris Risen's eyes around to the front of the room where the slightly fuzzy image of *Intrepid* is swimming into view, a telescopic shot from the Russian crew.

"Where are they?" Chris asks, moving alongside the controller, a sharp young female captain.

"Twenty-one miles and closing, sir."

"So, we've got a sudden telemetry reactivation, good pressure, Kip apparently back inside, and the cosmonauts within spitting distance. I'd say his impending demise has been greatly exaggerated."

The captain glances up at the four-star, wondering if she has permission to chuckle, or the need to give him a charity laugh.

She does neither.

"Bastardized Mark Twain," Chris explains. "Sorry."

"He has a chance, sir, provided he doesn't light off his engine."

"What do you mean?"

"Well, he's coming up to a retrofire point for coming down at Mojave in just six or seven minutes, and if he knows that, and doesn't know the Russians are coming . . ."

"And if he's fixed his engine as effectively as he's apparently fixed some of the radios . . ."

"Yes, sir. He might try to deorbit, and he's not a pilot. I mean, I understand he's had some glider training toward a license, but that's it."

The thought of an untrained, unlicensed pilot trying to guide a spacecraft through a precise series of return maneuvers sends a chill up his spine, and he forms a small prayer that, regardless of Kip's mechanical prowess, the engine won't fire.

"ASA is trying frantically to reach him and tell him to just sit tight," the captain adds.

"But no contact?"

She's shaking her head. "Nothing yet. The Russian crew is trying to signal him with a low-powered laser. But there's no response."

Chris Risen glances at the frozen crawl from Kip Dawson's laptop.

"And he's written nothing more."

"Yes, sir. I noticed that."

"Which means he's getting ready to try.

Captain, get a line to Baikonaur's Mission Control and make sure the *Soyuz* crew is informed what might happen."

"Yes, sir. See, that's what I was getting at, General."

"Sorry?"

"The *Soyuz* is behind *Intrepid*, a bit lower but right along his orbital path. If he retrofires at a slight downward angle, he may be thrusting right down the cosmonauts' throats."

"Oh, Jesus! Hurry up!"

Chapter 41

Kip sits in the command chair staring at the western edge of the planet, wondering why a bright blue light had been sparking intermittently on the horizon line.

But his mind is consumed by a thought that pulls him away from what he's seeing.

Here he is, ready to die. But what if he doesn't?

Maybe, he thinks, the CO_2 is winning at last. He feels clearheaded, yet his longing to return and have another stab at life — his desire to see his kids again and use the insights he's gained — seems somehow cheapened. It's as if his impending death has suddenly been deemed privileged and noble, and an escape back to life anything but. It's like the narrative he's been writing for some future reader — the angst of one solitary man — is actually somehow a small contribution to humankind.

This is stupid, he thinks.

But there's a part of him protesting that to

440

live through this is to cheat himself of a legacy, to be just a mere survivor, not an example.

An example of what? An example of foolishness? Crying in my laptop for days before figuring out what to do?

Yet the feeling is all too real. It astounds and depresses him. As if deorbiting would be a cop-out, a cowardly retreat.

Kip snorts out loud at the irony.

But that's not it, he realizes, his eyes flaring wide as he sits up a bit straighter with a smile on his face.

No, that's not it at all!

What it is, is his father again. It's his dad's template for life imprinted in his brain like an indelible operating program, looking for a way even in the eleventh hour to impose duty and sacrifice and stoic acceptance of responsibility over any breath of self-determination.

He is, he realizes, being drawn back to that myopic world like a sailor lured by Sirens, believing not what fills his eyes and his consciousness, but what fits his parental rule book yet again: That doing something for himself is wrong. That speaking his truth is wrong.

My God, I'm thinking like a Calvinist! Surviving is wrong if there's a chance I might enjoy the result. The only thing missing is a hair shirt.

How tired and old and sad his father had seemed toward the end, and suddenly he understands why. No wonder visiting him was like tiptoeing to the edge of a black hole.

My father's manual for enduring life. But this time I've caught you red-handed, Dad! He looks around at Bill's bagged remains as if the bag also contains the part of his father that he's never put to rest.

His voice booms through the diminutive interior. "No more, Dad! No more. I'm going to give this my best shot, and if somehow I succeed, I'm going to have a go at really living like you never did. Like you should have. And you know what? I'm going to do it, even if I die trying. I'm bidding you good-bye, Dad, wherever you are. I love you, but I'm not listening to you anymore. And it's . . . it's time for you to go . . . to the light, whatever that is, or wherever. Just . . . go."

There is a tear in the corner of his eye he didn't expect and the feeling of a weight lifting from him. Only his imagination, of course, but he could swear something slipped away from this small enclosure, something dark and sad.

He turns back forward with a renewed

442

spirit, the laptop keyboard beckoning. But there are only four minutes remaining.

For some reason it feels good to speak out loud, after so many days of silent thoughts, at full volume, and now that he's started, he likes the broken silence.

"So, are we ready?"

He looks at the attitude indicator, noting the target dot nestling snugly where it should be in the "V" for retrofire. Five minutes of rocket thrust at more than three g's of deceleration will be required to get home. If he's slow in firing, he'll drift eastward, away from Mojave.

He pulls the laptop over suddenly, unable to resist.

Okay, I have two more things to say. First, I've just been outside and tried to repair this little craft, and I have no idea whether I made any difference, but I'm going to try to fire the engine once more in a few minutes. Second, I have finally realized something that to me is very important: It turns out that I have never been Kip Dawson until now, until I was forced to be honest about my life. But a few minutes ago, in effect, I buried my father and gave him back his book — his operating program. I am electing life on my own terms, and even if I have only a few minutes of it to enjoy, it feels wonderful. I get the point now. Self does matter.

Just under one minute left.

Kip positions his hand on the sidestick controller, fanning his fingers and waiting as he forces from his mind the fatalistic "reality" that the motor will not fire. Of course it'll fire. He'll simply *will* it to fire. All positive thoughts. Mind over matter.

Faith can move mountains, but dynamite works better, someone once said. So he'll use both — faith and the dynamite of determination. He demands that the friggin' engine fires, so it damn well has no choice!

So there.

Why do they say T minus? What does the T stand for? He wonders, watching the secondhand crawl below ten seconds, unable to resist the urge to voice his own countdown.

"Nine, eight, seven . . ."

The words seem to echo in the small cabin, something he hasn't noticed before. He's bracing for the thrust in his back.

"Two, one, and we have *ignition!*"

Kip's left index finger shoots toward the

ignition sequence button and presses hard. He can feel the click of the switch.

And that's all.

For just a second he sits with his finger still depressing the switch, as if the engine is just thinking about it and may get around to firing in a few seconds. But the seconds start moving toward a minute as he pulls his finger back and presses the switch down again and again, not frantically, but with a determination to get his message across: *You are hereby commanded to fire!*

The engine, however, isn't complying, and where he's expected to feel either instant acceleration or great angst at a failed firing, he feels strangely composed and calm. Like he's entering a zone reserved only for fighter pilots and astronauts with Chuck Yeager's right stuff: perfect tranquillity in the face of disaster and anything but acceptance.

Kip pulls his hand away, his mind moving steadily back over the checklist items needed to fire the engine. The checklist is in his lap, and he finds the right page and begins moving down the list, double-checking every switch, aware that more than a minute and a half have already passed and he'll commit himself to landing somewhere way east of Mojave if they light off. The thought of waiting for another orbit flickers across his mind and is just as quickly swept away by the reality that he doesn't know how much breathable air he has left.

"Ignition primary and secondary bus transfer switches should be off. They are. Ignition emergency disconnect relay one and two guarded on. Where are those? Oh yeah, they're positioned right."

He stares at the switches whose name he just spoke. Small red plastic covers known as "switch guards" cover each toggle switch to prevent a sleeve or wayward hand from accidentally flipping the tiny lever.

So are they off or on when closed? he wonders, opening one of the guards to expose the metal toggle lever inside.

It's off. So when the guard is closed and down, the switch is off.

"Wait a minute." He flips open both guards and moves the switches to the "on" position, double checking the language in the checklist.

"For God's sake, don't tell me that's why the engine didn't fire four days ago!"

Were they open or closed then, those guards? He read the checklist items very carefully on the first day, but the image in his memory of the two little switch guards is flip-flopping between whether they were open or closed. Up or down. He can't remember.

At least now, he figures, they're in the right position.

His breathing has accelerated and he can feel his heart pounding and his face reddening, more from embarrassment than anticipation. All this because he didn't follow the checklist four days back?

Yet the thought is instantly calming, and in the space of only a few seconds he gets over it, embracing the thought that what he's learned in accepting his own demise is worth a lifetime, and the thought that if the problem is that simple, then hallelujah! He's going home.

Once again his index finger stabs at the ignition switch.

Aboard *Soyuz*, 10:39 a.m. Pacific

"One thousand meters, closing at five per second," Mikhail intones in the calm voice of a man serenely on the razor edge of his technology.

Sergei Petrov nods, his eyes still focused on the radar screen and the just-received message from Baikonaur Mission Control that is wrinkling his features.

"You believe we should drop down in case he retrofires?" Sergei asks, knowing the finite amount of fuel in the maneuvering jets and estimating how much it will take to change orbit even that slightly.

"The warning came from NORAD, no?"

"Yes. NORAD. Not from Houston."

"You've been watching with the binoculars, Sergei. Have you seen any movement? Any evidence that he's seen the laser I've been flashing?"

"*Nyet.* Nothing. But let me look again."

Sergei plucks the instrument from where it's been floating by his face and focuses once more on the forward windows of the backward-flying American space plane. The image steadies and suddenly looms larger, as if he's triggered a zoom lens, and he shakes his head in confusion before pulling the glasses away and finding the very same zoom happening in his unaided vision.

"What am I . . ."

"Sergei!" Mikhail is barking the words. "He's coming! Coming at us!"

The mission commander grabs for the controls, time dilation already slowing the sequence as the American craft looms larger in the *Soyuz* window, coming directly at them, Sergei recalling now the sight of a burst of *something* alongside the craft just as it started zooming in.

Sergei's hand reaches the firing control and jams their main engine to life, thrusting forward while canting the angle of firing downward, but the oncoming vehicle is accelerating toward them.

A rapid calculation flashes through Mikhail's mind pairing five hundred meters with the steady acceleration of the ASA ship and yielding a catastrophic closing speed by the time it reaches them.

Intrepid is looming large now, its relative closing speed marked more by how fast it seems to be growing in size than by any lateral movement, but at last the two cosmonauts can feel their craft thrusting ahead of the oncoming space plane's trajectory as it approached soundlessly.

It's too late to do more, and as the American spacecraft fills the forward window both men cringe in anticipation of a thunderous impact that doesn't come.

As if it were a holographic projection, as soon as *Intrepid* fills their eyes, it flashes past, missing their craft by a tiny margin they can only guess at, shooting through the empty space around them, no wake turbulence to rattle their craft, and nothing but the accelerated heartbeats in the *Soyuz* capsule to mark its passing.

"He fired his engine!" Mikhail says.

"You think?" Sergei says, staring into the same void with a death grip on the control stick. "The phrase they use in Houston is: No shit, Sherlock!"

Chapter 42

Kip doesn't have a spare second to be confused.

No time to wonder about what flashed past the forward windscreen less than a minute after ignition. Maybe a satellite. Maybe nothing. Whatever it was, it seemed so incredibly close, yet, it whooshed past without a sound, like an illusion — some computer-generated sequence projected on the windscreen. He still has the mental image of what the thing looked like somewhere in his memory, and it's a familiar shape somehow, but his attention is too focused on the forward panel to think it through.

Kip's right hand is working the sidestick controller constantly with small, intense movements, and there's a tiny flash of pride that he's already learned not to overcontrol. Three g's of thrust are pressing at his back and pulling at his face, but it's all as handleable as the ascent was four days ago.

The physical impact of the light off was nothing compared to the psychological shock that the engine really fired. His mind is still trying to work through how that happened. At the same time, he's trying to make sure he doesn't do anything else terribly wrong, like face the rocket engine the wrong way and boost himself on a one-way trip to outer space. He's already figured out that, with enough fuel left to subtract seventeen thousand miles an hour of momentum, this spacecraft, if turned in the opposite direction, could easily reach the escape velocity of twenty-three thousand miles per hour and soar away from Earth's gravity forever.

He double-checks that he's aimed *Intrepid*'s nozzles in the right direction, and holds the ship steady with a massive force of will, playing a video game with life-or-death consequences in keeping the tiny dot in the "V" on the attitude indicator screen. The nose slowly comes up, changing the rocket engine's thrust vector from all horizontal deceleration to a mix of both vertical and horizontal, keeping gravity from yanking *Intrepid* too rapidly back toward Earth.

The engine should cut out, the checklist says, when he's at eighty degrees nose up, still flying backward, at an altitude of ninety miles and dropping at less than three hundred miles per hour, with almost no forward speed. *Intrepid*, he knows, uses fuel and thrust to slow down instead of trading speed for heat — using the type of red-hot thermal braking through the atmosphere that incinerated the shuttle *Columbia* years ago. He'll have less than a minute, when the fuel runs out and *Intrepid* begins to freefall, to use the reaction thrusters to raise the tail and turn the space plane completely around. Then he'll be falling like some sort of man-made leaf into the upper reaches of the atmosphere, belly first, never going fast enough through the thickening air to melt the structure with frictional heating.

It's a hard concept to grasp, this frictional heating and airspeed. He knows, because he tried to explain it to Julie for a school science report one night as Sharon rolled her eyes and left for bed. He reruns the memory, every word of it ringing clear in his head, even as he works the control stick and watches the forward panel.

"Honey, below four hundred thousand feet above the planet Earth — eighty miles high — the atmosphere begins with just an occasional molecule of air. On a space shuttle reentry, every molecule gets hit at nearly orbital speed as the spacecraft descends lower and lower into more and more air, and with each tiny collision, there is a transformation of the massive speed of the collision into heat. At four hundred thousand feet it doesn't amount to much, but hitting two hundred thousand feet, where the still-thin air molecules are much more closely packed together means a lot more of those tiny heat-producing collisions are happening, and the heat begins to raise the temperature of the spacecraft itself thousands of degrees, each collision stripping away electrons from the molecules and creating a superheated plasma that can be seen from the ground as a long trail of fire. It was at two hundred and seven thousand feet over Texas," he told her, "that the Shuttle *Columbia* began to break up, killing the crew."

Julie had seen Sharon's response, and it had limited her attention span. He never had the chance to talk about airspeed, and why a spacecraft flashing through those edge-of-space altitudes at thousands of miles per hour could show an *indicated* airspeed of less than a hundred miles per hour, something that always fascinated him.

A calculation he needs to make in his head snaps him away from the memory. He was four minutes late firing the engine, and so the result will be a landing somewhere in eastern Arizona. He needs to know soon where he is, what state he's over. Unlike the shuttle, which starts down around the California coast in order to land in Florida, he remembers from his indoctrination that with *Intrepid*, he's just dropping into whatever state he's over.

There's a button to be pushed on the HSI — the horizontal situation indicator — when he turns the ship around nose down, and the screen is supposed to show the airfields he can reach, but he's getting ahead of himself with the engine still firing, and right now all he can do is play the video game and hang on, battling the feeling that he's not really here.

The three minutes elapse, feeling like ten. The nose-up angle is nearly thirty degrees now as he slowly arcs backward toward the planet. The numbers on the screen indicating forward velocity are down below eight thousand miles per hour, the stars still visible outside the window.

The chilling thought that keeps running through his head is that with or without the help of the map computer, he'll have only one shot at finding a place for *Intrepid* to land — let alone figure out how to fly her there.

But so far his control movements are

steady, competent, even professional, and he can't figure why. He doesn't know nearly enough to do this. Yet here is his right hand, moving the stick with calm competence, as if he's channeling a *real* astronaut — a golden connection, a reserve of assurance and intellect from somewhere beyond himself.

Suddenly the noise and thrust and shaking and moving numbers that are the cacophonous reality of this descent back to Earth begin to recede, as if a sound engineer somewhere was moving the master volume down slowly. He feels an unexpected tranquillity descending over him like a warm blanket — reassuring, comforting, validating that his hands really do have it under control and his mind is free to float so he can turn and watch himself. He's being enfolded by a peace he's never felt, and along with it there seems to be a rising, gentle chorus of voices against the sound of a thousand strings, like the most magnificent space movie on the most amazing screen he could ever dream up, the orchestral and choral harmony all around him now, as if the unity and connectedness of uncounted souls are trying to put his fear in a perspective he's never imagined.

It's a crystalline moment of aching, indescribable beauty, and, as has happened several times in this odyssey, tears come unbidden to his eyes.

They are, he realizes, tears of appreciation for just *being,* and for the first time in his life he finds himself overflowing with a love of the moment and of life as it is akin to nothing he's ever experienced — a love so deep, so complete, that even if it all ends within seconds, the contentment will have too much force not to live on. It's a place he's never been, a moment he never wants to leave, and one he's quite sure he was never supposed to glimpse.

Kip Dawson's mind returns to the reality of *Intrepid*'s cabin, the sounds rising in volume around him but altered now and somehow incapable of threatening him, even as his adrenaline flows like a flood-stage river.

He shakes his head against the steady g-forces. There's a strange comfort, he thinks, in the force of this rocket-propelled deceleration pressing him down in the seat — an affirmation that Newton's laws are still relevant. Back in the Mojave ground school he'd thought the math beyond him and was astounded to discover how straightforward the equations are for the dynamics that are shaking him now. So many thousands of pounds of thrust out of the engine nozzles for so many seconds in the absence of air raises or lowers speed predictably, and he's filled with awe that, in essence, *Intrepid* is merely coming to a stop before dropping back into the atmosphere. No screaming trail of charged, burning plasma across the sky. No three-thousand-degree temperatures to be absorbed and deflected. Just a small, private ship dropping back in like a badminton birdie.

The countdown to engine cutoff is on the screen and less than forty seconds away, the nose-up angle approaching sixty degrees. Forward speed is coming under a thousand five hundred miles per hour, and still he's hanging on and holding the dot in the V.

He wonders if any radar facility will pick him up, or if anyone at Mojave even has a clue he's not still in his stable orbit. If he can't find an airport and ends up hurt or dead in the back country of Arizona, he figures they won't find him for days or weeks.

Or maybe even years.

Poor old Kip, he thinks with a smile, *the boy just disappeared while on orbit and no one ever knew why.*

And still he can feel the serenity growing within. It doesn't matter. Everything is as it should be.

Ten seconds to cutoff. He almost doesn't want the thrust to stop, but the noise has been deafening and he looks forward to quiet.

Engine shutdown catches him by surprise, kicking him forward. Again he's in zero gravity and it seems wrong. Shouldn't he *feel* the downward pull of Earth — the increase of thirty-two feet per second in speed every second?

Technically he's still in space, just nowhere near high enough or fast enough to stay there any longer.

Kip checks the descent speed. Two hundred sixty feet per second. He sees the target dot on the ADI, attitude deviation indicator, blinking red as it starts moving down. He moves the sidestick controller to follow, startled when the Earth swims back into view. *Intrepid*'s nose changes pitch from near vertical through the horizontal and continues downward to twenty degrees below the horizon. He wants to look at the surface below and try to figure out where he is, but his eyes have to stay riveted on the ADI until he feels the ship stabilize. Funny how suddenly it seems so easy, and just a few days ago he'd been spinning out of control like a crazed gyro.

The steadiness of the ship now that the

engine is quiet is almost unnerving, and he remembers to consult the checklist Velcroed to his knee before reconfiguring the space plane and raising the tail structure to keep down the speed of reentry. Instead of his finger shaking like before as he points it at the next section of the reentry checklist, his hand is now steady, and his index finger tracks the next few steps as he reads through the verbiage, and triggers a small hydraulic pump.

A tiny whine akin to an energetic mosquito begins complaining from somewhere aft, confirming its operation. Lights illuminate on the forward panel and a series of lighted pushbuttons that control the process of feathering the ship light up as well. He pushes them in sequence, checking and rechecking each step and feeling the change in the tail structure as the twin-boomed empennage begins to rise to a nearly eighty-degree upward deflection.

Kip recalls the explanation almost verbatim: "As the air molecules begin to flash past, the tail will align vertically, leaving the body almost horizontal into the relative wind, the tremendous drag keeping the speed from building too high. Like a shuttlecock," the instructor had added, sending Kip to the dictionary only to discover that "shuttlecock" essentially meant the same thing as "badminton birdie."

Four hundred thousand feet . . . eighty miles, Kip thinks, *the upper beginning of the atmosphere.*

His gaze takes in the horizon once again as he uses the sidestick to bring the nose up, stopping at ten degrees down.

Speed is what? Okay, five hundred twenty knots and accelerating.

In less than five minutes, *Intrepid*'s heat-coated belly will peak at a temperature of just over a thousand degrees Fahrenheit — as long as he holds the right attitude. He thinks he can feel the molecules of air beginning to impact the fuselage, even though *Intrepid*'s relative, *indicated* airspeed is still not even registering. But the true speed through the near vacuum around him is now just under twelve hundred miles per hour.

The curvature of the Earth is still pronounced, the darkness of space beyond still stark and amazing, and he realizes he's seeing the same view as those who ride suborbitally to the same height.

Three hundred fifty-one thousand!

The ship seems to be moving ever so slightly now, not unlike an airplane in stable flight, but he knows the motion will increase along with the sound of the high-speed air impacting his fuselage.

Where am I? The question now becomes urgent. He cranes his neck to see better through the forward windscreen, looking for anything identifiable. The map display should be showing what he's over, but for some reason it's switched to some diagnostic screen and Kip punches first one, then another of the buttons around the perimeter to get the map back.

Oh my God, the seat!

He's almost forgotten to reposition it, rotating the bottom upward and leaning it back in accordance with the checklist and tightening his seat and shoulder harness against the five-g peak deceleration to come.

The thought of Bill Campbell's lightly restrained body behind him suddenly flashes in his consciousness. Only small Velcro straps are holding the plastic bag to the back bulkhead, and up to now all the deceleration has been backward. But when the real atmospheric braking starts, the body will tumble forward, and he wonders how to secure it.

He could strap it into his passenger seat close behind, but it's too late to get out of the harnesses. The thought of the body crashing forward and into his hand on the control stick worries him, but he'll deal with it when, and if.

Three hundred five thousand, velocity twenty-four hundred feet per second . . . sixteen hundred miles per hour straight down!

He can see a line of snow-covered mountains far below, and as he looks north, one of them resembles Pikes Peak and he wonders if he's coming down in the middle of New Mexico's Sangre de Cristo range.

But when he looks more closely, he realizes Colorado is apparently much farther north.

He could twist the sidestick controller around and yaw left or right to see better, but he's afraid of disobeying the V on the ADI in front of him and he stifles the need. He'll wait until *Intrepid* is an aircraft again with the tail aligned before looking for airfields.

A hint of slipstream noise is becoming more pronounced, a clear rising protest of assaulted atoms of nitrogen and oxygen shoved aside by a bow wave, a supersonic bow wave, as he descends below three hundred thousand feet, no longer in space but clearly still in the far upper reaches of the atmosphere. The speed is fairly steady now, just under Mach 3, and the indicated airspeed has begun to move upward in single digits.

A red symbol has begun blinking urgently on the forward display and Kip leans forward to read it.

WARNING: LEFT STRUT UP-LATCH NOT LOCKED.

He understands. The twin tail booms are in the up position for reentry, yet the left one is not locked, and the increasing pressure of the airflow is trying to force it down. If that happens, he'll start spinning and speeding up until either the gyroscopic forces or the overheating kills him.

Kip pulls the other checklist to his lap from its storage slot and pages through, amazed that he isn't frantic. He flips to the section covering major emergencies and locates the one labeled "Strut Up-latch Unsafe Warning during Reentry." The first step is to verify the hydraulic pump is still on, and he looks at the appropriate part of the panel.

The switch is on. But the pressure is zero, indicating the pump has failed.

Ever so slowly, as he looks at the horizon, *Intrepid* begins to rotate to the left.

Chapter 43

There is a manual procedure, Kip sees, listed in the text, and at first it confuses him. Apparently a cable of some sort can be pulled to secure the up-latch, but the g-forces have already begun to build, and, as the gyration to the left begins to become noticeable, the reentry deceleration force is progressively raising the weight of the arm he has to use to open a panel he's never seen beneath his left leg.

The fact that in less than a minute he'll be pinned to the command seat by upward of five g's registers, and Kip snaps off his seat belt and shoulder harness and dives forward, his hand scrambling around the lower left kick panel, finding several different recessed latches. He struggles to peer over the edge of the seat and read the verbiage on each of them, holding on to the checklist with his right hand. Constant control of the sidestick is unnecessary during this phase, he was told, and he hopes he's remembered

465

that correctly. The aerodynamic forces are now gripping *Intrepid*, and the flipped-up twin booms of the tail are the only thing keeping the space plane correctly aligned.

And clearly, the left boom is starting to retract under the air load.

The first panel yields nothing but switches and circuit breakers, but the second is the right one, and Kip finds the left boom T-handle and grabs it just as Bill Campbell's body tears loose from the Velcro and tumbles forward, slamming into the panel and jamming the little access door partially closed with Kip's hand still inside.

He feels a flash of pain, along with a burst of unpleasant odor, as the mass of plastic covering Bill's remains pins his arm, the loads now exceeding two g's. Kip releases the checklist from his right hand and struggles to shove the body back away from his trapped left hand. There is only one pull possible, and if the boom isn't in the completely extended position the moment he pulls, he'll close the locking jaws on nothing.

His fingers close on the checklist.

"Ensure aerodynamic control automatic engagement has occurred."

There is a light somewhere on the screen. No, not a light, a lighted message. His eyes are blurry, his body straining forward against two and a half g's now, but he finally sees the words.

Okay. Engaged.

"Pull nose up momentarily to twenty degrees nose high, then pull T-handle."

Oh, Jesus! Simultaneously, then.

He understands what has to happen. *Intrepid* is now spinning at several revolutions per minute to the left, and it will get worse as he pulls nose up. But with nose up, the boom should be slammed into the up-locks, and if he pulls on the T-handle at exactly the right moment . . .

There is no time to think about it and Kip stays hunched over in the seat and unrestrained as he grabs the stick and pulls it back, feeling an amazing increase in g-forces as the belly of the space plane becomes perpendicular to the relative airflow, slowing him. The spin to the left becomes a blur, and he's having to pull almost to the stops to get twenty degrees nose high.

Now!

His entire body is protesting at the elephant of force that's just jumped on his back, crunching him down as he hears the boom clang into position. He yanks hard on the T-handle, pulling it out to the stop before the sickening feeling of a broken cable registers in his head. *Intrepid* has transitioned back to slightly nose down again, and he realizes the T-handle has come completely out with no resistance on the line.

Oh no!

Something on the forward panel has changed, though, and as he strains to look, the warning light is gone. Somewhere on the left is supposed to be a locked indication, but he feels himself about to pass out, his vision reducing to a tunnel ahead of him as he leans forward against what feels like five g's, and finally spots it.

Locked! God, I did it!

Kip forces his torso back into the reclined command chair and fumbles for the seat and shoulder harnesses, the very act of getting back in clearing his vision.

One hundred ninety thousand feet, he reads. When his eyes have cleared, he realizes the left spinning is slowly stopping, the world outside slowing from a blur back to identifiable landscape, the curvature of the Earth still pronounced, but the horizon showing a distinct atmospheric glow.

The indicated airspeed is climbing through a hundred and ten knots now, the downward true through-the-airspace velocity slowing toward the speed of sound.

His entire body is hurting from the fight with the g-forces and he has to remind himself to look back at the checklist. The procedure is only half complete. If the hydraulic system can't lock a wayward tail boom, it can't unlock it and move it downward, either, and with the tail in the flipped-up position, *Intrepid* is uncontrollable.

The g-forces are slowly diminishing with his speed as he once again concentrates on the checklist items, wondering what other T-handles he'll have to find.

He's missed a section, Kip realizes. He never checked to find the circuit breaker for the hydraulic pump, and apparently there's a backup pump as well.

Once more he leans forward, remembering the slightly higher kick panel compartment with the circuit breakers before recalling the panel of breakers overhead. His head hurts but he forces himself to focus on the placards next to each breaker until he locates one that has, indeed, popped out.

Primary Tail Boom Hydraulic Pump. That's it!

He pushes the small round button-type breaker in, feeling the click and hearing the tiny mosquitolike whine once more as the forward panel shows the pressure rising.

Thank God! he thinks, realizing he's solved the problem perhaps too soon. The tail shouldn't be reconfigured until sixty thousand feet and *Intrepid* is only coming through a hundred and fifty thousand.

But he's steady at last, facing generally south, and he thinks he can make out the Rio Grande River as it defines the Texas-Mexico border around El Paso, somewhere to the southwest.

Which means I'm coming down in south-eastern New Mexico.

The computer map is still not showing and he attacks that problem now in frustration, searching for the right button before the map suddenly swims into view on the lower screen, his position clearly indicated over the moving map of New Mexico.

One hundred two thousand.

As soon as the tail is realigned he'll be a flyable glider with only one chance at landing. He can glide miles in any direction then, but where should he go?

Somewhere on the panel he knows there's a switch or a button that's supposed to project potential landing sites, but he can't tell where it is.

He strains to look outside, but he's still too high to make out a strip of concrete a mile or two long.

I can't be too far from Roswell, or maybe Cannon Air Force Base.

Surely, when he gets under sixty thousand feet, something will pop up. But why won't the computer help now?

He tries the checklist as he comes through eighty thousand, the downward speed now slowing transonically below six hundred miles per hour, but if there's a section on how to get the map computer to display emergency airfields, he can't find it.

Seventy thousand.

The tail boom transition will be at sixty thousand, and he checks his ears, straining to hear the tiny whine of the hydraulic pump against the roar of the airflow around the space plane.

Okay, let's see . . . I'll need to know where the landing gear switch is, and the approach speed.

The handle is easy. It's a small recessed switch on the left side of the panel, and he remembers enough to know there's some sort of air bottle that blows the gear down and in place. But he knows there are no speed brakes or flaps, and *Intrepid*'s speed just before landing will be close to two hundred miles per hour, its stubby wings providing lift only in the most cursory way.

The altitude is coming through sixty

thousand now, the ship buffeting slightly, and Kip goes back to the page on tail reconfiguration.

"Hold twenty-degree-nose-down attitude until booms unlock and hold attitude until down locks are engaged, then recover from dive being careful not to exceed three g's in the pull-up."

He pushes the stick forward, feeling the engagement springs working the manual flight control surfaces and watching the ADI for the appointed twenty-degree nose-down attitude.

There. Twenty down.

He pushes the buttons for boom release and retraction and hears the whine increase as everything begins to change. When he was hundreds of thousands of feet above, moving the booms upward caused little but mechanical shuddering, but now the nose is pitching down severely as the tail aligns and he can see the indicated airspeed rising and feel, and hear, the slipstream increase.

Two green lights flash on, indicating both tail booms are locked, and he pulls hard, feeling the g-forces climb as he searches for a meter or an indication of how heavy they are. He thinks he knows what three g's feel like, and he holds that until the nose is up and he realizes he's no longer riding a spacecraft, he's flying a high-speed, heavyweight glider, and probably headed in the wrong direction.

I don't want to go due east, do I?

He looks back down at the screen, relieved suddenly to see airfields indicated, apparently in response to the reconfiguration of the tail. But the direction he's now flying, at nearly five hundred miles per hour, is showing no airports within the purple arc on the screen that he assumes is his gliding range and he banks back left, startled at the responsiveness of the craft and frightened by the descent rate which is over twelve thousand feet per minute.

He can barely see anything through the small windows with the seat pitched back, and he remembers he's supposed to change it upright again. He moves the two levers on the right of the command chair, relieved when the seat slides back into a normal pitch.

He pulls the nose up more, diminishing the descent rate and the forward airspeed as he shifts his eyes to the screen.

There's got to be an airport beneath me somewhere! Kip thinks, trying not to imagine the consequences of impacting the parched landscape of western New Mexico at two hundred miles per hour.

Roswell is sixty miles to the west, and it looks like the biggest and maybe the only available runway. The purple circle has increased in size as his descent rate has decreased, and he slows more now as he brings *Intrepid* around to a western heading, hoping to expand the range circle by slowing until it includes Roswell's airport.

And finally it does! Roswell is within gliding distance.

But at what speed?

He's dropping through forty thousand feet with a forward airspeed of three hundred fifty miles per hour.

Slow more . . . under two hundred.

He's squeezing his memory for every ounce of his limited flying experience, and decides that finding the stall speed is the most important element.

He brings the nose up even more, now to almost twenty-degrees nose-high, watching the rate of descent decrease to nearly zero as he trades airspeed for maintaining altitude.

One ninety. She's still controllable.

He'll let her slow, he figures, until the nose drops suddenly and he's in a stall, then he'll simply recover like all airplanes recover. At least he's always assumed that's how it works.

One hundred sixty.

She's mushy now but still flying, the nose way high, and suddenly he realizes the descent rate has started increasing again quickly to four thousand feet per minute even with the nose up at almost thirty degrees above the horizon.

Somewhere he's read about this sort of thing, a stall in a high-speed jet with the nose up, and he feels the cold possibility that he's gone too far.

Kip shoves the control stick forward, but nothing happens. The nose remains high, the airspeed languishing at one hundred sixty knots. He's falling straight down with *Intrepid*'s belly in a nearly horizontal position, and the descent rate is now over ten thousand feet per minute as he comes through thirty thousand, feeling again fear creep into his gut. In a nanosecond his mind has dredged up all the old feelings of insecurity and assaulted the incredible idea that he could survive everything else and snatch defeat from the jaws of victory by screwing up basic flight. How dare he try something he didn't fully understand? Now *Intrepid* is stuck in a nose-up stall, and even as he starts rocking the wings back and forth, she won't come out of it. It's like he's back in the re-entry configuration, his ship's belly to the ground as he screams toward it. The impact will be too great to feel, of course. He'll simply disintegrate. But how damned unfair that he could come this far and still die.

Something in that last series of thoughts snags, and a kaleidoscope of images flashes through his mind until the tail appears clear and unmistakable as the solution. The hydraulic pump keeping the tail in a horizontal position for reentry is still on!

With one quick stab at the appropriate button he once more ports the hydraulic pressure to unlock the twin boom tail and move it toward the UP position, poising his finger over the opposite control switch as he feels the aerodynamics drastically changing.

Suddenly *Intrepid* flops forward, nose down, and just as quickly Kip punches the retract button as he keeps forward pressure on the stick, once again seeing the two green locked lights illuminate before pulling g's to raise the nose and slow the renewed airspeed that peaks at less than three hundred miles per hour.

But now he's below twenty thousand, and a quick glance at the map tells the tale. The purple glide range circle has shrunk drastically, and Roswell is completely out of reach.

There is, however, a new target colored red just to the southwest, and he understands: a short runway. But if he runs off the end of concrete at a slow speed, he might survive.

He knows now to keep *Intrepid* above a hundred and ninety miles per hour. Maybe even two hundred since he'll need energy to flare and bring his descent rate down to a survivable vertical speed at touchdown.

He banks to the right, bringing the ship to a southerly heading, the altitude now coming through fifteen, but the rate of descent only three thousand per minute and holding.

He sees a few towns below, and he can see roads and section lines and a few rail lines.

Eleven thousand.

He can see evidence of wind below, plumes of dust when he looks closely, indicating a strong west wind.

And he can see the purple circle retracting away from the airport he's trying to reach, the edge of the circle finally passing over it.

No more airports within the circle.

Kip feels his pulse rate climbing again as he begins searching through *Intrepid*'s windows. Empty fields everywhere. A few railroad tracks and a small number of cultivated fields, but, other than a few country roads, no runways, no airports, no ribbons of concrete.

Except for the highways.

He has no choice. There will be power lines and signs and maybe even an occasional overpass — not to mention cars and trucks going one heck of a lot slower than two hundred miles per hour — but he's through eight thousand feet now with nowhere else to go.

He searches for an interstate, but whichever ones may be around are probably too far north. He's close enough to the ground to confirm that the wind is still out of the west, and he sees a two-lane highway running east and west and turns to the east, paralleling it, putting what seems a comfortable distance for a turn between the roadway to his left and *Intrepid,* and at the same moment he rolls out of the turn it hits him that there's no logic in waiting until he's lower to turn into the wind. He keeps *Intrepid* turning left, bringing it around steadily and overshooting slightly, then moving left a quarter mile until he's tracking straight down the highway below and coming through four thousand feet. There's a small rain shower off to the south and what looks like a dust devil off to the right of the highway, and he can see a big truck moving toward him perhaps a mile distant.

Landing gear!

478

He checks the airspeed, holding at two hundred ten, and flips the switch for the gear. He hears a whooshing noise and several "thunks" and three green lights appear on the upper right-hand panel. Unlike the first private suborbital craft, *Intrepid* actually has a steerable nosewheel, and he reminds himself that the rudder pedals control it.

Three thousand.

The wind isn't exactly from the west, it's a quartering crosswind from the left. He'll have to steer aggressively to keep from running off the road.

Two thousand two hundred.

The truck passes safely beneath him but he can see another one coming at him, and he knows even *Intrepid*'s short wingspan is too wide to fit both of them on the same two-lane road at the same time.

One thousand five hundred.

The rate of descent is frightening. It's like he's just dropping at the roadway, and a brief glance at the vertical velocity indicator shows why: more than four thousand feet per minute descent rate. A normal airplane touchdown is less than two hundred feet per minute.

The truck is more distinct ahead, a tanker of some sort, the gleaming metal of his tank reflecting the afternoon sun. Kip is covering three miles per minute and the truck perhaps one, but it's more than a mile away and coming toward him. No other cars or trucks that Kip can see, but now, like a parade of apparitions, several more big rigs rise from the undulating heat waves over the highway, and of all things to encounter in flat eastern New Mexico, he sees an overpass crossing the highway probably two miles ahead.

Kip's fingers are fanning themselves on the stick controller, his eyes taking in the road, the truck, and the horizon before flitting quickly to the last items on the Before Landing checklist.

Gear down and locked, seats up . . . I think that's it.

Something to the right of the roadway a mile or more away ahead catches his attention, another roadway or something like it at perhaps a forty-five-degree angle. But there's no time to evaluate anything else and he locks his eyes back on the highway, wondering if the oncoming truck drivers have spotted him dropping from the sky straight ahead of them. If so, there's no indication. The big rigs are getting closer by the second, the plume of black smoke from the lead vehicle streaming from its stacks and its speed constant.

There's nowhere else to land, but he's too wide to simply use the right lane and pass them safely, even if he puts her down on the right shoulder. One or more of the eighteen wheelers will end up taking him out, or wreck themselves trying to avoid him.

Airspeed?

He's holding just over two hundred miles per hour, afraid to pull off any more, but it's clear that if he doesn't flatten the glide, he's going to take out the first truck.

The angled ribbon of concrete or black-top or something to the right looms in his mind and he focuses on it as an alternative. Whatever it is, even from a mile out he can see it's overgrown with weeds and cracks that will probably kill him.

The road ahead is impossible, and he makes the choice without another thought. Kip pulls on the stick gingerly, feeling the craft respond as he settles through five hundred feet, calculating how much bank to use and when to angle onto the other roadway. The thing seems to end barely a mile or more in the distance, like it's merging into the desert, but at least the terrain on the other end is flat.

The overpass is still ahead, about a mile or so distant, the beginning of the strip of angled road he's aiming at starting on the far side. He'll have to fly over the overpass before angling onto the road.

The road, he realizes, is an old runway, maybe military, and there are a few buildings along the far end.

He pulls his aim point to the right, just above the overpass, still aligned with the highway he can't use.

One eighty-five!

He doesn't dare get slower before being right over the threshold of the old runway. He feels the remaining two hundred feet of altitude more than reads it on the altimeter, his eyes focused now on missing the overpass as he turns toward the end of the old runway. He rolls right slightly, feeling *Intrepid* drop more as he stops the turn, coming through fifty feet as the concrete abutment of the overpass flashes beneath him.

And in an instant he's yanking *Intrepid* to the right, using the rudder to help skid toward the end of the concrete ribbon, holding his breath as the truck he'd been aiming at disappears behind him. The ship aligns with the runway and he snaps it back to wings level, yanking the nose up to stop the frightening rate of descent, trying to exchange speed for lift as the threshold of the cracked and broken concrete runway moves beneath him.

He feels the airspeed bleed away, unsure how far off the surface he is, amazed when the main wheels squeal onto the surface.

Suddenly it's like trying to control a kid's tricycle accelerated to a hundred miles per hour on a bucking surface. He plops the nosewheel on the ground only to find himself rocking wildly left and right and working the control stick as he fights to stop overcontrolling the nosewheel steering while racing over a washboard. He steers back close to where the centerline used to be, the speed now showing less than a hundred miles per hour and slowing, Kip unwilling to pull the nose up as he's seen the astronauts do for aerobraking.

Seventy.

There's a partially collapsed hangar to the right ahead and a still intact building of some sort; he sees a weed-infested taxiway leading to a ramp where two Stearman biplanes — crop dusters he hadn't noticed before — are sitting.

His speed is below forty and he gauges the fairly broad expanse of concrete in front of the building and decides to risk hitting the brakes, pressing on the top of the pedals as he steers right, bringing *Intrepid* off the runway and coasting to a halt in front of the old brick structure, kicking up a cloud of dust and dirt in the process.

And the unbelievable fact that he is once again sitting static on the surface of Earth, still alive, begins to sink in like a distant rumor gaining credibility.

Chapter 44

Arleigh is losing it, Richard DeFazio thinks, but who can blame him? The telemetry all the way down has told of an excruciating series of near disasters — the wrong entry point, the wrong attitude, a near fatal problem with the tail boom, and just before the datastream dropped out completely, the unmistakable signature of a complete stall and a spacecraft dropping uncontrollably toward a spot in eastern New Mexico.

And then nothing.

Frantic calls to Albuquerque Air Route Traffic Control Center produce a bit more information, along with confirmation that there was what appeared to be a precipitous drop toward the ground tracked by radar, but then Albuquerque watched what they thought was the same target fly west, toward Roswell, and disappear.

485

There are phones to both of Arleigh's ears as he tries to get more information. With the world aware that *Intrepid* has somehow boosted out of orbit and is reentering with an untrained Kip Dawson at the controls, the guesswork on where the spacecraft will come down has launched scores of camera crews in airplanes and helicopters, some merely circling their home cities, waiting for word. The moment New Mexico seemed to be the end point, an airborne armada headed in from all points of the compass.

In the meantime, a worldwide television audience too large to measure has been watching long distance images of *Intrepid* descending, turning, configuring, reconfiguring . . . the shots ranging through handoffs from satellite-borne cameras to ground shots with amazing clarity until *Intrepid* dropped below thirty thousand feet and out of sight of the installation at Kirtland Air Force Base in Albuquerque. With Kip's fate hanging in the balance, billions are holding their collective breaths in the most widely watched global cliffhanger since *Apollo 13*.

Richard glances at Diana Ross, who has been progressively destroying pencils. He knows better than to ask what she thinks.

She thinks what he thinks — that it will be a miracle if Kip survives.

But it's already a miracle that he figured out how to guide *Intrepid* through reentry.

A secretary has appeared at their side noiselessly with word that a car is waiting to take them to Richard's jet now fueled and waiting a quarter mile away. Diana almost pushes Richard over in her haste to get out the door, knowing that the flight will take nearly ninety minutes with no certainty how close they can land to the remains, she figures, of *Intrepid*, Kip Dawson, and Bill Campbell. All Richard knows for certain is the section of New Mexico into which *Intrepid* has disappeared, but the exact location of the crash should be known in an hour.

Somehow, Richard has already put a private jet on standby to fly Kip's family in from the Houston area, just in case — something he has yet to tell the family.

West of Gladiola, New Mexico, 11:04 a.m. Pacific/12:04 p.m. Mountain

The quiet is overwhelming. Somewhere behind the instrument panel, gyros are still spinning and cooling fans still running, but once he snaps the master switch off, the sound of his own breathing is startlingly loud.

Kip looks around at the plastic bag that contains Bill Campbell's body.

"At least we got you home, Bill," he says, as reverentially as he can. And just as quickly his need to be out of the tiny cabin overwhelms him, lest it suddenly burst into flames. The need for air alone dictates panic.

Kip works to open the inner hatch, glancing at the brick building through the window. The walls of the old structure are deteriorating, the stucco unpatched and crumbling, the windows tilted crazily as if the building was melting slowly back into the desert along with the rest of what had to have been a World War II Army Air Corps field.

Intrepid's inner door swings open easily and Kip pulls the equalization lever to make sure any remaining air pressure in the cabin is dumped before working the lock and swinging the outer door open. He's still wearing Bill's space suit, but now without the helmet, and the trip out through the open hatchway is quick. His feet land on a dusty slab of broken concrete, and he works to regain his balance, walking shakily to the edge of the slab and onto the sandy ground. His legs feel weak, strangers to gravity, and he sinks to his knees to scoop up some of the earth as if it will evaporate if he doesn't touch it. He lets it run through his fingers. Incredible feelings of relief and deliverance course through his body like an electric current, but he feels removed slightly, as if it were all happening to someone else. He remains on his knees looking up in the sky and letting the unfiltered light fill his eyes as he takes a deep breath of the sweetest air he's ever tasted. There is springtime in the flavor of it, oxygen-rich and redolent with life, even in the absence of greenery in the surrounding terrain. The stiff breeze that helped keep his relative landing speed down is still blowing out of the west and kicking up dust, but he gratefully breathes that in as well with a huge smile as he gets to his feet at last, aware of the approach of a vehicle somewhere behind.

He looks around as an old Ford pickup rumbles around the corner and squeals to a halt, its stocky occupant getting out carefully, as if approaching a suspected crime scene. Jeans and a flannel work shirt, Kip notes, wondering why he's even aware of what the man's wearing. The sight of another human is such a relief, it couldn't possibly matter. The man waves as if embarrassed, a grin on his broad, squarish face as he gives the spacecraft a thorough looking over and walks close enough to offer his hand.

"Hope you don't mind me dropping in like this," Kip says, his voice sounding strange and unused.

The fellow is probably younger than he, Kip realizes, his face tanned and deeply creased as if he's spent a lifetime on the open range. But there are laugh lines as well and the etched evidence of an easy smile.

"I saw you headin' for the runway. Man, you were smokin'."

"I know," Kip says, shaking the man's hand.

"What were you doing, two hundred knots on final?"

"Close. I didn't see the runway until the last minute."

"It's kinda overgrown all right. Sometimes at dusk I can't even find the damn thing. But you did good, man! Helluva landing."

"Thanks."

"You do know we don't have any services here, right?"

"Sorry?"

"We don't have any gas."

Maybe it's the sudden reapplication of one g to his body or a delayed reaction to the greatest stress he's ever known, but Kip suddenly feels light-headed, as if whatever the man just said has been completely garbled on the way to his ears.

"This . . . runs on a different type of fuel," Kip says, feeling idiotic.

"I'm just kidding you, Mr. Dawson."

"You . . . know my name?"

"Hell, yes! Who doesn't? I'm Jim Waters, by the way."

Kip looks around at the ship, as if *Intrepid* might have disappeared. But no, it's still there, looming behind him with the incongruity of a pink elephant in a parlor.

"I should have landed in Mojave, California," he says.

"Yeah, I know. But the interesting thing is, you landed your spaceship pretty damn close to Roswell," he chuckles. "That strike you as coincidental?"

The reference soars past. "I couldn't make Roswell," Kip replies, knowing he missed a point somehow. "I mean, I was just trying to find a runway."

"Well, boy, howdy, I'm really tickled you'd pick my little duster runway. Although there was a time it was a big military field."

"Where am I, exactly?"

The smile broadens as Jim looks down momentarily, taking his time with the best straight line he's had in ages.

"Why, this is a planet called Earth, Kip."

"No, no . . . I mean, obviously it's Earth. Dumb question. And I know this is New Mexico, but *where* in New Mexico?"

"Oh, about forty-five years to the west of the tiny town of Gladiola."

"I really need to use your phone, Jim, if you have one. You know, to let everyone know I made it down okay. They probably have no idea where I am or anything."

Jim is shaking his head. "You can use my cell phone if you like, but I really don't think it's going to be necessary, Kip."

"Why not?"

"Take a look." Jim gestures to the northwest, toward Roswell and Albuquerque, and Kip follows his gaze to where something undulates on the horizon, the shape indistinct in the rising heat, coalescing quickly into several objects. A small air force of helicopters rises into view, racing toward them, as a fixed-wing business jet swoops in low from the north and passes over the field with a deafening roar at the same moment Jim's cell phone starts ringing in his pocket.

Chapter 45

Air Force Clinic, Holloman Air Force Base, New Mexico, May 21, 12:30 p.m. Pacific 1:30 p.m. Mountain

Somehow, Kip thinks, the reaction of everyone he's met so far is wrong. Weird would be a better word.

There was all the excessive handshaking the moment the Air Force crew members tumbled out of their helicopter to prepare him for transport to the nearby base. It was as if some celebrity had suddenly shown up asking for their help, yet everyone seemed to be sidestepping his questions.

It was too loud in the helicopter to say much, and he'd written off their enthusiastic grins as nothing more than satisfaction that he'd made it down safely.

Even stranger, however, has been the greeting at Holloman. The wing commander and the base commander met him at the door minutes ago, fussing over him obsequiously as they ushered him into this private room where a Colonel Billingsley, the chief of the hospital, was waiting for him.

Now the doctor motions him onto an exam table and begins checking his vital signs, the craggy features and silver-gray hair suggesting a man in his late fifties.

"Doc, when did you hear I was coming down?"

"Excuse me?"

"You know, when did they alert you I might end up in New Mexico?"

"Oh, not until just before you landed."

"And . . . the whole base was alerted then?"

"Not at all. Just the rescue forces and the clinic. Breathe deeply for me. Now, hold it and let it out slowly."

"Okay."

Kip complies, waiting out the multiple stops of the stethoscope around his back before speaking again. "Everyone seems so . . . engaged with this, you know. Has there been something on television about me?"

There's a knowing laugh. "Yeah, well . . . that's one way to put it. I need you to turn around and sit on the side of the table now."

Kip repositions himself, looking back up at the doctor. "But . . . I really would appreciate an answer."

"To what?"

"Was there a lot on television about my

coming out of orbit today? Everyone seems to be so aware of it."

It's the physician's turn to look puzzled as he straightens up, the blood pressure cuff in his hands. "You mean, about the spacewalk, and your decision to try the engine?"

"My . . . *decision?*"

"You know, when you wrote that about burying your father and giving him back his operating system?"

Kip sits staring at Billingsley not comprehending.

"I thought that was well put, by the way," the doctor continues. "In fact, I think you're a good writer."

"How . . . how on earth could you know anything I said up there?"

Colonel Billingsley laughs, cocking his head. "You're kidding, right? I know you have a good sense of humor."

"I don't understand . . . how do you know I have a good sense of humor?"

"Kip, we may be out here in the wilds of New Mexico, but we have cable, so to speak. You wrote it up there and we read it down here."

The doctor starts to wrap a blood pressure cuff around his left arm, but Kip pushes him away slowly.

"Wait . . . you were able to read that

comment down here somehow? Did I say anything else? When did the radios start working?"

The cuff goes on the table and the doctor sits down carefully on a metal stool, his eyes searching Kip's face, the realization sinking in.

"May I call you Kip?"

"Well, sure."

"Kip, hasn't anyone told you yet?"

"Told me what?"

"I mean, we all know from what you wrote that while you were stuck up there you weren't aware there was a working downlink. But I figured someone had told you about it on the way here."

"Doc, excuse me, but what the hell are you talking about?"

The physician is smiling at him as he would to a child. He chooses his words carefully now that he's alerted to his role. There is only a decade separating them in age, but he has to fight the urge to address Kip as "son."

"Kip, for the last four days everything you wrote up there on your laptop was actually sent streaming real time back to a single channel monitored here on Earth."

"WHAT? The Air Force was able to read what I wrote? The whole *time?* How?"

Silence fills a dozen seconds as the doctor glances at his feet, then back.

"My God, Kip," he says softly, "I had no idea you didn't know. You see, every time you punched a key up there on your laptop, that letter appeared almost instantly on television screens and computer monitors and even outdoor signboards all over this planet. Worldwide, Kip. Billions and billions of people have been hanging on your every word, reading everything you wrote *as* you wrote it, sitting on the edge of their seats in pure terror, as you were at times, crying with you over certain things you said, and . . . basically . . . living vicariously through the whole experience. Not a whole lot of productive work has been accomplished on Earth in the past few days, thanks to you."

"Everyone's been reading . . . *everything?*"

"Yes. And thinking very hard about a lot of what you've had to say. Kip, simultaneous translators have been changing your words into, I don't know, maybe a hundred or more languages. The President, senators, kings, queens, billionaires like Gates — and damn near everyone at this hospital and base — I don't know of anyone who's been able to blink or tear themselves away."

"I was just writing for myself, and . . . and . . ."

"And whoever would find that hard drive fifty years from now. I know. We all know. That's what makes it so incredible. We were watching the real-time thoughts of a doomed man grappling with his fate and his life. And, I might add, a guy who utterly refused to give up. That makes you heroic in my book."

The physician can see the blood draining from Kip's face as it begins to sink in. He squints, looking at the doctor for signs that he's the butt of a joke, then moves back slightly, as if to distance himself from what he's heard.

"This can't be true! This *isn't* true! I had no communications up there. You must have just received something after I spliced those wires, or . . . or someone was playing a cruel joke on the world."

"Four days, Kip. From the very first sentence you wrote — although at first only a few were seeing it live. But all of it was captured and replayed endlessly. Even your first lines where you were saying something about having twenty minutes before you had to turn the ship around, and it was scaring you silly."

"I don't believe you! With all due respect,

Doctor, I don't fricking believe you!" He's gripping the sides of the table now with white knuckles, almost wishing for the security of the spacecraft again.

Everything I wrote?

He struggles to find his voice after long seconds of wide-eyed silence, aware that the doctor has given no sign of suddenly breaking into a grin and saying "April Fool."

"You're . . . *not* joking about this?"

"No, Kip. This is no joke."

He tries to call up a memory of everything he wrote but it's impossible, given the stream-of-consciousness that flowed through the laptop. But what he does remember is enough to curl him into a fetal ball.

Oh, my God! Sharon! The way I talked about her, and about Jerrod, and sex and everything else to the whole world! How can I ever face anyone again?

The doctor is clearing his throat in an unsuccessful effort to refocus Kip's nearly dilated eyes.

"Kip," he says at last, "I'd say that right now it's safe to say that you are probably the most famous living person on Earth. I realize you didn't intend that to be, and I realize it's like having the whole world read your diary, but that's what's happened. I know it's going to take you a while for this to sink in so you can come to grips with it."

"They broadcast everything?"

"Every word. And people were acting on it. For instance, you talked about your employer's misconduct with that bad batch of antibiotics, and federal indictments have already been issued."

"Against me?"

He laughs. "No, Kip. Against the guys in your company who did what they did. Hell, man, you're probably not even aware someone filed your divorce for you?"

"My . . . *divorce?*"

"You wrote out the papers up there and someone printed them out down here and raced to the nearest courthouse, I think in Tucson."

He feels the room getting a bit fuzzy. *What on earth will I tell Sharon?* "Do you suppose my wife knows?"

"Well, she's been interviewed on TV a dozen times, so I'd say she . . . you okay, Kip?"

"I . . . I don't know."

"Kip, breathe deeply a few times. There. Hey, fellow, the world isn't laughing at you, we all have great respect for you. You needn't be embarrassed."

"That's easy for you to say!"

"What's amazed all of us is the way you just told the truth about your life and your thoughts and everything."

"Doc, I feel like I'm standing buck naked in front of the whole world. You know that dream everyone has where you're suddenly out in public without clothes? But I'm naked in front of the whole planet."

"Hey, man. One of the greatest things about what you wrote was the glaring truth about your own feelings."

"But . . . I mean . . . how do I deal with this? What the hell do I do now?"

"You already know, Kip. You wrote the answer. You go out there with your head held high and live for yourself, knowing you're one of the few humans on the planet who's been truly honest with himself."

"Yeah. Honest. Any chance the government would let me disappear into the witness protection program?"

"You've got a booming voice now, Kip. Use it well. We're all listening."

Chapter 46

The White House, June 2

Suddenly Geoff Shear sees what he's walked into is an ambush.

He should have been clued in, he thinks, by the others already assembled in the Oval Office, and their tight-lipped response when he was shown the place of honor on the couch. The FBI Director, the Attorney General, and the White House Chief of Staff would not normally be expected to evaluate NASA's emergency scrub of a shuttle launch.

Nothing sinister had been reported by any of his sources in the last few days, but the fact that Dorothy Sheehan had evaporated has been scratching at him like a strange vibration in an airborne engine, vaguely threatening, though nothing has happened yet.

But now the President has entered with a tight-jawed expression and little more than a glance at him, and Geoff feels his blood running cold.

The President stands behind his desk, not even sitting, a bad sign.

"Geoff, you recall what you personally promised me when I took office and chose to keep you on as head of the agency?"

"Yes, Mr. President."

"I told you above all else, I demand two things. Honesty in communicating any disagreements or distasteful information, and complete lockstep obedience when I've made a decision."

"Yes, sir."

"You've violated both. Jim? Hand him the evidence."

The FBI Director leans over and wordlessly plops a manila folder in Shear's lap.

"Evidence?" Geoff feels his stomach flip-flopping.

"Yes, Geoff. From the woman you sent to sabotage the rescue mission I ordered by keeping it on the ground. I'm aware you'd never imperil the crew or the vehicle on purpose, but I consider you've done just that. She, and you, put at risk more than just my orders, and when you've had a look at that folder, you'll understand why I have a decision to make right now. One, to prosecute you to the fullest extent of federal law in what will be a slam-dunk case, and put your ass in a federal prison; or two, have you resign immediately and preserve the illusion that we know what the hell we're doing in this office when I and my predecessors appoint someone to high position on the presumption that they're honest."

"Mr. President . . ."

"Don't even think about oiling your way out of this, Geoff. You're busted. And you're going to twist in the wind for the next forty-eight hours while I decide what to do."

The others are already on their feet, following the President from the room as a secretary appears, quietly motioning a stunned Geoff Shear to an alternate exit.

Lawn Lake, Rocky Mountain National Park, Colorado, September 8

Jerrod Dawson smiles at the symmetry of the curve in his fishing line as it describes a lazy arc through the evening air.

He wonders what it would have been like to be here ten years ago. It does seem odd at age twenty to be learning how to fly-fish at the behest of one's father, but he's enjoying it — and he's getting better at it all the time. Now, instead of creating a safety hazard with every cast, he can lay the line down quietly on the surface of the crystal water, the small fly plopping in almost effortlessly, as if no filament was attached to it.

The afternoon has yielded nothing more edible than a granola bar, but he knows the resident trout of Roaring River are still down there, tantalizing them both by their refusal to follow yesterday's catch into the frying pan.

He lets the hand-tied fly drift past the pool he's been aiming for, and once he's sure that nothing below the surface is interested in it, he looks away, back at the campsite. Dad is waving at him to come in, presumably to help cook the three rainbows they pulled from the lake last evening.

He pulls in the line, cranking his father's old reel carefully to avoid snarling it. He starts walking toward the bank in the awkward hip waders, stepping carefully on the slippery rocks, feeling like a kid again — like the kid he should have been. Or maybe he's living someone else's dream of being on a camping trip with a loving father. Not that his father didn't love him in years past, but he can't recall much time with him during his early years.

Kip is kneeling over the campfire, smoke beginning to rise into the pristine blue-black of a perfect Colorado twilight. From the distance of a hundred yards, the man could be as young as Jerrod, his hair flopping down into his eyes, a pair of jeans and a flannel shirt outlining a fit body, his jacket hanging on an adjacent tree. Jerrod thinks he's never seen his father as happy and content. But then again, before the last few months, he's never really seen his father at all.

He pulls himself free of the water and shucks the waders before shouldering the creel and walking back.

There is a history here in this beautiful place he knew nothing about, a history his dad has been relating story by story. Lawn Lake and Rocky Mountain National Park. A history of Kip's father and grandfather having camped here, almost in the same spot not far from the base of a sheer cliff that drops almost vertically from the summit of Mummy Mountain three thousand feet above. A history of dealing with an inquisitive bear in this very clearing, yelling it away from their tents late one night. The decades in between have been muddied by so much, even before he was born, including the loss of the grandfather he never knew. Seeing the mist in his dad's eyes last night as he described that first camping trip with *his* dad was yet another small addition to the emerging mosaic of the man.

The thought embarrasses Jerrod now,

and he tucks it into a mental corner lest his father somehow sense the depth of his shame.

He remembers that sudden flight from Houston to Roswell by private jet and the run to the military hospital at Holloman Air Force Base, but mostly he recalls the utter shock of having his father rush through a door to hug him and apologize. How could that happen, he'd wondered. The man wearing his father's face seemed totally changed, offering his love, and no defense against the anger Jerrod had displayed for so long, and no longer felt.

The last orange streaks of slow-yielding sunlight flaring over the ridge line of the mountains to the west are gradually giving way to a stunning canopy of stars in a moonless sky, and Kip wonders if he ever really noticed such subtle gradations of color before his space flight. He glances at Jerrod, finishing the meal they cooked together, reveling in the easy way they're now communicating.

There will be a few chores before bear-proofing the campsite and stoking up the fire, and he's looking forward to lighting up post-coffee cigars, a habit Jerrod hasn't yet quite embraced.

Jerrod is quiet as he puts down his plate and studies his father's face.

"Dad, what we talked about last night? The truth is, at first, when I got to Houston, I was too scared to read everything you wrote. But about day three, I read everything. Even the embarrassing stuff."

"The things about you, you mean?"

"Naw. That . . . I think I needed to see that, Dad, to have any idea how much you were hurting. You know, to understand how much I was nursing a blind anger."

"Then, what was embarrassing?"

"The girl stuff about your dates in high school. Eeyyouu!" He laughs, holding his nose. "That was way more stuff than we needed to know! And the *names!* Good grief! Talk about the ultimate kiss and tell!"

Kip is shaking his head and laughing ruefully. "I never thought anyone in your lifetime would see those names."

"I hope you apologized to those poor women."

"I've apologized to everyone." Kip leans forward and puts a hand on his son's shoulder. "Including that Russian crew that was coming up to get me. I didn't know I nearly hit them blasting out of orbit. They went on the rest of their mission to the space station, but I think they had to shovel out their cockpit, so to speak."

"I heard."

"But, son, as for the other things I was saying to you and about you, I guess I would have never said it at all — never admitted it to myself — if I hadn't thought I was dying."

"I'm glad you did," Jerrod replies, intent on changing the subject. "By the way, I heard first-love Linda even forgave you in public."

"Yeah. On *Oprah*. Embarrassing is the right word. I never would have mentioned her name . . . but we've talked and she's okay with it."

"One other thing I've been meaning to say to you, Dad. I mean, I think you know it, but I need to just say it."

"Go ahead."

"I want you to be happy. You should be dating. And I don't care if the divorce from Sharon is final or not."

"It will be, in a month."

"Well, I just wanted you to know. Dad, I've buried Mom. At last."

Kip studies his son's eyes and Jerrod can see he's stunned that another taboo subject has been softly opened. Kip's hesitation is lengthy and Jerrod wonders how his father will respond. But there's no squaring of his father's shoulders, no edge-of-the-seat prelecture stance. What would have once been a small incendiary bomb — an invitation to be enraged by what he'd always considered his father's infidelity to his mother's memory by even dating Sharon — is now defused.

"So . . . should I accept one of those marriage proposals I'm getting daily from desperate women all over the globe?"

Jerrod laughs. "Yeah, at random, Dad. That would be real smart. Man, I can't believe those women."

"It's embarrassing, son. I can't even read them, some are so lurid. And the pictures they send . . ."

"Who's answering them for you?"

"Diana Ross, I think. Or a secretary."

"By the way, she likes you a lot."

"Who?"

"You know who. And I think she's cool, too. I like the way she treated me in the first weeks after you got back."

Kip nods. He's thinking about the awkward visit from Diana a few hours after his landing, when he wasn't even sure he'd come back to the same planet. The trip from obscure contest winner to perhaps the most famous living human on Earth scared the hell out of him, and it had been calming to hear her voice down the corridor and see her swing in the door and look so relieved, actually hugging him and hanging on. Kip marked it off to raw emotion and the intensity of the moment, but in the months since, she's become the scheduler for the media demands for his time, and their phone calls and meetings have grown constant.

The call of a nightbird snags their attention. The windsong through the pine needles rises as Jerrod looks at him quizzically.

"You were suffocating with Sharon, weren't you, Dad?"

"I was suffocating myself, son. Denying what I felt. Following my father's script. Life with her the way I was living it was like losing the last oxygen in orbit. At least up there I knew what was happening. In Tucson it was a slower death."

"You going to write that book? Have they finalized the contract?"

"I have to. No, wrong answer. I *want* to. That and the fact that I need the money, now that I've quit selling pharmaceuticals."

"So, what are you planning after that?"

"The same thing I want you to do, son. Something I didn't know how to do. I'm planning to appreciate every minute of this life."

★ ★ ★

Grand Central Station, New York City, October 18

For some reason he can't explain, Kip closes his cell phone and finds a phone booth instead. Maybe it's too many old movies featuring the grand old railway station, or maybe just a need to touch something corporeal, something connected by actual wires. Never mind the fact that his voice in digits is probably bouncing through satellites to reach her phone in California.

"So, what are you up to?"

Diana's laugh is like music, especially when she's feigning stress.

"Drowning, I am, in the process of setting up the next Internet contest."

"How many this time?"

"Four winners."

"And let me guess, this time ASA is guaranteeing at least four days of stark terror for each one while the world watches?"

"Well . . . I did take one of your ideas."

"Which is?"

"They get their own laptop while on orbit and can type directly into their own Web site during the flight. Of course, we just can't guarantee a two-billion-strong audience like you got . . ."

"Lucky me."

"Is the disguise working, by the way?"

"You mean the baseball cap and mirrored dark glasses you FedExed? No. I tried them in Denver two days ago. Four people came over immediately to say they really liked my new look."

There is a moment of silence.

"You said in your text message you had something serious and professional to ask me?" Diana says.

"I do. But first I want to know when I'm going to see you again."

"I could e-mail you a picture."

"You know what I mean."

"I get a lot of offers, too, Mr. Dawson, thanks to everything you wrote about me."

She pauses. "How about this evening?"

"Diana, I'm in New York."

"I know. So am I."

"*Really?* Where?"

"Turn around."

The grin on her face as Kip realizes she's standing right behind him is infectious, and he pulls her to him for a hug that becomes a tentative kiss.

"How did you . . ."

"I followed you from the publisher's office. You know, jumped in a taxi and had fun saying, 'Follow that cab!' "

"This is great."

"But . . ." she says, holding him back. "I need to know what that important professional question is you were so hot for me to answer."

"It's a serious one."

"Okay."

"I mean, considering all I went through up there."

"Uh-huh."

"And because I've been your poster boy ever since."

"You've done very well for us, Kip, especially considering the various ways we tried to kill you."

"I'm glad you appreciate the danger I was in."

"I do. *We* do. So, what's the question?"

He glances skyward, then back to her, eye to eye.

"So, when can I go up again?"

About the Author

John J. Nance, aviation analyst for ABC News and a familiar face on *Good Morning America*, is a veteran Boeing 737 captain, a decorated Air Force pilot, and a lieutenant colonel in the U.S. Air Force Reserve. He is the author of seventeen books, including *Pandora's Clock* and *Medusa's Child*, both of which were made into major television miniseries.

The employees of Thorndike Press hope you have enjoyed this Large Print book. All our Thorndike and Wheeler Large Print titles are designed for easy reading, and all our books are made to last. Other Thorndike Press Large Print books are available at your library, through selected bookstores, or directly from us.

For information about titles, please call:

(800) 223-1244

or visit our Web site at:

www.gale.com/thorndike
www.gale.com/wheeler

To share your comments, please write:

Publisher
Thorndike Press
295 Kennedy Memorial Drive
Waterville, ME 04901